THE WRATH
OF
LEVIATHAN

T0160159

T.C. Weber

See Sharp Press ∾ Tucson, Arizona

The Wrath of Leviathan is a work of fiction. Any resemblance to actual persons, living or dead, is purely coincidental.

For more information contact

See Sharp Press
P.O. Box 1731
Tucson, AZ 85705

www.seesharppress.com

Weber, T.C.
Wrath of Leviathan / T.C. Weber – Tucson, Ariz. : See Sharp Press, 2016.
324 p. ; 23 cm.
ISBN 978-1-947071-01-8

1. Anarchists—Fiction. 2. Musicians—Fiction. 3. Dystopias—Fiction.
4. Brazil—Fiction.

813.6

Cover design by José del Nido Criado (www.josedelnido.com)

For my wife Karen and all who resist

Acknowledgments

Thanks to Eric Bakutis and Andrew Cox for reading full drafts and providing feedback, and the critique groups at the Baltimore Science Fiction Society (www.bsfs.org) and the Annapolis Fiction and Poetry Writers, as well as others who read portions of the manuscript (especially Eric Guy and Alicia Kelley, who read large portions and provided feedback). Thanks to Thomas Budesheim, Adam Lippe, Andrew Jarms, Robert Brandon, Eric Callman, James Madigan, Cristiano Aranda Flaminio, Leo Teixeira da Cunha, Leonardo Salemi, Shelby Driscoll Salemi, and Fernanda Bezerra for legal, cybersecurity, cultural, and linguistic feedback. Thanks to Amelia Matthews and Jane Ryder for providing introductions to legal experts, and to the helpful staff at the Maryland State Law Library.

1

Kiyoko

"The CIA will snatch you up or shoot you in the head."

Pel's parting words echoed inside Kiyoko's ears as she rode the narrow, creaky elevator down to the ground floor of their São Paulo apartment building. Pel was always saying things like that, ever since they fled Maryland. But Kiyoko was a princess, and wouldn't cower, especially when she had important tasks to do.

The elevator stopped with a shudder and she entered the lobby, empty except for a bank of locked mailboxes, and Gabriel, their muscular ex-special forces bodyguard. Gabriel stood just inside the grated doorway, glancing up and down the street. His black-framed augmented reality glasses had 10X zoom with image enhancement and could identify any face with a criminal record or military background.

Still scanning the street, he thrust up a hand. "Hold on, I haven't finished the recon," he said in gracefully accented English.

"There's no bounty on me," Kiyoko reminded him.

Gabriel turned to face her. The dark-lensed data glasses obscured his eyes, which she thought were his best feature, closely followed by his Roman nose and prominent jaw. Spoiling the effect, huge ears jutted out from his close cropped brown hair like radar dishes. "I am responsible for your safety," he said, "same as Pel and Charles."

Beneath his loose-fitting blue shirt, Kiyoko knew, were two high-tech guns she hoped he'd never have to use. "Well, I do feel safer with you around," she said, "and appreciate all your help." He was certainly friendlier than Alzira, who worked Fridays and Saturdays and didn't like to talk or go anywhere. Gabriel was nice to look at too, except of course for the ridiculous ears.

He tugged on the curved visor of the blue baseball cap he liked to wear outside. "Are you really wearing that outfit?"

Kiyoko was wearing regal scarlet and gold robes she'd sewn back in Baltimore, and a bright red wig indistinguishable from human hair. She owned twenty wigs and changed them every time she went out. "Red brings luck. And this is the most respectable attire I own."

"You look good, of course," he said, "but the officials won't take you seriously if you wear that wig."

"But it matches my robes." *He said I look good.*

"And the—crown? Is that what you call it?" Gabriel's English was excellent, much better than her Portuguese, but his vocabulary had limits.

"Tiara. Princesses wear them to formal events."

"I suggest you not wear this tiara."

"Maybe you're right." Her realm was large and influential—at least it had been. But it was located in BetterWorld, Media Corporation's virtual reality. BetterWorld had over a billion users and an economy that was overtaking the physical world's, but some people were stuck in the past and didn't get it.

"But the wig must stay," she added. Her real hair, brown with rainbow streaks, clashed with the robes, and she didn't have time to change.

He shrugged, scanned the street again, and unlocked the door.

It was bright outside, no clouds. Squinting, Kiyoko followed Gabriel down the cracked tiled sidewalk along Rua dos Estudantes, inhaling the fruity, spicy smell of caramelizing sauce. Rini Takahashi, the petite cashier at the yakisoba stall, waved. "Konnichiwa, Pingyang-san!" They bowed to each other.

Liberdade, Kiyoko's adopted district in São Paulo, was home to the world's largest Japanese community outside Japan. Otaku heaven, leagues better than Baltimore. Japan, China, and South Korea wouldn't grant her asylum, so this was the next best thing. And once her eyes adjusted to the sun, the weather was perfect, especially now that the rainy season was over. No freezing cold, no sweltering heat.

Still, she missed her Baltimore friends, some of whom she'd known since elementary school. She might never see them again. Not to mention her poor sister, imprisoned and alone.

The yakisoba smells gave way to garbage and chlorine. They passed graffiti-covered walls, a crowded manga store, and an empty sushi restaurant. Kiyoko quickened her pace until she was next to Gabriel. "Do you think Pel's right about the CIA? Will they come after us?"

Gabriel turned his head. "Take it easy, they have not so far. But your CIA loves to meddle."

"So is that a yes or a no?"

"Risks probably outweigh the benefit. If one of their agents is caught, Brazil would take advantage. The USA would look like stupid outlaws to the rest of the world. But if my government did not think they might try, they would not have hired a close protection officer. Your friends are famous. The government would be embarrassed if they took no precautions and you were abducted."

"We've been here two months and nothing's happened."

He nodded. "Hey, either no one is looking for you or they haven't found you yet."

"Yet?"

"You are starting to worry as much as Pel. Relax, let me do the worrying."

Ahead and to the right, the canyon of whitewashed shops, restaurants, and apartment high-rises opened up into Praça da Liberdade, an aging tile and concrete expanse with withered cherry trees and teeming knots of people. Her uber-cute friend Reiko rushed toward her, wearing a red and yellow Super Fox costume. "Yahho Kiyoko-hime! Genki desu ka?" *How are you?*

"Hai, genki desu." *Good.*

"My boyfriend agreed we can keep your cat as long as needed," Reiko said in Japanese. "He wants to know when you will travel."

If they had to flee again and couldn't take Nyasuke, Kiyoko wanted him in caring hands. "I haven't planned anything. It's just in case."

"We have an appointment," Gabriel interrupted in English. He didn't know a word of Japanese beyond *biru kudasai*—how to ask for a beer. "Officials are not like other Brazilians. They expect you on time."

Good point. Kiyoko couldn't screw up her first audience at the Ministry of Foreign Affairs if she wanted her sister freed. She told Reiko she had an important meeting, and apologized for leaving.

They took the stairs down into the Liberty Metro Station, bare concrete plastered with ads. Gabriel bought new pass cards with cash, same as every trip. Kiyoko averted her face from the white surveillance cameras. They were in every Metro station and every train car, effective crime deterrents according to Gabriel.

Pel thought the CIA could hack into the Metro and traffic cameras and they should never leave their apartments without a disguise. In case he was right, Kiyoko made an effort to vary her appearance and avoid the cameras. Anything to keep Pel from losing the rest of his sanity points.

A northbound train arrived, shiny white and brightly lit. It was after rush hour so there were plenty of seats. They added some kind of lavender freshener in the air conditioning and it didn't stink of fast food and puke like the trains back home.

Kiyoko faced away from the camera on the rear ceiling. Gabriel sat next to her, in the aisle seat. Kiyoko opened her big Sailor Moon carry bag, another remnant from home, and plopped her tiara inside. She pulled out a faux-Victorian hand mirror and brushed her wig.

"We get off at Luz," Gabriel said. "Three stops."

"I know." He was always stating the obvious, as if she were a clueless tourist who'd never been in a city before.

He didn't say anything else until they arrived at the Luz station. "We can take the underground walkway."

That was a shame. Luz was European grand at street level, a huge arcing hangar of metal and glass, with a big clock tower outside. "Lead on," she said.

The round-ceilinged pedestrian tunnel was starkly lit, with bare concrete walls. It had moving walkways in the center that were motionless.

"This section isn't finished," Gabriel said. "But it goes straight to the Ministry."

The Ministry of Foreign Affairs had offices in a brand new skyscraper, along with other tenants. Kiyoko had waited over a month for an audience.

The tunnels were mostly deserted except for construction workers and the occasional homeless person laying on newspapers or cardboard. They took an escalator up, passed through a guard station with a walk-through body scanner, and rode an elevator to the 28th floor, arriving at yet another guard station.

"They're as paranoid in your country as they are in the U.S.," Kiyoko whispered as they waited in a square, formaldehyde-reeking lobby for confirmation of their appointment.

"I think it's more that security is a big industry in Brazil." Gabriel flashed a friendly smile. "Which is good because it pays well. Not enough to get rich, but SSG pays all my expenses, too."

He'd never told them how much he made, and Kiyoko considered it rude to ask. But the Ministry of Foreign Affairs was using some special fund to pay Serviços de Segurança Globais fifty thousand reais per month, some fraction of which went into Gabriel's bank account.

A young woman wearing a blouse and dark skirt entered the lobby. "Olá! Siga-me por favor." *Follow me.* She led them past busy cubicles to a corner office.

A pale, rounded, middle-aged woman in a crisp business suit stood up behind a polished desk with a big computer screen. Behind her on the gleaming white walls were pictures of her receiving or giving awards, and framed screens playing silent loops of children with puffy cheeks.

The woman shook their hands. "Miranda Rossi. São Paulo Bureau Chief, Department for Human Rights and Social Affairs, Ministry of Foreign Affairs." She spoke English with only a faint accent. "Your dress is very . . . elaborate."

Suddenly Kiyoko felt out of place. "It's traditional. But thank you."

Everyone sat, Kiyoko and Gabriel in blue padded chairs facing the desk. Kiyoko began formally, using the protocol she'd acquired as a princess in BetterWorld. "I thank you with all my soul for granting this audience. And as well for your government's granting of sanctuary."

Ms. Rossi's brow furrowed. "So as I understand it, you want Brazil to pressure the United States to release your sister, Waylee Freid, from custody?"

"That's it exactly. Yes." Doubts crept into Kiyoko's head. This wouldn't be easy. Maybe impossible. But she had to try.

Ms. Rossi stared at her desk screen and moved a finger along it. "Ms. Freid is being held by the U.S. government on charges of conspiracy, fraud, theft, assault, trespassing, various cybercrimes . . . I assume you know the list?"

Kiyoko still trembled and cried when she was alone in her bed and thinking about her sister's plight. But she wouldn't do that here. "That sounds so negative, the way you worded it. Waylee let people know how MediaCorp is trying to control the world. She's a hero. No one was hurt."

"It says here twelve people were injured, two of them hospitalized."

Guards mostly. No one had been seriously hurt. "An exaggeration. Waylee is a political prisoner and should be freed. I've been trying to get Brazil to help, other countries also."

With Charles's help finding addresses and disguising her location, she'd been contacting ministers and diplomats all over the world. She had also started petitions and fundraisers in BetterWorld and on the general Comnet, but most were deleted, probably on orders from MediaCorp management.

Ms. Rossi hadn't responded, so Kiyoko prompted her more directly. "Can you assist?"

The woman almost smirked. "Your government considers itself the leader of the world, not a follower, and doesn't release prisoners just because another country requests it."

Not going well so far. Kiyoko kept her composure. "Brazil is powerful, with much influence. An official request would at least be considered. You could make a case for exile instead of imprisonment, saying that Waylee was following her duties as a journalist to uncover the truth and let people know about it. She belongs with her family, not in a cell."

Ms. Rossi folded her hands together. "We have already received considerable pressure to return your friends Pelopidas Demopoulos and Charles Marvin Lee. Your government claims that we are harboring criminals."

"What we did was share information, let people know how they're being scammed."

"Scammed?"

"Manipulated."

"The U.S. government provided a compelling case," Ms. Rossi said, "and our asylum conventions do not normally cover persons under indictment, like your friends. It's only because our government considered their acts to be of a political nature that we granted asylum. I suspect this was to point out the hypocrisy of your government when they lecture others about human rights and democracy and so on."

"We greatly appreciate your hospitality. Couldn't you extend it to Waylee?"

Ms. Rossi half smiled. "She's in custody. There isn't much anyone other than her lawyers can do. Why not leave it to them?"

"You read the charges. They're overwhelming her."

"What do you mean?"

"The government came up with as big a list as possible to overwhelm her defense. Even if not all the charges stick, she could be in prison until she dies." Kiyoko fought an outbreak of tears. "She has this illness and might not survive long in prison."

"What illness?"

I'm a princess. Don't cry. "Cyclothymia. But Pel—Pelopidas Demopoulos—thought all the stress, when we were on the run, turned her totally bipolar. Bipolar two, it's called. She was doing fine last I saw her, but now she's all alone, and she's one of those people who hates being alone. When she hits the depressive cycle, she might kill herself."

"Maybe her lawyers should use a mental illness defense, then."

Kiyoko bit her lip and clenched her toes. "She'd never allow it. It would undermine everything she did. Can't you help?"

"Your sister should at least be treated for her illness, maybe put on suicide watch."

"She should be freed. She can come here and everything forgotten."

Ms. Rossi shot out a quick breath. Just enough to betray a sense of disdain. "I will see what might be possible." She glanced at her screen, rose and shook their hands. "Please leave your contact information with my secretary."

Kiyoko fought an urge to step up her arguments. That would only irritate her most important potential ally. "Thank you for your efforts."

On the way out, she prayed to Yudi, the supreme deity with many names. *Please guide Ms. Rossi's heart. Please give me strength. Please don't let my sister die in prison.*

* * *

Waylee

Gripping her by the arms, a burly white man and a burlier African American woman marched Waylee down a brightly lit concrete hallway lined with steel doors. Special Housing. Waylee's wrists and ankles were shackled, limiting her steps to inches. She carried a thin bed roll and a set of generic-looking toiletries, and wore a bright orange shirt, pants, and slippers.

The receiving guards had taken her original clothes, strip searched her, photographed her naked from every angle, led her past hoots and hollers to a shower, made her scrub with delousing shampoo, and blasted her with scalding water. After that, they gave her the orange uniform to wear. Most of the other prisoners wore asparagus green, but she was special, they said.

They halted in front of a door stenciled 1057. "Your new home," the male guard said. He had a dark goatee and shaved head with stubble on the sides that betrayed early hair loss.

Never in her life had Waylee imagined confinement in such a place, the high security wing of the Federal Detention Center in downtown Philadelphia. Back to her birth city, where she and her sister suffered years of abuse until she blinded her stepfather and escaped. *Wouldn't it be funny if Feng was in this prison too?*

"This place is an assquake," the female guard said, her breath stinking of fried sausage. "But wait 'til you get to ADX Florence."

Waylee wasn't sure where that was, but obviously it was bad. "I'm innocent until proven guilty."

The guards chuckled.

I should shut up. Her lawyers told her not to talk to anyone because every word would be recorded and used against her.

Baldy spoke into his wraparound mike, "Unlock 1057, please."

She heard a click, and the man opened the door.

Her cell had the length and width of a cargo van interior. It had white concrete block walls, a narrow slit window, a concrete ledge with a brown plastic mat, and a stainless steel toilet/sink unit. The door was solid steel except for a small plexiglass window and a metal flap at the bottom. It smelled like bleach.

"I'm not violent," she said. "Why am I in solitary?" Bad enough the magistrate denied bail, but why did they have to make things worse?

"All terrorists go to maximum security," Baldy said. "It's the rules." They ushered her inside the cell.

"I'm not a terrorist."

"Lunch will be delivered between 1100 and noon," Fried Sausage said. She turned Waylee to face the door and pointed at the flap on the bottom. "It will come through that slot. You have half an hour to eat and then slide the tray, plate, cup, and utensils back underneath. If you fail to do so, you will not receive your next meal. Do you understand?"

"Jawohl, mein Kleinlichführer." She didn't know much German, but some phrases stuck in her head.

Fried Sausage gripped her arm, the one that was shattered in the car accident, hard enough to choke off the circulation. Even though it was healed now, Waylee winced.

"Don't you get sassy with me," the woman said. "I will knock you into the next century. Do you understand me?"

Waylee was pretty fit before the accident, but weak now from three months in the hospital, and couldn't wriggle free even without the shackles. She embraced the calmness that had kept her sane since her capture. "Yes."

The woman let go. "Alright then. Just remember who's in charge if you wanna keep your teeth."

Baldy unlocked and removed her shackles.

"After lunch," Fried Sausage said, returning to bureaucratic mode, "you will finish your intake screening. You will review the Admission and Orientation Handbook and complete the inmate acknowledgment forms. Then you will meet your case manager and get your ID card."

Sounds fascinating. "Can I have a pen and paper?" Waylee had started a book while confined at the Homeland Security hospital on Marine Corps Base Quantico, about how people could create a better world. She'd given it to her lawyers since she couldn't bring anything when transferred. She had a good memory, though, and could start over.

"You can buy it from the commissary at the end of the week," the woman said. "You have to fill out a Commissary Sheet."

"How am I supposed to do that without a pen?"

The guards ignored her and left, locking the door behind them.

Waylee threw her bedroll and toiletries onto the plastic mat. She felt lonely already. She scanned the tiny cell and spotted a small camera lens in the ceiling, probably with complete coverage of the cell. She gave it the finger out of habit.

She peered out the narrow window, but the thick plexiglass was too scratched on the inside and too yellowed and dirty on the outside to see much. Unless her lawyers could pull a miracle and get acquittals on all charges, or get most of them dropped, she might be in a place like this the rest of her life. Her fingers shook and she fought for breath. Somewhere below, a scream, a guttural scream of terror, clawed toward the surface.

No. Fuck you. No. She brought her breath under control. In. Out. In. Out.

How long could she keep her shit together? Would they let her mingle with other prisoners? Even if she had to fight some of them, she had a lifetime of training at that, and it was a lot better than being alone fending off the enemy within.

She wouldn't have any visitors. Kiyoko, Pel, Shakti, and Dingo were all out of the country. Safe, hopefully. Anyone else who visited, M-pat for example, might be implicated and arrested. She couldn't allow that. Couldn't ruin any more lives.

She'd just do what she could. It was all anyone could do. She'd achieved the near impossible a few months ago. She was a nobody with no money and not much influence, but her conspiracy revelations struck a serious blow to the oligarchs, one which might ultimately topple them.

Anyone could challenge the system. Even in prison, she could reach out, show others the way.

Waylee unfolded her bottom sheet and wrapped it over the plastic mat. She laid her head on the small pillow and grasped the top sheet to her chest. She closed her eyes and tried to remember what she'd written in the hospital. It needed tightening and reorganizing.

Beneath her active thoughts, detectable if she stopped and focused on it, the feeling of dread wouldn't go away.

* * *

Dalton

Dalton Crowley sat strapped into his form-fitting passenger chair on the Ares International VTOL jet, staring out the rain-streaked window. They had just descended into the clouds, and the plane juddered in the wind. Dalton's eyes scanned the clouds for lightning flashes, not that there was anything he could do about it.

This had better be good. Vacations were sacred, especially when they involved two-on-one hookers and menus of designer drugs. But he'd been personally summoned by the vice-president of operations, Mikhail Petrov. You didn't say no to Petrov.

Dalton was the sole passenger in the VTOL's cabin. The other nine seats were folded up and the space filled with crates of food and other supplies, strapped to the floor inside webbing. The box nearest him was stamped 'Bermúdez.' Good stuff as rum went.

They exited the cloud cover. They were feet wet, over the Caribbean Sea. Through the rain, he saw green and brown mountains on the horizon. The southern coast of Haiti, only a couple hundred miles from the Dominican Republic sex resort he'd been staying at.

He had played a key role in the team assisting "General" Renaud, a well-funded ex-Haitian Army officer, three weeks ago. Renaud's Ares-trained mercenaries took the presidential palace and government buildings. Dalton had accompanied them to make sure they didn't screw up.

At the same time, Ares employees, well paid ex-special forces from around the world, secured the Port-au-Prince airport. With MediaCorp's help, cyberspecialists took over the Comnet feeds and now controlled all information leaving the country. There was still some resistance in the slums and countryside, but it would be quelled soon enough.

No worries about interference from Brazil or the other left-leaning countries in the hemisphere. The U.S. State Department had announced the change in government was an internal matter and foreign governments shouldn't intervene. Dalton's job was done.

Or was it?

The plane circled, and the *Polemos* came into view. Closest he had to a home. A converted container ship, it was one of the company's biggest. Painted a uniform light gray, it was nearly a thousand feet long and displaced over 60,000 tons when loaded, but massive turbines could give it a speed up to 35 knots.

A wide landing platform stretched from the bow to near midship. Behind this was a hangar for VTOL aircraft and helicopters, and a big cargo crane. The six-story bridge superstructure and twin smoke stacks were aft.

The ship was headed into the wind. The big jet engines at the ends of the VTOL's wings rotated until they faced down. The plane slowed, matched the ship's speed, then descended toward the yellow circle on the landing deck.

They landed with a mild thump. After the pilot switched the engines off, Dalton unbuckled his seat harness and unclipped his big duffel bag from its alcove near the back. Everything he owned was in there—he hadn't lived in one place since joining Ares six years ago.

The rear hatch opened and a gangplank dropped. Bag over his shoulder, New York Giants cap on, Dalton walked out into the rain onto the gray steel deck.

A tractor emerged from one of the big hangar doors to tow the plane inside. Dalton bypassed the hangar and entered the receiving station on the starboard side.

The antechamber was small, bare, painted gray like everything else, and smelled like disinfectant. Sensors ran along the walls. The ceiling was perforated with holes that could release incapacitating gas.

He posed in front of the interior hatch camera and entered the monthly password on a keypad. A light turned green and he pulled the hatch open. A young, white-uniformed guard sat at a computer console inside. Dalton handed his Ares ID to the guard, who placed it face down on the desk skin.

The guard peered at his big wraparound screen. "Welcome back, Mr. Crowley."

"Petrov wanted to see me."

"You'll have to check your weapons outside Command."

"Yeah, yeah, I know." Dalton had a custom semi-auto in a shoulder holster and an XD mini strapped to his ankle. Neither was loaded. He also had a serrated combat knife in a belt sheath and a neck knife beneath his left sleeve.

The check-in guard returned his badge. "Go on through."

The next door unlocked and Dalton followed passageways and ladders to the command deck, checking his pistols and knives at the inner guard station. He had to wait an hour in the lounge before a synthesized voice came over a hidden speaker, "Mr. Crowley to the executive conference room."

The conference room was dominated by a varnished table with a dozen leather chairs and individual data screens and touch pads. On one side, a picture window looked out to sea. It was still raining. Data screens covered the other walls. One displayed a map of the world, with business opportunities indicated by various icons. Haiti had an orange outline, meaning operation in progress but nearly complete.

Petrov was sitting at the far end of the table, an athletic but graying man wearing a dark Italian suit. Dalton wasn't enough of a connoisseur to identify the brand. An aide sat next to the V.P., face hidden by a mirrored augmented reality helmet, black leather body suit and gloves covering everything else. Judging by the curves, the aide was female.

Neither Dalton nor Petrov were technically military, so no one saluted. "Reporting as ordered," Dalton said.

"Sorry to interrupt your holiday," Petrov said. He had a fairly strong Russian accent even after ten years in international waters.

Dalton tried to suppress his irritation. "Duty calls, I presume." He sat at the near end of the table.

The V.P. gave a slight nod. "Good job in Haiti."

"Thank you, sir."

"We'll be staying a little longer to help Renaud stabilize things," he said, "and MediaCorp wants us to pump up security at their Gonâve facility."

Why MediaCorp had a research facility on a barren island in the Gulf of Gonâve, Dalton had no idea. But it wasn't his place to ask. "So you want me to go back?"

Petrov folded his hands. "We have another task for you. We'd like you to manage project 993."

That was probably good. Another rung toward senior management. "What's project 993?"

"To bring in a couple of fugitives." Petrov turned toward the robotic-looking aide, who moved her fingers in the air. Three faces appeared on the wall screen directly opposite Dalton and slowly rotated. Names and other information displayed underneath.

On the left, an attractive white woman with intense eyes and a lot of face jewelry. Waylee Freid, 28, 5' 5", 135 lbs. In custody.

In the center, an olive-skinned man with close-cropped black hair, long sideburns, a mustache, braided beard, and pierced eyebrows. Pelopidas Demopoulos, 26, 5' 11", 170 lbs. FBI Ten Most Wanted Fugitive. Reward $2 million.

Holy crap!

On the right, a pudgy black youth, light-skinned, short hair. Charles Marvin Lee, 17, 5' 5", 160 lbs. Another most wanted fugitive. Reward $2 million.

"Alive, I assume?" Dalton asked. Dead would be easier, but the FBI preferred arrests.

Petrov unfolded his hands. "Yes, alive, so they can turn over names and stand trial. Your background makes you a good fit for this."

Dalton had spent thirteen years on the Jersey City police, mostly as a detective, after his stint in the Army. Multi-talented, Ares HR acknowledged during his interview.

"They were part of a conspiracy to bring down the American president," Petrov continued. "Ms. Freid and Mr. Demopoulos assumed false identities and infiltrated an invite-only event, where they recorded damaging information. And they weren't content just to release it on the Comnet. They broke into Media Corporation's broadcast headquarters, incapacitated a number of employees, and replaced the Super Bowl signal with a hit piece aimed at President Rand and MediaCorp."

"I saw that." He'd had money, a lot of money, on his hometown Giants, who lost the game. The message neither inspired nor bothered him. He didn't really consider himself an American anymore. But he'd been impressed at the broadcast's audacity and professional look, and thought it a nice touch to wait until a commercial break to air it.

"Mr. Lee and Mr. Demopoulos belong to the inner circle of the cyber-activist organization called the Collective. As part of their operations, they stole information and money from some very influential people. The U.S. Department of Homeland Security is seriously embarrassed, and so is Media Corporation. They caught Freid but the other two escaped. The FBI placed a million dollar reward each on Demopoulos and Lee, and Media-Corp matched it."

Three more faces appeared beneath the first three. An Indian woman named Shakti Seecharan, 22. A mop-headed man of mixed ethnicity named Oscar Sanchez, aka "Dingo," age 23. And a beautiful Asian girl, cheery smile, named Kiyoko Pingyang, age 19. Japanese? Chinese? Korean? Dalton could never tell the difference, but wow was she a looker.

"These are three of their accomplices," Petrov said. "We know there are more, but they haven't been uncovered yet. Other than Freid, who's awaiting trial, the criminals fled to Guyana, where Seecharan and now Sanchez by marriage, have citizenship. Demopoulos, Lee, and Pingyang continued on to Brazil, where they were granted asylum."

"Is there a reward on the bottom three?"

"No, so they're not worth bothering with unless we need them as bait. So here's where you fit in. We were approached by contacts in the U.S. government and MediaCorp, requesting assistance. They want Demopoulos and Lee, but a rendition mission is too risky. They're not worth a diplomatic mess if anything goes wrong. Considering our developing relationships, we can't pass this up. Besides, it's an easy delivery."

"So they're in Brazil?"

Freid, Seecharan, and Sanchez disappeared from the wall screen. Demopoulos, Lee, and Pingyang slid to the right, making room for a map of South America. It zoomed in to São Paulo, a big blob along Brazil's southern coast.

"According to NSA intercepts," Petrov said, "they've been settled in São Paulo. But we don't know where exactly."

"That's a big city."

The faceless aide spoke for the first time. Female voice, Central American accent. "24 million people in the metro area. 13 million in the city boundaries alone."

Petrov kept his attention on Dalton. "You'll be the project manager, but we have an agent on site you'll be working with."

A balding, heavyset man with a dark mustache—possibly dyed—appeared on the screen. Beneath: Olivier de Barros, Inspector, São Paulo Polícia Civil.

"De Barros works for us, but he's a detective in the state investigative police. He speaks fluent English and obviously he knows the city. I don't trust him, though. Never trust a man with two masters."

"I'll keep him under control." Lots of Jersey City cops had worked side jobs—himself included—and the majority did it honorably.

"Good," Petrov said. "He'll get 20% of the reward after expenses, and you'll get 40%."

A million and a half, maybe. And he didn't pay taxes. If he succeeded, maybe he could retire—buy a cabana someplace cheap like Guatemala or Mozambique. At 43, he was getting a little old for field ops. He'd been angling for upper management, but beaches and hookers were better.

"Thank you, sir," he said. "I'll bring them in." *I can send Donnie and Madison all the money they need for college.* The government didn't provide financial support anymore and tuition, even at public schools, was absurdly expensive.

Petrov pointed a thumb at the aide. "Martinez will send you everything we have on the fugitives."

"The hot girl. Pingyang. If I bring her in too, can we get something for her?"

Petrov stared at him. "I told you Demopoulos and Lee are the targets. There's no reward for anyone else. If Pingyang gets in the way, do what circumstances dictate, but don't bother bringing her in."

That meant a bullet to the head. He didn't like killing women, but for $1.5 million he'd shoot a pregnant nun.

2

Charles

He's a lot bigger than me, Charles thought. And faster too.

In the center of Alzira's living room, Gabriel stood, feet apart, on the blue foam mat that covered the floor. He wore a white cotton jacket and trousers fastened by a black belt.

The furniture had been shoved into the bedroom, leaving only the wall screen and its twelve camera displays, plus a wooden cross and a velvet painting of Madonna and her baby, back when Madonna was young and had brown hair. Alzira was away—she was only here Fridays and Saturdays, and even then kept a low profile.

"Come get me," Gabriel said, sounding almost American.

Charles knew he'd get thrown, but it was the only way to learn. He ran into position and grabbed at his opponent's arms, while sweeping a foot toward his left ankle.

His opponent dodged the foot, grabbed him by the arm and threw him down onto the mat. Charles landed on his back. A thick, solid arm wrapped around his neck and a hand pressed his head from behind. Gabriel could snap his neck now.

Charles slapped a hand against the mat. Gabriel let go and leapt to his feet. "That is called mata-leão—kill the lion. Very useful move. Now I'll teach you how to do it."

Embarrassed, Charles got up and glanced at Pel and Kiyoko. Pel looked bored. He had stopped shaving again and his face was covered with dark stubble. He looked a lot different from the B'more days, when he had a braided beard, mustache, and eyebrow rings.

Kiyoko gave him a solidarity smile. When she wasn't worrying about her sister, she was always so cheery.

And she was so slammin' fine. Pink stretch pants clung to toned thighs. Her butt was a little flat, but he could live with that. She wore a white tank top with a dancing emoji panda. It showed a hint of cleavage, especially when she bent over. Her shoulder-length, rainbow-streaked hair was tied back in two bunches—twintails she called them.

Charles caught himself staring and turned back to Gabriel. "Show me."

"What good is wrestling against a sniper rifle?" Pel interrupted.

Their instructor sighed. "Brazilian jiu-jitsu is an effective defense if you're up close. Charles and Kiyoko have made good progress the past two months."

"We have stun guns and mace," Pel said.

"Which are not completely reliable. Even if you shoot someone with a pistol, they can still hurt you."

"This is also good exercise," Charles said. He had lost a lot of weight, part of his program since last December to be a king like M-pat and win Kiyoko as soon as he turned eighteen. Instead of flab, now he had some muscles. And he'd been watching 'how to game women' videos. Trouble was, Kiyoko was no corner crab. She was royalty. Not to mention his only friend other than Pel.

"And martial arts teach discipline and self-confidence," Gabriel said. "They helped me a lot." He waved Charles back over. "That's enough talk. Now watch close while I show each part of the technique."

Charles learned the day's throw and neck hold. Kiyoko and Pel did too. Gabriel coaxed Pel into teaching a Krav Maga throw.

"I know about Krav Maga," Gabriel said. "But in the Brazilian military, they teach Brazilian techniques."

"Our friend M-pat taught me," Pel said, seeming a little less cranky now. "He said it's the best for street fighting. I never really had time to practice it much, though."

"I'd find a teacher," Gabriel said, "but I'm in this apartment building or following Kiyoko most of the week."

Kiyoko made a pouty face, one of those cute expressions she had. "Is my company so bad?"

Gabriel blushed. "No. I didn't mean that. I enjoy your company. You are very . . . interesting."

"Interesting? Is that good or bad?"

"Good of course."

Charles tensed with anxiety. Did they like each other? How could he compete with someone who could whop him like a dog? Gabriel was an outsider, though, and didn't understand her like he did.

Charles followed Kiyoko to her apartment, just down the concrete block hall, on one of the corners facing Rua dos Estudantes. They had the whole fifth floor, all four apartments. The stairwell door was kept locked and they'd programmed the creaky elevator so it wouldn't stop on their floor without typing in a code.

"I'm just going to shower and change and I'll come over for dinner," Kiyoko said as she unlocked her door. She hadn't painted her name on it or a rainbow and unicorns like her bedroom door back in B'more.

"Can we talk real quick?"

"What about?" she asked.

"I have an idea." More than just an excuse to be alone with her. "About Yumekuni."

Following Waylee's SuperBowl broadcast, MediaCorp had put locks on Kiyoko's ultra-spectacular BetterWorld realm, her avatar, and her shopping mall. Even though there was no obvious connection, only circumstantial. There was a copy of Yumekuni on a darknet server, but no one else could access it. And what was the point of a realm without any people?

Kiyoko gave one of her heart-thumping smiles. "Sure, come on in."

Two of the apartments on their floor, Gabriel's and Alzira's, had only one bedroom. The other two apartments had two bedrooms. Charles and Pel shared one of them. Kiyoko got the other one, all to herself.

A short entryway passed the bathroom and kitchen and led to the living room. Charles and Pel had only collected what they needed, in case they had to move again. But Kiyoko insisted she was staying in Liberdade for life, or until she got a Japanese visa, and her apartment was bursting with stuff she bought at stores and market stalls. The living room walls were covered with anime posters, except where Ikea bookshelves stood crammed with toys and every kind of religious figure you could think of. On a tapestry hanging over the window blinds, a manga girl in a short skirt posed with a guitar.

Activated by the presence of Kiyoko's comlink, music started playing from hidden surround sound speakers, bubbly electronics and a girl singing in one of those Asian languages. Nothing like Dwarf Eats Hippo, the hard-edged band Kiyoko used to play in with Waylee and Pel.

Nyasuke strolled up and greeted them with a meow. Kiyoko picked up her white and tan cat and kissed him. "Konnichiwa, my little nyan-nyan!" She sat down on the bigger of the two sofas, still clutching the cat. Charles sat next to her.

He wondered if Nyasuke appreciated how much trouble it took to get him here. First there was the long boat ride from Florida to Guyana, which made everyone but Pel seasick. Then they crowded into Shakti's aunt's broiling hot house in Georgetown while they awaited an offer of asylum and got jabbed full of vaccines. Then, the long drive to the border with Brazil, bouncing over potholes in a cargo truck with broken shock absorbers. Charles ate something bad and had diarrhea the entire drive. The border guards refused to let the cat through, but Kiyoko begged and pleaded and finally cried and they gave in, probably because she was so damn cute. Two federal policemen drove them to Manaus, where they sat through a week of meetings and interrogations before they were flown to São Paulo.

Kiyoko picked up a book of matches from the low table in front of the sofa, which was piled with Chinese statues, framed prints from Baltimore and BetterWorld, little brass dishes, and candles. She lit one of the sticks of incense standing in a sand-filled jar. The curl of smoke reminded him of vanilla soft-serve and tree branches on the sidewalk after a storm. The cat settled into her lap and Kiyoko pressed her hands together in silent prayer. She was always doing that.

Her bedroom doors were closed. One had a full-body immersion suit, he remembered. Like the ones she and Pel had in Baltimore, on a bowl-like treadmill and connected to a big cage with carbon nanotubes that even let you jump and fly. Charles and Pel had loaded up on gear too, using their generous loan from the Brazilian Resettlement Program.

The other bedroom, which Charles hadn't stepped foot in yet, was where she slept. Was her bed big enough for two? His was pretty narrow. And just a mattress, not a proper bed. No matter the size, though, they could make space.

When Kiyoko finished praying, Charles spoke. "We should make Yumekuni the center of Franteera Nova." He struggled with the pronunciation. The grammar rules of Portuguese were no problem—they were rules just like computer languages had. But pronunciation, that was hard.

"Fronteira," Kiyoko corrected.

His cheeks flushed. It was hard enough talking in English.

"Sorry," she said. "Anyway, you were saying?"

"You spent years on Yumekuni, and Fantasmas doesn't have anything like it for Fronteira." He made sure to pronounce it correctly. "It's just skeletal, we're still working on the coding."

He, Pel, and Kiyoko all had jobs for Fantasmas na Máquina, a startup that was developing a Brazilian-based alternative to BetterWorld called Fronteira Nova, or New Frontier. Charles and Pel both knew Qualia and were writing scripts. Kiyoko was helping with design and artwork.

"Are you suggesting loading a copy of Yumekuni onto their servers?"

"More than that, making it the centerpiece of their whole world."

She leaned toward him and smiled. "That would be awesome. And it makes sense—Yumekuni is the loveliest realm in BetterWorld." Her smile disappeared. "MediaCorp had no right to take it offline."

"They can pretty much do whatever they want, it's in the user contract. And you did help my Club Elite hack. I wouldn't have been able to access the place without your password." Using AI bots, he'd taken over a bunch of admin avatars and gained access to the MediaCorp intranet, among other things.

"They don't know that," she said. "They just know you got the location and password somehow. And that I left the country."

"They don't need proof. You had VIP access and connections to us. They're mad at Waylee and me, so they're mad at you too."

She didn't respond.

"Anyway," he said, "I was also thinking we deserve shares in Fantasmas." *We could be rich.*

"But we didn't invest anything. And they pay well, especially considering the government covers our rent. Not to mention they let us work remotely and anonymously. Who else would allow that?"

"They can't pull it off without us. I'm not that impressed by their other coders. Without me, Fronteira would be easy to grief."

She grinned. "You should know, all the ways you torqued BetterWorld."

"Yeah." He had always been a step or two ahead of the security analysts.

Her grin turned to a frown. "We're living well and having fun, and my sister's locked up all alone. I remember what that's like. It was the most awful thing ever." She bit her lip. "What if she's being attacked by inmates or guards? What if they try to rape her?"

Charles put a hand on her shoulder. "She can defend herself." Which was true.

She looked at him with moist eyes. "Depends on where she is in her cycle. And I know her, being alone and feeling like there's no hope will throw her into depression. Pel said she entered full bipolar while we were on the run, which means one of those downturns she'll try to kill herself."

She can't lose heart. "What about that woman you met? Will she help?"

"Sra. Rossi? Haven't heard back yet."

"It's only been a couple of days. Look how long it took to get an appointment in the first place."

Still frowning, Kiyoko twirled her hair, another cute thing she did. "I should ping her. I'm gonna write Amnesty International too."

"Who are they?"

"Global human rights group. They organize letter writing campaigns for political prisoners. At least that's what I've heard." She started to rise from the sofa. Nyasuke leapt from her lap onto the low table and knocked over some of the candles and little bowls.

Kiyoko's eyes widened like someone was shooting at her. "Nyasuke! That's a no-no!" She lifted her cat from the table, set him on the tiled floor, and shook a finger. "Stay off the table!"

She straightened up the damage, then said, "I have to shower and send some messages. Let's talk after dinner."

"Yeah." If Kiyoko's main worry was her sister, he should find a way to help. Besides, he owed Waylee. He'd still be in juvie if she hadn't organized that breakout.

Course if she hadn't, he'd be out at eighteen, maybe sooner, and not exiled to some place where he couldn't even speak the language. Pel thought Waylee's crusade had been a big mistake. He was probably right.

* * *

Waylee

After breakfast on Waylee's third day in solitary, the guards shackled her and marched her to a meeting room. The room was small, with chipped white concrete walls, a stainless steel table, and three folding chairs with torn black padding. Ancient foot odor lingered beneath a dusting of Lysol.

Fried Sausage slid one of the chairs to the table, and sat Waylee in it.

"Who am I meeting?" she asked. "My lawyer?"

They didn't respond. Baldy checked the wrist and ankle cuffs, but didn't unlock them. He used another set of cuffs to fasten her ankle chain to a thick U-bolt in the floor. "They'll let us know when you're done," he said.

"Have fun," Fried Sausage added.

Some miscreant neurons in Waylee's brain told her to spit at the burly guard, but the thought was drowned by fear. She was alone, and weak from her injuries, and they could hurt her as much as they wanted. "Who am I meeting?"

The guards left without answering and locked the door.

Waylee waited. Hopefully Francis would walk in and tell her everything would be fine. Or maybe it would be more interrogators.

What were her chances? What would the rest of her life be like? She breathed in and out. *Stay calm. You can do it.*

The door clicked. Waylee's eyes fluttered open. How long had she been asleep? She was still shackled in the chair, and felt stiff all over.

The door opened and a fortyish frosted blonde in a blue business suit entered, carrying a folded black data pad. She pulled one of the other chairs to the table and sat opposite Waylee. "Hello. I'm Irena Van Hofwegen. I'm with Kramer, Goldberg & Ashcraft."

"And you're here to see me?"

"Yes." Ms. Van Hofwegen unfolded her data pad, half flat against the table, half vertical, pressed the power circle, and stretched the vertical portion into a shallow curve, facing away from Waylee.

"You work for MediaCorp," Waylee said.

"Media Corporation is one of our main clients, yes. How did you know?"

Anger gave her courage. So did knowing that this woman had no authority over her. "I know more about MediaCorp than most of their employees. Did Luxmore send you?"

"The firm sent me. But let's talk about you."

"I already have a legal team. Francis Jones is my lead attorney. Did he give you authorization to see me?"

"I'm not here as an attorney of record, I'm here under the rules for social visiting."

"I didn't put you on my visitor list. I don't even have a list yet."

The lawyer huffed. "I have permission to be here. I'm here to tell you Mr. Jones doesn't have a chance." Ms. Van Hofwegen stared at her data pad screen. "The grand juries returned more charges than I can count here. Every one of those is supported by evidence."

Another reminder of how fucked she was. "We entered pleas of not guilty." By video from her Quantico hospital room, since she'd been too injured to travel.

The lawyer kept talking. "You were caught fleeing the Media Corporation facility. Video and audio analyses determined with 99.9% confidence that you and your partner Pelopidas Demopoulos impersonated Estelle Cosimo and Greg Wilson to infiltrate a closed presidential event."

"Where'd you get that information?" It was news to her—although it had been a while since she last talked to Francis.

The woman ignored the question. "You secretly recorded conversations at this event and broadcast excerpts over a hacked signal."

Damn straight I did.

"The prosecution has a witness who says you planned the whole operation."

Thanks for letting me know Amy's their star witness. Amy Hill was a thin sixteen-year-old living at Friendship Farm, a cannabis farm in southern Maryland where Waylee and her friends hid after sneaking into the presidential fundraiser. Amy tried to turn them in for the reward, but they stopped her. At first, anyway. She called Homeland Security after they left.

"That's just for starters," Ms. Van Hofwegen said. "Is your attorney planning to plea bargain?"

"I haven't seen him since they moved me. You're obviously in the loop." There wasn't much separation between MediaCorp and the government. "When can I see him?"

The woman shrugged. "I can inquire if you like."

"Please." She wouldn't consider it a favor, though. And doubted the woman would follow through.

"I've been instructed to bring you an offer," Ms. Van Hofwegen said.

"Really? Aren't negotiations usually between the prosecutor and the defense attorney?"

"This is off the record. If you make a public statement that you faked your video footage and all the documents you cited and released, all charges will be dropped. You'll be freed."

Waylee almost chuckled. Pel would respond, 'she's already Freid.' "So you want me to lie on the air? How very MediaCorp."

The woman pivoted her screen so Waylee could see it. She'd hidden all her windows except a statement in a big serif font. "My name is Waylee Freid," the statement began. "I created and broadcast the video hoax that interrupted the Super Bowl. In my zeal to slander the American president and advance a socialist agenda."

"I'm not a socialist," Waylee said. Socialism, as typically practiced, replaced corporate control with state control. In neither case, could people truly control their lives.

"Just read it."

The "confession" went on and on. "President Rand and Bob Luxmore never actually derided people's intelligence or claimed to manipulate them. I spliced statements so they would be taken out of context. My hacker co-conspirators in the Collective manufactured key portions using computer graphics programs, like the ones used to animate movies and video games. The emails and memos were also faked."

"It doesn't sound like me," Waylee said when she finished reading.

The woman turned her screen back around. "We can work on the language. You should take this offer. Do you know how big the prosecutor's team is?"

It was big, that was all she knew. "How big?"

"The Attorney General himself is involved. It's his top priority."

That meant the president was pissed. And worried. She must have seriously hurt his re-election chances. On the other hand, it meant she was probably doomed. "Can you set up a meeting with my lawyer present, and the prosecutor, and put this offer on the record?"

The woman's face tensed. She drummed fingers arrhythmically on the metal table. "It has to come from you. I assure you it will be accepted."

If she claimed everything was faked, who would believe it? True she had edited her video for brevity, but she'd released the raw footage and it was equally damning, and too realistic to be fake. The emails and documents were route-stamped and interwoven with the ocean of other data on the Comnet.

Then again, people tended to believe what made them comfortable and fit their existing world view. It might be easier to buy a fake confession of forgery than admit to being manipulated.

"Tell you what," Waylee said. "If I get this offer on the record, I'll consider it. I just may take it." She would never do so, but what great ammunition! "But otherwise, I'd be undermining my defense team."

Ms. Van Hofwegen frowned. "Well you've heard the offer." She folded up her data pad and stood. "I suggest you discuss it with your attorney. I'll be in touch."

* * *

Pelopidas

Pel was immersed in his VR suit, testing a custom tree-rendering program, when he received a popup message from his news monitor. Waylee was featured on MediaCorp's Top U.S. News channel, which had over

WRATH OF LEVIATHAN ◆ 25

a hundred million subscribers. He touched the link, which brought up a window in visual center.

The MediaCorp News logo appeared, 'The World's Most Trusted News Source' beneath. Even their motto was a lie. The logo dissolved to the *Top U.S. News* anchors behind a broadcast desk, a beautiful blonde in her late twenties and a jock-handsome brown-haired man. If they were real, which they probably were, their faces were painstakingly chosen and embellished to appeal to viewers.

"Hello, I'm Brad Edwards," the man said.

"And I'm Vanessa Goodley."

Their bio links appeared below, but Pel had never bothered clicking them.

"This breaking news," Vanessa said in excited but comforting tones. The anchors' voices were probably modulated, with subliminal undertones added. "Just hours ago, we learned that Kirk Ortiz, President Rand's presumptive challenger this November, was discovered having sex with an underage prostitute."

Waylee wasn't the lead story. But this was bad news for any hope of replacing that asshole Rand.

A popup window showed aerial footage, probably from a news drone, of a sprawling mansion overlooking an ocean. "Last night, Mr. Ortiz attended this exclusive fundraiser at the California home of Liwei Chang, a financier and former executive at DragonWare."

A picture of a middle-aged Chinese man popped up, along with biographical information.

Pel had played plenty of DragonWare games. They were big five years ago, but couldn't compete with BetterWorld, especially with MediaCorp controlling Comnet access. Single or two-player games didn't have the appeal of MMORPGs and you needed fast connections for those.

Vanessa's co-anchor, Brad, turned to her. "DragonWare is based in China. Does that mean Ortiz is taking foreign money and violating campaign laws?"

Pel visualized Waylee yelling at the broadcast: Chang doesn't work for DragonWare anymore! And his bio said he was a U.S. citizen.

"Certainly there's been a lot of speculation about that," Vanessa said. "We know he's received money from individuals in Mexico."

No mention of whether the campaign kept this money or returned it, which was a lot more likely. Pretty doubtful a campaign treasurer would risk jail time. And it was legal, if unsavory, for American divisions of foreign companies to throw money at elections.

"A lot of questions have to be raised about foreign interference in an American election," Brad added, "and how this might influence Ortiz's decisions if he were elected."

A picture of a young Hispanic girl popped up. She was standing outside the Disneyland castle, holding hands with a big Mickey Mouse.

"This is Rosa Hernandez," Vanessa said. "By accounts, part of a sex ring operated by one of Mr. Chang's associates, one Richard Russell."

Another photo, a thin-faced Caucasian man, appeared.

"Ms. Hernandez is only sixteen." Vanessa's nose wrinkled with disgust. "Mr. Chang and Mr. Russell are cooperating with the police investigation and have admitted to having drugs and prostitutes on the premises."

"We have exclusive video," her co-anchor Brad Edwards said, staring at his hidden teleprompter, "and take you to the scene . . ."

A swank bedroom with closed curtains appeared. A girl—Hernandez—removed the tie of a slightly chubby middle-aged man—Ortiz. He swayed on his feet. They sat together on the king-sized bed and Ortiz took off his shoes.

Username and password prompts popped up near the top of the screen, with the message "Log in for the complete video. Material not suitable for minors."

There just happened to be a hidden camera in the room with a perfect view of the bed? The whole thing seemed like a setup. Why were politicians such morons? Why did so many people buy MediaCorp's crap? Waving fingers, Pel brought up the menu and clicked on the next story.

There was a little bit of overlap. "We'll return to this story," Brad said, "and keep you updated as it unfolds."

"Leading the regular news," Vanessa said, "some of you may remember the video hoax broadcast during the Super Bowl. While most of the perpetrators are still at large, hiding abroad, their leader, Waylee Freid, was caught fleeing the scene. She's currently awaiting trial on a long list of charges, ranging from fraud to assault."

"That's right, Vanessa," Brad said. "She and her co-conspirators shot or savagely beat twelve employees during their rampage."

We used stun guns!

Vanessa nodded and looked at the camera. "Well, we've got this exclusive biography of Miss Freid for you." She turned to Brad. "Turns out that's not even her real name."

The screen spiraled and reappeared as a mug shot of Waylee with a prisoner number beneath. A pleasant female voice, not Vanessa's, narrated, "Police apprehended the apparent leader of the Super Bowl hoax, People's Party activist Waylee Freid . . ."

MediaCorp was using the video as an excuse to go after the People's Party, even though they had nothing to do with it.

"But who is she?" A picture of a brown haired baby appeared. "She was born Emily Smith twenty-nine years ago in the slums of Philadelphia to Phillip and Lora Smith."

Captioned photos appeared of an attractive but unsmiling couple. It was Pel's first time seeing pictures of Waylee's parents or her as a baby.

"Her father was mentally ill," the narrator continued, "with depression and paranoid schizophrenia. He killed himself when Emily was six, jumping off the Walt Whitman bridge. Her mother was an alcoholic. Emily inherited both traits—"

"That's not true," Pel shouted at the window. Waylee wasn't an alcoholic and had never shown signs of schizophrenia.

"In fact," the narrator continued, "she blinded her stepfather, Feng Chang, when she was just sixteen, gouging his eyes out with her thumbs."

A photo appeared of Feng in a hospital bed with bloody bandages over his eyes. He deserved it, from the stories Waylee and Kiyoko told.

A well dressed woman interviewed a haggard looking Asian man with dark glasses. Feng. He claimed their household was happy except during Waylee's violent outbursts, and her attack was unprovoked. "My life is over now."

The screen showed pictures of heroin addicts and prostitutes. "Emily then ran off with her seven year old sister and got involved in the drug and anarchist scenes in Baltimore," the narrator said.

Conflating drug use and anarchism. Waylee used to rant about MediaCorp's propaganda techniques every day.

"Emily changed her name and her sister's to elude detection. She changed addresses frequently, staying with short-term boyfriends and drug dealers, dragging her sister along and denying her a normal life. . . ."

She mostly lived with other musicians, you assholes. She's not a slut or a druggie.

"She joined the People's Party, where she met her co-conspirators and learned about the Collective, the international cyberterrorist organization. Both the People's Party and the Collective would go on to support Waylee's operation, and are currently undergoing a sweeping investigation."

I knew that video would backfire.

"Now going by the name Waylee Freid, Emily was diagnosed with a form of bipolar disorder." A window opened with clinical descriptions of bipolar disorder. No mention of cyclothymia, the milder version which she was actually diagnosed with.

"There's no record that she was seeing a psychiatrist or taking medicine at the time of her rampage."

Pel slapped a virtual finger against the window and closed the hit piece. Still seven minutes to go, but he couldn't watch any more. At least not right now. No wonder Waylee hated MediaCorp so much.

Pel forwarded the link to Charles and Kiyoko, then recorded a follow-up. "They can't be allowed to do this."

MediaCorp or Homeland Security—or maybe both—had done something similar in Baltimore, though. The local MediaCorp branch had posted a video that humiliated Charles, an interview with a fellow juvie who accused him of being a bed-wetter. Charles had tried to delete the video, but his computer got infected with custom spyware that gave away his location.

Pel sent Charles and Kiyoko a second voice message. "We have to be careful, in case it's a trap."

* * *

Dalton

Dalton peered out the executive helicopter window at the city below. Skyscrapers, a forest of lights in the night sky, stretched to the horizon. Below, car headlights crawled along a grid. Above, the lights of helicopters, planes, and delivery drones—too many to count—moved in every direction.

Now this is a city. Bigger than New York. An economic powerhouse. Cosmopolitan. Probably girls from every country in the world, trained in every preference.

"We arrive at your destination in five minutes, Mr. Hill," a pleasant synthetic female voice said over hidden speakers, using the fake name on his passport. "Please keep your seatbelt on until we land and the blades have stopped turning completely."

There were three other seats in the helicopter cabin, but he was the only passenger. It was a lot more luxurious than the Ares VTOL jets he usually took. Plush white chairs. Wood paneling. AR goggles with Comnet feeds. Mini-bar with top shelf brands. And you could barely hear the rotors.

The flight from the non-commercial Campo de Marte airport to the Tiberio Hotel wasn't long enough to dive into the Comnet. Besides, he wanted to see the city. His prey was down there somewhere. He raised his nearly empty glass of Macallan single-malt to the window. "My last mission." He finished it off.

They approached a concrete and glass tower and landed on a blue helipad on top. Once the engine stopped, the door slid open and steps descended. A hotel porter took his big duffel bag, which was mostly full of clothes. Dalton held on to his gun case and carry-on.

A smiling young woman checked him in with a data pad and handed him two key cards. "There is no need for you to go all the way downstairs," she said in English.

Accompanied by the silent porter, Dalton took the elevator eight floors down to his room on the 14th floor. It was spacious, with a king-sized bed, sofa-chair set, wall screen with surround sound, a desk set in an alcove, and a big picture window that overlooked the endless skyscraper lights. A bottle of white wine sat on the table.

There was a heavy-duty safe—not like the flimsy jokes in most hotels— inside the closet. It was big enough to hold his guns and other gear, and was bolted to the wall.

His comlink beeped. Inspector de Barros was here. Dalton tipped the porter, threw his carry-on and most of his guns in the safe, and took the elevator down to the ground floor.

He found the detective in a corner table of the otherwise empty downstairs bar, as instructed. Balding, heavyset, dyed mustache, blazer, loose tie. Just like his photo.

De Barros thrust out a hand and introduced himself. "How was your flight?" He only had a trace of an accent. Must have spent some time in the States.

"There must be a thousand aircraft overhead," Dalton said, accepting the shake. "How often do they collide?"

"Believe it or not, almost never. The airspace is strictly regulated and all the aircraft have avoidance software." His shoulders thrust back, like he was proud of the fact.

"The Tiberio. My employer booked it. It seems pretty fancy." Ares was usually stingy on accommodations. They must have got some kind of deal.

The inspector nodded and chuckled. "It's one of the best in the city. And it has good security—you need a guest card to use the elevators or stairwell."

Probably Ares picked it for the helipad and security. "Can I have a couple of girls sent to my room?" According to the Comnet, prostitution was legal in Brazil, and Dalton intended to take advantage.

De Barros's smile disappeared. "Why are you asking me? Ask the bartender."

Dalton glared at the man, who unfortunately he knew little about. "Let's get to business then."

De Barros nodded. "Now before we start, I was thinking. I know everyone we need to know, and I'm the one who will make this work. So I was thinking 20% is too low. 30% seems more fair."

Dalton grabbed the fat detective's ugly tie and yanked his head forward.

"The fee is non-negotiable," he said, staring at the wide-eyed detective. "You've already accepted the contract. Should I remind you of how Ares deals with troublemakers?"

"Filho da puta! What is wrong with you?" He ventured a hand out but Dalton knocked it away.

"I'm not in the mood to get jerked around, that's what's wrong." He released the tie. De Barros scrambled back out of range.

"Now let's get to business," Dalton said.

"Chupa-rola," the detective grumbled.

"What's that?"

"Nothing." He paused. "Now the bartender is looking at us."

Dalton glanced over his shoulder. The black-uniformed bartender, a light-skinned, effeminate-looking man, averted his eyes.

"I don't like talking here," Dalton told De Barros. "Let's talk in my room."

De Barros nodded and they took the elevator upstairs. The fat detective eyed the bottle of wine on the table. "We should open this."

"Go ahead." Dalton had that glass of Scotch in the helicopter—too extravagant to pass up—and one drink was his limit. Best to keep a clear head while working and save enjoyments for off-hours.

De Barros opened the bottle with a corkscrew on the table and filled one of the wine glasses. Almost as an afterthought, he poured some in the other glass, but Dalton didn't take it.

De Barros took a long sip. "Not bad. It's Chilean, they make good wine. Now here's my plan. I know this group. Gang, you might call them. As Piranhas." *The Piranhas.* "They're one of the splinters from when the government broke up Primeiro Comando da Capital and put its leaders in solitary. As Piranhas specialize in kidnapping and they're safer than trying to recruit a group of police."

"Are they any good?"

"As Piranhas have a lot of practice. They make about one abduction per week, and they are very good, very efficient, you know." He chuckled. "They have girls but they aren't ornaments, they are the lethal ones." His smile faded. "When there are problems, I mean, like with other gangs."

"And you've worked with this gang?"

"We have a business arrangement, don't worry, man. They give me information on other criminals and don't kill anyone they kidnap, and I keep them out of prison."

Cops needed snitches—Dalton had had some regulars in Jersey—but he'd never have worked with kidnappers. He'd accepted freebies from hookers, but no one got hurt from a blowjob. "Send me everything you've got on them. Comnet account SharkFeed999, capital S, capital F. Encode everything."

De Barros nodded. "I think you will like their qualifications."

"I hope they're not too expensive." Subcontracts were necessary, but the greater the expenses, the lower his cut.

De Barros grinned. His teeth gleamed, like they'd been recently polished. "Easy, for me they will work for a bargain price."

"Let's talk about finding the targets," Dalton said. "I've been told you have a lot of official contacts."

"Of course. I rank high in the state police."

"And some of these contacts can help, I assume?"

The inspector snorted. "Of course. Don't worry, we'll find them."

3

Waylee

After another day alone, the guards brought Waylee back to the meeting room. This time, she recognized her visitors when they arrived. A dark-skinned man wearing a charcoal pinstripe suit—Francis Jones, her lead attorney and a friend from the Baltimore People's Party. And one of his Virginia colleagues, Miranda Cruz, a young Hispanic woman fresh out of law school. Both were working pro bono.

Seeing them made the world a little brighter. "I'd hug you," Waylee said, "but I'm feeling restrained."

Francis smiled, then frowned. "That's unnecessary and demeaning." He called to the guards outside the room. "Please unshackle my client."

"Rules," Baldy said from the other side of the door. "She's on the high security list."

"Don't worry about it," Waylee said. At least she wasn't fastened to the floor this time. "What's important is, when are you gonna get me out of here?"

"As soon as I can. It's one of my top priorities."

Not his only priority. But between assisting indigent clients and defending the People's Party from hostile officials, he'd always been busy.

Francis and Miranda sat at the stainless steel table and opened their data pads. "Do you mind if I set my data pad to transcribe?" Miranda asked her. "We're not allowed to record your voice, but there's no conditions against transcribing."

More stupid rules. "Go ahead."

When they were ready, Waylee said, "This woman came by from one of MediaCorp's firms, just a couple of days ago. Irena Van Hofwegen from Kramer, Goldberg & Ashcraft. She said they would drop all the charges if I lied about my video, say in public that I faked the whole thing." Waylee added as many details as she could remember.

Francis raised an eyebrow. "How did she get in here? On what authority would your charges be dropped?"

"It's another example of how there's no real separation between MediaCorp and the government. Luxmore or one of his stooges makes some calls, and someone in the government gets him what he wants." *Will this ever stop?* "I told Ms. Van Hofwegen I wanted the offer on record."

"And what did she say?"

"She was pretty cagey. She wanted me to make the offer instead."

"Don't talk to her again without me present." Francis glanced at his data pad. "We have a lot to go over. It's been a while since we've been able to talk."

Waylee hadn't seen her lawyers since the arraignment, and that only by video.

Francis looked in her eyes. "It sounds like you didn't say anything incriminating to this third party lawyer. Have you discussed your case or anything related to it with anyone else since we last met?"

Waylee shook her head. Over a dozen different Homeland Security suits had interrogated her while she was hospitalized, but she had refused to speak, invoking her Fifth Amendment right against self-incrimination. After a while they'd given up.

"Good. Now I'm reasonably confident we're not being recorded here. We're not on a military base any more, and I've asked around, there's no mikes or cameras in this room."

"There's a camera in my cell."

He shook his head again. "You don't need to be in high security. I'll ask them to move you."

"Thanks. I've been in solitary three days and already I'm getting twitchy."

Francis nodded.

"What's going on in the world?" she asked. "I'm cut off here. Have you heard from Kiyoko or Pel?" She hadn't heard from them since the birthday video that Miranda had played for her. They hadn't said where they were or what they were up to, just that they were okay but missed her.

"I'm not representing them—they don't have any representation at the moment – and I'm not in regular touch, but I did receive a message from your sister last week that they are doing fine and not to worry. They're still in Brazil as far as I know."

Vague, but better than bad news. "Thanks."

"Kiyoko and Pel are trying to secure your release through diplomatic channels," he said. "They've also started a crowdfunding site for your legal expenses. We'll still be working for free, but this will help cover travel expenses, and maybe we can hire an investigator."

"Thank you. And thank Kiyoko and Pel for me."

He nodded.

"Do you think the diplomatic approach will work?"

Francis shook his head. "I'm sorry to say, no. The U.S. government considers itself the leader of the world and never bows to foreign pressure."

"And their so-called leadership is toxic." The Rand Administration led the unraveling of climate change treaties and defunded the United Nations, and now the only global treaties were free trade agreements enforced by corporate tribunals. "Last time we talked, Rand's job approval rating was in the toilet and there were calls to break up MediaCorp or revoke their charter. Tell me that's still the case."

"We really should focus on you, Waylee."

"That is focusing on me." Her video had sparked a lot of outrage, hopefully enough to change things. She couldn't have sacrificed her life for nothing.

His eyes wandered. "Well, Luxmore seems to have weathered the storm. And the media focus is on Ortiz's underage hooker scandal now."

Kirk Ortiz was President Rand's main challenger. A douchebag, but less of a douchebag than Rand. Her heart sank. "What's that about?"

"He was videotaped having sex with an underage prostitute. He's probably going to have to withdraw."

Waylee almost chuckled. Pel would have made a corny joke about that. But it meant MediaCorp was still in control. "Was he really that stupid? Was it a setup?"

Francis shrugged. "Maybe a little of each. He was drunk, you can tell the way his voice slurs."

Like President Rand, who'd succumbed to Waylee's flirting at the Smithsonian and practically bragged about working with MediaCorp to manipulate the public and blackmail opponents.

"The girl's pimp got off scot free," Francis added.

"Obviously the whole thing was arranged. I wish I wasn't stuck here so I could look into it."

Francis sighed. "Yeah. So can we go over the charges now and put a strategy together?"

Waylee had a million things she wanted to talk about, but this wasn't a social visit. "Of course. I know we have a lot to cover." What if she could never have a normal conversation again?

He passed her a thick binder of paper. "This is your copy."

The first page was titled "UNITED STATES OF AMERICA VS. WAY-LEE FREID (1)," and began listing grand jury charges in double-spaced Times New Roman.

Francis stared at his data pad screen. "To summarize, the complaints say you harbored a fugitive and conspired to aid his escape from detention, then infiltrated a closed presidential event, directed a group of hackers to steal information and money from hundreds of people, led a break-in at Media Corporation's broadcast headquarters, injured or incapacitated twelve people, and replaced the Super Bowl broadcast with a video of your own."

All true, more or less.

Francis swiped a finger against his screen. "The U.S. Attorney's office is prosecuting first, but I've been told Virginia and Maryland are also moving forward."

Waylee's legs rattled in their shackles. She'd been hoping the states wouldn't bother. "I thought they deferred to the feds."

"They did, but they've decided to go ahead with the state charges when the federal case is settled. The Virginia charges, which include assault and battery and grand larceny among others, are more serious than Maryland's. But let's worry about the federal case first." He frowned. "Lachlan's a grade-A asshole."

Todd Lachlan, who Waylee had seen on video, was the Assistant U.S. Attorney for the Eastern District of Virginia. Francis had told her he'd never lost a case, and was working with a big task force and unlimited funds. He'd blocked Francis from challenging their evidence by bypassing the preliminary hearing and taking the grand jury route. Defense attorneys couldn't attend grand jury hearings, and Francis said they were typically rubber stamp processes and a way to intimidate witnesses. Lachlan had gotten indictments on all charges, even the ridiculous ones.

Francis looked back at his screen. "The feds are charging you with fifteen separate crimes. Some of them have multiple counts. You've been indicted for harboring a fugitive who has committed federal crimes, conspiracy to commit computer and wire fraud, entering and remaining in a restricted building with the intent to disrupt the orderly conduct of official functions—"

"I didn't disrupt their event," Waylee said. "I just asked some questions."

Francis looked up. "I agree. Mind you, these are all just allegations. The U.S. attorney only needs probable cause to get an indictment, but to get a conviction, they need to prove beyond a reasonable doubt. A lot of their case is pretty shaky. Let me finish the list."

Waylee nodded. "Go ahead."

"Illegal interception and disclosure of electronic communications, possession of prohibited communication intercepting devices . . ."

Those would be their ghost snares, which Pel bought on the darknet with BetterWorld credits. They'd recorded faint electromagnetic traces from VIP comlinks, which Pel and Charles used later to hack their users' accounts and computers.

". . . unlawful access to stored communications, wrongful disclosure of stored communications . . ."

They'd discovered all sorts of gems in MediaCorp and government emails and documents.

"Conspiracy to commit bank fraud and grand larceny . . ."

That was Charles and some of their allies in the Collective, who'd been able to access some of their targets' bank accounts.

"Disclosure of classified information, here defined as confidential communications between government officials. Advocating overthrow of the government—"

"I never said anything about using force," Waylee said.

Francis nodded. "We can get that dropped easily enough. The code is clear about inciting force or violence, which your video did not." He returned to his list. "And lastly, thanks to statutes enacted last year—cyber-terrorism."

"MediaCorp and the government throw that word around a lot. But I'm not a terrorist."

Francis read from his screen. "It's 'the premeditated use of disruptive activities against computers and/or networks, with the intention to cause harm or further social, ideological, religious, political or similar objectives.'" He looked up. "That's one we definitely need dropped. The penalty is up to twenty years in prison."

Anger displaced her fear. "Luxmore and his circle commit crimes with impunity, but I'm facing twenty years on some bullshit charge just because I let people know about it?"

"I know." He looked up. "Since our last meeting, Miranda and I have seen all the grand jury videos. The prosecution has a lot of evidence, and I doubt the videos cover it all. I've asked to see everything they have, but it looks like they'll delay as long as possible."

"Van Hofwegen said the prosecution has a witness who said I planned the whole operation." *Which wasn't true, although it was my idea.* "Amy Hill, I assume."

During Waylee's deepest depression, following Charles's admission that he couldn't broadcast her video without inside help, she'd told Shakti it was stupid to think they could take over the Super Bowl broadcast. Amy had overheard and it was probably why she turned them in. And the reward certainly played a part.

Francis nodded. "Yes, she testified before the federal and state grand juries in Richmond." He stared at his data pad. "So did a number of Media-Corp employees, including a technician who claims you shot him with a stun gun. He hit his head and was injured."

"I didn't intentionally hurt anyone."

He ignored the comment. "You were caught driving a stolen car—although they showed no proof you knew it was stolen. The prosecution said you impersonated an employee, Tania Peart, to sneak into the MediaCorp broadcast headquarters. They claim you participated in the re-routing of the Super Bowl signal and replacing it with the fake emergency broadcast. They can tie you to all this because a custom-made mask of Tania Peart was found in the car you were driving. They found your DNA on the inner surface. And your voice is on the video. Which brings me to the Smithsonian charges."

"Ms. Van Hofwegen told me that video and audio analyses confirmed it was me and Pel disguised as Estelle and Greg."

"That seems pretty ironclad. And in Maryland, the prosecution showed DNA evidence that Charles Lee stayed in your house after being freed from the juvenile detention center. They also played a security video of you fleeing together through a printing factory."

We were so careful. But not careful enough, I guess.

He finally looked up from the screen. "With your permission, now that you're out of the hospital, I would like to contact the federal and state public defender's offices and have them represent you."

What? "Why not you? You're a legal rock star."

"That's flattering, Waylee, but since you're eligible for public assistance, I'd be doing you a disservice by not taking advantage. It's true funding's been cut from the public defender offices, but even so, they know the system best. You have three cases moving forward under different jurisdictions, so you'll need three legal teams. I will continue to be there for you as a friend and pro bono consultant, though, if you like. And if you don't like your public defenders, you can ask the judge to appoint a replacement. And I'm willing to take over again if it comes to that."

Waylee tried not to show her disappointment. "You know the law better than me, so if that's what you think is best. I'd like you on my side, though."

"I'll do what I can."

Miranda swiveled her data pad so Waylee could see the screen, which displayed an official form. "There are three applications for public assistance," she said, "one for the federal office and two for the states. They're already filled out based on your prior paperwork, but you should take a look and make sure everything's correct."

Name, address, employment information, yadda yadda . . . No income, no assets. Waylee signed a box on the bottom with her right index finger.

Miranda turned the data pad back around. "We'll take care of it."

"In the meantime," Francis said, "we need to start thinking about a plea bargain. We can probably get a lot of charges dropped. It'll take some fancy footwork to coordinate with multiple jurisdictions, but it's certainly possible. Having PD's in each jurisdiction will help."

"Can you get all the felonies dropped?"

"We'll certainly try. It helps that you don't have any priors."

Waylee had quite a record as a juvenile, but it was expunged when she turned eighteen. She'd never been arrested as an activist like Dingo and some of her other friends—too worried about damaging her credibility as a journalist.

"And we can generate reasonable doubts about their evidence," Francis said.

"I don't want to lie about what I did. That would defeat the whole purpose."

He stared in her eyes. "I'm not talking about lying. You shouldn't say anything."

"How much prison time do you think I'll get?"

"Depends on what we get dropped and what the prosecution and court will settle for. If you plead guilty, maybe just a few years. If you go to trial and lose, which is the most likely outcome, you could spend the rest of your life in prison."

The rest of her energy drained away. "So you're saying it's hopeless."

"I'm not saying that at all. But we have to be realistic. And I think we can get you a light sentence."

"The guards said they'd send me to ADX Florence. Why would they say that?"

"It's the federal supermax. They just added a women's wing and they're probably looking to fill it. But you're not violent and not a terrorist. You don't belong there."

"I can't do solitary." *I'd completely lose it.*

"I'll keep that in mind. Now I know how you'll respond, but as your lawyer, I have to tell you that the prosecution might be lenient with you if you name all your alleged co-conspirators. There are rewards posted for Pel, Charles, Dingo, and Shakti, but there is also a reward for an unidentified man, tall and broad-shouldered, possibly older and Italian-American, but he could have been wearing a mask."

M-pat. "I'm not saying anything about anyone other than myself."

"I figured," he said. "Just had to mention it."

"Maybe I could plead guilty in return for charges to be dropped against everyone else."

"Why would you want to do that? They're safe as long as they stay where they are. They're outside U.S. jurisdiction. President Rand could send an illegal military team, but since your friends haven't killed anyone, or even seriously hurt anyone, there might be resistance from the Defense and State Departments. And if the operation fails, he'll be even more embarrassed and drop lower in the polls."

Good news. "What if we forgot about plea bargaining and went to trial?"

He stiffened. "That's extremely risky. I advise against it. If you're convicted on all counts, even most of them, you could be in prison the rest of your life. First, the federal government has a 99% conviction rate. Then, the prosecutor can argue for the maximum sentence—which I expect Mr. Lachlan would do—and the judge could grant it."

"You call this justice? Guaranteed conviction?"

"I agree our justice system has a lot to be desired. But we have to do the best we can here."

* * *

Kiyoko

Princess Kiyoko teleported to the BetterWorld embassy of China, arriving in a marble courtyard surrounded by gardens. Ahead was a brick wall with portraits of national leaders, topped by a pagoda. Photorealistic avatars, mostly Asian-looking, milled in the courtyard and spoke quietly. Kiyoko wore dark, formal robes to show respect.

A smiling young woman in business clothes approached. "Welcome to the People's Republic of China. How may I assist you?"

"Greetings. I am Princess Kiyoko, ruler of Yumekuni on the Fantasy Continent. I have an appointment with the consul."

The woman didn't blink. Probably a bot. She swept an arm toward the gate in the wall, which was flanked by two live dragons. "Please follow me."

The consul, Zhang Minsheng, was an attractive man in a business suit, standing in a palatial room. Given his position as the official representative of the People's Republic of China, and the economic and cultural importance of BetterWorld, he was probably a real human, although you could never be sure these days.

They nodded heads slightly and introduced themselves. Kiyoko would have brought a gift or at least a greeting card, but after Charles's vampire bot attacks, everyone was too paranoid now.

The consul motioned for Kiyoko to sit. They took chairs facing one another, a small glossy table between. In her VR webbing and conforming suit, the seat felt firm yet cushiony.

"Tea?" the consul offered.

"Yes please." Pleasantries were a critical part of any meeting, especially in refined cultures.

A young woman wearing a gold-embroidered jade-green dress and pearl earrings set out blue-patterned cups and poured oolong tea in them.

Kiyoko didn't have a taste simulator—the technology still relied on crude tongue electrodes that interfered with speech—so she didn't comment on what was probably the best virtual tea ever programmed. "Thank you for receiving me," she said. "As I told the greeter, I am Princess Kiyoko, ruler of Yumekuni."

"Yumekuni. I have not visited, but I understand it is quite enchanting."

"Thank you." She sipped her tea.

"And the largest realm on the Fantasy Continent."

"Yes, it is." Since her defeat of Prince Vostok six months ago.

"Kiyoko—an interesting name," the consul continued. "Pure one."

'Pure child' actually—which the consul surely realized. But she wasn't a child anymore, hopefully. "You are indeed astute. It is my name outside BetterWorld as well."

"And your family name is Pingyang."

The consul had done his research. Or he was accessing databases as he spoke. Kiyoko Pingyang wasn't her birth name, but after she and her sister fled their vicious parents, they purged their affiliations with them.

"Princess Pingyang was your age now when she organized an army to overthrow the Sui Dynasty," he continued.

"Yes, it was a campaign of liberation against an evil despot."

The consul nodded slightly. "Very interesting." He sipped his tea. "We do not receive many visitors from the Fantasy Continent. I understand you've had some troubles there."

"Yes. I have legal title to my realm, but MediaCorp has decided to seize it, putting a lock on it, and also locked up my avatar, my mall, and everything else I own." Charles had written fake user data into her duplicate avatar, hiding her, more or less, from the BetterWorld admins.

"There is precedence for such actions, if you violated the terms of service."

"I did not. I sent you evidence to the contrary."

"Yes, it was reviewed. They claim you are connected to the Collective, and its attacks on MediaCorp, including here on BetterWorld."

"They have no evidence."

Consul Zhang set his tea cup on the table and raised an eyebrow. "It is clear that your sister and your housemates were all involved in these attacks. You say you were not?"

"Yumekuni was not involved."

His face gave no indication how he interpreted her evasiveness. "May I ask, how you are able to appear here if your avatar was locked?"

"I still exist. And so here I am." She sipped from her tea.

"And what is it you request?"

"I request that you help facilitate the return of Yumekuni to Princess Kiyoko, its lawful caretaker."

He nodded. "I see."

"And there is another matter, in the outside world."

"Yes?"

"My sister Waylee Freid is imprisoned in the U.S." She repeated her well-practiced plea.

Consul Zhang sipped his tea before responding. "You have presented this information before."

"Not to you, though. I hope that with your compassion, wisdom, and influence, your country, which is the oldest and most populous in the world, might help secure my sister's release."

He set down his tea and rose, indicating that the meeting was over. "I will consider your plea and note it in my communications."

Kiyoko rose and bowed slightly. "The fate of Yumekuni and Waylee Freid lie in your hands."

The consul nodded. "Thank you for your visit to the People's Republic of China."

Just like everyone else Kiyoko had spoken with. Polite words, but no promise of help.

4

Waylee

Francis and Miranda returned the next day, about an hour after breakfast and cell inspection. According to the prison schedule, Waylee's only clock, that meant it was around 9 a.m. The concrete-walled meeting room looked even bleaker than before.

"Francis," Waylee began as her lawyers opened their data pads, "you've gotten protesters off. Dingo for example, more times than I can count."

"In state court, sure," he said. "They're short-staffed, and even though there's been a flurry of laws introduced to limit protests, the prosecution is usually happy to settle for fines and probation." His eyebrows raised like question marks. "Your case is a lot more serious, though."

Waylee wasn't entirely sure where to go with this. "I remember reading about this case, it was before the Rand Administration, where a group of people were arrested for protesting a pipeline, but were acquitted after testifying that their actions were justified by the threat of climate change. What if I tell the jury about the threat MediaCorp poses to free thought and democracy, and that they made it impossible to reach people any other way? What I did had to be done."

Francis loosened his tie, then swiped fingers against his data pad screen. "What you're talking about is a necessity defense, an argument that you have a necessity to act to prevent a greater harm." He met her eyes. "Unfortunately, it almost never works. I can cite some studies if you like. You need a sympathetic, or at least open-minded, judge. Most of the federal judges these days won't allow that kind of argument."

"Why not?"

"It's a strict line of thought, let's leave it at that." He exhaled. "It's irrelevant. Like I said yesterday, I advise against going to trial. If we did go to trial, I would not call you as a witness, and I expect a PD would feel the same way. Once you're on the witness stand, the prosecutor can pick you apart."

"And you don't think I can handle myself?"

Francis waved a hand. "You can discuss that with your public defender, if it comes to that." He glanced at his data pad again and cleared his throat. "There's one last strategy to consider."

"What's that?"

"I've been examining your medical records. You were diagnosed with a condition called cyclothymia?"

Her toes clenched in anger. "If you're talking about an insanity defense, no way. That would undermine everything I did. People would say, 'Oh, that video and all those documents were just a crazy person's manifesto.' Once I'm labeled as crazy, I'm irrelevant, and everything connected to me is irrelevant."

Francis waved his hands. "Yeah, yeah. I thought you'd say something like that, but I had to suggest it. Mental disorder defenses rarely work anyway." He paused. "Have you had any psychiatric evaluations since your arrest?"

"No."

"That's probably because the prosecution is afraid you might be considered incompetent to stand trial—"

"Is that what you think?"

"No, of course not. Let me finish. The prosecution has to share evidence with us, and if their psychiatrist deems you're not competent to stand trial, or your actions had mitigating factors, we could use it. It seems they're unwilling to risk that. So if you're willing to meet with a psychiatrist, it might make a good bargaining chip."

Waylee shook her head. "Forget it. I'd rather spend life in prison than discredit what we revealed."

* * *

Pelopidas

Pel didn't need VR to write code, nor especially prose. But with goggles and headphones on, distracting clutter and traffic noises disappeared.

'Waylee Freid is quite possibly the most courageous, selfless person of our time,' the light gray letters in the universe of blackness began. 'She overcame a difficult childhood, which gave her an innate urge to fight injustice.'

The corrective bio went on and on, Pel's longest prose work ever. He also wrote a condensed version, bullets that refuted MediaCorp's lies. A video might get more hits, but would be harder to find homes for, and he'd have to customize a new avatar. Besides, he didn't have Waylee's charisma or video skills—he'd probably put people to sleep.

Tears dripped out of Pel's eyes as he recalled the reasons he loved his girlfriend. He had to pull off his VR helmet to wipe them away.

Now for the hard part. He put the helmet back on and opened the minimalist interface of the Collective Router. It generated a fake Comnet address, computer ID, and geographic location, and opened a portal into the Comnet, a universe of icons and pathways, redshift-accelerating beyond anyone's ability to catalog.

Pel created a new Comnet account, 1Truth1, and posted Waylee's defense on forums he had addresses and passwords to. Then he cobbled a script together to find indie blogs and other non-MediaCorp outlets and list their addresses in descending order of traffic count. 99% of contact pages had video captcha codes and other defenses against bots and spam. AI was Charles's thing, not his, so he had to pitch Waylee's defense manually. A pain in the ass.

If he was lucky, he would reach 1% of the number of people that Media-Corp reached with their slander. He didn't have Waylee's knack for viral phrasing. Maybe an upvote campaign?

Pel logged on to the Collective's news net and requested help. But would anyone notice his request? The top threads were all about stepped-up attacks by MediaCorp and the government. Pel followed a link to Homeland Security's Comnet site.

A Homeland suit told a room of reporters, "As recent events have demonstrated, cyberterrorism is one of the leading threats to America. Particularly the cyberterrorist organization that calls itself the Collective, which was behind the Super Bowl hack and associated attacks on BetterWorld and massive thefts of information and money . . ."

We didn't get that much. We didn't even get enough money to break even.

". . . These attacks undermine America and cost billions of dollars. The goal of the Collective is nothing less than the destruction of our way of life."

The destruction of MediaCorp, maybe.

"It is imperative that we make every effort to combat this threat, and so we have made it our top priority."

Interpol made a similar announcement. "Cyberterrorism, particularly the Collective, is the greatest current threat to global security. Interpol is committed to the transnational fight against cyberterrorism and cybercrime, and is working with law enforcement agencies and private companies around the world to investigate and eliminate these threats on a global scale."

We should have addressed other countries, not just attacked the Rand administration. MediaCorp's tentacles and President Rand's free trade agreements undermined democracy everywhere.

Pel followed more links. MediaCorp news and discussion programs accused the People's Party of fomenting terrorism, and said the party should be outlawed. Both major parties piled on, calling for People's Party candidates to be removed from the ballot.

Just when they were picking up momentum. The People's Party had little chance of winning any seats in Congress, but had been favored in quite a few state and local races.

Pel continued his reconnaissance. In business news, things were picking up for Bob Luxmore. He took advantage of the drop in MediaCorp stock value by doubling his shares, pouring most of his fortune into it. In response, the stock price rose. Luxmore was now even richer and more powerful than before.

It looks like we ruined our lives for nothing.

* * *

Kiyoko

Dressed in long yellow robes with red trim and a gold headdress, Kiyoko stared in the wide-angle pinhole camera outside Pel and Charles's apartment door. It was one of many motion-sensitive cameras Pel had hidden around their floor or pointed out windows, all integrated into a security network.

"It's me," Kiyoko half sang to the nearly invisible lens. She typed in the combination to the digital lock and opened the steel-plated door. Gabriel followed her in.

Like her apartment, a short entryway passed the bathroom and kitchen and led to a living room with bedrooms on either side. Charles and Pel's living room was barren, though. It had a white faux-leather sofa, matching chairs, a table, and a big wall screen, but no decorations at all. Not a poster, not a souvenir, not a photograph. It was a living room without any sign of life.

You could tell Pel lived here, though. Fifty feet of high-tensile rope lay coiled inside a cardboard box and tied to a bracket beneath the covered window. Compact infrared binoculars hung from a hook next to the window, along with a flashlight and pack of spare batteries.

The binoculars were kind of a waste. He'd put thick white honeycomb blinds over all the windows on their floor and insisted they never be opened. They were cheap, and admitted some light, but couldn't be seen through and would supposedly prevent laser microphones from picking up their conversations. Pel's were coated with dust—he and Charles never cleaned anything except the dishes.

The wall screen was set to display the camera feeds. One showed her friend Rini Takahashi walking home, her yakisoba stall closed until tomorrow morning.

"Wall screen," Kiyoko commanded, "Episode 207 of Three Princesses." Her favorite new anime show.

"This show is the best," she told Gabriel as the catchy title song began.

"What is it about?" He looked sincere.

"It's about three princess sisters in medieval Japan with magical powers, fighting an evil shogun and his minions." Normally she'd say more, but she waited for a reaction.

He smiled. "Sounds like you and your sister. You only need a third."

She looked at him, surprised at his insight. "And magical powers."

"What you did with that Super Bowl video, that seems like magic to me."

The door to Charles's room opened and he stepped into the living room. Charles wore jeans and a plaid shirt. He ran a hand over his close-cropped hair and bowed. "Konbanwa, my princess!"

She returned the bow. They were equals. "Konbanwa, tomodachi-chan!"

"Three Princesses?"

"Wall screen, pause," she commanded. "Just started," she told Charles. "But we can watch it after dinner."

Speaking of which, no sign that anyone had started dinner. And she was hungry. "Where's Pel?"

Charles shrugged. "He's been in his room all day. I don't think he even came out for breakfast or lunch."

Kiyoko used to do that, get so immersed in BetterWorld she forgot to eat.

Behind her, Gabriel said, "We can always get takeout."

"Is he working or gaming?" Kiyoko strode to Pel's bedroom door, robes swooshing behind her, and knocked.

No answer.

"Uh, Kiyoko?" Charles asked.

She looked over her shoulder. "Yeah?"

"Did you see what those cheap bastards at Fantasmas said?"

"I saw your forward. It's not all bad news. They won't create new shares without more investment, which makes sense. But they're intrigued about including Yumekuni, and I bet that will bring in new investors." *And my realm will live again!*

She knocked on Pel's door again. "Are you alive?"

"Hold on," Pel yelled from inside.

After a while, he emerged, scruffy and barefoot. "What is it?"

Kiyoko threw up her hands. "It's dinner time and you're in there gaming."

Pel narrowed his eyes and clenched his fists. "I'm defending Waylee from MediaCorp's slander campaign. I'm sorry if that's more important than serving your royal highness a meal that you'll complain about anyway."

Jerk. "I hardly ever complain about your cooking. Even when it's bad."

That last part slipped out.

Charles stepped forward, his face in nervous knots. "We are pretty hungry."

Pel stared at him. "Are you that helpless? Am I the only one who knows how to put rice in a cooker?"

"I can do that much," Kiyoko said, "but we have an arrangement. I do everything that requires stepping foot outside, since you're so scared. You cook and Charles cleans up afterward."

Charles huffed. "The black man always gets the worst job."

Was he kidding or serious? "Don't say that," Kiyoko said.

"I suggest takeout," Gabriel repeated, his mediation skills meager but the effort admirable. "I will pay. No need to fight, we are all friends."

Pel smacked his bedroom door jamb with the bottom of his fist. "What the hell is wrong with you all? I told you what MediaCorp said about Waylee and I'm the only one who did anything?"

Beneath her floor-length dress, one of Kiyoko's shoes stomped against the tile floor. She stabbed a finger at Pel. "Waylee's my sister, you jerk! I write people every day trying to get her out of prison before it's too late. I go visit officials while you sit in your room too scared to help!"

"I'm helping," Charles interjected.

Kiyoko nodded. Charles had been covering their tracks, redistributing data and documents, and keeping tabs on their Collective allies to make sure none would turn.

Pel kept shouting. "You know Interpol is after us now too? How long before Brazil turns us over?"

Gabriel interrupted. "Come on, take it easy." He looked at Kiyoko. "I'm on your side, of course."

Pel ignored him. "You know the People's Party may be disbanded, people arrested, just because Waylee was a member? And guess what their response was?"

He didn't wait for anyone to respond. He pulled his comlink out of his jeans pocket and stretched the screen. "People's Party national site," he spoke to it.

Staring at his comlink, Pel read in a softer but still agitated voice, "'Contrary to allegations made by MediaCorp and the two corporate parties, the People's Party had nothing to do with the video released during the Super Bowl. While the video revealed how MediaCorp and the president's party actively work together to suppress democracy, a fact long pointed out by the People's Party, it was produced and broadcast without any consultation with Party officials. Waylee Freid may support our candidates, but she has no official position and acted entirely on her own.'"

"So even the People's Party are sellouts?" Charles asked.

Pel's whole body clenched. "Not only that, someone claiming to represent the Collective released a video saying we're rogues. We're losing all our allies."

"How can someone claim to represent the Collective?" Charles said. "We're structureless."

Pel nodded. "Maybe MediaCorp or Homeland infiltrated them. But no one's countered it."

"I'll do that right now," Charles said. "I got max creds."

"I got it," Pel said. "I'll be more careful, and besides, you can't even write legible comments."

"Fuck you, script kiddie."

Gabriel walked between them before the argument got physical. "Why don't you all sit and reconcile. Relax, and I'll come back with some food."

"I'll go with you," Kiyoko said.

"No," Charles said, "you should stay here. We, uh, need to talk about Fronteira and Yumekuni."

"Don't you think we have more important things to talk about?" Pel said.

"We can be rich and live wherever we want."

"What's wrong with Liberdade?" Kiyoko asked. She'd picked it out. It was almost like living in Tokyo.

Charles fidgeted. "Sure, Liberdade's better than my old hood in B'more. Got stores and restaurants, and almost never hear gunshots. But why not trade up if we got the money?"

He was probably just sick of sharing an apartment with Pel. Their friendship had always been a little rocky, and things were definitely getting worse.

Pel let out a huff and stomped back into his room, slamming the door and locking it.

Sad. "He used to be really mature," Kiyoko said. "I used to look up to him."

"Maybe he needs a good fuck," Gabriel said. "I can find him a girl." He looked at Charles. "I can find you one too."

Charles's eyes widened and he grinned. Then he met Kiyoko's eyes and turned away.

"Are you going to find me a girl too?" Kiyoko asked Gabriel.

His jaw dropped.

"Joke." If she wanted a partner she'd find one herself. "You know, Pel loves my sister. Are you trying to destroy their relationship?"

Gabriel shook his head. "No, no. But be realistic—who knows when they'll see each other again? I am sure she would want him to be happy."

Kiyoko's energy drained away and she collapsed onto the couch.

Gabriel sat next to her and put a hand on her shoulder. "I am sorry. I am no diplomat. I do not want to hurt your sister and didn't mean to upset you. But I worry about Pel's mental health and . . ." He glanced at Charles but didn't continue.

Kiyoko patted Gabriel's hand. He had good intentions, at least. She stood. "Let's get some takeout, like you suggested." She knocked on Pel's door. "We'll be back in a few."

Charles fidgeted as they left.

* * *

Dalton

Window blinds shut, Dalton set his laptop on the desk and stretched out the screen and keypad. Old-fashioned, but he didn't like being shut in

VR—too vulnerable to attack. He opened the onion router, logged onto a private Ares network, and checked SharkFeed999's message box.

Nothing from De Barros yet. Dalton hoped he wouldn't have to hunt for a replacement.

The Jersey City police had had plenty of cops like De Barros who were corrupt, alcoholic, or both. There had been a big scandal about under-the-table work and falsifying time cards that went all the way up to the captain level. It had tarnished the entire police force and Dalton had been forced to quit his side job as a security consultant even though he had nothing to do with the scandal.

Then there were the fights at home, the stormy affair with Mia, and things just kept getting worse. Dalton had arrested this drug dealer, a gang lieutenant who went by the dumbshit name of Grill-Z. He had a pretty solid case. But the dealer's douchebag lawyer got it thrown out on a chain of evidence technicality.

A few days after the trial, Dalton and his partner found Grill-Z on a stoop with his crew. They took him for a ride to an alleyway, where Dalton used a tire jack to mete out some street justice. Just smashed his diamond grill and a few teeth to let him know his actions had consequences. Far short of what the scumbag deserved. But the asshole's lawyer sued the city, and the dickless mayor pressured the department to fire him.

The hell with them.

A message popped up from Seeker111, who was Petrov's AR-masked aide, Martinez. The message was short: 'See attachment.' A file with no application icon was attached. A message popped up from the laptop's malware scanner: 'Attachment unscannable and quarantined.'

The laptop had a custom encryption/decryption program that Dalton was supposed to use for all internal communications, an extra level of security. Clunky but pretty safe. He countermanded the malware scanner, swiped the attachment into the decryption box, and entered the day's key. The file converted to a text message with screen captures.

According to Ares's contacts in MediaCorp, all known Comnet accounts of Demopoulos and Lee had been deleted. They had not appeared under their own names or known aliases on any message boards or blogs. Pingyang still had BetterWorld and Comnet accounts, but was locked out of them.

Dalton typed a question in the composition box and clicked the 'encrypt' button. He swiped the output file to his message box and sent it to

Seeker111. 'Can we restore Pingyang's accounts, then use them to track her?'

Seeker111 responded almost immediately. This time she didn't bother typing 'see attachment.' 'I will ask,' the encrypted portion began. 'Media-Corp has incentive to cooperate. And they have this tool that can monitor BetterWorld avatars.'

There must be other angles to pursue. Dalton wasn't a hacker, but had over a decade of experience finding people.

Lee was a loner and would be the hardest to find. But Demopoulos and Pingyang had played in a band called Dwarf Eats Hippo with Freid and, at first, a drummer named J-Jay. MediaCorp had taken down their Com-net site but sent a copy to Ares. Their so-called music—screeching guitars and vocals with layers of computer noise and audio samples—had grated against Dalton's ears.

Pingyang might be the easiest to find. She was a social butterfly in Baltimore and on BetterWorld, a time suck he'd never bothered with. Unfortunately, she made and modeled costumes for a living and changed her appearance almost constantly.

Even Demopoulos looked completely different with a buzzcut and braided beard on stage versus the young executive he'd impersonated at the New Year's fundraiser for President Rand. Hopefully the face recognition software on Dalton's data glasses would be up to the challenge.

Would Demopoulos and Pingyang be dumb enough to play in public, maybe for money? Would Pingyang get modeling work? Would they try to defend Freid? Communicate with her lawyer? Beg people for money?

'Can you find out who's been communicating with Francis Jones from São Paulo?' Dalton wrote.

'I can look. But remember Demopoulos and Lee are hackers in the Collective. They'll use encryption and random relays and hide their tracks.'

Dalton opened another Comnet window and searched for 'Waylee Freid.' He got millions of results. Besides news and opinion pieces, they included memes, most of them stupid, and weird shit like a sex game with simulations of Freid and President Rand. MediaCorp's biography video was the top ranked result, claiming more hits than the rest put together.

Dalton encrypted a quick summary and sent it to Martinez.

'MediaCorp manipulates the rankings,' Martinez wrote back. 'You won't find your quarry with their search engines.'

An hour later, Martinez sent SharkFeed999 a copy of the Collective Router and a list of hidden sites, 'courtesy of Homeland Security and Interpol.'

The Collective message boards were full of subversive thoughts and hints of illegal activity. But if they were shut down, the posters would just move elsewhere. Better to monitor them and gather intelligence.

After more consultation with Martinez, Dalton searched for darknet essays containing 'Waylee Freid,' 'hero,' and 'courageous,' with a high 'like' frequency that suggested a coordinated upvote campaign.

Dalton's algorithm found a long pro-Freid piece with a barrage of upvotes on several Collective boards. It was also posted on blogs in the legitimate Comnet.

'Waylee Freid is quite possibly the most courageous, selfless person of our time,' it began. It called her a hero.

Dalton ran a program that compared the wording to writing samples obtained of Demopoulos, Lee, and Pingyang. It definitely wasn't Lee, whose command of written English was poor and full of abbreviations and typos. Nor Pingyang, who used flowery, formal language. It was an 86% match with old posts and class assignments from Demopoulos. Not great, but well above random chance.

Could he track down the author? He put Martinez on it.

5

Waylee

Waylee's next trip to the visitation room was for a thirty-something couple in blue suits. The man, Indian in appearance with wire-rimmed glasses, introduced himself as Agent Kulkarni from the FBI's Philadelphia division. The woman, pale with short brown hair, introduced herself as Agent Morgan.

The two agents sat at the table with Waylee. Agent Morgan peered at her. "We're hoping you've changed your mind and will cooperate with our investigation."

A new pair of clowns. They never give up. "Investigation of what?"

"The broader organization you're a part of. The Collective, for starters."

"I'm not a member of the Collective. You have to be a hacker. I'm just a journalist."

"I see. Well, what is your connection with them?"

"Where's my lawyer? I can't speak to you without a lawyer present." *Should have said that as soon as they introduced themselves.* She was a little too desperate for conversation.

The agents looked at each other. "Ms. Freid," Agent Kulkarni said with a slight accent, "we just need some information for our investigation. Nothing you say will be held against you."

Waylee stifled a laugh. At least they were entertaining. "Trust the government, huh? Lawyer."

Agent Morgan spoke. "We know your boyfriend, Pelopidas Demopoulos, is a member of the Collective. As is the boy you freed from jail, Charles Marvin Lee."

Waylee sat back in her chair and watched their eyes.

"This is your opportunity to help yourself," Agent Kulkarni said. "Otherwise you will probably spend the rest of your life in solitary at the supermax."

Waylee forced herself to ignore the threat. Of course they'd try to rattle her.

"Fine," he said. The agents stood, their chairs scraping against the pitted concrete floor.

"We'll arrange a meeting with your lawyer present," Agent Morgan said. "How's that?"

Waylee maintained her silence and they left.

* * *

Kiyoko

Astride her white unicorn cat, Nyasuke, Princess Kiyoko led the Fantasmas na Máquina delegation back through the Palace grounds from the teleport pad. She wore a carnation pink gown with ribbons and flowers and a diamond tiara. Not very practical for traveling, but it looked fantastic.

Charles rode a chestnut mare beside her. He had resurrected a Better-World avatar, a big Zulu warrior named Iwisa, with dark muscled skin, striped loin cloth and feathered headdress. He carried a cowhide shield and spear. Manly looking, Kiyoko had to admit.

Pel had refused to come, insisting he had more important things to do. *Uncool to abandon your friends, jerkface.*

Princess Kiyoko looked back at the delegation. First behind her was Fronteira Nova's producer, a Viking explorer. Next to him, the director, his avatar a figure of fire astride a flaming horse. On feet turned backward, an orange-haired child, the lead designer. Then other designers, artists, and programmers, one of which was a rolling head with long hair and wide eyes.

Fifteen in all, a big group to keep focused. Almost like herding cats. Kiyoko winked to herself.

"We return to the throne room to confer," she told the others. "I hope you enjoyed our brief tour of Yumekuni." Although most of her audience spoke English, her avatar spoke in Portuguese through a real-time translator that mimicked her voice.

To save time, they hadn't ventured far from any teleport pads, most of which were new. But they saw the realm's highlights—the Palace and capital, the Magical Woods, the Crystal Hills, the Vale of Waterfalls, the main towns . . . "We missed like 99% of the realm. But you can explore as much as you want now that there's a copy on your servers."

Her unicorn cat meowed, not the high-pitched squeak of normal cats, but a low, goosebump-raising timbre. "Nyasuke enjoyed your company," she told the others.

"How long did it take you to create all this?" the Viking-attired producer asked.

Kiyoko decided to estimate on the long side. "I started on BetterWorld when I was 14." The minimum age back when there was a minimum age. "At first, I just had a quarter acre." She patted Nyasuke's head. "I started expanding after completing my quest to free Nyasuke. So you could say four years."

Really, most of the design, artwork, acquisition, and coding took two years—still a big time investment, though. "Now of course," she continued, "I can build environments much faster. And Iwisa here is the best coder on the Comnet."

One of the programmers, a blue-and-yellow head-dressed native woman, looked Iwisa up and down."Your avatar—Zulu?"

Charles held up his spear. "Yes. I am a Zulu warrior. We forged a powerful kingdom under Shaka and humiliated the British colonialists in battle."

"As we hope to do against MediaCorp," the flame-covered director commented.

He turned to the producer and the native woman said, "The British won in the end, you know."

Guards in formal attire bowed to Princess Kiyoko and her company as they passed through the tourmaline-encrusted inner gate of the palace walls. Charles had helped her upgrade the NPC's, stitching in scripts from the Collective Emporium and improving virtual intelligence and subtleties of expression. Her guests had actually carried on conversations with capital and town leaders, convincing enough to pass a Turing test.

"The AI chatbots require a lot of processing power," Kiyoko admitted to her guests. "But emotional connections are more important than scenery to draw people in."

Her guests nodded in agreement.

A marble path led through a garden of flowers and past pools with leaping dolphins and singing salamanders, to the sprawling pink palace with its intricate latticework and spiraling towers. Inside, chandeliered halls and tapestry-walled antechambers led to the long throne room, pink silks hanging from the vaulted ceiling high overhead. Stained glass windows on either side cast patterns of colored light on the floor and columns. Butterflies flew loops and barrel rolls.

Princess Kiyoko halted in front of her golden throne and turned to face her guests. An angel-winged NPC attendant brought a gem-covered wooden chest and opened it.

Kiyoko reached inside and passed out silk-wrapped scrolls of gold lettering. "The gifts I promised you. A thousand cho—about a thousand hectares—of land, all of it agriculturally productive and rich in *qi*."

Purely symbolic at this point of course. But once Fronteira Nova went online, they could draw income from the land and use the *qi* to weave spells, once she taught them how.

"Most important," she said after distributing the gifts, "since I hold the copyright to Yumekuni's design, we can make it the fully realized centerpiece of Fronteira Nova. I am prepared to share all the parameters and code so we can replicate its magic throughout your brave new world."

No one had ever done this before, since BetterWorld was the only Qualia platform able to support complex realms and large numbers of users. Until now.

"We will create a virtual world," she continued, "that is more beautiful, more magical, and more fun than BetterWorld. All at a lower price. And we can give the users full rights to their creations, without the type of arbitrary clauses that makes MediaCorp so totalitarian." That was a condition she wouldn't waver from.

"You said you own the copyright to Yumekuni," the Viking producer said. "MediaCorp will not challenge that?"

Good question. From what she'd read, trade agreements made everyone, including Brazil, subject to common copyright provisions. These provisions protected her design work but also gave multinational corporations the right to sue. And MediaCorp had more lawyers than any other entity on Earth. "We should be okay. But we should discuss it with your legal staff. We could change the name but I don't think that's necessary."

"Follow up," one of the designers asked. "Yumekuni, does it still exist on BetterWorld?"

"MediaCorp suspended my account and locked up my realm there. No one can access it or message me."

Much to her archrival Prince Vostok's delight. He had even filed a dubious claim to the territory. Maybe that was why MediaCorp hadn't deleted it. It certainly wasn't because they were honorable.

The disembodied head, scroll in its teeth, rolled up to her. "Question. The people we met besides you and Iwisa are all bots?" The scroll didn't affect its speech.

"Yes. Iwisa is the best when it comes to programming bots."

Murmurs of appreciation from the guests.

Princess Kiyoko spread her gowned arms. "Shall we move forward, then? Forward together?"

The Viking producer bowed, followed by the others.

"We predict a big migration from BetterWorld in Brazil," the producer said, "and your realm and more like it will speed the process."

"Not just Brazil but users everywhere," Kiyoko said. "I have many followers in BetterWorld."

She locked eyes with Iwisa/Charles. Moving an entire realm and hordes of users? That was the equivalent of war. And Fantasmas na Máquina was a gnat compared to MediaCorp. Not only could MediaCorp sue in Brazil and the International Court of Arbitration, they could block access to their servers and routers, and thereby most of the world's customers.

They would have to keep a low profile until they had the infrastructure and following to withstand an attack.

* * *

Charles

"Can you please help Pel defend Waylee?" Kiyoko video messaged Charles from her apartment.

Immersed in his VR suit, Charles assented. It was disgusting, how MediaCorp spread lies about the bravest person he'd ever met.

Pel had recruited some Collective members to help spread and upvote his truth piece. But they were outnumbered by trolls that bashed Pel's words as soon as they were posted, and wrote dumb-ass shit on message boards like "ur a retard" and "Wailey Freed is a lying crazy nutjob, everyone knows that," or created memes that tried to paint her as a hypocrite. Like a doctored mug shot of Waylee with the captions 'Complains about the media / Uses the media to complain.'

Well, how the hell else was she supposed to get her message out? Knock on a billion doors?

Pel had said MediaCorp funded a shadow army of trolls who created fake accounts and bots to spread propaganda supporting asshats like President Rand and attacking any opposition. They were paid by the number of views, in cryptocurrency or BetterWorld credits. Of course MediaCorp went through a shitload of proxies so you couldn't pin it on them, but their dick print was all over it, Pel had said.

Time to measure up and kill some trolls. Blogs and forums had defenses against bots, so posters there were most likely real people hiding behind aliases. Brainless people, judging from their potato-headed comments.

First thing was to put a package together that when activated, would infect the pwned bitch's computer, send the virus to all their contacts, and post their personal information and documents on public file depositories, tagged with a cartoon troll in chains. Then it would wipe the computer and anything connected to it without a firewall. Charles started with pre-existing scripts but customized them so they wouldn't be in any malware databases.

And now to deliver the package. The latest video captcha technology on most message boards took too much computing power for an AI, so he'd have to post the virus link manually. Or he could direct message the trolls—bots could do that, and it would also eliminate collateral damage.

Charles opened up a machine learning tool called PhishPhactory that automated target discovery and spear phishing. He had to modify the code a little. He set it to deploy bots that would search for accounts that posted anti-Waylee or anti-Collective shit. Then it would search all postings by that user, examine timings and network paths to see if the user had other accounts, and create a profile. Then it would message the user with something enticing, like cheats to their favorite game, seemingly sent from a friend, or the closest a troll could have to a friend. The message would contain a hidden link to his virus package.

One nice thing about PhishPhactory was that it collected analytics and improved its performance as it worked. Charles double checked everything and deployed his weapon.

"Some trolls are going down!" he shouted to himself. Maybe just the gullible ones, but word would spread, and people would know they'd pay if they dared trash Waylee or go up against the Collective.

* * *

Dalton

Dalton sat at the alcove desk in his spacious hotel room, typing on his data pad and drinking a Coke. The clock in the lower right corner of the screen said 7:39 PM. De Barros was supposed to pick him up at 8, but would message him when he arrived. He was driving, and São Paulo traffic meant arrival times were never more than approximate.

Dalton logged onto the Ares network and pinged Martinez. 'Any luck?' he typed. His laptop had voice recognition but he almost never used it, not wanting to be overheard.

The response came almost instantly, probably voice to text. 'Freid's lawyer encrypts, too many bits even for Homeland. No traffic pointing to São Paulo. Could be anonymous routing. And your blog poster leaves no trails.'

Not surprising. Homeland Security had been chasing Lee and the others since last year and they had no doubt become extra paranoid.

'Some good news,' Martinez added, 'MediaCorp agreed to reinstate Pingyang's accounts and their cybersecurity experts filled them with custom viruses to track her location. It worked with Lee not once but twice last year.'

'Then why didn't they catch them?' Dalton typed. According to records and camera footage Dalton had reviewed, the FBI and city police had dedicated nearly thirty officers to arrest Lee and his accomplices at a house owned by Demopoulos's family. Yet their quarry managed to escape.

'MediaCorp wasn't privy to ground ops. They just assisted the Comnet ops.'

'Won't they be wary of a trap?'

'Lee and Demopoulos, yes,' Martinez responded. 'Pingyang, maybe not. It's worth trying.'

'Agree.' It might tip them off that they were being hunted. But they already knew that; they'd been hunted for six months.

A message popped up with a red header bar. Inspector De Barros. 'Five minutes from hotel. Meet me outside front doors. Black supercar.'

Dalton stowed his laptop in the room safe and put on his holsters and blazer jacket. In case of trouble, he was fully packed. Two guns, two knives. Data glasses with a camera and Portuguese translator. His jacket and slacks had a nanotube weave between the outer and inner liners that could stop most handgun ammo. Rifles or armor-piercing rounds were another matter, but this wasn't a combat mission.

He took the elevator down and exited the lobby. It was warm outside for a jacket, but it resembled standard business attire, and the concierge and door guard didn't deviate from their usual expressions of boredom. He spotted the inspector's car, a slick design with dark-tinted windows. The passenger door swung upward as he approached.

Dalton hopped in and the door closed. The leather interior smelled faintly of pot smoke.

"Ready?" De Barros's breath stank of alcohol, but his red-rimmed eyes were focused and speech unslurred.

A practiced alcoholic. Ares should cut him loose after this. "Your car?" Dalton asked.

"Like it? It's custom built. Viper V-10 engine, Formula 1 suspension. And it's bulletproof, even the windows. Adaptive copolymer laminates. Impossible to carjack."

"All you need is a bumper sticker that says 'I take bribes and work with gangs.'"

"Vai se fuder."

"Go fuck yourself," the bone transducer against Dalton's left ear translated.

"You've heard of translation programs?" Dalton said.

De Barros turned red. "Let's go."

Dalton kept one eye on the car's GPS display, projected on the windshield, as De Barros drove away from the hotel. His data glasses had a navigation program too, but there was no need to activate it. "Where are we going?"

"Nowhere. The car is a safe place to talk. And you can view our lovely city."

"I've already taken a tour." Several, actually, hiring private drivers to take him places that so-called musicians like Demopoulos and Pingyang might hang out at. The 'bohemian' Vila Madalena and Santa Cecilia neighborhoods seemed promising, but no luck so far.

De Barros kept his eyes on the road. Rua Oscar Freire was a one way, two-lane street lined with tall luxury hotels and apartment buildings. Expensive looking.

"Any luck?" Dalton began.

"No one's heard of Lee or Demopoulos, at least not in the state police. I think because asylum is a federal matter, and they only tell us things when they want."

Unfortunate. "Do you have colleagues in the federal police you can ask?"

"Yes, I know someone in DPF. He is on vacation so I must get his personal contacts." De Barros turned right down a street that looked a lot like Rua Oscar Freire.

"And there are others not on vacation?"

"Yes, but they are not necessarily friendly." He yammered about his experiences with DPF and how they were full of themselves.

De Barros turned right again, onto Rua Estados Unidos. United States Street. It was lined with mansions on one side.

"I've seen some security cameras and traffic cameras," Dalton said. "How many are there? Can you access them?"

"Yes, there is a citywide surveillance system. High-definition cameras in public circulation spaces—the Metro system, the parks and plazas, some of the streets, some of the buildings. And there are many, many private cameras. State police can access most of these over the network."

"Perfect. Can they be scanned with recognition software?"

"Yes, we have facial recognition programs."

"Run through past footage. Look for Lee, Demopoulos, and Pingyang."

He coughed. "How am I supposed to do that without someone noticing and asking questions, man?"

"That's your worry. Make something up. Spread money around if that's what it takes."

Permission wasn't their only worry. What if their quarry had changed their appearance or wore disguises? Freid and her accomplices had worn photo-realistic masks when breaking Lee out of jail and when sneaking into the MediaCorp broadcast center.

Everyone made mistakes, though. A methodical search would find them.

6

Waylee

Do you feel like plankton in the sea,
Tossed helplessly or devoured
By a voracious Leviathan?

That's how I felt.
Plankton. Chattel.
Chattel on a dying planet.
Straining against shackles,
Vocals strangled silent.

WHY?
Why fight?
Why not surrender to MediaCorp's fetid embrace?
Shut up and let the men of gold do your thinking.
>   *Toil and consume!*
>   *Vote for Product A.*
>   *Toil and consume!*
>   *Vote for Product B.*
>   *Toil and consume!*
>   *Everything is better in BetterWorld.*
Surrender is easy.

But I realized otherwise.
I, you, WE, ARE MORE POWERFUL than they.
The few cannot constrain the many.
Especially when we transform
Self-mutating
Into legions of heroes.

Using the pen and paper Francis had bought at the commissary, Waylee kept scribbling. She had intended to write a treatise against the Media-Corp-led plutocracy, but the thoughts came too fast to organize.

Hypomania. Her cyclothymia was back. These past months of calm and control, all a mirage.

The door opened. Her guards entered.

The burly black woman smirked. "Did you forget your appointment?"

"I don't have a clock in here."

"Time to go." The bald male guard put on her ankle and wrist shackles.

"What are your names?" Waylee asked. Names were better than uniforms.

"None of your goddamn business," the woman said.

The guards brought her to the visitation room and locked her inside. Francis Jones and his assistant Miranda Cruz were sitting at the metal table with their data pads. Well groomed as always, but their faces drooped.

"How's the case?" Waylee asked, worried they had bad news. Just seeing them, though—allies, friends—she wanted to break off her chains and dance around the tiny concrete block room with them. Shackled, she couldn't even hug them but clasped their hands as they stood to greet her.

"Did you know the FBI tried to interrogate me the other day?" Waylee said.

Francis's eyebrows rose. "No. Did you say anything?"

"Of course not. But they said they'd arrange another meeting with you there."

The lawyers sat back down. Francis motioned for Waylee to take a chair on the opposite side of the table.

Waylee sat and told them everything the FBI agents said. Other thoughts jumped out too, about Ms. Van Hofwegen's offer, about government collusion with MediaCorp, about fighting the plutocracy, about poetry and music. *Hypomania. Control it. Focus on the FBI meeting.*

Miranda took notes, lips pinched together in apparent frustration.

When Waylee finished, Francis thanked her and said, "Let me start with the good news. I contacted the federal and state public defender offices. They're reviewing your paperwork."

"When will they start?"

Francis let out a breath. "Since you have no money or assets, it should have been a quick decision, but the courts are investigating whether you have any hidden assets from criminal activities."

What? "I don't. That's absurd."

"Yes, and I expect it to be resolved in your favor, but it's caused a delay."

"That was your good news? I take it there's bad news?"

His face tightened. "Homeland Security ransacked my office and took my computers and all my data cubes. All my paper files too. Everything."

She leapt from her chair, scraping it backward over the concrete floor. "What the fuck?"

"Your book materials too, I'm sorry to say. They claimed their invasion was part of an ongoing terrorist investigation, and had a warrant. I filed grievances and requests for release right away but don't expect a positive response. The government overreaches every chance it gets."

Waylee paced the room, her steps constrained by the leg shackles. "Well, yeah. Why do you think I'm here?" She did break some laws, and was willing to pay for it, but the march toward totalitarianism had to be stopped.

Francis didn't respond, eyes following her.

"You lost everything?" she asked, still pacing. *Lions do that too when they're caged.*

"I have backups but the AUSA could have everything related to your case now. He shouldn't, but he probably does."

"AUSA?"

"Sorry," he said. "Assistant U.S. Attorney Lachlan."

"I bet we can use this to our advantage."

He smiled. "That's why I like you, Waylee."

"Thanks, Francis. You copied my book notes, right?"

"Scanned them, yes."

When was the last time this room was painted? The fluorescent-blue white walls were streaked by gray exposed concrete. Mostly at the same height as the crest of the chair backs.

"Lachlan's working with a DHS task force," Francis continued. "It's possible the seizure was unrelated, part of the government's persecution of the People's Party. But if the agents were on the task force, I might be able to get your case thrown out for prosecutorial misconduct."

"And even if you can't, you can bring it up to the jury, paint the government as abusers of power."

"If we go to a jury trial. I told you how risky that is. The feds almost never lose."

"I'm not selling anyone out. You just don't do that. And I'm not retracting my message or lying about it."

He nodded. "I grew up on the Baltimore streets too. I know all about the code. And I know you. So I'm not going to ask you to do something that I know you won't do."

"Thank you Francis."

"But we can plea bargain, and that is a much safer option than going to trial."

She smacked shackled fists together. "Plea. Bargain. Throw myself at their mercy."

Francis pressed his lips together.

"Go on," she said.

"I should let you know, the ACLU and People's Party are no longer supporting your case. I can't call on them for help anymore, and they've suspended their Comnet campaigns. It's just me and Miranda and my support staff now. At least until the PD's start."

She halted her pacing and stared at him, feeling besieged by swarms of hornets. "What happened?"

"They're overwhelmed. The government and MediaCorp accused them of supporting terrorists—"

"I'm not a terrorist. I didn't kill anyone or blow anything up." *Maybe I should have, but violence would just embolden them.*

"I explain that whenever I can. Anyway, there's a lot of pressure. The People's Party is focusing their resources on ballot access—most of the state legislatures are making it harder for third parties."

"It was already hard enough."

He nodded, then continued. "And the ACLU has so many cases these days, they've marked yours as a low priority."

"They think I'm a lost cause?"

"You're not a lost cause. And you do have defenders." He passed her sheets of paper stapled together. Printouts from a blog, *The Vanishing Voice.*

'Waylee Freid is quite possibly the most courageous, selfless person of our time,' the entry began.

Pel. It has to be. She sped down the lines of text. It was definitely him. Her skin flushed with warmth. "He still loves me!"

"You can keep the printout and read it whenever you're feeling down. The warden gave permission."

Much better than re-reading the thick binder of indictments. She rushed toward him, intending to kiss him on the cheek. "Thank you, Francis! I love you."

He put up a hand.

She halted her advance. "Sorry. Carried away. Are you gonna stay on?"

"Of course."

"Did you get anything from the crowdfunding site?"

He exhaled. "It was taken down and the funds were frozen. Homeland claimed it was supporting terrorism."

"Fucking kleptocrat weasels." She strained against her shackles. "So you won't even get gas money. How is that legal?"

"I'll help you no matter what, Waylee. Just like you, I hate bullies."

Miranda looked up from her data pad. "We need Ms. Freid's permission to negotiate."

"That's right," Francis said. "We left it open last time."

"I'd like to make a statement on the Comnet and explain myself."

"Unfortunately, that's against the rules. Like Miranda explained last time, we have to disable our cameras and microphones before entering the prison."

"Why?"

"The authorities make whatever rules they want. That's one of them. Now, about plea bargaining?"

"I'll do two years in general population. I'm not sure I can handle more. And please, you've got to get me out of solitary."

He nodded. "We'll do our best."

Back in her cell, which had developed a distinct odor of stale sweat and urine, Waylee wondered if she should have asked Francis to get medication for her cyclothymia. She'd forgotten. Maybe subconsciously she was too embarrassed to bring it up.

Medicine had never helped before, but there were drugs to even out the swings and ones to treat depression, which would come as soon as her hypomanic phase crashed. Her last two depressions, when they were on the run, were horrible. Soul-crushing to the point of catatonia. The next one might be worse yet, since she was all alone in this tomb-like cell.

Of course she had no way to pay for medicine. She had the blog printout, which she'd read like a Bible. And her pen and paper. Could they overcome programmed biology?

She paced her tiny crypt, tried to peer through the scratched, yellowed window slit, then snatched up her ballpoint pen and resumed writing.

* * *

Kiyoko

Kiyoko stood in the center of the big club stage, hundreds of diversely attired BetterWorld residents dancing and swaying below. Her VR gloves replicated the pressure of guitar strings against her left fingers as she tried to replicate her sister's chord progressions. The hard part was singing at the same time.

Marching from sunlight
Into the rain
Embracing the torrents
Of endless pain

Dark, even by Waylee's standards. Probably written during a depressive cycle.

To Kiyoko's left, clad in black leather, Waylee was playing bass. Not Kiyoko's bass with the Hello Kitty and unicorn stickers, but a generic black and red Fender. To the right, Pel stood behind banks of keyboards and computers, throwing in rhythm and mood layers and sampled voices from around Baltimore.

It wasn't live, just a replay of one of Dwarf Eats Hippo's handful of BetterWorld gigs, but Kiyoko was teaching herself how to front a band. Next step, write her own songs. They'd be cheerier than her sister's, no doubt about that.

She finished the show, tired from trying to imitate her big sister's jumping and gyrating, and sat down to check her messages.

First thing was to check Crypt-O-Chat, a darknet service where Pel had set up a private, encoded chat room. Kiyoko had a new message from M'patanishi—M-pat—the "Chief Facilitator" of their Baltimore neighborhood, a former gang enforcer, and an essential part of Waylee's team to fight MediaCorp. Kiyoko missed him, and missed her old neighborhood and house, even though she yearned to leave when she lived there.

Ujamaa1: Hauled in and questioned. Out now. Everyone interrogated. Laying low.

He didn't propose a live chat time. Kiyoko wrote back.

Princess_Kiyoko: Want to know more. When can we chat?

She logged off. Everything she read would be automatically deleted.

Next up, Princess_Kiyoko@mico.net.br, her public account. Amnesty

International finally wrote back, saying they wouldn't call for Waylee's release, since she was not just a prisoner of conscience. They would create a petition asking for a fair trial, though, and that she be treated for depression.

Better than nothing.

And she received an email from a BetterWorld admin, forwarded from her Comnet account. "After careful review of your case," the message stated, "we found no clear evidence of wrongdoing on your part. We have therefore decided to restore your BetterWorld avatar and properties, including the realm of Yumekuni."

Kiyoko jumped up and clapped her hands. "Yayyy!!"

She'd have to tell the others. Especially Nyasuke. She pulled off her helmet and climbed out of the VR suit. "Nyasuke! Where are you, my little soulmate?"

She heard a meow in the living room. She bounced out and picked up Nyasuke, held him close. "Everything's gonna be okay! Waylee's getting a fair trial, she won't hurt herself, and I'm back in BetterWorld!"

A knock at the door. The wall screen in the living room brought up the camera feed automatically, a feature that Pel had programmed. It was Gabriel, staring in the tiny camera lens with eyebrows raised.

Kiyoko was only wearing a T-shirt and panties. Best cover up a bit before answering the door. Although it would be nice to see his reaction, and maybe he could take some clothes off too. He looked fantastic that time she saw him without a shirt. She shook the thought away and threw on her one pair of shorts.

"I was coming over to see what you were doing, and heard you shouting," Gabriel said when she opened the door.

She pulled him inside and hugged him. "I'm back on BetterWorld!"

He hugged her gently, as if she were something breakable. "That is why you shouted?"

Their eyes locked. His irises were circles of different shades—a narrow band of russet on the outside, then a band of bronze, then dark chocolate, and finally, black pupils like portals to a far-off universe.

Her body moved on its own and she kissed him. His lips were soft for someone with such chiseled features.

At first he didn't respond. Then he kissed her back, lips pushing, hot breath entering her mouth. His tongue followed, grazing against hers.

It didn't feel right, the reluctance and then the sudden switch. Vague anxiety soured her desire. She let go and backed away.

He blushed, kind of cute for a lethal warrior. "Did I do something wrong?"

Kiyoko tried to fend off disaster. "No, no, I'm sorry. I didn't mean it." What a mess.

Gabriel shifted on his feet. "I do not think my supervisor would approve if he knew we were attracted to each other."

"You're attracted to me?" Of course he was, it was obvious. But he was making her seem like the bad person.

"Yes, certainly, but there are rules. Let's start over. You have your avatar back?"

Time. They needed a little time to sort this out. "Well I already had a copy of it," she said, "but now it's legit again. And I'm only half in exile now."

"How did this happen?"

She motioned for him to join her on the sofa. Maybe they could kiss again—first times playing a video game rarely went well, and kisses were no different. Especially considering they were from different cultures. But Nyasuke jumped up and sat between them.

Just as well. I don't want to get him in trouble. Kiyoko brought up the admin's email on the wall screen.

"You told me you were going to place Yumekuni on Fronteira Nova?" Gabriel said.

"Yes, I've already committed to do that."

"It is okay to do both?"

"I don't see why not. I can change the name if I have to. You should create an avatar and you can be my champion. Like you are here in São Paulo."

He blushed again. "You know, I don't always understand you. But I would be happy to make an avatar. You know I collect superhero comics."

She smiled. That was one of their first conversations when they met two months ago. He had a big comic book collection at his parents' house in the suburbs, and had talked about the X-Men and Avengers. She talked about Cyan and Rukia and how she used to sleep with a big Ren Tsuruga pillow when she was in middle school. Then she had gotten embarrassed about seeming childish in front of this professional soldier, and had switched subjects.

"We should talk to Charles first," Kiyoko said. "He can keep you from grief."

"Pardon?"

"Make sure you don't get infected with malware." New worries shoved aside her worries about the clumsy kiss. "He should check my avatar too."

Who knows what the admins might have done to it. MediaCorp was run by snakes. Maybe Charles could compare it to her downloaded copy and see if any of the code had changed.

* * *

Charles

"Of course I'll help," Charles, as the Zulu warrior Iwisa, told Princess Kiyoko. She had summoned him over their local network to a pared-down copy of her Yumekuni palace stored on a data cube in her game room. As always since settling in São Paulo, they didn't meet in her throne room, but met in her flower garden as equals.

Princess Kiyoko, wearing her customary pink robes with a diamond tiara, curtsied. "Thank you, my capable friend."

Charles/Iwisa bowed. "You're smart not to trust MediaCorp. Give me the passwords and I'll check out your avatar in the sandbox."

She squinted. "Sandbox? What do you mean?"

"Virtual machine." He summoned a virtual spray paint can, set the nozzle to fine, and summoned a whiteboard which floated in the air. There wasn't any breeze in the garden—Kiyoko was running off a game console, not a server farm—so he had no worries about random fuzziness.

Charles sprayed a big rectangle on the whiteboard. He activated voice to text, and labeled the rectangle 'LAPTOP.' "One of my computers," he told Kiyoko, "is set up just for testing and spoofing."

Inside the big rectangle, he drew a smaller rectangle and labeled it 'VIRTUAL MACHINE.' He drew another rectangle next to it and labeled it 'FAKE COMNET.' Then he drew arrows between the two, and arrows between 'VIRTUAL MACHINE' and another label, 'REAL COMNET,' that he placed outside the LAPTOP rectangle.

"I'll download your avatar to the virtual machine," he said, "which will look just like a real computer as far as anyone outside can tell, only with an address in China, and using fake Comnet accounts."

Princess Kiyoko nodded. "Like we do already, spoofing our location and hardware IDs?"

"Yeah, but the VM is self-contained. If it gets compromised by malware, it's no big deal, it's already quarantined."

With a pink-nailed fingertip, Kiyoko inscribed glowing letters and numbers in the air: Comnet and BetterWorld IDs and passwords. "I'm going to trust you with these," she said. "If I can't trust you and Pel, I can't trust anyone, and then what's the point of anything?"

"I got your back, you know that. Stay away from BetterWorld and don't download anything until I give the okay."

"I know, stay safe." She curtsied. "I thank you, Iwisa!"

Charles bowed, then logged out of the simulation. He took off his VR gear and powered on his test laptop, stretching the screen to full size. He opened the virtual machine window, started up the address spoofer, and selected a location from a map of China. The spoofing program would figure out an appropriate Comnet address and serial numbers, and load that into the fake operating system and hardware memory.

Preliminaries out of the way, Charles logged onto BetterWorld as Princess Kiyoko and downloaded her avatar using his BadPackets program. He'd written BadPackets himself—it was pretty simple. It would copy and assemble all the incoming data packets but randomly fail to send acknowledgments near the end, then cut the connection once all the packets arrived so it looked like the download failed.

Once the avatar finished downloading and BadPackets disconnected him from the Comnet, Charles unplugged the optic cable and disabled the Wi-Fi to be safe. He compared the new avatar to Kiyoko's local copy. The new one was bigger. Why? What did they add?

BetterWorld had a program called Sentinel embedded beneath the Qualia code that parameterized each avatar. MediaCorp claimed that Sentinel was only used to patch errors, fight malware, and prevent the use of cheatware to violate BetterWorld's 'laws of physics.'

That was bullshit. Sentinel was spyware at a James Bond level. It could snoop through the user's computer, copy everything on it, and request all sorts of payloads from the MediaCorp controllers. Unless you disabled it, and installed your own version, there was no chance of bypassing BetterWorld's rules. Of course that was a challenge he'd beaten years ago.

Charles ran his SentinelBuster program with the latest patches from the Collective boards. MediaCorp constantly updated their software and the Collective almost immediately found a way to crack it—part of the nonstop arms race between rule makers and people who didn't like playing by rules.

Sure enough, there was a Sentinel payload embedded in the Princess Kiyoko avatar. But it was encrypted and SentinelBuster didn't have the right decompiler. Charles might be able to crack it, but even if Pel helped, it would take time—maybe a lot of time.

Normally about now he'd open a bag of Utz chips or pack of Berger Cookies while he strategized. But São Paulo didn't have any of his favorite snacks, and besides, he didn't want to get fat again. He loaded a second virtual machine that replicated a VR headset and gloves. Too complicated to replicate an entire suit and support cage, but the user interface would only load what the hardware and rendering software—or simulated equivalents in this case—could handle.

He set up a monitoring program between the BetterWorld interface and the simulated hardware and operating system, and started recording. What's this avatar's spyware gonna do?

First thing it accessed was the fake GPS chip. Charles and Pel had disabled the GPS's in everything they owned, so that wasn't a worry. Although it confirmed MediaCorp was trying to find them. The Sentinel also accessed the virtual network card and Comnet address and attempted to transmit the data. If they were real, MediaCorp would have bypassed the anonymous pathways of his onion routing and pinned his location within a block.

Charles put his VR gear back on and voice messaged Kiyoko and Pel. "MediaCorp set up a trap. They're trying to find us."

Kiyoko summoned them to her flower garden again. "Do they know where we are?" she asked.

Pel's avatar, the old white man called William Godwin, stared at Charles/Iwisa. "You didn't give us away again, did you?"

"Fuck you."

"Well?"

"No, I ain't stupid." Charles told them about his precautions and what he'd found.

Kiyoko frowned and her shoulders drooped.

"I can replace the Sentinel spyware," Charles said, "with our own version that sends back fake information."

She sprang into perkiness. "Then there's a way I can return to BetterWorld?"

Pel crossed his arms, not a gesture he used in real life. "Won't MediaCorp have ways to know it's not legit?"

"We could run some trials and see what the avatar sends to the servers," Charles said, "then replicate the same protocols."

"Can I run my avatar from your virtual machine?" Kiyoko asked.

"Trouble is, it needs to communicate with your VR suit. That's the real problem—if you wanna interact in BetterWorld, you can't be isolated. We have to disable the spyware somehow without MediaCorp knowing, or fool it into sending fake information."

Pel shook his head. "Why are we even bothering? Lots of risk with no benefit."

"What do you mean no benefit?" Kiyoko said. "I have a lot of influence in BetterWorld, and can use it to help Waylee, maybe help the world."

Pel threw up Godwin's hands. "But you've already been on BetterWorld as Princess Kiyoko."

Her stand-in avatar looked a lot like the original, but didn't have any spyware and submitted fake user information. If they wanted, the admins could scan for avatars that resembled Princess Kiyoko. With a billion users and billions of NPCs, they would have to dedicate a lot of AI power, though, and Kiyoko had changed her avatar just enough that none of the parameters exactly matched the old one.

Kiyoko seemed to read Charles's mind. "I can't spend much time there. I just visit embassies. If the admins spot my avatar in a scan, or someone reports me, they'll delete it and block any duplicates from returning."

"Well it's good to know MediaCorp is laying traps for us," Pel said. "They matched the FBI bounty, so I'm not surprised. Now let's delete the damn thing and stay off BetterWorld."

"I told you," Charles said, "there might be a way to fool them."

Pel raised his volume. "And what about the unknowns? What makes you think you can figure out everything that spyware does? MediaCorp has over a million employees. They could easily have dedicated a team of hundreds just to fuck with us. There are only two of us, three if you count Kiyoko."

Kiyoko rolled her eyes. "Thanks."

Pel ignored her. "What are the odds two are smarter than hundreds? They found us in Baltimore with custom payloads; they can do it again."

"Depends on the two," Charles said. "But I feel you."

Kiyoko sighed. "I'll stay off BetterWorld until you figure this out, assuming you have time."

Charles shook Iwisa's spear. "I'll find the time."

Pel/Godwin's eyes narrowed. "Look, fools. If MediaCorp is trying to access our location, it means they have a plan to kidnap or kill us. I don't care how safe you think you're being, the minute you access the Comnet with that avatar, I'm out of here and you can fend for yourselves."

* * *

Kiyoko

VR suit on, Kiyoko met Francis in a darknet chat room. It had no furniture, just floral wallpaper and daylight-spectrum ceiling lighting. Francis had a generic avatar, a thirtyish Chinese man with every feature—eyes, nose, cheeks, chin, lips—barely deviating from the mean.

Princess Kiyoko appeared as herself. She curtsied. "Thank you for taking the time to meet me, Francis."

"You're welcome. You're not being charged with anything, so it doesn't violate any rules." Even though Francis was born and raised in Baltimore, his avatar spoke with an English accent, in near monotones. His body didn't move at all, just the face.

"How's Waylee doing?" she asked.

"Surprisingly energetic. Which is good, I think."

"Maybe not." Kiyoko opened a window that only she could see and brought up a diagnosis of hypomania. "Did she talk non-stop and really fast?" she asked Francis. "Did she keep changing the subjects? Did she pace or drum her fingers?"

"You think her cyclothymia is back?"

"Things like that never go away, it's just how well she can control it. The hypomanic phase is just irritating, but when she enters a depression, especially a bad one, that's when I worry. And depression always follows the hypomania, at least for her."

"I'm not a psychiatrist," Francis said, his avatar expressionless.

"Amnesty International said they would create a petition asking for a fair trial, and that my sister be treated for depression."

"They should contact me so we can coordinate."

"I'll let them know. And if you'll excuse my curiosity, what's up with your avatar?" Even Kiyoko's earliest peasant NPCs in the most remote reaches of Yumekuni were more interesting.

Generic Chinese Man didn't change expression at the insult. "Just using defaults and a comlink. Homeland Security took my computers so I'm a little hampered. Avatars are the least of my worries."

"What?"

"They ransacked my office and took everything but the furniture. Claimed it was part of an ongoing terrorist investigation. I filed grievances and requests for release right away but haven't even received a response yet."

"That's crazy. How can they do that? Especially since you're a lawyer."

"It's a short goose step from one-party rule to totalitarianism. The Rand Administration thinks they can do whatever they want."

"The government's still claiming Charles and Pel are terrorists," Kiyoko said, "even though they've never hurt anyone. And MediaCorp launched this awful hit campaign against Waylee."

Charles and Pel were doing their best to counter the trolls and fake news, but it pained her to tears.

"I saw the video," Francis said. "It was full of inaccuracies. Waylee should file suit for slander. I'd be happy to help."

"You're the best." She returned to the more pressing problem. "How long until Waylee gets medicine?"

"I don't know. Amnesty International campaigns can take months, if they succeed at all."

"That's too long!"

"I'll bring it to the warden's attention that the whole world is watching him and he needs to provide Waylee the medicine she needs. And I'll make sure the court knows this trial is being scrutinized."

"Is she still in solitary?"

"Yes, but I'm trying to get her transferred to the general population. And she'll get help from the public defenders' offices. It's taking a while, but I'll make sure it happens."

"You're my hero," Kiyoko said. He had freed her from federal confinement. Maybe he'd free Waylee too. "I'll see if Amnesty can contact the prison today. And let me know if there's anything else I can do."

* * *

Dalton

Dalton hopped into De Barros's black sports car. Another warm night. "You said you have good news?" he asked the fat inspector as they pulled onto Rua Oscar Freire. He'd been in São Paulo twelve days now and operation expenses were mounting.

"Yes, I am the guy here," De Barros said. "We found something on the cameras."

De Barros had bribed an IT technician to look through the city camera footage. The technician been running an AI program for a week now, scanning live and archived footage from over a hundred thousand police-accessible cameras.

"No matches with Lee or Demopoulos," De Barros said as they crawled along with the traffic. "But we found Pingyang on archived footage from sixteen days ago. They keep it for ninety days before it's overwritten."

"Where?"

"Picked her up on a hidden camera in the Luz station. They're not all obvious." He pulled into an ethanol fuel station and parked against the wall of a service garage.

De Barros pulled out his comlink and stretched the screen to maximum size. "DCL, exibe Pingyang na Estação da Luz."

A striking Asian girl with bright red hair, wearing a fancy Chinese gown, walked across the frame. She had Kiyoko Pingyang's face, although he couldn't be 100% sure. She was accompanied by a big guy wearing dark data glasses and a Miami Marlins baseball cap.

"You're certain that's Pingyang?" Dalton asked. In images and video from Baltimore, she changed her hair, clothes, even eye color, almost constantly.

"99% match."

"Who's the guy with her?" He had a military haircut and strode with a straight posture, shoulders back, data glasses scanning the surroundings. Ten to one he was a bodyguard with a lot of training.

"Don't know."

"Find out."

De Barros grunted. "Do you want to hear my report or not?"

The fat detective never ceased to irritate. "Continue," Dalton said.

"We checked the rest of the Luz cameras. She avoids them, you never see her face. But in some you can see her dress and the red hair. Sticks out like a fucking macaw. We're checking the other Metro cameras for the same hair, to see where she entered and exited the system."

"Nice work." Dalton meant it. "How often does she use that station?"

"She only shows up once there, but from the pictures you sent me, she likes to change her appearance."

"Let me know when you find out more. And we need to know if the Marlins fan's a bodyguard."

Z

Kiyoko

The aquamarine-robed priestess, her face and hands smooth and age-less, onyx hair whipping in the salt wind, strained to carry a thick disk of dull grayish lead. She knelt with it in the upper reaches of the surf and positioned it on wet sand between jumbles of dark, pitted rocks. "You must stand on this," she said, "or it will see you. You don't want it to see you."

Princess Kiyoko, sandaled and cloaked in oiled wool, didn't entirely un-derstand but followed the woman's instructions, stepping onto the disk. It was barely wide enough for a single person but looked heavy, much too heavy to move unaided.

A chill wind assaulted her from the ocean and she closed her cloak tight. Stretched along the beach to either side, others stood silent amidst the rocks, faces cowled, backs hunched, webbed feet greeting the incoming waves.

"You are very lucky," the priestess told Kiyoko. "Your ancestry and the trained configuration of your mind will allow you to observe. Most cannot. They would see only what they are doomed to see—ordinariness, lack of import. They suckle conformist distractions and grasp desperate sanity."

Standing on the platform, elevated above the terminal reach of the waves, Kiyoko abstracted questions within questions. "Why is this?"

The priestess did not answer. She held up her hands, palms facing the sea, and fell into a silent trance.

Beyond, the waves whipped into a frenzy. About a mile offshore, some-thing monstrous arose from the depths, gibbous and clawed, amorphous head with gaping tentacled mouth, water streaming down glistening skin. Scudding over the sound of crashing water, dissonant guttural rumbles chilled her skin and inner ears. A foul stench blew in with the wind, the stench of things long dead beneath primordial muck.

The thing was bigger by far than any ship Kiyoko had seen. It oozed malevolence. Yet she was too astonished to feel fear.

Human-faced, gnat-bodied creatures flew to the monster from places beyond her tunnel vision and down from low-looming grey clouds. They buzzed around it and dropped strings of colored lights on its head and hunched back, decorating it like a Yule tree. The thing lumbered forward, toward the shore at an angle. Toward the city.

Waves washed in. Chilly brine splashed over the platform. Kiyoko struggled to keep her balance but slipped off. Sandals slapped the water and sank in the sand as she fought to keep erect.

The monstrosity halted, turned and gazed at her with vacant eye sockets, black portals to a nether universe where the constellations were wrong and futures crushed into tortured knots.

She panicked at last, bladder threatening to discharge, knees rattling beneath her cloak.

The thing blinked in and out of visibility, a rapid strobe, then it disappeared, along with its gnat-winged attendants. The sea and sky continued to writhe but on their own now.

"I saw it," she told the priestess.

The priestess turned an impassive face toward her. "And it saw you. I warned you."

* * *

Kiyoko woke in her room, shaking with horror, sheets damp with cold sweat. She sat up and saw Nyasuke, her faithful nyan-nyan, curled at the foot of the double bed. She hugged him until the fear subsided. She didn't usually have such vivid dreams, maybe because BetterWorld was her dream, or because she spun dreams into the world around her to make it better.

What did it mean? She stumbled out of the bed and lit a cone of incense.

The multiverse was an interwoven pattern in space and time, too intricate for humans to fully grasp, but there nevertheless. Everything was interconnected and part of the whole. People were born with free will but it was hard to move in the webbing, and your best bet was to hitch a ride with one or more of the gods as they glided from destination to destination.

Kiyoko typically prayed to the Japanese kami and Chinese deities, but all gods had power. The key was knowing which ones to address for a given situation, and then getting their attention. "Omoikane-sama, Great Chandra, O Morpheus, hear my humble petition . . ."

When she was done praying, she dressed in golden robes, draped a blue eye talisman around her neck, and knocked on Alzira's door. Gabriel was off today and visiting his parents. Hopefully not meeting girls.

Alzira opened the door and eyed Kiyoko up and down, saying nothing.

Kiyoko hardly ever saw their backup bodyguard, who was almost as antisocial as a hikikomori. She was a little younger than Gabriel, and dark skinned with frizzy hair bound in a ponytail. She wore a silver crucifix around her neck and a silver band—her engagement ring—on her right ring finger. "Diamonds invite trouble," she'd said when Kiyoko first asked about it.

Kiyoko clasped her hands together. "Oi, Alzira."

"Olá."

"I would like to buy a Ba Gua mirror. But I know I must be accompanied when leaving the floor."

After a pause, Alzira replied, "Yes, you must. What is a Ba Gua mirror?"

"I had an inauspicious dream." To phrase it mildly. "A Ba Gua mirror over the front door will protect us. It will counteract the negative *qi.*"

Alzira squinted. "I do not understand."

Kiyoko pulled out her comlink, opened the translation program, and tried explaining the Taoist cosmology in Portuguese. She didn't get far.

"Forget these superstitions," Alzira said. "Trust in SSG and our Lord Jesus Christ."

Kiyoko tried to explain some more but Alzira cut her off. "I am busy."

Doing what, Kiyoko wanted to ask. "Maybe a little later then?"

"I will accompany you outside if you need to do something important, but otherwise you can wait until Gabriel returns. Someone must monitor the cameras." Alzira shut the door.

Such a rude woman! The cameras, at least the interior ones, had motion detectors. They didn't need constant monitoring.

Kiyoko returned to her apartment. She sat down with pens, paper, and scissors, and created her own octagonal Ba Gua of trigrams. She cut a hole in the middle and taped the octagon over her faux-Victorian hand mirror, then nailed the whole thing to the outside of her door.

"Mission accomplished!" she told Nyasuke.

Her cat, who was very sensitive to spiritual matters, meowed.

Then, when Kiyoko checked her messages, the dream monster revealed itself to be MediaCorp. At least it was the prime contender.

Dear Ms. Pingyang,

Media Corporation is challenging Fantasmas na Maquina for copyright infringement on a number of fronts. The nature of their claims suggests that they are fully aware of all our company's activities. Among their claims, they list the inclusion of products developed in BetterWorld or using Qualia or Edict, computer languages which Media Corporation developed. They claim these languages and packages cannot be used without permission, and expressly cannot be used to compete with their products or services.

Until these matters are resolved, we must regretfully pause deployment of Yumekuni and associated products, and rethink our general strategy as we move forward with Fronteira Nova. We are exploring the legal issues and the possibility of developing our own computer language. I request your patience in the meantime.

With apologies,
Augusto Monteiro
Founder and President, Fantasmas na Maquina

Kiyoko also received a message sent to all employees and contractors, saying that most work would temporarily cease. Contractors—and this included Kiyoko, Charles, and Pel—would have to wait until operations resumed.

No! How will we survive?

Kiyoko pinged Charles, also immersed in the Comnet. Much easier than getting out of her suit and knocking on his door.

A window appeared with Iwisa standing on a rooftop with short spear in one hand, big cowhide shield in the other, São Paulo cityscape in the background, the words 'Private chat' beneath.

"Hi Charles," Kiyoko spoke, trying to keep the dejection out of her voice.

Iwisa bowed. "Princess Kiyoko."

"Did you get the message from Sr. Augusto?"

Iwisa smacked his spear against the shield. "Yeah, what the fuck? How can MediaCorp sue a company in Brazil?"

"National borders are irrelevant as far as commerce goes. Free trade agreements and all. You should know that. It's like the Comnet."

"Qualia and Edict are computer languages. They don't belong to MediaCorp. I ran a search. Oracle vs. Google, 2016—a jury found that reimplementing APIs is fair use."

"MediaCorp claims otherwise," she said. "And they have an army of lawyers. Not only that, they've been getting President Rand to stack the courts." One of the many facts Waylee had uncovered about their nemesis. "They pretty much own the trade tribunals too. But I'm going to write Sr. Augusto and tell him not to give in. You can't just give in to monsters, no matter how terrifying they seem."

Iwisa rattled his spear. "I'll let the Collective know. This sort of fight is what we live for. And the Open Network legal groups. It would take years and a shitload of money for Fronteira to develop and test a new language. And you can bet MediaCorp would find ways to make it incompatible with the Comnet. So the legal route's the only workable option."

Charles's defiance made Kiyoko feel a little better. But they had no savings to fall back on. They spent money as fast as it came in, and had to pay back their settlement loan.

"What are we going to do for money now?" she asked. "How are we going to buy food?"

Charles/Iwisa waited several seconds before responding. "We'll figure something out."

* * *

Dalton

Sitting on the plush sofa in his room, Dalton opened his unlabeled pill box and popped a green THC pill, a pink stimulant, a white focus enhancer, and a light blue performance booster. In front of the big bed, two girls stripped off their tight clothes. They were both young, with light caramel skin and dark nipples. He'd ordered them from a Comnet site, paid with cryptocurrency, met them in the downstairs bar, and brought them up to his room.

Everything in the world was for sale, he thought as the girls knelt before him and got to work. In São Paulo, ordering girls was like ordering a pizza. They even had menus and specials. This was a buy one, get the second half price.

The shorter of the two teenage girls stopped and looked up at his eyes. "You like?"

"Did I tell you to stop?" Dalton growled.

She cringed a little and returned her attention where it belonged.

His job made real relationships impossible. He'd given up on relationships anyway after the messy affair with Mia and the even messier divorce from Jane. He hadn't seen or heard from his ex-wife or two kids for seven years now, even though he paid thousands of dollars a month in child support.

Good riddance as far as Jane went—they fought all the time anyway—but he missed Donnie and Madison. Every now and then, mainly when drunk, he'd message them. But they never wrote back. Goddamn Jane, even though she was too self-absorbed to be a decent parent, turned them against him.

The hell with it. He stood and ushered the hookers to the bed.

Dalton was pounding the taller of the two girls when his comlink played the Pink Panther theme. He'd tagged each contact with a unique sound file, for occasions like this where he couldn't see the screen. Pink Panther—Inspector Clouseau, actually—signified Inspector De Barros.

Dalton didn't stop to answer the ring—he preferred to talk privately—but finished up as quickly as he could. He slapped the hookers hard on their asses, gave them a generous tip, and sent them on their way.

Once he was back alone, he called De Barros. "You got something?"

"I have good news, mano. Pingyang entered the Metro system at the Liberdade station at 1016 hours on May 6. There's no video of her exiting Luz, which means she either met someone in the station or used one of the new walkways, which aren't all monitored yet. She returned to Liberdade and exited at 1323 hours."

"Then she lives in Liberdade?"

"Possibly. That neighborhood doesn't have many cameras, but I'll check the ones they have."

I have them! "Did you ID her companion?"

"Gabriel da Silva, former sergeant in Primeiro Batalhão de Forças Especiais. Current employer unknown—we only have his military records. He is not in the police."

"Mercenary?"

"Private security of some sort, most likely."

"Thank you," Dalton said. "I'll look him up. Let me know if the street cameras in Liberdade pick up Pingyang. I'll be in touch." He terminated the connection.

Dalton looked up da Silva's unit on the Comnet. The 1st Special Forces Battalion was Brazil's primary special operations force, analogous to the U.S. Delta Force and Britain's Special Air Service. Experts at sabotage, intelligence, recon, counterterrorism . . . pretty much everything. Only a tiny percentage of applicants made it through the selection process and training.

Dalton logged into the Ares network and searched their databases for da Silva. He had received commendations for operations in the Amazon against animal smuggling syndicates and illegal mining operations. And he led one of the squads that freed a cruise ship from a band of well-armed hijackers off the coast of Bahia.

Not an ordinary bodyguard. Da Silva could be a problem.

8

Waylee

Sometime in the afternoon, Waylee's guards marched her back to the meeting room. Her hypomania had dissipated and she felt normal—except for the first hints of dread that meant an approaching plunge into depression. The only question was, how bad would it be? *Dead suns collapse / Light entombed eternal*, she'd written in her song *Event Horizon*.

Ms. Van Hofwegen was sitting at the stainless steel table, talking into her data pad. The lawyer looked up. "Hello, Waylee."

"Is Francis here?"

"Not today."

The guards sat Waylee on the opposite side of the table and fastened her ankle chain to the floor. Just like their last meeting.

Ms. Van Hofwegen faced her screen toward Waylee. There was a camera lens above it—small, but bigger than normal for a data pad.

A grey-haired, beady-eyed man in a business suit appeared on the screen. Bob Luxmore, CEO of Media Corporation. Her nemesis. "Hello Ms. Freid, or Smith, should I say."

Was this a recording or was he live? "Freid. That's my legal name."

"It's been a while."

She'd almost thrown a drink in his face at the New Year's fundraiser. Too bad she'd had to restrain herself.

"I do hope you're uncomfortable," Luxmore's image continued. "By the look of those shackles, I think I can guess the answer to that." He smiled with narrowed eyes.

So he was live. Probably. "Enjoying your fall from power?"

He chuckled. "I built the world's most powerful company from scratch. Our assets are worth more than most countries' combined. And we're on the verge of a breakthrough, the biggest since Charles Babbage invented the first computer."

Fear knotting her stomach, Waylee spoke quickly. "What's that?" *The neural interfaces he talked about with the president? Will he be able to control people's brains directly now?*

Luxmore ignored the question. "Do you really think you can trouble me? My first wife was a lot more trouble than you." He laughed.

He was definitely live, unless it was an AI. If only the bastard was here in person so she could strangle him. "Obviously you're worried enough to talk to me in person, or close to it. What do you want?"

"I want to give you a chance to save your sister and boyfriend from life in prison, and to know that I have the power to stop that from happening."

Waylee's heart seized. "They have asylum. You can't touch them." Her ankles strained against their shackles.

"You know I can. I know where they are, where they live and work, and it's already arranged. Unless you cooperate by recanting your video. We can do it right here. Look into the camera and recite the speech we've prepared for you."

Ms. Van Hofwegen slid over a printed version of the "confession" she showed last time, saying Waylee faked her video footage and forged the documents she released.

Waylee's hands shook. "I thought you weren't allowed to record here."

"That's a special condition to prevent terrorists from communicating with their followers," Luxmore said. "I'm not a promoter of terrorism."

Waylee's molars ground from the audacity. "You're the biggest terrorist in the world. Thanks to you and your lackeys like Rand, the world is turning to desert and people are starving to death." He was wrecking the world and making sure no one cared.

His beady eyes narrowed. "Yes or no?"

Was he bluffing about being able to reach Kiyoko and Pel? Could he do it? If he wasn't bluffing, would he keep his word if she recanted her video? Or would he have them extradited anyway? "I have to talk to my lawyer about this."

"Not an option. This has nothing to do with your trial, although certainly the previous offer is also still valid. Give the speech and I'll put in a good word with the A.G." He leaned back and smiled.

"You fucking bastard. You're the one who belongs in prison." *Slipped. Don't lose control.*

Luxmore raised an eyebrow. "Choices. Free will. It's a bitch, isn't it? Our greatest asset and our greatest burden."

Waylee choked out a laugh. The world's biggest enemy of freedom lecturing her about free will.

He frowned. "Well? What's it to be? You can swallow your pride or you can condemn yourself and everyone you care about to life in prison."

"I have to think about it." Could she derail the movement she ignited against MediaCorp and President Rand? And for what? How could she make him keep his word?

"Doesn't seem like much of a choice to me," he said. "But fair enough. You have twenty-four hours."

* * *

Pelopidas

Immersed in his VR suit, Pel flipped through the morning's stories that contained one of his keywords: Waylee Freid, Charles Lee, Collective, and eleven others. Most of the stories were MediaCorp propaganda, but he had decided to adopt Waylee's habit of monitoring it.

"Know the enemy," she used to quote. Waylee followed that part of Sun Tzu's advice diligently but struggled with the "know yourself" part. Pel wasn't sure he was good at either.

A window with flashing red borders popped in front of the Interpol text releases he was skimming. MediaCorp's corporate logo and the words 'BREAKING NEWS' filled the window's interior. It stopped flashing and the mannequin-like lead U.S. anchors, Brad Edwards and Vanessa Goodley, appeared behind a faux-wood table.

"This breaking news," Ms. Goodley said in excited but vaguely seductive tones. "Kirk Ortiz is set to make an announcement over the Comnet."

Curious about MediaCorp's anchors, Pel had confirmed they were real people, just enhanced with makeup, lighting, and digital effects. He'd run their voices through a frequency analysis program, one he used back in Baltimore to help layer Dwarf Eats Hippo songs, and compared them to a database of vocal emotional expressions he pulled off a university server. Sure enough, not only had the anchors trained their voices, but the signal was modulated to amplify the feeling of anger, fear, trust, or whatever in the listener.

Mr. Edwards spoke with an authoritative but intimate voice. "Speculation has been rampant that he would drop out of the presidential race following the disclosure that he paid to have sex with an underage prostitute.

With more than half the delegates in his corner, Mr. Ortiz was his party's presumptive nominee, but polls show unfavorability ratings over 80%."

"We take you to the announcement now," Ms. Goodley said.

Pel pressed a finger against the corner of the Breaking News window and decreased its size. He slid it out of the way and resumed reading Interpol announcements while a trembling Kirk Ortiz apologized for his behavior and announced his withdrawal from the race.

"What happens to your delegates?" a reporter asked him after the statement.

"Are you endorsing Kathleen Woodward or Sean Bowers?" another asked.

Ortiz looked at the cameras. "I'm not taking a stance. That's a decision they'll have to make at the convention. Whoever the nominee is, the important thing is to get Al Rand out of the White House."

The other news was equally grim. Interpol, Homeland Security, and others announced the arrest of multiple hackers belonging to the Collective. Pel didn't know any of them by name but recognized some of their avatars, like Yosemite Sam and the hipster named Hopper. Yosemite and Hopper were among the inner circle's elite, and had helped him exploit the trove of comlinks from the presidential fundraiser he and Waylee crashed on New Year's. They should have been uncatchable.

Pel tried to find out more on the Collective message boards. But they were all down. And the Emporium closed.

According to polls broadcast by MediaCorp, which were typically bullshit but the only ones widely available, over 95% of Americans and 90% of people worldwide approved of the crackdown against the "hacker terrorists." 80% thought the People's Party should be disbanded, and over 70% thought their members should be jailed.

The world was seeming more and more hopeless. Waylee, he recalled, felt this way during her depressive episodes—given, much more severely—but at least it was balanced by times of energetic optimism. The last time Pel had felt optimistic was when their video aired. Before Waylee was captured.

He forwarded the news to Charles and Kiyoko. They were both on the Comnet also, Kiyoko from her apartment and Charles from the adjacent room.

Charles's Zulu avatar, Iwisa, appeared next to him, only visible on their local network. "Collective's been driven underground."

Pel activated his avatar, the eighteenth century philosopher William Godwin, and placed them in his wood-paneled library. Pel stood up in his VR cage. His avatar replicated the movement, getting out of an armchair and standing on the Persian carpet. "More underground than before, you mean," he said. "But yeah."

Iwisa's eyes scanned the virtual room. Pel had the same habit from a lifetime of gaming.

"Everyone's hiding," Charles/Iwisa said.

"The ones who haven't been caught."

"How'd they catch Yosemite Sam?" Charles/Iwisa asked. "I wasn't that impressed by Hopper, but Yosemite took five comlinks from your New Year's snares and turned that into fifty owned chumps, some of them MediaCorp admins."

"Fifty-two. Yeah. Wish I knew how they caught him. Hope he doesn't talk."

"Or turn."

True. Homeland Security had a knack for convincing hackers to work for them rather than go to prison.

The library's polished oak door swung open and Princess Kiyoko walked in, diamond tiara on her head, long pink robes swishing over the Persian carpet. "I don't believe those poll numbers."

"You shouldn't believe anything MediaCorp broadcasts," Pel/Godwin said. "They're a lie machine."

Princess Kiyoko paced the virtual library. "Seventy percent of Americans think people should be jailed just for belonging to a political party? That can't be constitutional."

Pel opened a window and placed it in the library as a wall screen. "VR, wiki search political parties banned in the USA. Go."

The virtual wall screen displayed information about the 1954 Communist Control Act, which outlawed the Communist Party of the United States and criminalized membership in, or support for the Party or "Communist-action" organizations. However, the law was never enforced, and a federal district court declared it unconstitutional.

"It's all hype," Pel concluded.

"Are there polls other than the ones broadcast by MediaCorp?" Kiyoko asked.

"Maybe. You can look."

Charles/Iwisa shook his spear. "We need to be proactive with this shit.

See if we can take over MediaCorp's feed again."

"And how are we supposed to do that? We can't break into their head-quarters again, especially while we're stuck in Brazil."

"We'll find a way. Least I'm gonna do is set up some DDoS bots and au-tospammers to grief their facilities and PR flacks."

"That's not going to accomplish anything. And what if they trace your location?"

"Give me some credit. That's like entry level shit. And it's better than do-ing nothing." Charles teleported out of the room.

Princess Kiyoko stared at Pel. "Do you have a better idea, Mr. Godwin?"

"Let's start by countering MediaCorp's polls."

"I checked while you were arguing with Iwisa," she said. "There's lots of electoral polls out there but I couldn't find anything about the Collective or People's Party besides the ones published by MediaCorp."

"Maybe dig a little deeper." *How much research could she do in two min-utes?*

"I shall. Let us stay true and never give up." Kiyoko turned, pink robes swishing, and left through the door.

Kiyoko messaged him later via video chat. "I did find a couple of inde-pendent polls done by academics. Still negative numbers about the People's Party and the Collective, but not quite as bad. And I messaged some other university pollsters and statisticians—I created a profile of a journalist in Iceland so don't worry—and asked if they could do some independent re-search. I told them people desperately need unbiased information."

"Good for you," he said. "Your sister would be proud."

"Thank you for the compliment."

Pel shrugged.

"I'm going to the market now," she said. "Do you wanna come with?"

"Are you kidding? We have so much to do."

"It's good to get out and mingle, don't you think?"

Not that again. She was going to get them killed or kidnapped. "No. Maybe if it had some purpose to warrant the risk. But you're not very care-ful."

Her face tightened. "You're such a stick. What about the hacker spaces? Why don't you and Charles go make some friends?"

"I don't speak Portuguese, and more important, there are bounties on our heads. We have to keep a low profile."

Kiyoko huffed. "Zannen, jiji." She signed off.

What the hell did "zannen jiji" mean? If she was going to insult him, she could at least do it in English.

* * *

Gabriel

Tired from a night of drinking with friends, Gabriel followed Kiyoko as she picked her way through the crowd. Her ribboned pink hair and flowery kimono made her easy to spot if they got separated, although she was far from the only one with antique Japanese clothes or colored hair.

He accompanied Kiyoko to Feirinha da Liberdade, the Liberdade Street Fair, every Sunday. It was his first task of the week after hearing Alzira's report from Friday and Saturday, checking the cameras and locks, and sweeping the building. Alzira always ended her shift by telling him, "Go to mass today—it's not too late to save your soul," but he'd stopped doing that when he left home and wasn't going to start now.

The fair was a security nightmare, thousands of paulistanos and a few tourists, mostly from Japan, crowded between red and white tented food and craft stalls. Kiyoko stopped at nearly every one, making this an all-day task. She also stopped to chat with her friend Reiko, who was dressed as a ranger from *Attack on Titan* this time.

A program on his data glasses ran background checks on every face. Reiko and Kiyoko's other friends, most of them young, were harmless. Occasionally a name and other details would pop up: a security guard, an undercover police officer, a released felon. None ever showed interest in Kiyoko beyond curiosity or desire. And if one approached her and seemed like trouble, all he had to do was open his unbuttoned outer shirt and flash one of his shoulder holsters to scare them off.

Routine. But it was his job to keep Kiyoko and her friends safe. And if anything happened to her . . . he didn't want to think about it. He'd never met anyone like her.

And there was the kiss. She obviously liked him and he would have kissed her long ago if not for the problems it might cause. She kissed him instead, then changed her mind. Was it the tongue? Was it a gringo thing, fear of intimacy? Or was it because she was only 19 and he was pushing 30?

Since he was her protection officer, he couldn't push it. He was a professional.

Kiyoko turned and smiled at him. "Vamos almoçar." Let's have lunch.

"Good idea," he said in English. "I'm hungry." A few more months, hopefully, and they'd speak each other's languages like natives. She had a lot of catching up to do, but she was smart. And far ahead of him on Japanese.

Kiyoko entered one of the nearby food lines. Japanese of various ages—possibly a family—worked a grill and cash register. "What do you want?" she asked him. "My treat."

"That is not necessary. SSG pays my food while I work so I should buy for you."

Her eyes widened. "Work? I thought you liked the fair."

"Oh I love it. . . . It is the most difficult security situation I can imagine." He opened his wallet and handed her a twenty reais note, yellow with a young woman on front and a golden lion tamarin on the back.

He scanned the crowd as Kiyoko waited in line. One stood out, a tanned northern-looking man wearing dark data glasses. He was a little on the short side, with a receding hairline, but had a solid build. No name or occupation popped up. But he had the look of a security professional.

The man picked through a trinket stand, not obviously guarding someone and not obviously watching them.

Kiyoko handed Gabriel a paper boat with six sauce-covered dough balls and a plastic fork. "Takoyaki."

"You remembered I like it."

"Of course."

Gabriel looked for the man with the data glasses, but he was gone. Still scanning, he ate a forkful of batter-covered octopus. Crispy on the outside, a little chewy on the inside, tomato barbecue sauce the main flavor.

Kiyoko had ordered the same thing. She stood next to him and waved her fork. "There's such a diversity of people here. I love it." She popped a takoyaki ball in her mouth.

Ninety-five percent of them harmless, but unfortunately not 100%.

"Do you think Pel wants to replace me?" Gabriel asked. He had tried setting Pel up with Maya, an ex-girlfriend who liked to party, but he wouldn't go meet her. Said he'd never betray Waylee like that.

Kiyoko held up a finger until she finished chewing. "Of course not. He knows how capable you are, and that's all that matters to him. I told him you were just trying to help."

"I couldn't find a girl for Charles. I don't know anyone his age. But I could rent him an escort."

Kiyoko lifted an eyebrow. "You mean a prostitute?"

"It is legal in Brazil."

"I know, but I don't want him to think of women as something to pay for."

"Are you his mother?"

"No, but he's one of my best friends."

"Why don't we let him decide?"

She shook her head. "I think it's wrong and I don't want you to do it."

Kiyoko could be stubborn. Best to drop it. But Charles did need to end his obsession with her, so he'd find him a girl anyway, and keep the payment part of it secret.

They finished eating and walked to a stage where Japanese men and women in loose-fitting uniforms pounded mallets against huge drums. A crowd was gathered and Gabriel had to scan every visible face.

Kiyoko bobbed her head to the rhythm. She put a hand on his shoulder and spoke in his ear, her breath warm and smelling of takoyaki. "I miss playing music. We should buy instruments and jam every night. Pel would enjoy that."

No apparent threats in the crowd. Not at the moment, anyway. "I don't play anything."

"I'll teach you guitar. Or you could be our drummer."

It looked like a great workout, the way the performers smacked the drum heads and jumped around.

"Do you have a lot of girlfriends?" she said when the drummers finished.

"Four."

Her mouth dropped.

"Just kidding," he clarified. Kiyoko didn't always pick up paulistano sarcasm. "I mean, I've had some, but none right now."

"You don't go pick up girls and take them to your bed?"

An odd question. "I've been focusing on my job. I haven't had time for a girlfriend. And I like to know a girl before, uh, taking her to bed."

She twirled a finger in her pink wig. "I'm sure you could have any girl you wanted."

"What about you? You could have any man you want." She turned a lot of heads, and occasionally got propositions.

"That's not how I work."

"Well, me neither." At least not since he left the army and thought about settling down.

He slapped himself mentally. More and more, he had this tendency to focus on Kiyoko instead of the surroundings. *I should tell her not to talk to me when we're outside. But that would make me even more obvious as a bodyguard. I can do both, it just takes practice.*

The drummers finished and bowed to the crowd. Most of the spectators dispersed, but an overweight balding man remained on the periphery, glancing over every few seconds. He had a dark mustache and wore a light blue shirt and tan slacks. Gabriel's data glasses displayed the name Inspetor Olivier de Barros, São Paulo Polícia Civil.

SSG had a one year federal contract to protect Kiyoko and her friends. Local police didn't even know about them. Or did they? "Follow me," Gabriel told Kiyoko, then strode toward the inspector.

The man's eyes widened and darted as they approached. "Bom dia, Inspetor," Gabriel said.

"And you are?" His breath smelled of alcohol, even though it was midday.

"What's going on?" Kiyoko said in English.

Gabriel continued interrogating the inspector in Portuguese. "You must know who we are. Are you following us?"

"No I am not. It's my day off. Why, should I follow you? Are you a criminal?"

That wasn't the answer he expected. "Run my picture on your comlink and you'll see I am a decorated veteran. I work for Serviços de Segurança Globais now."

He nodded. "I believe you. Is this your girlfriend?"

How to answer? "She wanted to see the fair. Now tell me, why are you watching us?"

"I can't help it, your girlfriend fascinates me. There is no need to be angry."

"Why does she fascinate you?"

"Why do you think? She is very traditional Japanese but with pink hair. And she is very beautiful. You are very lucky."

"Obrigado," Kiyoko interjected, obviously following at least some of the conversation.

"We're leaving," Gabriel told the inspector. "I don't care if you are police, I don't want to see you watching her again."

The inspector shrugged. Gabriel led Kiyoko away from the stage.

"What was that about?" she asked as they threaded through the crowd on Rua Galvão Bueno.

"Police inspector. I wanted to know what he was up to."

"Did he say?"

"Said it was his day off. I think maybe he was drunk and *lascivo*, I don't know how you say in English."

"Lecherous?"

"Lecherous. It is my job to be careful, though."

They stayed at the fair until late afternoon. He didn't see Inspetor Olivier de Barros again.

Kiyoko bought him a hanging tapestry with Mt. Fuji on it. "Your walls were bare last time I saw."

"Please, it is not necessary to buy me things. You have no job at the moment."

"It wasn't expensive. I just thought your walls needed decoration."

Why argue? She looked sincere. "Thank you, Kiyoko. Perhaps you could help me find a good place for it."

She smiled and his heart pounded. That smile of hers.

* * *

Dalton

"I thought you were a fucking professional," Dalton told Inspector De Barros back in his car.

The fat detective shrugged. "Da Silva must have face recognition on his data glasses and access to our personnel files."

"Well we do, so why shouldn't he? He works for a security company, you moron." Dalton's data glasses, still on, could access all kinds of files, as well as having real-time A/V translation.

"Fuck, I don't think you need to be so rude."

Dalton almost punched the bastard in the nose. Instead, he took a breath and looked out the front window. *I have a job to do. I need this asshole.*

"He saw you too, porra, didn't he?" De Barros said.

"Yeah, but I'm not in any databases. Ares had my old personnel files purged and all images of me removed from the Comnet." Thanks to their connections in Homeland Security and MediaCorp.

"He didn't seem to suspect we are surveilling."

How could he be sure? Dalton looked in De Barros's beady brown eyes.

"We should take him out."

"SSG is very well connected. No way we should kill one of their employees. There would be consequences."

Working in places like Haiti and Somalia was so much easier. You could kill whoever you had to and no one would hassle you about it. "Alright then, we'll set up cameras and figure out where Demopoulos and Lee live. When they're home and unprotected, we'll nab them. You said they have these street markets every Sunday?"

"Yes, the fair is every Sunday."

"That gives us a week to get ready." And if Da Silva got in the way, Dalton would kill him no matter what the fat inspector said.

9

Waylee

Waylee still hadn't heard from Francis when the guards escorted her back to the meeting room and chained her to the floor. Her twenty-four hours were up, she presumed, and she had to make a decision. By herself, with no legal counsel.

Her period had started that morning, but she didn't have any pads or tampons. Since she only had one pair of semi-clean prison panties left, she'd stuffed toilet paper inside. Uncomfortable and embarrassing, especially while trying to walk.

Ms. Van Hofwegen arrived and opened her data pad. She sniffed the air as if Waylee was some sort of mangy animal. "Hello again, Ms. Freid."

How nice to only spend an hour or two a week in this shithole, then return outside, able to feel the sun and semi-fresh air on your face and do whatever you wanted. "I need to see my lawyer," Waylee managed. "The guards won't let me make any calls."

"You're in high security," the frosted blonde said. "And you're associated with the Collective hackers. They're not going to let you near a Comnet interface."

The toilet paper had shifted during her march to the meeting room, releasing a trickle of goo that pooled beneath her. "I have the right to see my attorney. We still have a Constitution, right?"

"Why wouldn't we?" Ms. Van Hofwegen turned her data pad toward Waylee and started a video that filled the screen. "This was just released on the Comnet."

On the screen, a giant bald eagle swooped with a rider on its back over an endless field of ripe wheat, shining golden in the sun. The view zoomed to the rider: President Rand. The resolution and animation quality were as realistic as any she'd seen. "Beats the hell out of Air Force One," he said.

The video faded to black, replaced by words in white font, 'Anyone can fake video. #SuperBowlHoax.'

Forcing out bravery, Waylee shrugged. "Nice try. But truth is self-evident."

"You can be simulated too, you know. They don't need you to confess; they have your image and voice from my last visit, and computers can do the rest."

She was right. That was probably the main reason for the videoconference with Luxmore. "Then why bother coming today?"

"Mr. Luxmore made you a promise, so here I am."

Waylee almost laughed. Bob Luxmore with any ethics beyond survival of the fittest? "No, you can't fake a so-called confession from me. Either the prosecutor or my attorney would include it as evidence. No matter how real looking, their experts would discover you faked it. And it would explode in your face. Now if you'll fetch the guards, I'd like to exercise my rights and contact my attorney."

"Francis Jones? He was arrested for aiding and abetting a terrorist organization."

Waylee strained against her shackles and gasped for air. "You're lying!"

"I'm not. Homeland Security found incriminating evidence on his computers that he worked with the Collective. Your boyfriend belongs to their inner circle and they conspired together, via your sister."

"You're full of shit!"

"And they found a manifesto you wrote that presumably he was planning to publish."

Waylee's throat tightened. "He was just keeping it for me."

"Mr. Jones and his team are under investigation and will not be able to represent anyone. However, my firm could represent you. Pro bono. And we are the best in the business. All you have to do is cooperate."

"I'll go with a public defender, thanks." No way would she sell out to MediaCorp.

"Mr. Luxmore requires an answer from you. Will you cooperate, or do your sister and boyfriend end up in prison? With life sentences for all three of you, plus your friend Charles Lee who you broke out of juvenile detention? And that's just the beginning. There's a massive investigation going on, and everyone you know is getting swept up."

"You're bluffing. You don't have them in custody, and you can't just kidnap them." But her stomach contracted to a pit. What if she was wrong? And why was she even talking to this woman?

To keep from collapsing in tears, Waylee gathered all the saliva her dry mouth could muster, and propelled it toward the stooge's data pad. It splattered against the center of the screen and dripped down over '#SuperBowl-Hoax.'

Ms. Van Hofwegen wrinkled her nose in disgust. "Have it your way." She pulled a handkerchief out of her suit jacket and wiped off her data pad, then folded it up. "I tried."

Why did I spit on her data pad? What do I do now? Francis, poor Francis. The room grew cold and her throat closed, making it impossible to breathe.

* * *

Charles

Virtual reality helmet and gloves on, Charles skimmed the "Brief of *Amici Curiae*" floating in front of him, skipping the citations and footnotes. "Functional requirements for compatibility between computer programs are not protected by copyright." That was good.

Fantasmas na Maquina had refused help from the Collective, saying it would make them look bad. But the more mainstream Free Internet organizations had filed legal briefs in support of Fantasmas. Thanks to him and Pel, maybe the company and Fronteira Nova would be saved. Trouble was, they needed money now and they had to earn it anonymously somehow.

He and his Collective comrades had taken over hundreds of computers and comlinks during their fight against MediaCorp, some of them leading to bank accounts or credit cards. Unfortunately, none of them were accessible anymore, either purged or wiped.

There was always BetterWorld, where he'd risen to god level after their attack on Club Elite. Trouble was, MediaCorp's new patches were extremely thorough this time and he couldn't infect other avatars anymore.

Charles dropped two avatars and the latest client software into his sandbox, complete with their anti-malware modules and spyware. He had old copies of BetterWorld's login and data server software, which he'd update as soon as he found a way back in. He loaded a heap viewer and some other diagnostic tools, and started probing and dissecting. How could he get a package past the layers of defenses, and how could he get it from avatar A to avatar B?

The feed from their apartment door camera popped up. Gabriel was outside the door with a short girl, Kiyoko's age or younger, wearing a low-cut blouse and tight skirt. Did he have a girlfriend now? As long as he wasn't banging Kiyoko . . .

Gabriel knocked. Why? He knew the keypad code. Maybe he didn't want his girlfriend to know it. Or maybe he wanted their attention. Charles logged off the Comnet and pulled off his VR suit.

Pel was already in the living room by the time Charles had combed out the helmet indentations in his hair and opened the bedroom door. He was arguing with Gabriel and his girlfriend. "You can't just bring strange girls in here."

"Adrianna is very nice," Gabriel said. "You can trust her." He gripped a brown paper bag.

"Are you Charles?" Adrianna smiled. She was hot, maybe not beautiful like Kiyoko, but had a kickin' body with supersized tits. She had light brown skin—a little African—and plain brown hair that hung down past her shoulders. And that smile seemed just for him.

"Uh, yeah, how did you know?"

"Gabriel told me." She had a strong accent but he was used to it now.

"Adrianna is a friend of a friend," Gabriel said, "and likes to have a good time."

Charles remembered Gabriel was going to find girls for him and Pel. Is that what this was? "So she's not your girlfriend?"

Gabriel shook his head and pulled a bottle labeled *Única* and four plastic cups out of the paper bag. He sat at the kitchen table and poured a little bit of strong-smelling clear liquid into each cup. "Do you have limes and sugar?"

"Isn't it early to be drinking?" Pel asked. "And aren't you on duty?"

Gabriel's eyes narrowed.

Pel better back off, Charles thought.

"Alzira's here," Gabriel said. "She wanted all next weekend to visit the beach with her fiancé, so she's working today and tomorrow. I'm staying also because we need to be friendlier."

"What?" Charles wasn't sure what Gabriel was trying to say.

"You are less a team every week."

Waylee's not here. She had a talent for keeping people together and focused.

"Just 'cause you were an army sergeant doesn't mean you can run our lives," Pel told Gabriel.

Adrianna slipped fingers into Charles's and directed him to the sofa. "Where are you from?"

"Gabriel didn't tell you?"

She poked him in the chest. "No, but I am guessing U.S. America, you sound American. Home of the brave."

"Uh, yeah."

"You are very handsome, you know."

What? No one had ever told him that. He tried to keep his eyes away from her rack. "You are very beautiful." *Is that the best I can do?*

"Thank you."

"Muita bonita," he added, hoping he got the pronunciation right.

Pel was still arguing with Gabriel. "You know you have your own apartment."

"Don't be like that. I can bring you a girl. I told you Maya wants to meet you. And I know others."

Did that mean this fine shorty was here for him?

Pel bit his lip. "Just leave me alone." He stomped into his room and locked the door.

"More for us then," Gabriel said. "He's too stubborn."

He handed cups to Adrianna and Charles. "Forget the capirinhas." He held up his cup. "Saúde."

Adrianna tapped her cup against his. Charles joined them.

It tasted like paint thinner. Or auto fuel. Charles tried not to cough or spit it out. "What is this stuff?"

"Cachaça," Gabriel said. "The national drink of Brazil. It's distilled from sugarcane juice."

"It's better in capirinhas," Adrianna said. "Unless you buy gold, but that is very expensive."

Obviously this wasn't the expensive stuff. "So what do you do?" Charles asked her.

She looked at him.

"Your job?"

She glanced at Gabriel. "I serve drinks at a bar. And I dance."

Good to know she wasn't some street whore Gabriel picked up. She didn't have that street look, she had nice skin and perfect teeth and smelled like fruity perfume.

Adrianna pointed at the rope fastened to the wall and leading into its cardboard box where the rest was coiled. "What's that for?"

They had a rehearsed explanation. "This building don't have a fire escape. That's so we can get out if there's a fire." That was actually a more likely emergency than being attacked by CIA agents.

They finished their paint thinner, by which time the room was unsteady. Adrianna leaned over and kissed him, tasting like alcohol. Charles tried to remember what Kiyoko taught him about kissing back in Maryland. He hoped she wouldn't walk in.

They kissed for a long time, then she pointed to his half-open door. "Is that your room?"

"Yeah." His heart pounded. Did she want to have sex?

Adrianna squeezed his hand. "We could have more privacy there."

He'd be a fool to pass up such an opportunity. He led Adrianna into his bedroom and closed the door. The room was messy, with clothes and stuff strewn all over the floor. Why couldn't Gabriel have given him time to clean up?

Adrianna stripped off her clothes and lay back on his mattress. His knees shook. Kiyoko was beautiful, but no way did she have tits like those.

He just hoped she didn't find out about this. On the other hand, they weren't boo cakes and had yet to come close. Heart hammering and iron hard, Charles pulled off his clothes as quick as he could and followed Adrianna's lead.

* * *

Gabriel

Gabriel didn't really want to listen to Charles and Adrianna having sex. He hadn't had time to pursue any girls since starting this bodyguard job. And now he couldn't get Kiyoko out of his mind.

He found the living room Comnet interface and woke up the wall screen. It was on default, showing a four by three grid of camera feeds, one embedded in each apartment door, one pointing down the hall, one in the stairwell, and six pointing out windows. Nothing to see in any of them.

"Audio," he commanded, "Chico Science, Da Lama Ao Caos, mid volume." Pel had set all the commands in English.

Chico Science were from last century, but their classic manguebeat kicked the tiny nuts out of the electropop shit most paulistanos listened to these days. Pounding snares and syncopated guitars drove him to dance around the room. On the wall screen, the camera view windows shrank and rearranged onto a single row on the bottom. Above them, abstract shapes pulsed and transformed to the music. Gabriel grabbed Pel's abandoned cup of cachaça and downed the firewater a little at a time.

After going through the whole album, he let the music wizard pick, and sat down to play a shooter game. It was more fun playing with others, but Charles was busy and Pel was being a ball sack.

Anything, though, was more fun than shooting people in real life. Like the *Tropical Breeze* fiasco.

The *Tropical Breeze* was a 110,000 ton cruise ship with three thousand passengers and a thousand crew. Colluding with the ship's security chief and two of his guards, a well-armed group of pirates seized the liner off the coast of Bahia, took the bridge and engineering room, and emptied the safes. The Brazilian Navy showed up before they could escape, and things got messy.

The pirates stuffed most of the passengers into the main dining room and demanded free passage and $10 million in cash. Not a lot of money, considering. But anxious to show off, the Brazilian government sent in special forces the next night. Through messages from crew and passengers, they knew the pirates were spread thin: including the insiders, eighteen men to hold a ship almost 300 meters long.

Half of Gabriel's battalion boarded helicopters. They launched drones, some of them smaller than a dragonfly, and with the help of the cruise company, hacked into the ship's camera system. While one group diverted the pirates' attention with a fake money drop, Gabriel and dozens of comrades donned jet packs, lightweight armor, and augmented reality helmets, and launched from the helicopter skids.

Gabriel's squad had the most critical assignment—to take out five men watching the crowd of passengers with AK-47s. They blasted holes in the big stern windows and flew right into the huge two-level restaurant, firing laser guided, gyroscopically stabilized assault rifles at the enemy.

It would have been a huge success if one of the hijackers hadn't gone berserk and emptied a clip at the hostages. Three were killed, including a school-age girl.

The official press release said the deaths were regrettable but that 99.9% of the hostages were saved. Medals were handed out like tinsel on carnaval. Gabriel never put his on.

Gabriel had told this story to Kiyoko, Pel, and Charles soon after starting his bodyguard job. He promised if they were kidnapped, their safety would be his only priority.

"Oi Gabriel!" Kiyoko's singsong voice from the kitchen.

Gabriel paused his game—he was stuck on this level anyway—and checked the clock. Dinner time. The music wizard kept going, playing some baile funk/synth-jazz song he didn't recognize.

Kiyoko bounded into the room, wearing a red and pink silk dress, slippered feet bouncing to the music. She had a pink wig with red bows bunching the sides, and matching pink lipstick and contact lenses. "Where is everyone?" She pointed at the half full bottle of cachaça. "Have you been drinking?"

"Only a little." *Actually quite a bit.* Which explained why he kept dying in the game. "You look very, uh, pink today."

Her head cocked. "Audio, mute volume."

The music stopped. Moaning came from Charles's room. Adrianna was on the loud side.

"Is Charles with a girl in there?" she asked.

Still sitting on the sofa, Gabriel nodded. "They've been in there for hours. I kind of forgot about it."

Her eyes were wide. "And where'd this girl come from?"

"A friend at SSG recommended her. She is Charles's age and speaks English."

"What do you mean, recommended her?"

Gabriel started to make up a story but decided he didn't want to lie to Kiyoko. He stood, wobbling a little on his feet. "She works at a luxury club. My friend said, um, she's very good. I looked at the catalog. He was right, she has top ratings from customers."

Her jaw dropped, then her eyes misted. "You ordered a girl from a catalog?"

"No, I told you, my friend recommended her."

"I asked you not to do that."

"Charles doesn't know I paid. He will never know unless you tell him."

"It's not right."

"What's not right is you cooking that boy in the water bath. This is good for him."

"What do you mean, cooking in the water bath?"

The cachaça forced him to concentrate. "He has hopes for you which you do not discourage. You don't tell him to give up."

Kiyoko bit her lip. "I know he's in love with me but I told him we could only be friends. I mean, he's not even eighteen. Is it legal, hiring a prostitute for someone who's underage?"

"Come on, this is Brazil. The age of consent is fourteen. This isn't the United States."

"I wish you would stop treating me like a tourist. I'm a Brazilian too now." She frowned. "I didn't know you go to these sex clubs. How often do you buy a girl for yourself?"

He squelched the paulistano urge to answer with sarcasm. "I never do that, come on." Not since he left the army and his parents gave him the big "save your money, settle down with a respectable girl, and make us some grandchildren" lecture. He drew close enough to feel Kiyoko's breath. "Are you, by any chance, jealous?"

Her eyes narrowed. "I don't get jealous. That's a bad emotion."

"I think you don't want me with another woman."

"That's none of my business." Her eyes darted away.

"And I think you are jealous Charles is having sex with another girl."

"I am not. He's not my boyfriend."

"It's not only about Charles. I was going to get a girl for Pel also but he is too damn stubborn." *Just like you.*

She stared at him. "And what about me? Do you know how hard it is to find someone who won't just use me, won't lie and cheat on me?"

They'd commiserated about bad relationships not long after moving into the building. Kiyoko's last boyfriend, back in Baltimore, had slept with two of her friends. Her prior boyfriends—and girlfriends—hadn't been much better.

Gabriel put a hand on her shoulder. "I'd never do that." He looked in her pink-irised eyes so she'd know he meant it.

She smiled and gazed back. "Are you saying you'd like to go out with me?"

"Go out with?"

She blushed. "You know, like on a date." She glanced down, then met his eyes and exhaled through her nose. "No one needs to know."

Kiyoko was so beautiful, so interesting, so strong. And they liked each other. "I was afraid of the conflict," Gabriel began, "but forget that. I think about you all the time. I see you when I close my eyes."

She drew closer, her exotic, flawless face filling his view. Her pink lips parted.

He kissed her. She kissed him back, this time with passion. He threw arms around her, held her close, wanting her more than anything.

What if Alzira walked in? They were supposed to be friendly with the clients but avoid romantic entanglements. If she told his supervisor, he'd be reassigned.

No, Alzira was not very social and was probably sitting in her apartment watching the camera feeds and talking to her fiancé on her comlink. Even if she did walk in, they were comrades and she wouldn't rat on him. No one at SSG would know. And if they did find out, who cared? Kiyoko was worth any trouble.

"You taste like alcohol," Kiyoko said when their lips separated.

"I love you," he said. The words solidified the feeling. *Te amo.* This was it. Kiyoko was the girl he'd finally marry.

She stepped out of his embrace. "I should leave."

His muscles tensed and the hazy euphoria vanished, like he'd wandered into an ambush. "Why? I don't understand."

"I don't like being played. I thought I told you that."

"What are you talking about? Why are you trying to spoil things?"

Her mouth opened, then shut, and she hurried out the door.

What just happened? Gabriel walked over to the cachaça bottle. He almost dashed it against the wall.

But that would be a waste. He sat down on the couch with the bottle and stared at it. *I've had enough of this job. I should quit.*

But it was such a sweet assignment. Free room and board. No real dangers. Kiyoko. Did he really love her or was it just the cachaça and her constant proximity?

He poured another cup, turned the music back on, and resumed the shooter game. Tomorrow. There was always tomorrow.

* * *

Dalton

There were two types of people Dalton could always pick out: combat vets and whores. One of each exited the front door of his targets' apartment building. Talking to each other but not touching.

The combat vet, Gabriel da Silva, didn't have his data glasses on, and swayed a little. Drunk, perhaps? The whore was short, young, and busty with tight clothes and high heels.

Sitting in the passenger seat of a generic-looking Ford rental, Dalton pointed his small directional mike at them. They spoke in Portuguese and his ear bud translated—an American female voice for the whore and a male voice for the bodyguard. Next to Dalton, behind the wheel, De Barros fiddled with his data glasses.

The whore smiled and spoke, "Obrigado pela gorjeta."

"Thank you for the tip," the female voice translated.

"You were in there a long time," da Silva said. "Sounded like Charles had the time of his life."

Charles? Jackpot! The long hours of sitting in cars or monitoring microcameras had finally paid off.

The whore smiled. "Oh, he did. We had fun. He wants to see me again."

"You did not tell him you are an escort, I hope?"

The whore ran a hand up da Silva's arm. "No, you told me not to." She looked him up and down. "I am available now if you are."

He shrugged off her hand. "What is your number? It wasn't on the catalog."

"No number. Find me on BetterWorld. Sexy Adrianna. I am the one with the most likes by far." She blew him a kiss. "Or message me on the Comnet, Sexy Adrianna GSP."

"What does GSP mean?"

She smiled. "Gostosas do São Paulo."

"And Charles knows how to contact you?"

"I just gave him my Comnet address."

"You'll have to arrange payment with him," da Silva said. "I should have told him the truth and now it's a mess."

"Does he have money? I'm trying to save money to start my own club, you know."

"By yourself?"

She touched his arm again. "Yes, but I'm looking for investors."

He frowned. "Try a bank. We are not swimming in money."

A taxi arrived and Sexy Adrianna got in.

"Follow that taxi," Dalton told de Barros.

De Barros grumbled under his breath but followed at a discreet distance. They drove half an hour south to an apartment building, where she got out.

"Going in?" De Barros said.

"No need. I'll just message Sexy Adrianna and have her come to me."

10

Waylee

Waylee lay curled beneath her blanket on the sleeping ledge. She couldn't eat or speak or move. Thoughts moved like dark sludge. She'd had some bad depressive episodes before, but this was worse. Even worse than her collapse when she thought she'd never get her video out.

Shakti and Pel helped her then. She was all alone now. Alone forever.

And during her last meeting with the MediaCorp lawyer, the guards had searched her cell and taken all her writings. Her offering to others, her purpose in life. They'd taken Pel's support essay too. Her last connection to the man who loved her.

Life was over. They'd even taken her pen. She'd be in a barren cell like this until the urge to end her life eclipsed her survival instincts. Kiyoko and Pel and everyone else she cared about would suffer the same fate. Luxmore would make sure of that.

Her video was being discredited. The movement against MediaCorp and President Rand had collapsed. If it ever existed at all.

The plutocracy was stronger than ever. They would rule humanity until they destroyed the world through their greed and recklessness.

Luxmore would deploy his neural interfaces and monitor everyone's thoughts, even control them. Democracy was gone forever. So was hope.

Pain overpowered thought, crushing her into the plastic mat. Nothing existed but eternal agony.

* * *

Kiyoko

Kiyoko knocked on Gabriel's door the morning after their argument. Gabriel opened the door, close-cropped hair pointing in haphazard directions, chin dark with stubble, and right eye more open than the left. He had only boxers on, displaying his broad shoulders and muscular torso.

She caught herself staring and returned to his eyes. Those expressive eyes with their three bands of russet, bronze, and chocolate.

"What is it?" he asked.

"I . . . I wanted to apologize for yesterday. I can come back later."

Gabriel pressed fingers against his forehead and stepped back from the doorway. "No, no, come in."

His apartment, which she rarely visited, was uncluttered and spotless—no dirt, no dust. It smelled like lemon freshener. The living room was as spare as Pel and Charles's, with stock furniture and a wall screen displaying the camera feeds. The Mt. Fuji tapestry she'd bought him hung on the far wall, the only decoration. Kiyoko sat on the white faux-leather couch and Gabriel trudged into his bedroom.

He emerged a minute later wearing an olive drab T-shirt and dark gray running pants. "Please give me a minute."

"Of course."

Gabriel walked past the living room into the bathroom. She heard a cabinet open, followed by running water and the brushing of teeth. He returned looking much fresher, although still unshaved.

He sat on the sofa next to her. "Sorry," he said. "I am not feeling well. I had too much to drink. I am afraid I will have to cancel today's martial arts training."

"That's okay. It's supposed to be your day off anyway."

He nodded. "Thank God."

"Just get some rest. Do you need anything, like for the pain?" She'd never had a hangover but plenty of her friends in Baltimore had.

"I took some medicine. I just need to sleep it away now." He sighed. "I'm sorry, I know I should not have drank so much. And I should not have kissed you. It is against the rules."

Her heart stopped. She gripped his forearm. "But you like me, don't you?"

"Yes, very much."

Relief mixed with hope mixed with anxiety.

"I've never done long-term close protection before," he said. "I'm not sure I'm suited for it."

"You're not leaving, are you?" *Did I jeopardize his career?*

He stared in her eyes. "I don't quit."

"I'm sorry I was so unfair last night," she said. "I'm too suspicious. It's just that I've been lied to so many times, and with you buying a girl for

Charles, and then all of a sudden saying you love me—it's like you were manipulating things. I kind of panicked."

He laid his hands over hers. "Forget it. I know you had problems with men in the past, and your situation here, uh, so much thinking about security and being careful. But please believe me, I try to help you, Charles, and Pel every way I can. Maybe I don't want Charles to be obsessed with you because that can create problems for everyone and it isn't healthy. But I am not a 'player,' as you put it. I looked it up on the Comnet."

"I believe you. You've always looked out for us." She gazed in his wide, tender eyes. "You said you loved me. Is that really true?"

"I'll be honest. I was a little drunk. But I do like you very much. We should talk when I am less tired."

Her throat tightened. "You just want to be friends, then."

He squeezed her hands. "No—eu gosto muito de você. More than friends."

She knew the phrase. A stage toward love. Her cheeks and forehead flushed with warmth. His face was so ruggedly handsome. Despite the ears. His torso was sculpted like a warrior god. Her heart pounded like a taiko drum ensemble. *Oh, gods, why am I the most unchilled person on this planet?*

Against her hands, Gabriel's palms felt moist with sweat. The battle-hardened warrior was as nervous as she was!

"I was thinking," he said, "Alzira can be your bodyguard and I can be Pel and Charles's. That way, there is no conflict. If it's fine with her to work more hours. Anyway, it is difficult with just one bodyguard here."

"I thought the budget was too low for two bodyguards at the same time."

"If my boss insists on it, I can reduce my official hours, even if I stay here all the time, and Alzira can work more. I have a higher salary than her, so it should be no problem. Pel and Charles never go anywhere, so they will be easy to protect."

"Compared to me, you mean."

He smiled. "Yes, compared to you. You are very difficult to guard, you are too social."

"I don't want you to lose income because of me."

"It is the only way we can have a relationship. Besides, my housing and food is free, it's not a worry. I like you. You are the most interesting girl I've ever met. And I admire what you and your sister and friends did. I would never have attempted such a thing."

She'd never wanted someone so intensely. "Will you promise to keep being honest with me?"

"Yes, of course."

She closed the rest of the distance between them and kissed him. He tasted like mint toothpaste. He wasn't as enthusiastic as yesterday, but he still had that conflict and he had a hangover.

She stood. "I'll let you go back to bed. If you come by my apartment later, I'll make you some tea. Or coffee, we could buy some." And they could talk some more, and see what would happen.

* * *

Dalton

Dalton was just going to recruit Adrianna to help his operation. But she was so hot, with big tits and an "I love fucking" smile, that he had to do her first. Normally he liked having two girls. Double the pleasure. But Adrianna was good enough by herself. She was in great shape, seemed to enjoy sex with strangers, didn't mind him being a little rough, and didn't fake her orgasms while his cocktail of drugs let him go on as long as he wanted.

Eventually he was spent. They lay on the sweaty sheets together. "You are incredible," he had to admit.

She sat up. "Can I use your shower?"

"We're not done yet."

She frowned, then glanced around. "You have a very nice room."

Ares didn't normally spring for five-star hotels. He wondered what kind of deal they got, if they had worked for the owner. Dalton rolled out of bed, opened the room safe and fished out one of his fake IDs. "I'm with Interpol."

"Who are they?"

"You're kidding, right?"

Her eyebrows squished like she was getting more and more confused.

Dalton set his comlink to translate English to Portuguese, his translated voice coming out of the tiny but full-spectrum speaker. "Interpol is an international police organization. Brazil is a member."

He displayed pictures of Demopoulos and Lee on the comlink. "These two men are wanted terrorists."

She blinked, obviously nervous. "They are?"

He went over the charges, which included assault and cyberterrorism.

"You met them, right?"

"That's not your business."

The answer he expected, more or less. Dalton re-opened the safe and tossed her 3,000 reais. About a thousand bucks. Her eyes widened as she counted the bills.

"You're working for me now. 3,000 reais a day." Which was not even a blip compared to a $4 million bounty. "I need intel on Demopoulos and Lee, what rooms they're in, if they have guns, what sort of locks, that sort of thing. I'll give you a video camera to wear, on a necklace or something. You'll visit them and report back to me."

She looked confused again so he repeated it with more precise phrasing. The translator needed work. "I need you to return to that building and bring back video I can use."

She got up and walked to the coffee table by the window. The sway of her naked ass aroused him again. She slipped the money in her purse and sat on the sofa, away from the bed. "Charles said he wanted to see me again. He's been messaging me but I haven't replied yet. It's a business opportunity but Gabriel paid me not to say I'm a pro."

"You'll figure something out. You've got 'till tomorrow, when I get your camera." He had some cameras and mikes, and just needed to buy the right kind of necklace and install one.

She nodded.

"I'm going to fuck you too whenever you come over," he said. "That's part of the price. Now get back over here."

11

Kiyoko

Kiyoko skipped the usual group dinner and went out with Gabriel for sushi. Alzira had departed without saying goodbye, and wouldn't be back for a week and a half. Why was she so anti-social? How did she manage to land a fiancé?

No matter—Alzira had agreed to Gabriel's proposal. As soon as she returned, he would guard Pel and Charles and she would accompany Kiyoko outside the building.

"Our supervisor, Sr. Iago, also agreed," Gabriel said quietly at their table. "I told him it's not safe to have just one person working. He agreed as long as the budget is the same. That means there will be days when you can not leave the building, however. You can't leave when Alzira is not working."

"That's what the Comnet is for," she said. *And I'd rather spend my time in your arms than anywhere else.* "Will this hurt you financially?"

He shrugged. "No, as I said, SSG pays my expenses. I'm saving for a house but this will have a very small effect."

After finishing their celebratory meal and splitting a small flask of sake, Kiyoko directed Gabriel to Charles and Pel's apartment instead of hers. "I need to tell Charles about us," she said as they exited the elevator holding hands. "That we'll be dating."

They'd only kissed so far, but it was definitely the beginnings of a relationship. "Namorar" was the Brazilian term, to become girlfriend-boyfriend. Her skin tingled and she felt giddy, like her prior relationships had all been hollow or fake but Gabriel was the real thing, the companion she'd always wanted. The gods were being nice for once.

Kiyoko entered the keypad code and opened the door. Pel and Charles were standing in their living room arguing.

"We need money," Charles said in a strained voice.

"Common sense," Pel said. "You have none of it."

"What's going on?" Kiyoko asked. She realized she'd let go of Gabriel's hand.

Pel looked at her. "I'm the only one here who's careful. I should take off."

Gabriel held up a hand. "Tell us what is happening."

"Charles is trying to take over BetterWorld avatars. It's going to backfire, I know it. We've been over this. MediaCorp is sparing no expense to find us and take us out."

"I have faith in you," Kiyoko told Charles. "But Pel's right that we should be careful."

"I tested everything in the sandbox." His eyes glittered. "I cracked the new client defenses. I can take over an avatar and get code onto the user's computer. Trouble is, the user has to accept it. I can't just transmit by contact anymore."

"And you have a plan for that," she said, "like the way you took on those trolls?"

"Bunch of ways. Fake avatar updates. Free mods. Nearly everyone's a sucker if the shit's cool enough and it's all slicked over. We can even limit the targets to people who deserve the grief."

"It's not worth the risk," Pel said. "There's other ways to make money without going up against MediaCorp."

Charles ignored him, looking Kiyoko in the eyes. "Why didn't you eat with us?"

"Good grief," Pel said. "Give her some space. And don't change the topic."

"Yessa, massa."

Pel threw up his hands. "Here we go again."

Charles's comlink, minimized and strapped to his wrist, buzzed. He looked at it and smiled. "I'll be right back." He rushed out before anyone could question him.

"We have to do something for money," Kiyoko said. "We don't have any savings."

"You worked as a model in the U.S.," Gabriel said. "Models in Brazil make good money."

"That was just modeling costumes. It's not the same. I can't wear a bikini and look sexy."

"Why not?"

"I don't know how."

Pel frowned at Gabriel. "Don't make her do that. Besides, she should keep a low profile. Bad enough she prances around Liberdade wearing those costumes."

Kiyoko ignored Sir Grumps-a-Lot. "I can freelance design. It won't be enough for all of us to live on, though."

Charles returned holding hands with a caramel-skinned girl wearing a glittery cleavage-brandishing blouse and hip-hugging skirt. Just above her breasts, a filigreed silver heart hung from a thin chain. It was encrusted with diamonds, presumably fake.

Was this Adrianna? She was gaudy, but pretty. And very shapely.

Charles's smile vanished when he caught Kiyoko's eyes. He looked away.

"It's okay," Kiyoko began, but decided to wait for introductions to say more.

Gabriel stared at the girl, although not at her cleavage. "Oi."

The girl smiled and kissed him on the cheeks. "Oi, Gabriel, prazer em vê-lo novamente." *Nice to see you again.*

Kiyoko's stomach hardened.

Instead of returning the girl's kisses, Gabriel made introductions. "Kiyoko, this is Adrianna. Adrianna, this is Kiyoko."

Adrianna leaned forward and blew a kiss against Kiyoko's right cheek. "Prazer."

Standard social greeting. Kiyoko did the same.

Gabriel addressed Adrianna in Portuguese. "Você está aqui para ver o Charles?" *Here to see Charles?*

"Sim." *Yes.*

Kiyoko forced herself to relax. Petty jealousy was beneath her, especially when unwarranted.

The girl addressed everyone in English. "Charles helps me with my BetterWorld avatar and site."

"What's your avatar?" Kiyoko asked.

"Sexy Adrianna."

Of course. Did Charles know she was a prostitute? Was he paying her? Was Gabriel? "Is your site, um, related to your work?"

"What's that supposed to mean?" Charles interrupted.

"Well, I assume you saw it."

"Yeah. So she's a sex worker. So what?"

"How long have you known?"

"Uh, as soon as I saw her site. But I ain't a customer, it ain't like that. She did say Gabriel gave her some money the first time, but once she met me, she got to liking me. Then knowing I'm a Comnet grand master—we did some talking—she asked for my help."

Adrianna nodded.

"She wants a hidden page to book clients on her own," Charles continued, "instead of going through the club. They take a big cut."

Kiyoko decided to be nice. She held out a hand to Charles's new friend or whatever. "I am Princess Kiyoko of Yumekuni."

"Charles told me." Adrianna shook her hand.

Kiyoko decided not to ask about her sex career or lecture her about how prostitution turned women—all women—into objects. That would be rude. Instead, they talked about BetterWorld. Adrianna frequented the virtual clubs but she also had a level 60 half-elf wizard named Allannia on the Fantasy Continent.

"We must meet as soon as my avatar is reinstated," Kiyoko said. Assuming she wasn't banished from BetterWorld and Fronteira Nova forever.

Adrianna turned to Gabriel.

"Você mora aqui?" *Do you live here?*

Gabriel paused. "Sim, sou o vizinho deles." *Yes, I'm their neighbor.*

"Neste edifício?" *In this building?*

"Sim. Porque?" *Yes, why?*

Adrianna glanced at Kiyoko, then back at Gabriel. "Apenas conversando." *Just making talk.* She slipped fingers into Charles's and smiled at him. They went into his room, Charles with a huge grin on his face.

Gabriel addressed Pel. "Maya is coming over for dinner next week. Be nice to her."

Pel pressed his lips together, not saying anything.

"She's not a girl with a program," Gabriel said.

Pel looked confused. "A what?"

"Prostitute. She is very nice, you will like her."

Pel's eyes narrowed. "I have a girlfriend, we're practically married. You're our bodyguard, not our social director. I have to get back to work." He went into his bedroom.

"He is very rude sometimes," Gabriel said after the door closed.

"Yeah, well, consider his circumstances," Kiyoko said. "But you're right, that was a mean thing to say."

They returned to her apartment. Kiyoko greeted Nyasuke and led Gabriel to the sofa. He sat but she didn't. Her stomach tightened again. "Adrianna seems very interested in you."

His eyes widened, then narrowed. "We have already talked about this."

True. "So you weren't expecting her?" He had looked surprised.

"No. This was her doing."

She sat next to him on the sofa, not wanting to seem like a police interrogator. "And it's not a business transaction?"

"It is probably a skills trade. Although Charles is too young to realize it."

"So he thinks she likes him and he'll get hurt when he realizes otherwise."

"He is enjoying life now, that's what matters. And maybe she does like him."

"If he gets hurt, it's your responsibility to help him through it."

He nodded. "Of course. I want everyone to be happy."

He was such a nice guy. As chivalrous as a high-level paladin. "I'm sorry for doubting you, and being so bossy." She hadn't mentioned they were dating, either.

He smiled and drew close. "Forget it."

They embraced. It was okay to have a little happiness in a dark sea full of monsters.

* * *

Kiyoko

Invited back to the Ministry of Foreign Affairs, Kiyoko took a seat in conference room #2. It was just big enough to hold a faux-mahogany table, eight padded swivel chairs, and a curving wall screen. A window looked out to the skyscraper forest of downtown São Paulo, most of it below their floor.

Gabriel took the chair next to her. "You look lovely."

Her heart fluttered the way it always did when he complimented her. "Thank you."

Kiyoko was dressed in red robes again, but instead of a wig, had dyed her hair bright red. She needed the luck, and wigs demonstrated lack of commitment. She'd also prayed to Kui-Xing, the Starry-Eyed God of Official Documents and Paperwork, and offered a homemade sponge cake.

Miranda Rossi, São Paulo Bureau Chief, Department for Human Rights and Social Affairs, entered and closed the door behind her. "Good afternoon," she said in English. "I'm sorry there's no refreshments in here."

"That's okay," Kiyoko said. *Thank you for receiving me again.* "Obrigado por me receber novamente."

Ms. Rossi raised her eyebrows. "Your pronunciation is very good."

"Obrigado."

Ms. Rossi spoke some commands in Portuguese. The window darkened, the front overhead lights dimmed, and three faces appeared on the wall screen, each sitting in a different office. On the left, a light-skinned, ginger-haired man with freckles, young for an official. In the center, a middle-aged woman with glasses. On the right, a stern-looking man with a dark beard and mustache.

Ms. Rossi looked at the screen, then at Kiyoko. "I was able to convince some colleagues in Brasilia to join us remotely. May I introduce Arthur Bitencourt from the Office for the United States."

"Hello," the ginger in the left portal said. He sounded like an American.

Ms. Rossi continued. "Isabella Pedrosa from the General Secretariat's office." The woman in the middle greeted her. "And Nicolas da Costa from the Office of the Legal Counsel." The bearded man on the right.

Ms. Rossi introduced Kiyoko, but not Gabriel, and gave an overview of her case.

"Thank you for taking the time to speak with me," Kiyoko said. "I am honored. Does this mean you have decided to pressure the U.S. until my sister, Waylee Freid, is released?"

Eyebrows raised. Not a good sign.

"I have reviewed the case," Mr. Bitencourt said, "and it does not appear that Ms. Freid's human rights are being violated."

Kiyoko jumped in. "She was shot at from helicopters and almost killed, then thrown in prison."

"She was escaping a crime scene and a grand jury indicted her on the evidence. It's not arbitrary."

"Ms. Freid is being charged under domestic U.S. law," Mr. Da Costa added, "and it would set a poor precedent for Brazil to intervene."

Her prayers must not have worked. "She's a political prisoner. She didn't hurt anyone, just let people know how dangerous MediaCorp is."

Eyebrows raised again.

"Even here in Brazil," she continued, "MediaCorp is too powerful. They attacked the company I was working for and now I don't have a job."

"Brazil is subject to a host of trade agreements," Ms. Pedrosa said. "It is difficult for many of our companies. I sympathize."

Kiyoko nodded and kept going. "Waylee wanted everyone to know about the secret deals MediaCorp cut with government officials during the Internet upgrade, how they took over the backbone and switches and used that to control the content. They did the same thing in other countries. Now they can control what people think."

"Why break into a private facility and hijack a broadcast?" Mr. Bitencourt said. "Why not just write articles about it?"

"Because no one sees anything that doesn't make money for MediaCorp. Waylee used to work for the *Baltimore Herald*, but MediaCorp took over the paper and fired her. She tried writing articles on her own but thanks to MediaCorp's stranglehold, couldn't get any readership. The only solution was to reach people directly."

"Your sister was charged with a long list of crimes," Mr. Da Costa said. "Would you like me to read them?"

"All alleged," Kiyoko said. "None of it's been proven."

"If she were imprisoned just for writing an article," Ms. Pedrosa said, "it would clearly be a violation of human rights. But the fact is, and we all agree on this, that she was charged for violating a number of U.S. laws, and there was enough evidence to indict her."

Mr. Da Costa nodded. "And many of those laws have analogs in Brazil."

Kiyoko pressed on despite the obvious hopelessness of her position. "I implore you to help. She's in solitary confinement and it could trigger a suicide attempt."

Ms. Pedrosa looked down, then back at the camera. "I noted that Amnesty International created a petition asking for a fair trial, and that she be treated for any illnesses she might have."

"Yes. Can Brazil ask the same things? And ask that she be taken out of solitary?"

"It's not our position to dictate what a fair trial is," Mr. Bitencourt said.

"Why not?"

"Our ministry generally works through the United Nations or Organization of American States rather than bilaterally," Ms. Pedrosa said.

"That's perfect. Get the whole O.A.S. to issue an opinion."

"I'm afraid that's outside their scope."

Ms. Rossi spoke for the first time. "We're nearing the end of our allotted time."

Kiyoko had researched the Ministry quite a bit since her last visit. There was one thing that shouldn't be such trouble. "You can make a public statement. Release a statement that you hope Waylee Freid will be treated fairly and her human rights respected. Surely that's feasible."

The three bureaucrats agreed to discuss it, and gave their farewells.

Kiyoko stared at the blank screen. Would they do anything at all? Did they have paperweights for hearts?

Gabriel patted her hand, transferring a little energy to her spirit. Kiyoko thanked Ms. Rossi and planned to contact Kui-Xing's boss in the Chinese pantheon, Wen-Chang.

* * *

Waylee

Waylee's burly guards entered her cell. "Why ain't you eatin' your food?" the female one said.

She forced her head toward the woman. "Can I have my things back?"

"What things?"

"My papers." *All I had left.*

"I ain't got any papers of yours. Now eat your damn food."

Her writings were lost forever. "I need medication," Waylee managed. "I need to see a doctor." She didn't have the energy to cite the eighth amendment, which should guarantee her access to medical care.

"You got a fever or some shit?" the woman asked.

Forget it. Waylee buried herself under the blanket. She heard the guards march out, slam the door shut, and lock it.

After a while, she opened her eyes and looked around. The food tray was gone.

Sometimes, she'd heard, prisoners fashioned their bedsheets into a rope and hanged themselves. Her cell didn't have anything she could tie a rope to, though.

Could she use the stainless steel toilet-sink unit somehow? The sink had an edge she could bash her forehead against.

It would hurt. Unlikely to kill her though. Would just make things worse. Blackness. She started to cry.

Maybe she could climb on top of the sink and jump down in a way to break her neck. It was worth a try.

* * *

Dalton

With his data glasses enhancing his night vision, Dalton scanned the narrow street for trouble as De Barros knocked on the metal door of a do-it-yourself fortress. Dalton's bullet-resistant jacket was mostly unzipped so he could whip out a pistol if needed. The solid-looking door was the only visible entry to a three story building constructed from red bricks roughly cemented together. Narrow windows punctuated the wall above, too small to climb through but perfect for pointing guns out of.

According to his data glasses, they were about forty minutes southeast of his hotel and thirty minutes from Liberdade. From Liberdade, it would be another twenty minutes to Campo de Marte Airport.

Up and down the uneven concrete street, men stared back from alley corners and upper floor windows. Names and links to criminal records appeared above some. But no one approached.

A tattooed dark-skinned man opened the door. João Melo, according to Dalton's database connection. His name linked to a long rap sheet, not worth reading at the moment.

"Boa noite, mano," Melo said.

"Evening, bro," the bone transducer against Dalton's left ear translated.

They entered a dimly lit, poorly ventilated room that reeked of marijuana and tobacco smoke. Hip hop music played from a small white box in the far corner. Five men and four women, all young, sat on mismatched sofas. Some played a shooter game on a big wall screen, others passed joints or drank beer. The men had pistols in holsters or thrust in their belts. Automatic weapons lay on tables or were propped against the wall.

The oldest of the men, a clean-cut man in his late twenties, shook De Barros's hand. De Barros introduced him as O Capitão, chief of As Piranhas. *The Captain.* According to the database, his real name was Danilo Machado, wanted on charges of kidnapping and drug trafficking. Probably De Barros was keeping him on the street in some kind of business arrangement.

More people came down from the stairs, boosting the total to thirteen. The Captain looked at Dalton and spoke in Portuguese. The data glasses translated. "You have a job for us?"

Dalton spoke in English. "Yes. Two men in Liberdade. We need to secure them alive and transport them to Campo de Marte Airport. They can't be killed or we won't get paid."

De Barros translated.

One of the gangsters set up their wall skin to receive wireless data and Dalton displayed photographs of Demopoulos and Lee. "These are the targets. They have stun guns and some rudimentary hand to hand skills, but will probably piss their pants when we break in. No combat or police training."

"How about street training?" the Captain said.

"They're computer nerds. They're not like you." From the files De Barros sent, what As Piranhas lacked in formal training and discipline, they had in toughness and experience. "That doesn't mean we should be careless, though," Dalton added.

"Quanto custa essa brincadeira?" the Captain asked. *How much for this joke?*

"Joke? This is no joke, and you'd better not treat it like one."

The Captain's eyes narrowed.

"But it's only one day's work," Dalton continued. "Flat fee, 100,000 reais." About $35,000, well below De Barros's suggested price of $50,000, but it was just a starting point.

"For all of us? Are you crazy, bro? No way."

"I don't need all of you. I need eight, your most experienced. Two drivers, four to carry the targets, and two sentries who are good shots. More than that will get in the way."

De Barros said something that translated to, "We may perhaps give you a little more, but remember that you would go to prison without my good graces."

They haggled over the price a while, finally settling on 100,000 up front and 100,000 upon delivery to the airport. A big markup but a necessary investment—they needed the manpower.

"We'll do it Sunday," Dalton told the assembled gangsters, "when their bodyguard is at the street fair. They have a fill-in shift bodyguard but she won't be there either." One of the gems Adrianna had discovered.

Dalton displayed maps of Liberdade, a 3-D rendering of the targets' building, and the route they would take in and out. Lastly he showed video shot from Adrianna's necklace camera, which covered the way to their apartment and what it looked like inside. She'd turned it off before having sex with Lee.

"The elevator doesn't stop on the targets' floor," Dalton explained, "and the stairwell door is kept locked with a deadbolt." He pointed to De Barros. "The inspector will provide a hydraulic spreader to break the door jamb. The apartment door is a little more challenging. It's got steel plating and framing and an electronic lock."

Unfortunately, Adrianna hadn't learned the combination. It would have been too obvious to ask, and Lee was savvy enough to cover the keypad with his hands while typing the code. The door looked spreader and battering ram resistant, so they might need explosives, which could be messy and would require a special delivery from Ares.

"Easiest way in," Dalton said, "is if my operative opens the door for us. But in case something goes wrong there, I'll bring plastic explosives. Either way, you'll need to rush in as soon as the door opens. We have to be in and out before anyone arrives to interfere."

The Captain nodded. "Yes, we know how to be fast."

Dalton brought up a photo of Gabriel da Silva. "And speaking of worst case, this is our targets' bodyguard. He works for a private military company called Serviços de Segurança Globais. He's got special forces training."

The Captain frowned. "I thought you said the bodyguard wouldn't be there."

"He won't," Dalton said. "But in case the targets call him, and he's able to get to the building before we leave, we have to be prepared. If the sentries see him approach, they should contact the rest of the team, then shoot him."

De Barros waved his hands. "No, no, I told you SSG is well-connected. There will be problems if we kill one of their employees."

Stupid fuck! Dalton glared at the fat detective. "This is my operation. Don't question me again." He looked around at the others. "We'll do what's necessary to succeed."

12

Charles

Encased in his immersion suit and hooked to the metal frame that took up half his bedroom, Charles deployed a new version of his PhishPhactory tool, which automated target discovery and spear phishing. Griefing trolls was as fun as it got, but with most of the Collective servers offline now, he needed an army of zombie computers to support any sizable campaign to make money or fight their enemies. He wouldn't hurt any of these targets, just use a little CPU time here and there when it wouldn't be noticed.

Then he ran the tool through a translator to convert the Edict code to Qualia so it would work on BetterWorld. He dove into the Qualia code, which needed a complete interface makeover. Maybe he couldn't take over avatars without the owner's permission anymore, but he could always trick them into accepting his Trojan. Some gift they couldn't refuse, tailored to the user. And once they accepted it, he'd have root access to their computer.

His concentration wavered. Kiyoko and Gabriel were at the Sunday market again. They spent an awful lot of time together. Charles almost never saw her anymore. They weren't fucking, were they? His heart clenched.

But it would serve him right. After all, he'd been fucking Adrianna—whose real name was Maria Ledo—all week and he practically flaunted it.

As if summoned, a window popped up with a picture of his bang honey giving a "come here" smile, nude but cropped just above the nipples, *Sexy Adrianna* written beneath. The picture switched to video. "I'm here," Adrianna said, meaning she was just outside the building and would be at the stairwell door soon. "Can you let me in?"

He was expecting her, but had lost track of time. Always happened when working. "Give me a couple of minutes," he replied with his Zulu avatar.

Charles closed his Comnet connection and pulled off the VR suit. This would be day number five. They would work on her BetterWorld site and then fuck like the end of the world was coming.

Maybe she was more than a bang honey. Maybe they could get serious. Kiyoko and Pel didn't seem to mind her being around.

Charles straightened his clothes, then went to the stairwell door and opened it. Adrianna was pacing, even though she couldn't have been waiting more than a couple of minutes. She wore a halter top and jeans, and that heart-shaped necklace. Less revealing than usual. Maybe because it was Sunday?

Her eyes darted, then she came in. Charles kissed her but she didn't kiss back.

"What's up?"

"Nothing." She kissed him, thrusting her tongue against his, her mouth warm and minty.

"I'm gonna make a drink," she said when they entered the apartment. "Want one?"

"I'll pass." He was with Kiyoko on keeping alcohol out of his brain.

∗ ∗ ∗

Pelopidas

Immersed in the Comnet, Pel redistributed his article countering MediaCorp's misinformation about Waylee. Someone had deleted it from half the sites he posted it on. Petty bastards.

Pel had his VR helmet and gloves on, but not the whole suit. It was a pain to put the whole suit on and hook it to the support frame, and there was no point in doing it if he wasn't gaming or testing Fantasmas code.

He responded to some comments, ignoring the obvious trolls, then sent a message to Kiyoko to ask Francis for an update on Waylee and to give her his love. Francis would only communicate through Kiyoko, citing some arcane lawyer rule.

Having run out of productive tasks, he checked the anonymous dropbox where his cousin Despina had been storing video clips from her comlink. There was a new file.

His defense programs found no viruses or other malware. As he normally did to be safe, though, he streamed the video indirectly through a converter on a remote server so the data wouldn't reach him, only a translated playback.

It was wedding footage. His cousin Jimmy, Despina's brother, was married at St. Nicholas, the Orthodox church in Baltimore's Greektown. Married to Alyssa Galanis, who was far too nice for him. Pel's parents, sister, and the rest of the clan were there, and lots of old friends.

I should have been there. Me and Waylee and Kiyoko. We had such a great life. Our own house, the band, lots of friends, Orioles games with old buddies. Not sleeping alone, not hiding someplace I don't belong.

He willed himself not to cry. *At least I'm not in prison like Waylee.*

Why'd we have to listen to her? We're all fucked and nothing good came of it, only bad things.

The stairwell camera feed popped up. It was Adrianna again, wearing jeans for the first time, tapping a foot, then pacing. Through the other cameras he saw Charles exit their apartment and let her in the hallway.

Adrianna wasn't so bad as long as Pel's VR suit drowned her out when she and Charles were at it. She wasn't out to scam them. Charles deserved his fun. And it cut back his obsession with Kiyoko.

The stairwell door display popped up again. A dark shape flashed across, followed by uniform blackness.

Shit. Pel pulled up the other cameras. In the hallway, Charles and Adrianna were entering the apartment. In the exterior feed, two white cargo vans, no logos, were among the vehicles parked in front of the building. Two girls, both wearing unzipped jackets, stood next to the vans and trained dark data glasses at his apartment windows.

The stairwell door smashed open, pieces of door jamb flying into the hallway. *Holy fucking fuck!*

Six men entered the hallway, wearing crude plastic masks of people he didn't recognize. They wore gloves and carried leather bags and guns. What timing—Gabriel was off at the market and Alzira was at the beach.

"Gorilla snot sandwich!" Pel shouted. His safe phrase, one unlikely to be uttered by accident, activated a routine to wipe their computers, delete his Comnet accounts, upload the video camera feed to a remote server, and warn Charles, Kiyoko, and Gabriel with the code '911.' "This is Pel," he said, leaving a voice message rather than waiting for them to pick up. "Apartment's under attack."

Everything turned black, his computer dead. He pulled off his helmet and gloves, thankful he didn't have his full VR suit on.

Back in his bedroom, his home in exile. Should he put his bug-out bag— his backpack full of road necessities—on? Not if he had to fight—it would slow him down.

He fumbled for his stun gun and the extra charges. Maybe he should have bought a regular gun like Gabriel suggested. There would be consequences for killing someone, though. More importantly, he wasn't a trained killer like Gabriel, or M-pat back home. Most inexperienced people couldn't bring themselves to kill another human being, even in self-defense, and he almost certainly fell in that category.

Stun gun in trembling hand, he unlocked his bedroom door. He inched it open. Charles stood in the living room staring at the wall screen. "Get your gun," Pel told him.

He opened his door the rest of the way, swinging it inward. He glanced around the corner at the apartment door just past the kitchen and bathroom. Adrianna was in the kitchen, biting her lip and pacing.

Three loud raps echoed from the door.

"Don't answer it!" Pel said.

Adrianna looked at him, then started for the door. Charles stood in the living room, eyes glued to the wall screen that Pel couldn't see from his vantage. "There are people in the hallway," he said.

No shit. Pel aimed his stun gun at Adrianna. "I said don't answer it!"

More knocking.

Her eyes were wide. "Is that a gun?"

"Back away from the door." His hand shook but she was only ten feet away and hard to miss.

"They put tape over all the door cameras," Charles said, "but they missed the one at the end of the hall. They're getting stuff out of their bags."

The knocking turned to pounding.

Pel turned to catch Charles's eyes. "Get your fucking gun!"

There was the climbing rope fastened beneath the living room window, but the intruders were watching the windows and they'd certainly have guns. He hadn't expected such a big team.

Adrianna was still near the door, staring at the gun in his hand.

Pel willed his feet to move. He ran to Adrianna and shoved her inside the bathroom. "Lock the door and hide."

He shut the door on her and ran back to his position in the bedroom doorway. The front door was as solid as money could buy. They'd have a hard time getting in. Who were they? There were too many to all be CIA agents. Mercenaries?

If only he'd built a trap door to the apartment below. Everyone else, including Gabriel and Alzira, had vetoed the idea when they moved in, saying the building owner and downstairs neighbors would get angry. The only option, then, was to delay the attackers until SSG or police reinforcements arrived.

* * *

Kiyoko

Lunch at Feira da Liberdade was a serious matter. So much to choose from.

Kiyoko settled on vegetarian gyoza. Couldn't go wrong with dumplings. And she could pick something more substantial for dinner.

"How do you eat so often and stay so thin?" Gabriel asked as they dove into their food.

It was another perfect day; a little rain overnight but now the sun was out. "I'd say it's age related, but my sister's thin too. A blessing from the goddesses I suppose." She looked in his dazzling eyes. "They brought you to me too."

His face melted. "I can't wait for Alzira to return, and my conflict worries end."

She couldn't wait to have sex with him. It had been so long since the last time, almost a year. Gabriel made her heart flutter. A champion, better by far than anyone back in Baltimore.

I love Brazil. All we need is to get Waylee here and get MediaCorp off our backs and everything will be perfect. There was even a group of activist journalists called Mídia Ninja, one of the few alternatives to MediaCorp and Globo, their local subsidiary. Waylee could learn Portuguese and work with them.

Kiyoko's comlink beeped. She almost never got calls, since she had to keep her address secret. And the beeping wasn't a cute jingle. It was the monotonic repeating notes of Pel's alert signal.

The screen displayed '911.' *Please be a mistake!* She pressed it.

"This is Pel." No video. "Apartment's under attack."

Gabriel stared at her. He'd received the same message.

They were only a few blocks away. Kiyoko dropped her food and started running for their apartment building, as fast as her robes and slippers would allow. Gabriel ran faster, leaving her behind.

"Wait for me!" she shouted.

He glanced back.

That was stupid, he's the one with the guns. "No, never mind, go help them!"

* * *

Pelopidas

Pel trained his stun gun at the front door. The pounding stopped. Charles finally ran into his bedroom and returned with his.

"Where's Adrianna?" he squeaked, gun shaking in his hand.

Pel whispered, "Bathroom. Hiding."

Charles nodded.

A loud boom. The door blew open and acrid-smelling smoke billowed in. *Fuck. Fuck. Fuck.*

Figures rushed in, plastic masks on, stun guns in hand.

I'm committed now. Pel fired at the one in front. His stun gun buzzed and the man fell to his knees, then dropped to the floor.

Charles stood in the living room, trembling.

Pel shot at the next one. He fell.

The next figure aimed a stun gun at Charles, who hadn't tried to find cover. His arms jerked and he dropped.

Pel shut his bedroom door and locked it. He yanked the expended capacitor out of his gun and slapped a new one in.

The flimsy door flew open with a crack. Pel dropped to his knees and fired at the man coming through.

The man stumbled forward and crashed to the floor. Another was right behind him, pointing a gun.

Pel's muscles seized, like sudden cramps. He lost his balance and everything went black.

* * *

Dalton

Dalton was pissed. Three men down, including the gang leader. Three men felled by one amateur. He shook the Captain, prone on the floor between the kitchen and living room. "Get up."

The Captain groaned. Dalton wished Inspector De Barros was here, but he had refused to take part in the extraction, saying he couldn't be seen. *Pussy.* Dalton had hired two more Piranhas to compensate. He'd take it out of De Barros's cut.

On the bright side, the fat inspector had passed along all the address-es and passwords Martinez and the other hackers at Ares needed to take down the police dispatch system. No one could call in, and they'd have a hard time coordinating any response.

"Find the whore," Dalton ordered the three still on their feet. He injected Demopoulos with a fast-acting sedative, sticking the needle into his ca-rotid artery. He did the same with Lee. They'd be out for a while.

A big wall screen in the living room showed twelve camera feeds, not all of them blank. They'd missed a camera in the hallway and ones pointed outside. No matter, and no time to disable them now.

"Encontrei," a voice came from the bathroom. "Found her," Dalton's ear bud translated.

Dalton joined the Piranha man, who was masked as Bruno something or other from the telenovelas. His real name was Orlando. He pointed a pistol at Adrianna, who was cowering and trembling in the shower stall.

"What do we do with her?" Orlando said.

Adrianna clasped her hands together. She spoke in Portuguese, "Pelo amor de Deus . . ." "For the love of God," the translator said. "I'm sorry I didn't get the door. They pointed a gun at me. Made me come in here. Please, please."

What to do with her? She was an unreliable loose end. And she didn't do what she was supposed to. "Consider your contract terminated," he said in English.

"I don't understand."

Dalton looked at Orlando. "Shoot her in the head." His data glasses translated and a small speaker in his mask broadcast, "Atira na cabeça dela."

She shook her head. "No! Please no!"

Orlando sighed and fired his gun. A hole appeared in her forehead and blood and brains spattered all over the tile wall. The body slid down into the tub. Orlando shot her again to make sure. Double tap—the man knew his craft.

Damn shame, though. She was a fine piece of ass.

13

Gabriel

Gabriel left Kiyoko behind. Unlike Pel and Charles, there was no reward for her. Gabriel dodged around people, trying to get through the crowds.

They didn't always move as expected. He bumped into a man his age, who spilled a half-full plastic cup of beer.

"Filho da puta!" The man hurled down his cup and swung a fist.

No time for this. Gabriel grabbed the man's arm, twisted, and threw him to the ground. He took off again.

I can't believe this shit is actually happening. And timed while he was away—it had to be deliberate. He tried calling Pel while running. "DG, call Pel," he commanded his augmented reality glasses.

No answer. He shoved his way through a food line blocking the street. More curses thrown his way. "Police! Out of the way!" he shouted.

Seemed to work, even without showing a badge. Attitudes toward police varied, but only well-armed gangsters were willing to challenge them.

He kept running, the rows of overhanging white lanterns marking his progress. "DG, call SSG emergency dispatch." His company had set up procedures in case of trouble he couldn't handle himself.

The connect icon flashed. "Serviços de Segurança Globais," a woman's voice said. "Please state the nature of your emergency."

"Da Silva. Condition Red. I need backup in Liberdade immediately. You have the address. Unknown number of assailants attempting to kill or kidnap Demopoulos and Lee. Need a helicopter team."

He turned onto Rua dos Estudantes, their street. No tented stalls, but it was still crowded with pedestrians. Only a few more blocks, though. And it sloped downhill.

"Helicopter?" the woman asked.

He abandoned the crowded sidewalk for the street, which was blocked off for the fair, but lined with cars anyway. "Yes, Da Silva Condition Red. Possible kidnappers, probable head start. Hurry, I am alone!"

Gabriel kept running. He dodged between groups of people bound for the fair. With luck, the SSG helicopter would arrive from their Congonhas base in fifteen minutes. They always kept at least one on rapid response, and it was only an eight kilometer flight.

He called the state military police, Águias da Cidade, next. They had a helicopter base at Congonhas Airport too, having just moved from their old facility at Campo de Marte.

No answer. What was the problem? And no police visible. Where was that Inspector De Barros when they needed him?

Gabriel approached their six-story apartment building and zoomed in on his data glasses. Nothing unusual. No smoke, no noise, people walking up and down the sidewalks as if it were any other day.

Two white cargo vans were parked on the street, one next to their building and another three spaces up. Also not unusual, except for the tattooed girls standing next to them and glancing back and forth. Both wore dark data glasses with wraparound mikes, unzipped leather jackets, and bulging cargo pants. The closer one was young, with cinnamon skin and black hair tucked under a red bandanna. The further one was older with dark skin and long purple box braids.

Were they armed? His data glasses couldn't identify Bandanna Girl, but Purple Hair had a long record, including an arrest for illegal firearms. The two women stared at him and tapped their data glasses.

Gabriel turned away and pretended to look at building numbers. "DG," he whispered, "display feed from Pel 2SQ1BZ23." Pel's emergency activation streamed his security camera feeds to a Comnet site that he and SSG headquarters could access.

Swiping a finger along the right arm of his data glasses, Gabriel panned through the camera feeds. Five were out. Still transmitting but no picture.

But the hallway camera showed people emerging from Pel and Charles's apartment. The door was off its hinges and smudged black. Seven people exited, four of them carrying Pel and Charles, who looked unconscious. The intruders wore street clothes, not uniforms, wore gloves, and were masked as telenovela stars. Three moved slowly and stiffly. They entered the stairwell through a shattered door frame.

Shit. They're already leaving. It would take them a while to get downstairs, though. The elevator wouldn't stop on their floor without a code, and could only hold three people anyway.

Gabriel was outnumbered at least nine to one. But all he had to do was delay them until reinforcements arrived from SSG and the police. Pin them in the stairwell? Or take out their transport?

I'll go for the transport. Gabriel strode toward the closest van, which had no windows in the back.

The tattooed women stared at him, then reached into their jackets.

Fuck. Gabriel whipped out his pistols. In his right hand, a Glock semi-auto with dampened recoil and a full clip of hollow-point. In his left, a long-barreled needlegun with a big magazine of guided fletchettes with explosive heads. Both guns had laser targeting systems integrated with his data glasses and able to adjust for range and wind.

Purple Hair drew a polymer submachine gun. Bandanna Girl, who was less than ten feet away now, pulled out a sawed-off shotgun.

Holy shit. Gabriel's arms acted on reflex. He swung the needlegun toward the greater danger, the girl with the shotgun, red crosshairs in his augmented vision sweeping toward her chest. He flipped the switch to full auto. At the same time, he swung the Glock toward Purple Hair. He pulled both triggers.

Neither gun had much recoil but they made plenty of noise. Just as Bandanna Girl leveled her shotgun, half a magazine of explosive fletchettes ripped into her torso and exploded in a spray of red. He hit Purple Hair too. She staggered backward.

Bandanna Girl dropped to the sidewalk, blood gushing out of her jacket. *I killed her.* He squelched the thought for now.

Wide eyed, Purple Hair shot back, *dakka dakka dakka,* spraying bullets in his direction. Plinks against parked cars and thwacks against concrete.

Gabriel felt a sharp pain in his upper right arm. He fired the Glock at Purple Hair again and dashed behind the nearby van.

People screamed and ran. On the sidewalk to his right, a middle-aged Japanese woman lay on her back, bleeding from the stomach. On the street, a school-age girl grasped her forearm and wailed. A lanky teenage boy tried to pull her away. A familiar image flashed into his mind, a dead girl in the *Tropical Breeze* dining hall, blood soaking the carpet around her.

Gabriel glanced at his arm. It burned like fire and blood dripped from his torn shirt sleeve, but it wasn't bad enough to worry about yet.

The bystanders would most likely survive. "Everyone get out of here!" he yelled.

He glanced around the side of the van. Purple Hair was gone, either retreating or reloading. Bandanna Girl lay in a spreading pool of blood, motionless.

"Gabriel!" Kiyoko's voice. *No.* He turned.

Kiyoko was running toward him in her pink kimono. Her eyes were wide.

I thought she was staying put. Gabriel waved his arm. Pain. Wrong arm. "Get out of here!" he yelled in English. "Take cover!"

She nodded and veered toward the minimarket where they did most of their shopping.

Gabriel peered around the van again. Purple Hair was waiting for him. He snapped back behind cover.

Dakka dakka dakka. More plinks and thuds and screams.

Kiyoko was in that direction! His heart seized. He whipped his head around and saw her just outside the grocer's. Unharmed but exposed. Someone had pulled down the corrugated metal shutter door that graced every store in the neighborhood.

Kiyoko banged on the shutter door. "Let me in! Me deixe entrar!" She followed with something in Japanese.

"Take cover damn it!" Gabriel shouted.

She ducked behind an old Camry hybrid next to the market. Safe for now.

Gabriel looked around the other side of the van. Someone shot at him with a pistol. The bullet whizzed by his ear.

Fuck. The driver, leaning out the window. A girl, light skinned with long dark hair.

Gabriel holstered his Glock and tried the back door of the van. The handle was unlocked. Made sense, they were expecting passengers. He whipped the door open, needlegun in his left hand.

The girl turned around, teenage face rigid with surprise. Too late. Crosshair on her head, Gabriel fired a short burst.

Her head exploded, blood and bone fragments and brains splattering the windshield. One eyeball flew into the empty back of the van and bounced toward him. Gabriel almost gagged but emptied the rest of the magazine into the console. Plastic and metal fragments flew everywhere. The dashboard lights went out.

One van down. He could take out the tires of the other. He couldn't see them from this vantage, though; he'd have to cross the street. "DG, call SSG emergency dispatch."

"Serviços de Segurança Globais," the dispatcher began.

He interrupted her. "I need that backup."

"On its way."

"Patch me through."

"Pistario here." *First good news.* Pistario was an old comrade from the special forces, team leader, damn capable. SSG didn't have ranks like the military and although Nicolas Pistario supervised more people, he and Gabriel were equivalent in the field.

"Da Silva. Eight to ten assailants, heavily armed. Two white cargo vans. I took out one, will try to get the other."

"Copy that. We are loading, and airborne soon."

They hadn't even left the base yet, and then they'd need another few minutes to get here. "Couldn't get through to police," Gabriel said. "Can you give it a try?"

"Copy that. Will pass it to dispatch."

Da Silva clicked off. He slapped another magazine in the needlegun.

More shop owners closed their shutters. Lots of people would be calling the police. And nearby patrols would hear the gunshots and radio headquarters. For a shootout, they'd bring armored vehicles, maybe helicopters.

Gabriel crouched, ready to dash across the street. *Wish I had a smoke grenade.* He glanced around the left side of the van.

Tatta tatta tatta. He ducked back behind the van. Another teenage girl, standing in the street with an AK-47. She was bronze-skinned, with blonde-streaked hair tied in a bun. Not the type you'd expect to carry an AK-47.

An icon of Kiyoko's beautiful face popped up. He'd disabled video; it was too distracting. "Are you safe?" Her voice trembled.

"Yes. Stay behind cover. Don't stick your head out."

"Please don't die."

"I won't." He tapped his glasses arm, terminating the connection. *If I try to cross the road I'm dead. If I stay here they might get away.*

Someone peered from the glass front doors of the apartment building, just ahead and to his right. "DG zoom," he commanded.

It was a man wearing a Tony Santos mask, everyone's favorite telenovela billionaire. Holding a matte-gray submachine gun. He peered out the door but made no move to exit.

What was he waiting for?

The side entrance. If Gabriel were running their gang, he'd send some men out the side to flank him. He'd be surrounded. And dead.

Gabriel abandoned his position and ran back up the street toward the plaza, keeping the van between him and the machine gunners. He glanced into the side street between the apartments and the building with the grocery store, seeing two masked men with pistols. They saw him too and fired.

And missed. Not enough time to aim and no targeting glasses.

Gabriel ran behind the sun-blotched Camry next to the grocery and crouched behind the trunk. Shitty cover compared to the van. Kiyoko was still there, eyes wide.

She looked at his arm. "You're bleeding."

He could still move it fine, although it hurt. "Just a scratch." Had she seen him kill those two girls?

Kiyoko pulled off the flowery sash around her waist that cinched her dress. Even though he'd said not to worry, she wrapped it over his arm wound and tied it tight. "I'll take a better look as soon as I can."

"I'm good for now." He glanced around the car.

The streets and sidewalks were deserted now except for the Japanese-looking woman motionless on her back and the dead bandanna-wearing girl, shotgun by her side. And up ahead, Purple Hair and the teen-age blonde-bun girl with their machine guns. He had hit Purple Hair in the torso with a 9 mm plastic-tipped hollow point round. Why wasn't she down? Wearing armor?

"I called the police," Kiyoko said. "Was going to use my auto-translate app. But no one answered."

"They're probably overrun with calls," Gabriel said.

Masked men exited the front door of the apartment building, holding the unconscious forms of Pel and Charles toward him as shields. He had promised their safety, so he didn't shoot.

One ran to Bandanna Girl's corpse and knelt by her, shouting. Another ran to the van and looked inside. More shouting.

The guy looking in the van was unprotected. Gabriel popped a couple of rounds into him and he dropped.

The two masked men in the side street whipped around the corner and fired at him. Bullets whizzed over his head and plinked into the car. They kept shooting, perforating the car but so far not hitting him or Kiyoko, who curled up in a ball. *Dog fucking sons of a whore.*

Someone opened up with a machine gun and Gabriel hugged the back of the car, hoping its engine block and the slope of the road would keep them safe. A couple of rounds bounced at him from beneath the car, one striking his right boot but deflecting off it, its energy depleted.

Gabriel heard sirens in the distance. *About time.*

An icon of Nicolas's harpy eagle avatar appeared on his data glasses. "ETA two minutes."

By now the kidnappers would be loading Pel and Charles in the surviving van. "They'll be in a white van headed east on Rua dos Estudantes, then I don't know where. Do not, repeat, do not, light up the van. They have our clients inside."

"Copy that—white van, do not fire on."

More bullets hit the car. If he stuck his head out, they'd put a bullet through it.

The drone of helicopter blades approached from the south. The gunfire ended. "Here come the reinforcements," he told Kiyoko.

He smelled gasoline. The car was full of holes and leaking fluids.

Kiyoko half stood in a crouch. "I smell gas."

"Me too." It trickled downhill toward the kidnappers. What if they set it on fire?

Gabriel peeked around the side. No one there. The helicopter grew louder.

He stood. The white van was driving away, too far now to risk a shot at the tires.

"We've got to go after them," Kiyoko said.

"Yeah." They also had to get away from this leaking car.

Gabriel had a company vehicle, a locally built electric two-seater. He almost never used it, the metro being much less of a hassle than São Paulo traffic or searching for a parking spot or vacant charging station.

He checked again for gunmen. Seeing none, he bolted for his car, parked on the side street next to their building. It was plain white except for the undecipherable graffiti someone tagged it with a few nights ago. At least it hadn't been stolen; you'd have to be a Charles-level hacker to fake the ignition card.

Kiyoko ran after him and jumped in the passenger seat. "I'm coming with you."

"No way. You can't."

"They're my friends. I'm coming."

Too stubborn and brave for her own good. He didn't have time to argue, though. "As long as you stay in the car and do what I say."

"I understand."

He threw the car joystick into drive, the ignition card in his wallet automatically detected. He pulled onto Rua dos Estudante, the little car making only a faint whining noise, and pressed the accelerator all the way to the floor.

He heard a helicopter overhead. He contacted Nicolas. "I'm in the toy-mobile giving chase. Where's the van?"

"I see them now. Headed north on Rua Anita Garibaldi. We're trying to coordinate with the police but their dispatch seems to be down."

"Still? Try the military."

"Copy that."

Gabriel took the next left, swerving around other cars, scraping one in the process. "My car is even uglier now."

Neither one of them laughed at the poor joke. "Where are they headed?" Kiyoko asked.

"They're going north. Either out of the city or to Campo de Marte."

"What's that?"

"Old airport, the first airport in São Paulo. Just used for private flights now, mostly helicopters." Only eight kilometers away. It would be his choice to get Pel and Charles to the U.S.

One thing worked on their side. The 4th Command of the Brazilian Air Force used part of Campo de Marte for transport and passenger operations. "Call Fourth COMAR, Fourth ETA," he radioed SSG dispatch. "Tell them there's kidnappers headed their way, maybe foreign spies, and ask them to shut down the airport."

"They don't control civilian flights," came the delayed response.

"This is an emergency."

He turned to Kiyoko. "Help me navigate to Campo de Marte airport. I am not used to driving around here."

She nodded and spoke into her comlink. Gabriel brought up a map on his data glasses. "DG, plot route to Campo de Marte."

Predictably, it displayed a different route than the one the kidnappers seemed to be taking. He ignored it and wound his way to Rua Anita Garibaldi.

Unlike most of the streets in their neighborhood, this was a wide avenue lined with trees. And it was choked with traffic. No sign of the van.

He heard machine gun fire up ahead. He called Nicolas. "What's going on?"

"Taking small arms fire. Looks like the engine's hit." After a pause, "Pilot wants to return to base."

Gabriel cursed. Nothing was going right.

"If they're headed to the airport," Kiyoko said, "why don't we get off this road and try to beat them there?"

"Good plan." He spoke to Nicolas again. "Can you make it to Campo de Marte? Without being obvious you're going there?"

After a pause, "Yes. We'll see you there."

With Kiyoko's navigation help and a traffic report from the SSG helicopter, Gabriel took a combination of back streets and major roads to the Avenida Santos Dumont bridge over the channelized Tietê River.

"They're on the other bridge," Kiyoko said.

He glanced to the right. He saw a white cargo van on the next bridge, amidst slow-moving trucks and cars. "We're ahead of them."

He drove around a traffic circle. The airport was to the left, but there didn't seem to be a way to get to it. He cursed, then asked, "Where's the entrance?" At least they were on an eight-lane road with light traffic.

Kiyoko swiped fingers on her comlink screen. "It's the other way. On Avenida Olavo Fontoura." She mangled the pronunciation.

Gabriel cursed. He whipped the steering wheel to the left. The little car jolted over a curb and onto a grassy median full of trees. They ran through some shrubs and plopped down on the other side, going the opposite direction.

A sedan honked and swerved out of his way. Gabriel stepped on the accelerator and sped back to the traffic circle, dodging through honking cars.

He exited the circle onto Avenida Olavo Fontoura, a six lane road with a barbed-wire topped wall on the right, three-story concrete buildings rising beyond. "How far?"

"One kilometer."

The wall on the right gave way to a tall, heavy fence studded with sensors and fronted by vehicle-proof concrete poles. Paulistanos took security seriously. Beyond the fence were round-topped hangars.

Was the kidnappers' plane in one of those hangars? More likely it would be on the tarmac ready to go.

Up ahead, a green sign, 'Campo de Marte Hangares.'

Gabriel called Nicolas. "We're coming up to the entrance."

"Control tower put us in the southwest corner."

"See any planes ready to take off?"

"Can't see shit where we are, trees and buildings in the way. The runway was empty when we were coming in, but I saw many planes and helicopters outside the hangars."

Gabriel approached a big overhang, 'Aeroporto Campo de Marte,' entrance and exit gates beneath, guard station in the middle. The green outer gates were open, but a thick boom barrier blocked the entrance.

He pulled in. What if they were wrong and the kidnappers were going somewhere else?

A guard peered at him from the open window of the guard station. He was young, wearing a uniform, badge and holstered sidearm. "Who are you here to see?"

Gabriel showed him his SSG badge. "One of our helicopters just landed. Engine trouble. I'm here to help."

He stared at the graffiti-covered, scratched-up little car and frowned. "In that thing?"

"I know, I need a new car."

He peered at Kiyoko. "What about her?"

"Visiting dignitary. Wants a helicopter ride."

Kiyoko bowed. "Konnichiwa."

The guard turned to his computer console. "Let me check."

"We could just wait here," Kiyoko whispered. "The van can't get by you."

A possibility. They could also take over the guard station and shut the gates. But better to trap them inside.

The boom swiveled up and the guard waved. Gabriel drove inside. Two ways to go, straight ahead or turn right. He contacted Nicolas. "We're inside. Can you meet us at the entrance?"

"Already on our way. Helicopter out of service. We'll be there in five minutes."

Too long. "What about the Air Force?"

"Sent a team to flight control to lock down the runway."

Gabriel parked thirty meters past the gate, facing the road, between a tree and a big metal building. He looked at Kiyoko. "You should get out and hide."

"They're here," she said.

He turned. The white van was pulling up to the gate. The cross bar tilted up a few seconds later. *They must have a pass.*

Instead of driving forward, past them, the kidnappers turned right down a road that paralleled the fence, towards the south hangars. Gabriel radioed it in as he pulled out to follow them.

They turned left into a parking lot between two hangars. Most of the spots were full. A chain link fence stretched across the far end. A man stood at a big gate in the fence and slid it open. The van slowed.

Gabriel stopped before entering the parking lot. He handed Kiyoko the ignition card. "Take the car. Get as far away as you can."

Not waiting for a response, he jumped out and drew his guns.

The man finished opening the gate. Gabriel fired into the van's rear tires, popping both of them.

The van lurched forward, bouncing through the gate on flapping rubber. The man at the gate ran away to the left, leaving the gate open.

Gabriel updated Nicolas and contacted Kiyoko. "I need the car back."

She swung into the parking lot. Gabriel ran to the driver's side and waved Kiyoko out. "Stay here. Take cover."

"You're so fickle." She followed his instructions though.

Gabriel mashed down the accelerator and sped onto the tarmac between two rows of hangars. It stretched into the distance in both directions. Helicopters and small planes, mostly propeller-engined, were parked outside the hangars. A feeder taxiway ran down the middle. Somewhere—he couldn't tell where—it connected to the runway.

The van crossed the tarmac onto the taxiway, the driver ignoring the flats. They turned left. Gabriel paralleled them, keeping parked aircraft between them.

They turned into one of the hangar lots on the far side. Headed for a sleek blue and white jet, twin engines already on. The door was open, steps down. A camouflage-uniformed man stood in the doorway with an automatic rifle, grenade launcher slung beneath.

Uniformed Man jumped out of the plane and aimed at Gabriel's car.

Fuck me! Gabriel yanked the wheel to the right as a puff of smoke emerged from the man's grenade launcher. The little car fishtailed as he angled away.

A loud explosion behind him. Smoke and pieces of metal flew through the air. Something smashed through the rear window. In the rear mirror, flames erupted from a parked helicopter.

That would bring the Air Force if nothing else did. Gabriel floored the car toward the other side of the tarmac and put the jet between him and Uniformed Man.

People were piling out of the white van. Gabriel got a clear shot at the jet, a hundred meters away, and aimed his needlegun at the starboard engine.

He emptied the magazine. The fletchettes tore through the aluminum exterior and into the delicate compression blades and combustion chambers inside, where they exploded. Sparks flew out of the back of the engine, then flames and black smoke.

Take that, you bastards. Gabriel reloaded.

Men with masks fanned out and fired submachine guns and pistols at him. Uniformed Man sprinted from behind the smoking jet, along with the girl with the AK-47.

He was pretty far away but bullets ripped into the car. He dove out the passenger side just as the girl opened up with the AK-47. He ran, keeping his head down, and the car between him and the plane.

Behind him, an explosion. A rush of hot air and smoke almost knocked him over. Something sharp struck him in the back.

At least the smoke would make him impossible to see. Ears ringing, he kept running, ignoring the pain in his back and right arm.

An icon with Kiyoko's face appeared. "What's going on?"

"Lost the car. But I may have grounded the kidnappers." He wasn't sure if they could take off with one engine. In case they tried, he'd find a hiding spot and take out the other engine before they reached the runway.

Behind him, more shooting. He heard the sweet cracks of HK418's, the SSG battle rifle of choice, on full auto. Nicolas's team had arrived.

Ahead, six-wheeled, olive drab armored personnel carriers appeared beyond a hangar, rumbling down the taxiway, presumably scrambled from the Air Force base on the other side of the airport. One, two, three of them, each armed with machine guns and a light cannon, and a squad of infantry inside. He heard helicopters too.

It's over for the kidnappers. He prayed that Charles and Pel would survive, and messaged Nicolas to be careful.

14

Kiyoko

Heart pounding, Kiyoko raced through the open gate onto the airport tarmac. She'd followed Gabriel's instructions and waited for the shooting to stop. This wasn't a VR game.

She continued her prayers as she ran. "Great Amida Buddha, by the power of your goodness, may all dangers to Pel, Charles, and Gabriel be averted, and no harm come to them."

An asphalt strip ran between long rows of hangars, with helicopters and planes parked in front. Two of the helicopters and a small plane were shattered wrecks, belching flames and acrid, oily smoke. What was that burning pile of metal ahead and to the right? Gabriel's car? She didn't see his little white car anywhere else.

Her heart seized. "Gabriel!" she screamed. "GABRIEL!"

She kept running. Her slippers had come off somehow but she couldn't feel the concrete. "Tàiyī Zhashén, Heka, Kamrusepa, Agwu, and Bahamut, by your power, protect Gabriel, Charles, and Pel from harm."

Three six-wheeled, olive drab troop carriers were ahead and to the left, along with a jet plane emitting smoke from one engine. Men in uniforms and combat gear were everywhere. The kidnappers' white cargo van sat next to the plane, intact. Bodies lay on the ground nearby.

She repeated her prayer, then heard the rising and falling wails of approaching ambulances. And the rapid pulses of police sirens. Her feet propelled her toward the kidnappers' cargo van.

The nearest soldiers, five men wearing camouflage uniforms, pointed automatic rifles at her. "Pare! Pare!" one in the center shouted.

Kiyoko stopped and threw up her hands. *Don't shoot. I'm friendly.* "Não atire. Sou uma amiga."

Ambulances raced onto the tarmac from the left, followed by police sedans.

"Fique parado aí!" the center soldier commanded. *Don't move.*

He and two others strode toward her, gun barrels pointed down at an angle. Two behind them kept their guns trained on her.

Kiyoko didn't lower her arms. But Gabriel could be dead or dying. Pel and Charles too. She fought the tears. *I'm a princess.*

"Preciso ver os meus amigos," she said when the soldiers arrived. *I need to see my friends.*

Their dark-skinned leader was young, and his camouflage uniform had blue patches on the shoulders with three silver wings nested atop each other. The other two with him didn't have patches at all.

Their leader said something but it didn't register. A man was running toward them. He wasn't wearing a uniform. It was Gabriel. Kiyoko's sash was still tied around his right arm.

Gabriel!

He reached her and they threw arms around each other and she gripped him so he would be safe forever, thanking the gods for listening. The happiness overwhelmed her and she cried.

"It's over," he said.

"Pel and Charles? Are they okay?" *Great Amida Buddha, please!*

"Yes. They're unconscious but they are alive."

＊ ＊ ＊

Waylee

Some part of Waylee confined her to the sleeping platform, kept her from climbing on top of the sink and trying to break her neck. It was a stupid plan anyway.

She smacked her head against the concrete wall. It hurt—a lot. Physical pain to accompany her anguish. *I don't normally do this.* But there was no one to stop her. No one to care.

Kiyoko. Pel. She'd never see them again. Tears exploded out of her eyes and drenched her cheeks.

She bashed her head again. And again.

The door opened and Waylee's guards dragged her down the hall. She was too tired and weak to react. Her head ached but the guards seemed not to notice. They hauled her into a brightly lit room and strapped her to a gurney.

A man and a woman in blue hospital garb and surgical gloves scowled at her. "If you're not going to eat, we're going to have to give you nutrition the hard way," the man said.

He was a doctor and didn't bother examining her? She didn't have the energy to protest, though.

The man sprayed something in her nostrils, then took a plastic tube and shoved it up her nose, all the way through her sinuses and into her throat. She gagged but couldn't throw up or speak.

The woman started a machine and musty-smelling brown liquid globbed down the tube and slid down her throat in lumps.

Waylee felt violated, ashamed. She'd never been raped—although her stepfather and a later acquaintance had tried—but that's what this felt like.

"It would be a lot easier for everyone if you just ate your food," the man repeated.

This was how she'd spend the rest of her life. No longer human. A slab of tortured meat kept alive for the state to keep torturing.

* * *

Kiyoko

Kiyoko sat in the waiting room of the Air Force hospital next to the airport, her feet sore and filthy. Gabriel was in surgery, his wounds thankfully minor. Some of his armor-clad comrades, led by a burly man named Nicolas Pistario, had checked on him, but were gone now.

Charles and Pel were still unconscious and being examined by doctors. She'd only seen them from afar but everyone said they'd be fine; they'd been injected with a sedative that should wear off.

Tàiyī Zhashén, Heka, Kamrusepa, Agwu, and Bahamut, by your power, restore Charles and Pel to full health.

She felt so tired. She couldn't wait to go home and go to sleep.

Could she go back? Was it safe? Who were the kidnappers? Would they try again?

She couldn't just sit here. She had her comlink but the Comnet signal was jammed. The handful of magazines and newspapers were all in Portuguese.

Kiyoko started the translation app on her comlink and pointed the camera at one of the magazines. It had a bunch of uniformed men with guns on the cover. Her screen, stretched to full size, showed an exact duplicate except with all the text in English. The translations were rarely exact but were close enough to get the ideas across, and wasn't that the point of language?

Soldier of Fortune. Thinking about Gabriel, her *coração*, she flipped through it. Mostly ads inside for "security companies" like Global Security and Ares International. SSG had a half-page glossy ad too. The magazine had an article titled "The War Against Cyberterror," about the campaign against the Collective. Pel and Charles would be interested, assuming they didn't know already.

Interpol and governments around the world have proclaimed cyberterrorism, particularly the organization called "The Collective," as one of today's major global threats. Law enforcement agencies and private companies around the world have made this a priority and mobilized to investigate and eliminate these threats.

"This is an excellent opportunity for cybersecurity professionals."

A slender man in a light blue shirt, dark blue pants, and gold-trimmed pilot's hat walked up to Kiyoko. "Excuse me," he said in accented English. "Would you come with me?"

Where to? "Aonde?"

He smiled. "We need to ask some questions."

He looked insistent, but not particularly threatening, so Kiyoko followed him down several hallways to a small conference room. She sat at the faux-wood table, the officer opposite. Cameras were mounted in the wall above him.

The officer introduced himself as Captain Magano, and asked her name and where she lived. Then, "Please tell me everything that happened today from your perspective."

No need to lie. The Brazilian Air Force and SSG had saved Charles and Pel. Thanks to Gabriel. Without Gabriel, a champion even above Waylee and Francis Jones's levels, Charles and Pel would be on their way to prison. She started crying again. She couldn't help it.

Captain Magano flushed with embarrassment. "Shall I get you some tissues?"

She shook off her loss of control. *I'm a princess.* She reached for her Sailor Moon carry bag to get a handkerchief. Except her bag was no more, incinerated in the blast that destroyed Gabriel's car. Another part of her Baltimore life gone.

She wiped her eyes with one of the long-hanging sleeves of her dress, and looked at the captain. *We're all safe now. Except for Waylee, but we'll get her out no matter what. Maybe SSG can free her.*

* * *

Pelopidas

Pel rose out of haze. He was lying on a firm cot with a thin blanket, a white curtain surrounding him on three sides. Behind him, a monitor attached to the tan wall displayed numbers and waveforms in different colors. None of the waveforms were flat or irregular.

He was alive. But where the hell was he? He'd been kidnapped. He still had the same clothes on. No comlink, but a thick matte-black bracelet was wrapped around his right wrist.

He got out of bed, feeling woozy, and parted the curtain just enough to peek through.

A woman, young, wearing blue scrubs, brown hair tied in a ponytail, sat at a small desk, staring at a screen and typing on a keyboard mat. To Pel's left and right, more curtains. A young man, also in blue scrubs, peered inside the curtains to his immediate left. The man turned and met his eyes.

Pel stood his ground as the man slid the front curtains aside and said something in Portuguese to the woman at the desk. The woman got up and joined him.

"Where am I?" Pel asked. "Where's Charles?"

"Seet down pleese," the woman said, pointing at the bed. Pel's knees wanted to give out so he followed her instructions.

The woman, presumably a doctor, tapped a comlink fastened to her wrist and said something in Portuguese. She spoke to the man and looked at the wall monitor and her comlink. She faced Pel. "You are safe. Your friend also. You were tranquilized but it is wearing off."

She didn't answer my question. "And where are we?"

"Hospital da Aeronáutica de São Paulo. We are next to Campo de Marte airport. I am Dr. Almeida."

"Yo, is that you, Pel?" It was Charles's voice, coming from beyond the left curtain.

Pel got up, eliciting a frown from the doctor, and pulled the curtain aside. Charles was lying in an identical cot. He didn't look hurt. "Looks like we're safe," Pel said.

"What happened?"

Pel looked at the doctor.

"You were kidnapped," she said, "and the people tried to fly you away. There was a battle. The kidnappers are dead or in custody."

"Can we go home now then?" Charles asked her.

"You must stay here until the matter is sorted."

They should have stayed on a military base in the first place. Pel addressed the doctor, "Do you have my comlink?"

"No."

"What about Kiyoko?" Charles asked her. "Adrianna? Where are they?"

"Your friend Kiyoko is in the next room visiting another patient. There is no one here named Adrianna. Was she one of the private soldiers?"

"She's not a soldier." Charles frowned, then fixed wide eyes on Pel. "Think she's a'ight?"

"They must not have found her," Pel said. "The kidnappers I mean."

Or she was part of their crew, their inside operative. *The kidnappers knocked before blowing down our door. Why knock? Why the warning? Adrianna was by the door. Was she supposed to let them in?*

But she didn't. *Maybe because I pointed a gun at her. She might not have known it was only a stun gun.*

There was nothing to be gained by mentioning his thoughts to Charles. *What about Gabriel? He brought that woman to our apartment.*

Which meant Gabriel might be on the inside too.

* * *

Kiyoko

A gray-uniformed state military police officer, a young woman named Sgt. Leal, drove Kiyoko and Gabriel back to Liberdade. They sat in the back seat of the electric sedan, clutching hands.

Gabriel's wounds were minor. A bullet had grazed his right arm and a piece of car metal had lodged in his back, but not very deep. The doctor had cut his shirt and undershirt away. A nice view except for the bandages. His guns, holsters, and data glasses were stuffed in a paper shopping bag on the floor by his feet.

"How long will they hold Pel and Charles?" Kiyoko asked her champion. The tranquilizers had worn off but they hadn't been released from Hospital da Aeronáutica, and two Air Force guards were posted outside their room.

Gabriel frowned. "I don't know. Maybe someone is unhappy I allowed them to be kidnapped."

She squeezed his hand. "You saved them. You're a hero." They were okay, that was the important thing. Kiyoko had hugged them and plastered their faces with kisses, then thanked the gods and goddesses.

They pulled onto Rua dos Estudantes. A two-block stretch was cordoned off and full of police, mostly standing around and chatting. They must have finished taking photos and interviewing people and all the other stuff cops did.

Sgt. Leal stopped at the cordon and let them out. She said something in Portuguese about the civil police wanting to talk. Gabriel nodded. "Entendo. Obrigado."

They took the elevator to the fifth floor, entering the access code. On their floor, the stairwell door was broken off the hinges. "We'll have to get that fixed," Kiyoko said.

"And strengthened, if we stay here."

Good point, will we stay here? Might as well spend the night at least. The place was surrounded by cops. And Pel and Charles were the ones with bounties, not her.

A bulky man with data glasses, a holstered pistol, and a flak vest inscribed "POLICIA" nodded at them and said something in a wraparound mike. Gabriel said something about living there.

Kiyoko peeled black electrical tape off the tiny camera lens on her door. How did they know it was there? Across the hall, the steel-plated door of Pel and Charles's apartment was blackened and hanging inward from the wrong end. Police were inside, walking around.

A balding overweight man in a blue blazer strode out of the apartment.

Gabriel's eyebrows raised. "Inspetor de Barros. Interesting to see you again."

The police inspector shook their hands. "Sim. Inspetor de Barros, São Paulo Polícia Civil. I am investigating this case." His English was almost unaccented. "I get most of the cases involving foreign nationals."

"Kiyoko Pingyang." She curtsied. "I live here. What happened?"

"We're still trying to determine all the particulars. I understand you two were involved in the rescue operation."

"Mostly Gabriel and his company," Kiyoko said. "And thanks to the Brazilian Air Force."

"I need to get your statements." He pointed at her door. "May we?"

Kiyoko unlocked her door and they entered. Nyasuke greeted her with a meow and she picked him up. She pointed toward the living room. "Have a seat."

Nyasuke's food dispenser in the kitchen was still half full, and the self-filling water bowl still working. "Tea?" she called out.

"No thank you," they both replied.

Carrying Nyasuke, she joined Gabriel on the bigger sofa. Inspector de Barros sat on the perpendicular smaller one. He had data glasses on now, with a red "record" light on.

"Please tell me everything that happened today. Include every detail."

Gabriel replied first. "Estávamos na feira." He glanced at Kiyoko and switched to English. "Pel contacted us and said someone was attacking them."

The inspector leaned closer. "Can you recall his exact words?"

"'Apartment's under attack.' That was it." Gabriel described how they ran to the apartment building and were shot at, and how the men coming out wore masks, and how they pursued them to the airport.

"Who fired first?" the inspector asked.

"They pulled guns on me and I had to defend myself or they would have killed me."

"So you fired first?"

"They raised weapons at me. I had to shoot. Otherwise I would be dead. You are a police officer. Surely you understand."

"But according to witnesses," the inspector said, "you drew first. So perhaps the girls you shot were the ones defending themselves."

Gabriel gritted his teeth. "They went for their guns first, I was just faster. They were part of a kidnapping gang. I was trying to save my clients."

"Your clients being Sr. Charles and Sr. Pelopidas?" he asked.

"Yes."

"So that is your reason for starting the gunfight?"

"I didn't start it."

The inspector asked question after question, asked to see Gabriel's gun and private security licenses, then turned to Kiyoko. She didn't have much to add, but described how she ran to the scene, took cover behind a car, and helped navigate to the airport.

When she finished, the inspector stood. "I apologize. My video memory is almost full, and we are not permitted to upload testimony without a secure connection." He shook their hands. "I will be in touch. Please do not leave the city. Five people dead and five injured, two of them bystanders, is a very serious matter."

Gabriel crossed his arms and shuffled his feet.

"And I will need your weapons, of course," the inspector added, looking at Gabriel's bag.

"Why?"

"Ballistics testing and crime scene simulation."

Gabriel argued with him in Portuguese but more police entered and he surrendered his guns.

After the police left, Gabriel said, "I don't like it. The police taking my weapons and trying to blame me for what happened."

"You didn't do anything wrong," Kiyoko said. "You were a hero."

"That inspector interrogated me like a criminal," he said. "It is good I have more guns."

Our champion. "You're a one man army."

Gabriel put his face in his hands, then shook them back to his sides and edged toward the door. "I need a drink. I'm going back to my apartment."

Kiyoko shook her head. "Don't leave." She opened her bedroom door, wanting him in her arms until the end of time. "Please stay."

He followed her into the bedroom. Without speaking, they removed each others' clothes.

* * *

Dalton

In complete darkness and stuffy, sweat-stinking air, Dalton powered on his data glasses. 0300. Should be safe now. He hadn't heard any boots stomping around the plane for over twelve hours.

"Opening the hatch," he said quietly to Yegor Kozachenko, the 40-year-old Ukrainian vet asleep next to him in the cramped smuggling compartment. Demopoulos and Lee were supposed to be in here, not them.

"Pro chas," Kozachenko grunted. *About time,* Dalton's data glasses translated.

Dalton slid open the hatch, then pushed aside the carpet that the pilot, another Ares employee, had placed over the hatch. If the pilot had talked to the police, he hadn't mentioned the smuggling compartment.

Dalton filled his lungs with fresh air. The compartment's ventilation was terrible with the fans and air conditioning off. He peered out, data glasses set to low light. The cabin appeared abandoned. Probably the Brazilian Air Force, police, and Ares's dummy subsidiary, Friendly Skies, were fighting over the plane.

He looked out the windows. No one visible, but the area was well lit and full of cameras and motion detectors. "We're going to have to run for it," he told Kozachenko. "We won't have long."

Instead of putting his plastic mask back on, he rummaged through the overhead bins and stripped the cases off two pillows. He tossed one to Kozachenko. "Cut big eye holes in that and put it on."

Kozachenko unsheathed his combat knife and cut holes in his pillowcase. He stared out the windows. "RPG's gone," he said in English.

"Of course it is. You think the police would let something like that lie around?"

"No. But I miss it. We had some good times together."

Neither Dalton nor Kozachenko had been injured in the fiasco. But the rest of the team were killed or captured. Worse, he'd lost the bounty. At least temporarily.

Dalton had committed the biggest sin of military operations—underestimating the enemy. He had prepared in detail for every eventuality—except that Demopoulos would be so well prepared, and able to delay his team by a good five minutes.

And how could one man, Gabriel da Silva, be so damn lethal? A normal bodyguard would never have gone up against overwhelming odds. Too bad da Silva was working for SSG and not Ares.

Maybe Dalton could get SSG's contract canceled somehow. He had to do something. If he gave up, his career was finished, not to mention his chance at early retirement.

He turned to Kozachenko. "Ready?"

"Da."

They put on their makeshift masks. Dalton opened the hatch, leapt to the ground, and started running.

15

Waylee

The door to Waylee's cell opened. Her guards brought a tray and set it on the narrow shelf beneath the opaque window slit. She sat up and examined her breakfast—a plastic bowl of off-white mush and a paper cup of thin milk. Even though the mush was cold and looked like day-old vomit, she'd eat it.

Being force fed was degrading and painful. And she needed the nutrients. Why should she help the government destroy her?

The thought almost made her smile. A tiny remnant of determination had survived the worst depression of her life. Or maybe it was acceptance.

A cylindrical white pill sat on the tray next to the cup of milk. The female guard pointed a stubby dark finger at it. "You're supposed to take these pills with your food now."

"What is it?"

"It's an antidepressant. Supposed to make you less of a baby."

A prison doctor must have prescribed it, whether on his or her own initiative or ordered by someone else. Waylee took the pill and spooned down the tasteless mush. Even if the medicine had side effects, it couldn't be worse than how she was feeling now.

* * *

Kiyoko

Kiyoko opened her eyes. Stubborn scintillas of light filtered through the red velvet drapes on her bedroom windows. She was nude in her double bed, left arm draped over her champion's broad shoulders, sheets crumpled on the floor.

Gabriel was fast asleep, lying on his stomach. Further down, gauze was taped over his back wound. His arm dressing leaked red. Time to change it.

They had gone through every position they could think of that didn't press something against his back or right arm. It was a little awkward at first, but they kept at it until the sun rose, ginseng, açaí, and enthusiasm compensating for his painkillers. She lost count of her orgasms, well into the double digits, some of them leaving her breathless.

Even though she felt fatigued and a little sore, Kiyoko ran a hand over her champion's warm skin until he turned to face her, brown eyes fluttering open. He rolled on his side.

"We should have started doing this weeks ago," she said.

He grinned. "I know." He cupped her left breast and ran a thumb against the nipple. "We should never leave this bed."

At some point they'd have to get up and deal with the disasters looming everywhere. But not just yet.

* * *

Gabriel

That afternoon, Gabriel's manager called him to SSG headquarters at Congonhas Airport south of Liberdade. Gabriel booked a taxi on the Comnet and brought Kiyoko along, not wanting to leave her alone. "We cannot show affection on the base," he warned her in the taxi.

"Rules for everyone or just us?"

"Rules for everyone. It is like the military."

They checked in at the guard station and passed bunkers, a hangar, and helipads, six of them occupied by surplus Mi-38s, AW139s, an EC725, and an NH90. They were all painted light blue with the company logo on the doors. The two V-22 Ospreys were either in the hangar or on duty somewhere.

Security and support personnel waved to him or gave him the thumbs up. "I hope my supervisor is that supportive," he told Kiyoko.

Kiyoko gave one of her beautiful smiles. "Why wouldn't he be? You're a hero."

Did heroes kill teenage girls? "I'm not a hero. I was just doing my job. And we had a lot of help. But we should have waited for Alzira to return before going to the market."

"I'm sorry," Kiyoko said. "I didn't know. We went two months without any sign of danger."

He rubbed her shoulder. "Forget it. It's my fault, I'm the security professional."

The main office building was eight stories of plexiglass, concrete and steel, plus four floors below ground. The hidden magnetic sensors above the plexiglass front doors could read his ID card from at least ten meters away, but he had to place his eyes in front of the retinal scanner.

The doors slid aside. Chilly air blasted his face. "You'll have to wait in the lobby," he told Kiyoko as they entered.

"That's fine."

The well lit main lobby was small and bare, with a chrome-plated reception desk and two elevators at the far end. Lafayette Chaves, a military pensioner who'd worked for SSG five years now, sat behind the desk and smiled at him. To the side, Alzira sat in one of the waiting chairs, wearing a SSG T-shirt and tan cargo pants, data glasses obscuring her eyes. She rose.

"Oi Gabriel," she said quietly as he approached.

"Oi."

"Olá," Kiyoko added.

"Do you have an appointment also?" Gabriel asked in Portuguese.

"Yes, after you." She paused. "I'm very sorry you had to face those kidnappers alone. If I was there too, maybe I could have held them off."

"Forget it. Besides, they might have killed you."

"The contract was too cheap," she said. "We needed two bodyguards on duty, like you said."

"You are right about that."

"I didn't think our clients would actually be attacked, though. I thought it would be easy. We have to find out who was behind it."

"That is my plan. I will find out who attacked us. And I will ask for more guards and permission to take the fight to the enemy." He turned to Kiyoko. "You can wait here."

Kiyoko sat next to Alzira and started asking about her beach trip and upcoming wedding. Gabriel walked over to the reception desk. Sr. Lafayette checked him in, told him where to go, and called down an elevator. Gabriel didn't have an office so his badge only gave him access to the lobby.

Gabriel took the elevator to the top floor and proceeded to Conference Room Amazonas in the center. The Operations VP, Altair Balfager, sat at the head of a long polished table. On the sides sat Gabriel's supervisor, Iago Ramalho; the Human Resources director, Carla Teixeira; and a graying man in a pinstripe suit.

Sr. Altair began the meeting and introduced the sixtyish man in the suit as an SSG attorney named Eduardo Bicudo. "Since we have an attorney present," the VP added, "we can speak frankly."

The lawyer nodded. "Everything will be confidential."

Must be nice to collect a big paycheck just by sitting in a room, Gabriel thought. But it wasn't a good sign that SSG was worried about legal repercussions.

They started with small talk and questions about Gabriel's injuries. Then Sr. Altair steered the conversation to yesterday's shootout, which was the top trending news in Brazil. "Please recount for us everything you remember," he told Gabriel.

Gabriel described the day's events and answered their questions.

"The government doesn't want a repeat," Sr. Altair said. "All the ones who died were scum. Good to get them off the streets. But bystanders were hurt, and three of our men, yourself included. Not to mention the property damage. It should never have come to that."

Gabriel kept quiet. You didn't interrupt your superiors at SSG.

The VP's face tightened. "Our contract was terminated."

Gabriel felt crushing disappointment. Instead of the detail increasing, it was being abandoned? "Permission to speak?"

"Go ahead."

"What happens to Lee and Demopoulos now?"

Sr. Altair shrugged. "Not our concern."

In other words, he had no idea and hadn't bothered asking. "Can we appeal the termination?" Gabriel asked. The contract agreement was for a year, and they were less than three months in.

An eyebrow raised. "You should know the federal government can end contracts at any time. And we certainly don't want to anger our biggest customer."

That's it, then.

Sr. Altair glanced at his comlink screen. "I was told you have a lot of leave time?"

Another bad sign. The HR director looked at her comlink and nodded. "He has 220 hours of vacation and comp time, and is also entitled to leave for injuries sustained on the job, until they heal."

Sr. Altair looked at Gabriel. "Take some time off, then. A month on the beach, perhaps?"

"I'm fine." He had managed a long and vigorous night with Kiyoko. Remembering how great it was, how beautiful her naked body was, he smiled inside. "And obviously the kidnappers are finished. We caught them all, right? Do we know who they worked for?"

"At least two escaped. But the point is, we no longer have a contract. I don't like losing contracts, even small ones. It makes us look bad."

Was he fishing for an apology? It wasn't Gabriel's fault. Or was it? "Sorry sir," he managed.

Sr. Altair waved it off.

"Do we know anything about the kidnappers?" Gabriel repeated. "Like who they worked for?"

"That's a question for the police. We're done for now. Enjoy your leave. Post some photos so we can all be jealous." He smiled.

Gabriel returned to Kiyoko in the lobby, feeling lost.

* * *

On the way back to Liberdade, Gabriel told Kiyoko that SSG lost the bodyguard contract and they put him on leave. "They want me to spend the next month at the beach."

Kiyoko stared at him. "Is that it, then? Are we on our own now? You aren't going to leave me, are you?"

He squeezed her hand. "Of course not. I cannot be happy without you. It will take much more than a personnel manager to keep me from your side."

They kissed all the way back to the apartment building.

The door to Pel and Charles's apartment was still off the hinges. The police had departed some time last night, but had fastened yellow "local do crime, não atravesse" tape across the doorway.

"Do you mind if I take a look?" he asked Kiyoko. They hadn't been inside since before the kidnapping.

"Won't you get in trouble?"

He scanned the doorway and hall, then shrugged. "I don't see any cameras."

Considering how many crimes occurred in São Paulo—two thousand murders alone last year—the police didn't have the resources to monitor inactive scenes.

Gabriel ducked underneath the tape and entered the apartment, Kiyoko following. Out of habit, he edged his way in, checking for threats before exposing himself.

The apartment didn't look much different. But it smelled faintly of gunpowder and overripe fruit and burnt metal.

Behind him, Kiyoko gulped.

The smell came from his left, from the open bathroom door. No one visible inside. He put up a hand. "Stay here."

The tiled wall of the shower was spattered with blood and specks of pale yellow that dripped down to the tub. One of the tiles was cracked, with a hole in the center. The bottom of the tub was almost solid red. No body, but whoever was shot here had bled out.

"Don't come in." He pulled the shower curtain shut. Whose blood was it?

"What's in there?" Her voice trembled.

"Someone was shot. Body's gone." He exited the bathroom and shut the door.

Kiyoko pulled her comlink out of the cut-resistant purse slung across her body. "Pel and Charles are both alive, thank the gods."

Gabriel checked the rest of the apartment. VR gear and other electronics still here. No comlinks or stun guns. Pel's rope and binoculars were gone too.

"Oh no!" Kiyoko's voice sounded from the entryway.

He hurried to her. "What is it?"

She looked up from her comlink, tears filling her eyes. "Adrianna was killed. The police found her body here." She cast wide eyes at the bathroom door. "In the bathroom."

Gabriel's stomach contracted. He focused to keep from retching.

Kiyoko started crying. Gabriel's eyes filled with mist. *That poor girl. She's dead because of me.*

He caught himself and let Kiyoko do the crying for both of them. He held her close and pressed his face against hers.

Her crying tapered off and she sniffled. "Poor Charles. I wonder if he knows?"

"We should leave." He helped her back under the police tape.

They stopped by his apartment, where he fetched a bottle of cachaça from the cabinet. They continued to Kiyoko's apartment and sat on her sofa, legs touching. As Kiyoko hugged her cat, Gabriel poured himself a shot of cachaça and threw it back. "Want some?"

"No thanks. Well, okay, but not straight."

He found cashew juice in her refrigerator, poured a big glass with ice, and mixed in a shot of cachaça. Kiyoko drank with him, kissed his cheek, then lit candles and incense on the coffee table. She pressed her hands together, bowed her head, and closed her eyes. "Stars above, stars so bright, fill the world with silver light. Hear me, O gods. Hear me, O spirits. Embrace Adrianna and welcome her into the starry heavens."

She prayed for a long time. Gabriel downed more cachaça.

When she finished, she turned to him, eyes dry now. "Meu corazón. Meu campeão. I need to talk to Charles. And Pel."

He'd never felt so close to someone before. "About Adrianna?"

"I hope Charles already knows. I don't want to tell him. But I need to know how they're doing."

"Do they have their comlinks? I didn't see them at the apartment."

"I don't know. If not, I'll call the hospital."

Neither Charles nor Pel answered her call or returned texts. She put her comlink on speaker and called the Air Force hospital. "Alô," she said. "English?"

"No English," a woman's voice responded.

The comlinks had translators, but Gabriel took over, asking to speak with Charles or Pel.

"They've been discharged," the woman said in Portuguese.

"To where?" If they were discharged, why hadn't they called Kiyoko?

"That's all my records show," the woman said.

"Did they leave with someone? Police? Civilians?"

"I have no idea."

Next to him, Kiyoko looked alarmed. "Where are they?"

Gabriel asked to speak with others but no one else knew either.

16

Charles

Charles's room in the Brazilian Air Force section of Campo de Marte airport was nicer than his apartment room. Certainly a lot bigger, with a queen-size bed; spotless, fresh-smelling carpet; and his own bathroom and kitchenette.

The downside was, they were confined to one floor of the base's guest quarters. "For your own safety," an officer had claimed. Guards were stationed by the stairwell and, visible through the window, patrolled the grounds outside. The exterior doors were monitored with electronics although he and Pel didn't find any obvious cameras or mikes in the rooms. Not surprising, Pel had said, since they were intended for visiting officers.

They had no comlinks. By now, their links at the apartment would be wiped. Pel had set them to reformat after three unsuccessful attempts to log in or 48 hours without use.

They had asked if they could contact Kiyoko but as with everything else, their protectors/captors turned them down. The rooms had a pared-down Comnet interface: a small box, wall screen, and a plastic keyboard with a pointer pad and wireless transmitter. They could watch a menu of movies or shows on it, all in Portuguese without a translator, play games, or use a word processor. But no access to the net.

Someone knocked on the door. It was Pel, wearing a green T-shirt and camouflage pants and jacket. Charles was wearing Air Force fatigues too, at least until his regular clothes were washed.

"Come over," Pel said.

"What for?"

"Found something interesting on the TV."

Charles shrugged and followed him into the adjacent room. It looked exactly the same as his, down to the photos of camouflage-painted fighter jets over rainforest or ocean.

Pel closed and locked the door.

"Sorry I kind of froze when those men broke in," Charles said. *Am I a coward?* "I'll man up next time."

"Forget it. I was scared shitless myself."

"Yeah, but you shot at them and took some of them down."

"Flight was impossible, so fight it was. You can't just give up." Pel picked up the thin remote control lying on his bed. He pressed a bunch of keys.

The wall screen displayed a blue background with a menu in white letters. "Service mode," Pel said. "I kept trying key combinations until I found it. Info Menu Mute Power."

Fuzzing. "Right on. I was looking at the box in my room. It's ancient. It has USB and micro ports in the back though."

"They all do," Pel said. "Comes standard. Wi-Fi too."

"Too bad we don't have a data stick with Linux."

Pel nodded. "Yeah, we could open up the box, hot wire the motherboard and bring up the BIOS, then boot from the USB. But there's alternatives. This feeble excuse for an entertainment system almost certainly has a Linux or FreeBSD kernel, with an API and application layer built on top."

None of the apps would help them get hold of Kiyoko. Or Adrianna. Charles hoped the kidnappers hadn't found her. Or if they had, let her be. She wasn't their target, after all. "How do we drill to the kernel?" he asked Pel.

"I was hoping you could help with that. Service mode gets us below the app level at least."

Charles examined all the menu options. The Wi-Fi was disabled and the input set to cable. He enabled the Wi-Fi, but couldn't find any unencrypted connections.

"Yeah, I looked at that too," Pel said. "I can build a wi-fi antenna to expand our range."

Charles nodded. "Hey, I have an idea. We don't even need to get fancy." A lot of shows had story syncs, and infotainment programs were full of hyperlinks. They had share links too. Their ticket to the wider Comnet.

He exited Service Mode and scrolled through the entertainment channels until he found one, a Brazilian travelogue, with Comnet links for more information.

The links didn't work. No net access. "Damn."

"Yeah, that was the first thing I tried," Pel said.

Charles ignored him and went through all the channels, trying to follow links or click on adware. None of them worked. "I was hoping we could keep following links until we got to a Comnet search engine or something," he said. "They must have a firewall on the cable that blocks links and downloads. But if we're on Wi-Fi we won't have that problem."

"Alright," Pel said. "Let's see what we've got in the kitchen. Antenna-wise, that is."

* * *

Pelopidas

Pel had built plenty of antennas in his day. Wi-Fi was one of the easiest, although typically he had basic hardware and connectors on hand.

Thankfully the kitchenette was reasonably well stocked. No sharp knives, but they'd left stainless steel butter knives. They made poor weapons but could cut wire and remove screws if you were patient. The kitchen also had a wire mesh colander and aluminum foil that he fashioned into a parabolic dish.

Pel opened the entertainment box and found the built-in wi-fi antenna, which was soldered to the wireless card. *Why'd they have to solder it on? Bastards.*

Using a knife, he cut the power cord from one of the lamps, then cut off a short length to use as a solder iron. He stripped away the insulation on the ends and touched one end against one of the old-style electric stove burners. Protecting his hand with a towel, he used the other end to melt the solder holding the wi-fi antenna to the circuit board. It stank, but copper was an ideal heat conductor, and the stove had a ventilation fan. He removed the antenna and its short co-ax cable, placed it at the makeshift parabola's focal point, and reconnected it using the remaining wire from the power cord.

Finished, Pel disconnected the wall cable, set the box input to Wi-Fi, and pointed the improvised antenna out the window. It felt good to be doing something constructive, instead of just worrying.

Someone knocked on the door. Pel's heart stopped. *Shit!* The door was locked but the guards would have keys.

Sitting on the bed, Charles cringed.

"Olá? Tudo bem?" a man's voice sounded from the hall. He wanted to know if something was wrong. The smell? It must have been noticeable outside.

"Coming! Uno momento por favor!" Was he saying that right? Pel hid the antenna behind the curtain and reconnected the wall cable. An airline commercial played on the screen, a white and red jet marked "LATAM" flying through the night sky and trailing a rainbow.

Pel heard a click and the door opened. They hadn't waited for him. Two young soldiers in camouflage fatigues and caps entered, automatic rifles in their hands but pointed down. One sniffed the air and looked at the kitchenette.

"I was testing the stove," Pel said. "Do you mind if we go to the store, so we can eat what we want?"

Waylee told him once that politicians did this all the time—change the subject before it got uncomfortable.

The sniffing guard stared. "No English."

Pel walked past him and opened the kitchenette cupboards, which were mostly empty. "Food. Comida. Compramos comida."

The guard squinted. "Não entendo. Nós trazemos sua comida. É grátis."

Pel kept asking to go to the store in fragmented Portuguese and Spanish until the guards threw up their hands and left. "Fica aqui," one said as they shut the door.

After an hour, Pel re-locked the door and looked out the window. No one was watching. He set the entertainment system to Service Mode and pointed the parabolic antenna outside.

A lot of connections appeared on the wall screen. He moved the setup until an unencrypted signal appeared, Hipster_Cafe. Pel chuckled as he connected. "We're in business."

Charles grabbed the remote and sat on the bed. "You the man." He flipped through channels and settled on a steamy beach telenovela titled *Gostosas do Rio*.

"Your favorite show?" Pel had watched it halfway through once before getting bored.

"Good way to learn Portuguese." Charles clicked on the story sync link. It worked, taking him to a menu dominated by short video loop inserts of hot girls in bikinis. "Adrianna should be on this show. She's as fine as any of these."

Pel sat on the bed next to Charles and passed him the thin keyboard. "Just get us to the Comnet. We should hurry."

Charles nested the keyboard on his lap. He ran a finger over its touchpad and clicked on different links, navigating the labyrinth of *Gostosas do Rio* and their advertisers until he found a Comnet search engine. "What first?"

"Text site," Pel said. "We need to get hold of Kiyoko and tell her where we are. See if we're still in danger, and what's going to happen to us. Go through a proxy to be safe."

* * *

Charles

Brazilian keyboard layouts were almost the same as American ones. Charles routed through an anonymizing proxy server, logged onto their private room on Crypt-O-Chat, and sent a message to Princess Kiyoko.
```
Iwisa: Come chat ASAP.
```
A few minutes later, she responded.
```
Princess_Kiyoko: This who I think?
Iwisa: Aint ur nyan-nyan
Princess_Kiyoko: R U OK?
Iwisa: @ campo de marte AFB.
Iwisa: nice digs but they wont let us leave
Iwisa: how r u?
Princess_Kiyoko: doing ok. can I visit?
Iwisa: plz. Dont say we msg, its on down low.
Princess_Kiyoko: have u seen news?
Iwisa: which news?
Princess_Kiyoko: I can't say it. I'm very sorry. :(
```
Still sitting next to him on the bed, Pel leaned forward. "What happened?"

Charles resumed typing.
```
Iwisa: u have to tell
Princess_Kiyoko: #Tiroteio_em_Liberdade
Princess_Kiyoko: Gotta go. See you soon.
```
Feeling anxious, Charles moved the pointer to the search engine and typed #Tiroteio_em_Liberdade. It brought up coverage of their attempted kidnapping.

He'd been told the basics already, that a group of gangsters kidnapped them but Gabriel and his company stepped in. There were two big shoot-outs, one outside their apartment building and one in the airport. The Brazilian Air Force sent in security troops that finished the matter.

MediaCorp Brazil seemed to have scooped the local outlets and mentioned his and Pel's names. The site had a pull-down menu that listed a bunch of languages. In case a bot was monitoring, Charles skipped English-US and picked English-UK.

"My man," Pel said.

An attractive light-skinned woman and a well-dressed man sat behind a desk with a city skyline behind them. "Massive shootouts erupted in the São Paulo neighborhood of Liberdade and the Campo de Marte airport." The woman's lips didn't move in sync with the words, but the dubbed voice sounded natural, like a British actress.

The woman described the event as an attempted kidnapping gone bad. "Sources tell us the kidnappers were members of a local gang called As Piranhas and the intended victims were two fugitives from U.S. justice named Charles Marvin Lee and Pelopidas Demopoulos." The screen displayed rotating photos of them and links to past stories.

"How'd they know that?" Pel asked.

"Don't interrupt."

On the screen, the woman went into details about their supposed cyber-terrorist activities. Charles fast-forwarded.

The man turned to the woman, like they were having a conversation. "Criminals kidnapping criminals?" His voice sounded like James Bond.

"So it appears," she said. "It's just too bad innocent people were hurt in the process and property destroyed."

The woman went into more details about the gunfight in Liberdade. There wasn't any footage of the actual battle, nor any mention of Kiyoko or Gabriel by name. Just a lot of CGI reconstructions and interviews of "survivors."

"It appears that most of the dead were affiliated with the kidnapping gang," the woman said. "Another woman was found dead in the victims' apartment—"

No.

"Police identified her as 18-year-old Maria Ledo, a sex worker who went by the name Adrianna."

"No, no, no!" The screen blurred and shook.

"Oh man," Pel said next to him.

Charles tried to keep from bawling but couldn't.

* * *

Dalton

Dalton was staying in a cheap guesthouse in the Parada Inglesa neighborhood, northeast of the Campo de Marte airport and a short walk from a Metro stop. The guesthouse took cash and didn't ask for an ID, although he had plenty of fakes. Kozachenko was staying at a different place a few blocks away. Dalton had ordered him to stay out of sight until they had a new plan.

Dalton downed a sandwich he'd bought that afternoon, then group messaged his kids. They never responded, thanks to his bitch ex-wife, but he did it anyway. He was their dad, after all. He had to keep his employment and whereabouts secret, but there were plenty of other things to talk about.

Donnie, I know you're headed to college next year. Where do you want to go? What do you want to major in?

Madison, it's not far off for you either. Not too early to start preparing for the SATs. You're smart but those tests are hard from what I hear.

Both of you, don't worry about expenses. Go wherever you want. I'll wire whatever you need. Miss you both. I think about you every day. Love, Dad.

That done, Dalton left the guesthouse and walked up the poorly lit narrow street. It didn't seem like a bad neighborhood but the close-packed houses and apartment buildings were all secured behind walls and sturdy gates, with no accessible windows. No one was visible. Water trickled along the left curb and stank of sewage.

He waited at the intersection with a cracked two-way street with no dividing line. De Barros drove up in his flashy sports car and Dalton got in.

"You sure fucked that up," the fat inspector said as he made a U-turn and drove back the way he had come.

Dalton had already been chewed out by Petrov, who'd said this job was one of the company's top priorities. De Barros had some nerve piling on. "Your fault hiring those Piranha jokers. Next time we're using professionals."

"They are professionals."

"Half of them got stoned before the op, then they couldn't handle one untrained asshole and one bodyguard."

De Barros kept driving straight. It all looked the same, interspersed two-story houses and tall apartment buildings behind walls and security sensors. They weren't headed anywhere in particular, but the inspector swept his car daily for bugs and hadn't found one yet, making it a relatively secure place to talk. "So there's a next time?" the inspector asked.

"I need the money. Move Lee and Demopoulos from the base and we can intercept them during the transfer. You got anyone on the force who can help?"

"For the right price. And I have a nephew in the military police. But how am I supposed to get authority to transfer them?"

"Figure it out. It's your fucking city."

De Barros glanced over. "If I have to take more risks, I want more money."

"And Ares wants that plane released. Jets are expensive."

"It's evidence. How am I going to manage that?"

"I don't know, but I was told Ares is willing to pay a half million dollar fee."

De Barros pursed his lips. "I'll see what I can do."

"Now what about those Piranha assholes? Are they going to finger us?"

"Pardon?"

"Name us. Fuck us up the ass."

"Not if they know what's good for them. Brazilian prisons can be dangerous places." He turned left down a street that looked just like the last one.

"Can you get them released?"

The inspector huffed. "Not easily. The mayor and governor are angry. Liberdade is a tourist area. The surviving kidnappers are to be made examples."

"Shit. That means they might talk."

"Evidence can disappear. And they have a good lawyer."

"They were caught red-handed."

"Pardon?"

Dalton sighed. "They were caught shooting guns and with two kidnapped people in their van."

De Barros nodded. "True. But they surrendered when the Air Force showed up with their APCs and helicopters, and it's not clear who did what. Maybe they can blame everything on the ones who were killed."

The road curved to the right and stretched into the distance.

"Tell them they'll get huge bonuses if they keep their mouths shut." Dalton had no intention of paying it, but promises were free.

"How much?"

"Make a number up, whatever makes them happy. Let me know how they respond."

De Barros grunted.

"Excuse me, I didn't hear you."

"I don't even know if I can talk to them."

"Well, try. Now how about that asshole Da Silva? Can you arrest him?"

"I am investigating him. It would be difficult to prove that he did not act in self-defense. But maybe we can get him out of the way temporarily. It's a mute point—"

"You mean moot point?"

"Listen, my English is much better than your Portuguese."

"Like I give a shit. So what about Da Silva?"

"SSG lost their contract, I found out, and Da Silva was placed on leave. He's irrelevant now."

"Good." It would be prudent to kill him, though. Send him to hell where he belonged. "But we should make sure he doesn't interfere again. A bunch of Piranhas stayed home. Tell them Da Silva killed their friends and cost them a shitload of money."

De Barros smiled and nodded.

17

Waylee

The guards shackled Waylee and hauled her to back to the meeting room. A young ginger-haired woman sat at the stainless steel table with a data pad.

As soon as the guards left, the woman stood. She didn't offer a handshake, tapping her fingertips together and twitching her jaw instead. "I'm Jessica Martin. I'm an Assistant Federal Public Defender from the Federal Community Defender Office. I've been assigned to your case. We can speak confidentially."

Waylee still felt overwhelmed by hopelessness, but the medications had diminished the crushing sadness and suicidal urges. She could at least claw portholes through the fog. But her sister, boyfriend, and Charles were in no less danger than before, and her prospects no less dismal. "Are you working with Francis? Francis Jones?"

"He's being held on felony charges. He can't assist you until that's resolved." She sat and motioned for Waylee to take the chair on the opposite side of the table.

Waylee felt dizzy and exhausted, her limbs heavy as lead, but didn't sit. Ms. Martin's fidgeting set off sympathetic waves and caused her own fingers to shake. "That's bullshit. You must know that."

Ms. Martin grimaced. "Uh, okay. Well, we are a nation of laws and you have rights under those laws." She glanced at her screen. "I have your application, and it's been approved. Sorry it took so long."

"I'm sure the court did their best to fuck me."

Ms. Martin pointed at the empty chair again. "You can sit, you know."

Waylee sat, not trusting her legs to hold her up. Her body was still adjusting to the medicine. "They're giving me medicine," she told Ms. Martin. "For depression. But they didn't tell me what it was. Or what to expect. What the side effects are."

Ms. Martin swiped fingers against her data pad. "It's a fairly new drug called Uplift. Nothing here about side effects, although it's not my specialty. It's being administered as part of an agreement with Amnesty International."

Waylee's body lightened, limbs floating away from the grip of their shackles, like she'd been transported to a world with less burdensome gravity. Amnesty International was helping her? Kiyoko and Pel's doing, no doubt. "What's this agreement? No one told me."

The young lawyer bit her lip. "I'm sorry, I don't have the information with me and I can't access the Comnet here."

"If you come back, could you bring a copy of the agreement?" She paused, her thoughts struggling to reach her lips. "Also, could you help me get my papers and pen back? The guards took them."

"Your what?"

"I had this printout I think my boyfriend wrote. And I was doing some writing. It was keeping me sane. Can you get them back for me?"

Ms. Martin typed on her data pad. "I'll look into it. But listen, your case is what's important. Shall we go over the charges?"

"Francis left me a copy of the indictments. I've pretty much memorized it." *Never had so much empty time.*

She nodded. "Uh, good. Now I talked to the prosecuting attorney and he is willing to plea bargain."

"Let me guess. I recant my video, tell the world I fabricated everything. And they reduce the charges."

"Sort of. Where'd you hear that?"

"A MediaCorp lawyer came here and told me that. She threatened me. And put Bob Luxmore on the screen. If I were you, I'd investigate that. Prosecutorial misconduct."

Her eyebrows raised. "This private lawyer wasn't part of the prosecution team, I assume."

They probably skated the edge of legality but didn't cross it. "I bet they're communicating. Even if it's informally."

"Do you have any proof I can examine, to back up your misconduct claim?"

"Check the visitation records. Irena Van Hofwegen from Kramer, Goldberg & Ashcraft."

Ms. Martin typed something, then said, "I think you should take the plea bargain offer. It's extremely generous. Most of the charges would be dropped and the remainder served concurrently, for a total of two years, assuming the judge agreed. That's it. With good behavior, that's . . ." She tapped fingers against her data pad. "20 months."

"I told Francis—I can do that as long as it's not in solitary."

"All you have to do is recant your actions and testify against your co-conspirators. You don't have to lie about anything."

That again. "No." Waylee tried to stand but lost her balance and fell back into the chair. Her face burned with embarrassment. "I keep telling people—I'm not going to do that. I'm not going to rat on anyone or let everyone down. And MediaCorp is too dangerous; that's more important than what happens to me."

Ms. Martin blinked, not saying anything in response.

"If you want to help," Waylee continued, "get Francis Jones released. See if the prosecutor's team is in an inappropriate relationship with Media-Corp. Have my blog printout and writing materials returned. Tell me what this Uplift drug does and what to expect."

The attorney nodded. "Maybe we can come up with a plea settlement that the prosecution will accept and is a little more appealing to you."

"As long as it doesn't include lying about what I did or repudiating it. Or testifying against anyone else." Waylee felt pride that she could think logically again and defy, at least temporarily, the inner clamors to curl up and die. "Do you have a trial strategy?"

Ms. Martin stared at her. "You want to go to trial?"

"Have you prepared anything?"

"Look, I just started, I don't have much in the way of help, and I assumed you'd take the prosecutor's offer."

"I didn't pick you, Ms. Martin. But my fate is in your hands."

"I'll come back. But I highly advise that we plea bargain." She paused. "If we do go to trial, the fact that you're on medication could help with an insanity defense—"

Waylee cut her off. "Please. Don't mention that again. I went over it with Francis. I'm not going to undercut everything I did."

Back in her cell, Waylee sat on her thin mattress and focused. *I may never get out of prison. But I'm not going to give up. I'm not going to kill myself. I figured out how to control my brain before. Can't I do that again? Especially if this drug helps more than it hurts?*

Acceptance gave way to defiance. Once she pulled out of this depression, she'd start writing again. She'd write something inspiring but rational, and get it circulated. And if she went to trial, she'd switch the focus, show how Luxmore and Rand were the true criminals. A necessity defense, Francis called it.

She hoped Luxmore was bluffing about being able to reach Kiyoko, Pel, and Charles. They were resourceful, especially Pel, and had the protection of the Brazilian government.

Was that enough? The world had never been cursed with someone as powerful as Bob Luxmore.

* * *

Kiyoko

Nyasuke woke Kiyoko the next morning, meowing in her ear. He had an automatic feeder and water fountain; it was just attention he craved.

Kiyoko had decided not to visit Charles and Pel last night. She wasn't used to alcohol and didn't want to talk to officials while drunk. And they might not let her in after hours.

She nudged Gabriel, naked in her bed again. So fine. And he was so good last night, even better than the night before. Unfair that she had so much to do.

He opened his eyes. "Good morning, my princess."

She kissed him. "Can you come with me to the base, my champion?"

"Of course. Let me get some clean clothes from my apartment." He ran a hand along her thigh. "You are so beautiful."

She rolled out of bed, wanting him but deciding on a compromise. "Go get some clothes and then we can shower together."

Once ready, they took a taxi to the Campo de Marte Air Force Base. A delta-winged fighter jet was anchored on display outside the entrance, angling up toward the sky. Ahead, the entrance was blocked off with big metal tripods. Camouflage-uniformed guards with assault rifles stared at them.

The middle-aged taxi driver half turned toward her and Gabriel, holding hands in the back seat. "Devo deixá-lo aqui?"

"Espere aqui, por favor," Gabriel responded. *Wait here.*

They got out and the driver pulled against the curb. Kiyoko set her comlink to translate. Data glasses, like Gabriel and Pel had, would have been a lot easier. *That's it, I'm getting data glasses as soon as I get some money, even if they do look dorky.*

The guards and Gabriel spoke in Portuguese. They followed one of the guards to the entrance gate just around the bend.

"We need to show our papers," Gabriel told her. "The base is on alert, so they might not let us in."

"They have to," she said.

Black and yellow striped booms blocked the lanes in and out of the base, which was surrounded by a white concrete wall topped by coiled barbed wire. A small tower sat to the right and a guard bunker in the middle, topped by a Brazilian flag and a big sign lettered "Força Aérea Brasileira." Guards manned the gate. Beyond were parked a pair of six-wheeled armored personnel carriers with cannon turrets on top.

Gabriel handed his ID to a young guard in the bunker. He wore data glasses with thick black frames and a thin wraparound mike. Kiyoko passed him her refugee visa. "We're here to see Charles Lee and Pelopidas Demopoulos," she said. "Pelopidas is my sister's husband."

An exaggeration, but five years together might as well be marriage. Kiyoko's longest relationship had only been six months.

The guard stared at her and spoke in Portuguese. "You're not a Brazilian citizen?" her comlink translated.

"Ainda não." *Not yet.* She, Charles, and Pel had filled out application papers, but were told they first had to live in Brazil for four years and have stable jobs.

"Passaporte?"

She didn't own a passport. "Não tenho."

The guard frowned and pointed to a small grassy area to the left of the gate. "Espere lá por favor." *Wait there.*

The taxi driver honked his horn. Gabriel went over to pay him and he drove off.

"I must owe you so much money," Kiyoko said when he returned. "And I haven't found a new job yet."

"I told you, you can make lots of money as a supermodel. You just need a tan, you are too pale." He smirked.

She smacked him on the chest with the back of her fist. "Don't be a jerk."

After a while, one of the guards waved them back over to the bunker.

The guard inside returned their IDs. "Sr. Pelopidas não é casado." *Pel isn't married.*

"It's called common law marriage," Kiyoko replied, using her comlink to get the Portuguese phrase right. "You don't need the government's approval to have a life partner."

"That's what we call boyfriend-girlfriend. You are not related." His eyes were only barely visible through the data glasses, but his forehead furrowed. "Why did you try to trick me?"

"I didn't. Please, can we see them? Maybe they could come to the gate and we could talk here."

"You must leave now."

Kiyoko's jaw clenched. Why was everything so difficult? "Let me speak to your commander."

Gabriel touched her shoulder. "Don't anger him," he said in English.

The guard spoke quietly into his wraparound mike and his right hand slid down out of view, either to an alarm button or a sidearm.

I should have let Gabriel handle this, he knows the protocols.

Two more soldiers approached from inside the base, holding automatic rifles. Neither was an officer. "You must leave now," the bunker guard repeated.

Gabriel guided her away from the bunker. "We can come back when the shift changes," he said in English.

They stopped beneath the slate-gray fighter plane, impressive in its defiance of gravity. It was anchored to the ground through the rear exhaust nozzle by a thick metal bar like a congealed contrail. They queried their comlinks and found an eatery a block away, a small shop that served empadas, pastries stuffed with different fillings.

It was too early for lunch, and the shop was deserted except for the middle-aged woman at the counter and, from the sound of clanking pans, at least one person back in the kitchen. Kiyoko ordered a heart of palm empada and a can of Antártica guaraná, and Gabriel ordered a chicken empada. They sat in the far booth and chatted about their lives and all the things they liked about each other.

"Do you respect me, Gabriel?" she asked in English.

His thick eyebrows rose. "That is a strange question. But I told you earlier, you are more than beautiful. You are smart and brave, and you care about others."

He looked sincere. But he was more than a great lover, they were comrades too. "I never feel brave. Waylee's the brave one."

"You are brave. That's something I know about."

"Can you teach me to be a soldier?"

He chuckled. "You want to join the army and go through at least a year of training?"

"Even if I had a year to spare, I assume you need citizenship."

"Yes, I was joking."

"You've taught me some Brazilian jiu-jitsu. What else can you teach me?"

"I cannot be your drill instructor. But you can practice discipline and teamwork. And have more confidence in yourself."

"I try," she said, "but it's hard."

Kiyoko didn't like to talk about her awful childhood in Philly or her evil parents, but since Gabriel was her boyfriend, he had a right to know. "I have to confess I come from evil stock. I've transcended it, but it was very hurtful and I still have bad dreams about it."

"What are you talking about?"

How would he react to this? Would he think less of her? She pushed on and told him how her father, mother, and sister used to scream at each other. And with alcohol or meth addling his brain, her father, Feng, escalated to slaps and punches. Her mother, who was almost constantly drunk, passed the abuse on to Kiyoko, who was little and couldn't defend herself.

"Waylee gave me a kitten when I was five, this super cute calico. I named him Squeaky-Squeaks 'cause he made these adorable squeaks. Then Feng took him away, saying he wouldn't shut up and was driving him crazy. 'Just like you, you little brat,' he told me. I still remember that. Waylee kicked him in the shin and then Feng hit us and hit us and I never saw my kitty again."

"What kind of a man beats a five-year-old girl?"

"A monster, that's what kind. Waylee used to call the cops on him or child services. I was too young to do anything but she's nine years older—she had a different father—he, uh, jumped off a bridge."

Gabriel's mouth opened but he didn't speak right away so Kiyoko kept going. "So sometimes they'd arrest Feng, but he always came back and then he hated us that much more. And mom was a good talker and the authorities didn't really care anyway so she never lost custody.

"Finally, Feng came home drunk one night and tried to rape Waylee, even though he was supposed to be her protector and she was only sixteen. Our mother was passed out in the bedroom or she might have tried to stop it. But Waylee—uh, fought back. She hurt him. Bad."

"How?"

She paused, but decided to answer. "She . . . gouged his eyes out. With her thumbs. She stuck them in as far as they would go and started digging. It was horrible. He screamed and thrashed around with his right eye hanging down his cheek and blood spurting everywhere." Kiyoko had wet herself, it was so scary, and it had given her nightmares for years.

Gabriel stared at her with arched eyebrows.

"Waylee emptied my mother's purse," Kiyoko continued, "and we took a bus to Baltimore, as far as we could get and still have money for food."

In Baltimore, they'd squatted, stayed in shelters, or lived with Waylee's boyfriends or musician friends. The last five years, with Pel in the band house, were by far the best. Kiyoko's belly fluttered as she remembered she might never see her old friends again. Never sew costumes with Jayna, or dance to J-pop at Club Kuro Neko, or play music to fans at Bar Zar or house parties.

Gabriel's face was soft with sympathy. "You're lucky you turned out so well. You are the nicest person I know."

He wasn't scared off! "Thank you. It's because of Waylee that I turned out decently." And her anime heroes, and her connections with the gods. "I love you, Gabriel," she said. "I'm completely in love with you." It was a worthwhile trade, a city of friends for this incredible man.

"I love you too, Kiyoko." He looked sincere. "You are everything to me."

She reached across the table and twined her fingers in his. "You must promise to never cheat on me or lie to me or break my heart."

"Of course. I am not such a fool."

All they had to do was free Pel and Charles and Waylee, and, if they could, end MediaCorp's tyranny, and life would be perfect.

"How can we find out more about the kidnappers?" she asked her soul mate in quiet tones. "The news said they were a gang called As Piranhas."

"Yes," Gabriel said, equally quietly. "I never heard of them. But I don't work in the police."

"Who do you think they were working for? The CIA? MediaCorp?"

"Maybe, or maybe they did it on their own to collect the reward."

"They had that jet waiting. Whose jet was that? Where were they going to fly it? Did anyone talk to the pilot?"

"I've been wondering that too," he said.

"And most important, will they try again?"

"I could make some calls and find out more. I don't think I can access the Piranhas in custody, or the pilot, but if they have associates, I could track them down and shake some answers loose."

"That sounds dangerous. And a job for the police. Maybe we should talk to that Inspector De Barros."

Gabriel frowned. "I don't trust him. He took my guns and asked if I fired first. Anything I tell him could hurt me." He lowered his voice. "The police comms were down during the kidnapping and this inspector must have known I would be away from the apartment, at the fair."

"So you think he's involved with the kidnapping?"

"It is possible. Corruption is a big problem in Brazil."

"It is everywhere," she said. "We need to learn more about Inspector De Barros, if he's working with the kidnappers. Do you know anyone in the police we can trust?"

"No. But SSG has many contacts. I will ask some co-workers, but I have to keep it secret from my superiors. They won't want anyone spending time on it."

After four hours in the empada shop, they returned to the base. As Gabriel predicted, new guards were on duty. The new shift was not any more cooperative.

Gabriel requested the officer of the guard. An underling, a sergeant, arrived. They talked in Portuguese for a while, then the sergeant gave them visitation forms to fill out.

"We have to be cleared to enter," Gabriel told Kiyoko. "We can come back tomorrow and see if we've been cleared."

"All I want to do is talk to them!"

"The sergeant said they are in a secure area and can't come to the gate."

"What a bunch of bureaucratic crap."

Gabriel put a hand on her shoulder. "There was a battle here and people were killed. Of course the Air Force is being careful. We must be patient."

They ordered a taxi on Gabriel's comlink. For now, she'd have to settle for Crypt-O-Chat to talk to Pel and Charles. Were they safe? Or would some corrupt bastard sell them off?

* * *

Kiyoko and Gabriel returned to her apartment. Kiyoko pulled her 'bug-out bag'—a mid-sized backpack full of travel necessities—out of her closet for the first time since Pel prepared it for her. It had copies of her residency documents, a comlink with fictitious user codes, a chip card with crypto-currency, 500 Brazilian reals in cash, a first aid kit, food and water, clothes and hygiene stuff, and a compact kit of wilderness survival gear. And Pel's favorite necessities—a multi-tool and roll of duct tape.

She gave Pel's backpack to Gabriel. "Someone might as well use this."

He looked through it. Pel's was lighter on clothes than Kiyoko's, and heavier on tools and electronics. "I should make my own, I don't know how to solder or hack computers."

Kiyoko removed the wilderness gear from hers. She had no intention of fleeing into the Amazon. Even so, there wasn't enough room for all the things she wanted to keep if she had to run. "I'm going to buy a bigger bag."

As she sorted through her things, Kiyoko's comlink sounded the conch shell pitches for a high priority message. When she checked, it was from her former employer.

Dear Ms. Pingyang,

As you know, Fantasmas na Maquina suffered severe financial difficulties as a result of legal challenges from Media Corporation. More recently, our creditors demanded repayment and we faced court-supervised liquidation. Our only option was to accept an offer from Media Corporation to become a subsidiary. While far from ideal, this allows much of our work to move forward, and allows continued employment for many of our staff. Under the alternative, liquidation, all of our work would have been in vain.

Unfortunately, only a select number of employees will be retained and I regret that you did not make this list. I wish you the best in your future endeavors.

With apologies,
Augusto Monteiro
Founder and President, Fantasmas na Maquina

All their hopes for a BetterWorld alternative, gone. All her hopes for Yumekuni, gone. Tears poured down her face and her breath turned to wet sobs.

Pel and Charles certainly wouldn't be employed either, not by a Media-Corp subsidiary. They had no future.

Gabriel hurried over. "What's wrong?"

"Everything. Everything's wrong. Except for you."

Gabriel held her and she cried in his arms. Even in Brazil there was no escape from MediaCorp's talons. How could she do anything? She couldn't even feed herself if that was Bob Luxmore's will.

18

Pelopidas

Pel knocked on Charles's door. No answer. The guard at the end of the hall, standing by the stairwell door, stared at him but didn't approach.

He tried the doorknob. It was locked. "Charles. It's Pel. Open up."

No answer. The guard fingered his rifle strap.

"Come on," Pel said to the door, "I want to talk." *We can't just sit and wait for the next shit sandwich.*

The door opened. Charles stood there, eyes red-rimmed, clothes rumpled, shoulders slumped. "What?"

"Can I come in?"

Charles shrugged and turned around, leaving the door open. Pel entered and shut it behind him.

"You know I'm really sorry about Adrianna," he said.

Charles turned and blinked. "It ain't fair. Why'd they have to kill her?"

"I know. I was wondering if you could help me find her killers. Our kidnappers. You know, they might try again."

"I thought they all got nabbed."

"Two escaped. And there's probably more out there."

Charles threw up his hands. "What the hell can we do about it stuck here?"

"I know this is a long shot," Pel said, "but maybe the kidnappers, the killers, visited Adrianna's Comnet site."

Especially if they recruited her to help them. Gabriel couldn't be on the kidnappers' side—he stopped them. Quite likely Adrianna was an insider, though. She almost let them in. And would she really have spent so much time with Charles to tweak her Comnet site, giving up hours she could have been spending with clients? She was probably recruited after her first visit.

Charles frowned. "Why would the kidnappers have visited her Comnet site?"

Pel decided not to share his suspicions. "They would have been surveilling us, and they would have looked up this girl who kept visiting."

After a pause, Charles nodded. "Makes sense."

"I assume you can get back in and pull up a visitor log and whatnot." He had examined Adrianna's site, but Charles had rendered it impervious to SQL injection, cross-site scripting, and everything else Pel could think of.

"Yeah," Charles said. "I have admin privilege and the password."

"You know, I really am sorry."

Charles didn't respond.

"Come over," Pel said, "and let's find her killers."

Charles followed Pel back to his room. Pel retrieved the makeshift Wi-Fi antenna from its hiding spot and logged onto the Comnet.

He passed the keyboard to Charles, who logged onto Adrianna's site as an admin. "I set her up to book indie," he said, "but she didn't get a chance. Bookings went through the club, and they took a big cut."

"What does that mean? Are we stuck?"

"I can view all her club info. It's linked. We're Adrianna as far as the club knows."

The site log wasn't particularly helpful, not without cross-checking the visitors' Comnet addresses, some of which were no doubt fake. But Charles brought up a list of recent clients, with names, addresses, voice numbers, dates, times, and "preferences." Her last appointment, five days before the kidnapping attempt, was with John Hill at the Hotel Tiberio. Not necessarily a real name, but the location should be real. No room number given, just instructions to call when she arrived.

The appointment before that was to Pel and Charles's building, no apartment number given, booked by Paulo Garibaldi. A name Gabriel must have invented.

"Why no appointments after the one at the Tiberio?" Pel asked.

"She was hanging with me," Charles said.

"But not all night."

They checked her club schedule but she hadn't been there either. "Maybe she was tired after me," Charles said.

Pel refrained from commenting. Then Waylee flashed in his mind, how insatiable she was when she was hypomanic. "This guy John Hill at the Tiberio, can we figure out who he is? He has an American name. English-speaking, anyway."

Charles opened a search engine. There were thousands of John Hills.

Too common a name and nothing else to go on. Probably a pseudonym anyway. "If we could get to the Tiberio," Pel said, "we could get a description."

"We're stuck here."

"Text Kiyoko. Gabriel could do it."

＊ ＊ ＊

Kiyoko

While Kiyoko was scooping her cat's litter box, her comlink alerted her about a text from Pel. She flushed the poop down the toilet and logged on to Crypt-O-Chat.

```
Godwin: Adrianna's last appt was some asshat named
John Hill at Hotel Tiberio. Can Gabriel check into it?
Princess_Kiyoko: What exactly do you need to know?
Godwin: Description. And if he's CIA. Good chance he's
connected to the kidnappers.
Princess_Kiyoko: On it. Any other info about this guy?
Godwin: Thats it, just name & address.
```

Before talking to Gabriel, Kiyoko checked her public account to see if Francis Jones had written. It had been three weeks since his last update about Waylee.

Nothing. She emailed him again. Then she went to his office's Comnet site, sent a message there, and found the office phone number. She called via a series of anonymizing proxies.

No answer.

Next step, call the Maryland People's Party office. Their Comnet site was down, but she found a cached copy.

A woman answered the phone. "Maryland People's Party. How may we help you?" Her voice sounded young, from inner Baltimore.

"Hi. I'm trying to reach Francis Jones. No one picks up at his office."

The woman didn't respond right away, but Kiyoko's voice was being bounced all over the world. "May I ask who's calling?" she asked.

"One of his clients. Motoko Kusanagi." First name that came to mind.

The woman chuckled. "How can I help, Major?"

She knows Ghost in the Shell. I should have picked something more obscure, or just made up a name.

The woman continued before Kiyoko could respond. "Our phone line is probably tapped, just so you know."

"Do you know a way to reach him? Your Comnet site is down, by the way."

The woman sighed. "Yeah, our site's been under attack for weeks now. Right-wing hacker group, far as we can figure. And Francis—Homeland Security took him away for aiding and abetting terrorists. That's what his assistant told us. Even though the man never hurt anyone in his life."

"How can they do that? That's ridiculous."

"No doubt. Lot of that going around. People brought in for questioning. Surveillance. Confiscations."

"What?"

"I'd tell you to read our blog but it's probably been knocked offline again. MediaCorp and the government claim the People's Party supports terrorism, thanks to that reckless Waylee Freid."

"She opened people's eyes!"

The woman's voice grew angry and rapid. "We had nothin' to do with Waylee Freid's video but we gettin' all the pushback, just 'cause she was a member. Major parties tryin' state by state to get us off the ballot, and now they got extra ammo. Friendship Farm was confiscated, and that's our main source of income."

"It was confiscated?"

"All the adult residents were arrested and charged for harboring fugitives. They out on bail now, but we lost our best attorney."

I have to find a way to help somehow.

"Hold on," the woman said, "I got another call."

"You don't know how I can get in touch with Francis?"

"Only Homeland Security knows." She put Kiyoko on hold.

Kiyoko cut the connection. Obviously she couldn't call Homeland Security. *What now?* Waylee was being held in the Federal Detention Center in Philadelphia. Kiyoko looked up their phone number.

"FDC Philadelphia," a man answered.

"Hi, I'm calling about an inmate, Waylee Freid. Is she still being held there?"

"May I ask who's calling?"

"Her sister, Kiyoko." She'd be on their list of relatives.

"Your Social Security number?"

"I don't have one."

"How can you not have one? Are you not a U.S. citizen?"

"I'm a citizen, I just don't have a Social Security number."

"I'm going to need some sort of verification."

"If you let me talk to my sister, she can verify it's me."

"Inmates can't receive calls and Ms. Freid is on a special watch list and can't initiate calls."

"Well then how am I supposed to speak to her?"

"You can come here in person during visiting hours. They're posted on our Comnet site."

Kiyoko fought from screaming. Waylee surely would have screamed by now. "Could you give me the name and number of her lawyer?"

"I'm sorry, I don't have that information."

Kiyoko gave up and called Amnesty International and asked to speak with whoever was handling Waylee's case. They transferred her to a young-sounding woman named Bethany.

"Have you had any luck yet?" Kiyoko asked.

"Yes, as a matter of fact. You'll be happy to hear our petition and lobbying was 100% successful."

"It was?" Kiyoko hadn't heard anything. "That's awesome!"

"We just heard today, in fact. I was going to have someone contact you. Ms. Freid is going through the standard legal process and is receiving medication for her depression."

A strange mix of joy and frustration rushed through Kiyoko. "The second news is great. I was really, really worried she'd end up hurting herself, all alone in prison with her condition getting worse and worse."

"Glad we could help," the woman said.

"But why do you think she's going to get a fair trial? Did you know her lawyer, Francis Jones, was taken away by Homeland Security and no one knows where he is? For aiding and abetting terrorists, I was told."

"I spoke with him just a few days ago. He mentioned he was being investigated, but . . . taken away? No, I didn't know about that."

"Did he say anything about Waylee's case?"

"He said the government labeled Ms. Freid as a terrorist leader and was throwing everything they had against her to discredit her and make an example. They claim she deserves life in the federal Supermax."

Kiyoko nearly dropped the comlink. "No, no way."

"Mr. Jones," the woman continued, "asked us to help with the public relations aspect."

"And did you?" MediaCorp spun her sister's Super Bowl revelations as 'a vicious cyberattack on America.' No wonder Waylee hated them so much.

"The more people that counter MediaCorp's lies, the better. It wasn't terrorism. No bombs set off, no one killed."

"We looked into it," the woman said. "Some people were hurt, so it was decided that we would limit our involvement to ensuring a fair trial and that Ms. Freid receive medical treatment."

Cowards. "She's not gonna get a fair trial, especially without her lawyer. Can you find out what happened to him and help him?"

"Let me get my supervisor on the phone."

* * *

Pelopidas

A pair of camouflage-uniformed soldiers escorted Pel and Charles to a small meeting room in the base's headquarters building. An overweight mustached man in a blue blazer and striped tie rose from the faux wood table and shook their hands. He wore old, bulky data glasses and the red 'record' light was on.

"Hello," the man said in barely accented English. "I am Inspector De Barros from the São Paulo State Civil Police."

"I thought São Paulo was a city," Charles said.

"It is. But there is also a state called São Paulo. It has the biggest population in Brazil, which keeps us very busy." The police inspector sat back down and opened his hand toward chairs opposite him. Pel and Charles sat.

"Someone already took our statement," Pel said. "Two people, actually, one from the Air Force and one from the police, and they recorded it on video."

"Yes, but I am in charge of the case and I need to interview all the witnesses." He asked them to recount the day's events, same as the previous interviewers.

The details were still fresh in Pel's mind, probably because the event was so traumatic. He described everything except wiping their computers, pointing a stun gun at Adrianna, and the way Charles froze.

"Who killed Adrianna?" Charles asked the inspector, voice cracking.

"The woman found in your bathroom? That is still under investigation."

"Do you know who they were working for?" Pel asked.

"I'm afraid I can not comment on an ongoing investigation." His face hardened into an 'I'm asking the questions here' position. He looked at Charles. "Now I need to hear what you saw and heard."

Charles more or less repeated Pel's story, in less detail.

"Thank you for the information," Inspector De Barros said afterward. He rose from his chair. "We are done examining the crime scene so you should be allowed to return to your home. I will speak to the military about it."

Pel wondered if it was safe to return, but they could always leave for someplace else, or maybe just stay on the move.

The inspector handed them each a business card. "Please contact me if you remember anything else. We need to stay in touch until the case is completed, so if you are released, please do not leave São Paulo. Call me right away and let me know where you are."

19

Waylee

Waylee's cell door opened. Her guards shackled her wrists and legs, and marched her downstairs to a concrete block room with bright overhead lights. Another guard, a fortyish woman with blonde hair drawn back in a tight bun, stood inside with gloves on. They removed her shackles and her male guard left the room.

"You know the drill," the woman said. "Strip and put your hands against the wall."

After the humiliating cavity search, she told Waylee to put her clothes back on. Two men, one Hispanic, the other African-American, entered. They wore blue jackets with yellow circled stars on the left breast and 'PO-LICE U.S. MARSHAL' in big yellow letters on the sleeves and back.

"So long," her burly female guard said.

Too bad that didn't mean she was being released. It must be time for her transfer to Virginia for trial.

Yesterday, Ms. Martin told her the prosecution had rejected any possible plea bargain unless Waylee publicly recanted her video or testified against her co-conspirators. No way, Waylee had repeated. Ms. Martin also said the prosecution had entered Waylee's missing writings as evidence. She'd moved to suppress, but the judge had denied the motion, saying prisoners weren't entitled to search and seizure protections.

The marshals put shiny new shackles on Waylee's wrists and ankles and a chain around her belly. In case that wasn't enough, they placed black plastic boxes over the keyholes.

"Lucky you," the African-American marshal said. "You're taking ConAir and you've got a plane all to yourself. Bet you'll feel like a big shot."

She didn't answer. It hurt, having her writings taken away and used against her. But what hurt more was losing Pel's support essay. It had been her talisman, her only connection to the love of her life. And that might be used against her too.

The marshals filled out forms on a data pad and escorted her through an electronically controlled gate. They shuffled along a white concrete hallway and out a steel door into a big enclosed garage lit by bright LED's. The air was warm and humid. She'd originally come in this way. They shoved her in the back of a black SUV with dark tinted windows and marked "U.S. Marshal" on the side.

She had the back seat, covered with squeaky vinyl, to herself. The windows were armored with thick plexiglass and steel mesh. The air smelled like pine-infused Lysol.

Could she escape? She was shackled inside a reinforced chamber designed to hold prisoners a lot stronger and more skilled than her. A bungled attempt would be used against her at trial.

The SUV drove up a ramp and a metal gate opened. Two more marshals stood outside, holding shotguns. The SUV didn't stop, turning left onto an alley, tall buildings on both sides.

It would have been nice to feel the open air even if it was overcast and probably muggy. Baltimore was hot and muggy in the summer and Philly was only fifty miles north. She'd probably never see Baltimore again, and it was possible she might never feel open air again.

If the worst happened at trial, maybe she could find a way to escape wherever they sent her. She couldn't do it on her own, though.

* * *

Gabriel

The taxi pulled up to a narrow glass skyscraper with a black helicopter platform on top. The tall building and its neighbors blocked the midmorning sun, casting the street in shadow. "Hotel Tiberio," the driver said.

In the back seat of the taxi, Gabriel squeezed Kiyoko's hand. As usual, she had insisted on coming along, but it was probably safer than leaving her alone. She had pinned her bright red hair into a bun and tucked it beneath a big floppy hat, and wore a long sleeved pink blouse and dark blue skirt.

Gabriel was well dressed also, wearing dark gray slacks and a matching blazer, his outfit for formal events. More importantly, he had borrowed two adaptive fiber undershirts from SSG. The latest thing in body armor, they contained carbon nanotubes designed to flatten bullets and spread out the impact. Over twice as effective as graphene or Kevlar, he'd been told. Should have been assigned them on day one.

Gabriel still hadn't recovered his primary guns from the police, but carried his two backups, an HK semi-auto with a 20 round magazine of armor-piercing fragmentation ammo, and a stun gun with ten charges. In her new carry bag, Kiyoko had a fast-discharging smoke grenade, a pepper spray gun with the hottest available formula and a thirty-foot range, and a stun gun. Plus a roll of duct tape, in case they captured their quarry.

Kiyoko paused on the tiled sidewalk as the taxi pulled away. A uniformed guard stood next to the front door, pistol in a belt holster.

"Don't worry," Gabriel told Kiyoko. "He's just a crime and beggar deterrent."

Gabriel led her past the guard, who said nothing. A concierge in a black tie greeted them and they entered the hotel lobby.

It was Gabriel's first time in a luxury hotel. The lobby had a high ceiling but not much decoration. "Not as fancy as I expected."

Kiyoko looked around. "Minimalist. My palace in Yumekuni is much more impressive. But I bet the beds are comfy."

This whole mess was his fault. He'd brought Adrianna into their lives, and it looked like she might have been recruited to assist the kidnapping. And what if John Hill was CIA, like Pel suspected? No way could Gabriel match their resources.

"They say in war to take the initiative," Kiyoko had reminded him that morning. "That's how I defeated my archenemy in BetterWorld."

They walked up to the check-in desk, which was manned by two women and a man wearing black uniforms. The plan was to lure Hill into the lobby and photograph his face, so Kiyoko or Pel could look him up on the Comnet. If they could lure him someplace private, like his room or a bathroom, they'd stun him, wrap him in duct tape, and question him. Gabriel hoped it wouldn't come to that—it wasn't his thing.

The clean-cut male clerk greeted them. "Bom dia."

"Bom dia," Gabriel responded. "Is there a John Hill staying here?"

"I'm sorry. I can't divulge guest information."

"He's expecting us," Kiyoko said in English. She wiped her right palm, which glistened with sweat, on the opposite sleeve, and held out the hand. "Chunhua."

The clerk hesitated, then shook it.

"Can you have him come down?" she asked. "My comlink is dead. I forgot to charge it last night."

"One minute, please." The clerk spoke perfect English. He checked his computer terminal. "I'm sorry, there's no one named John Hill here."

Kiyoko licked her lips. "That's weird. Did he check out?"

"I'm sorry, that's all I can say, he isn't here."

"Uh, thanks." She looked around, then headed for a lounge area.

Gabriel followed. "Where are you going?"

Kiyoko glanced back over her shoulder. "Plan B. Hill either checked out or is using a different name."

Plan B was to question anyone who might have seen Hill, and get whatever information they could.

The lounge was mostly empty. Three groups of well-dressed people sat at small tables with candles. Kiyoko went up to the bar, which had no seats, and spoke quietly to the black-uniformed, light-skinned bartender.

She whispered in Gabriel's ear when he joined her. "I think he's gay. Flirt with him." She didn't laugh like she was joking.

He thought about asking how she could tell, but decided to trust her.

The bartender spoke. "You can sit where you want and I'll come over."

"Here is fine." If they sat, it would be a lot harder to ask questions. He ordered a Brahma Chopp, his default beer, then introduced himself. "I'm Fabinho. This is my friend Chunhua."

"Andre." He filled a glass with beer and set it on the counter. Kiyoko ordered a papaya juice.

The bar had a shelf of books below the gleaming white counter. Strange. "Do people read books at the bar?" Gabriel asked.

Andre chuckled. "That's just to show we're sophisticated. Some of our guests borrow books, though."

"Do you like working here?" Kiyoko asked him in Portuguese. "Do you work here a lot?"

"Actually, I do." His eyes drifted to Gabriel. "I haven't seen you around. I'd remember."

"You have a good memory, then?" Gabriel asked.

The bartender shrugged. "Part of the job. You have to remember people's names and what they like." His eyes lingered a bit too long for comfort.

I should flirt back. Gabriel could no more flirt with a man than breathe underwater, though. "Do you see a lot of foreigners here? Like Americans?"

"Why do you ask?"

Kiyoko intervened. "Do you speak English?"

"It is required here," Andre said in American-sounding English. "Spanish also. We have many foreign guests, mostly businessmen, and Portuguese is not a common language outside Brazil."

"I'm Canadian," Kiyoko lied in English. "Ex-pat from Toronto."

"You sound like an American."

"Canadians are a lot like Americans, only more polite."

"Do Canadians tip well like Americans?" The bartender winked.

Gabriel looked at Kiyoko. Except for the optional 10% *serviço* added to bills, tipping was uncommon in Brazil. A tip would make a nice impression here.

Kiyoko put a ten real note on the counter, which was almost as much as her juice. "If the service is good, we add an extra 20%. Otherwise waiters and bartenders in our countries wouldn't earn enough to live on. So you get Americans and Canadians here and they give you nice tips?"

He shrugged. "Some of them."

"We're actually here to meet an American, friend of a friend, but it seems he's checked out already. Maybe you've met him. Name's John Hill."

His lips pressed together. "Doesn't sound familiar, but I don't get everyone's name."

"I don't have a picture," Kiyoko said. "But he, uh, would have had a visitor. Short, young, light brown skin, very curvy, probably wearing tight clothes."

Andre snapped his fingers. "Yes, I remember her. A garota de programa. They come here sometimes if they're invited and do not bother the other guests."

"Do you remember what the man looked like? So I can find him? I just have his name, we haven't met yet."

"You said he's a friend of a friend?"

Kiyoko nodded. "Yes. My friend at the modeling agency."

He stared at her. "You should be careful with this guy. He does not seem very friendly."

"What do you mean?"

"First time I saw him, he grabbed a man by the tie." He pointed at one of the far tables.

"An argument?" Gabriel asked.

He rolled his eyes. "Obviously."

"What were they arguing about?"

"I couldn't hear what they were saying, not that it was my business anyway. They went upstairs together so they must have worked it out."

"There is no worry," Gabriel said. "But we need to find Sr. John, if you could describe him for me." He laid a fifty real note on the bar top.

Andre smiled as he pocketed the note. "He was white. Strong-looking like you. But shorter. And older. Receding hair—he should get that fixed."

Sounded familiar. The man at the Liberdade Street Fair that he couldn't identify? "Did he wear data glasses?" Gabriel asked.

"No. Well, he did once. Thick rims, dark, that's all I remember."

Too bad Gabriel hadn't saved a picture. But now he knew who to look for. "The man whose tie he grabbed, do you remember what he looked like?"

"You're police, aren't you."

"We just need your help to find these guys. It's important."

The bartender sighed. "Well, I can tell you the man's tie was pretty damn ugly. Aside from that, he was balding and kind of a whale."

Inspector de Barros? He was at the fair also. "Did he have a big mustache?"

"Sounds like you know him."

"When was the last time you saw him? Either one of them."

"The fat guy was only here once. And your friend of a friend, he was a guest for a while, longer than usual, but I haven't seen him lately. Maybe a week ago? Something like that."

"Thank you." Gabriel paid the bill for the drinks and rounded up.

"We have overwhelming evidence now," he told Kiyoko on the way out. "The police, at least Inspector de Barros, but probably others too, are working with the kidnappers. And Inspector de Barros is in charge of the case. We have to warn Pel and Charles."

* * *

Kiyoko

As soon as they exited the hotel, Kiyoko pulled out her comlink and tried to reach Pel and Charles via Crypt-O-Chat. They weren't online. She left a message: Beware Insp. De Barros—Working with kidnappers!

She wished her sister was here. Waylee always knew what to do, and wasn't afraid all the time.

Gabriel hailed a taxi and they returned to Liberdade. Hungry, they stopped for lunch at the Ichiban Bakery. It was a small place, mostly for takeout, crowded with glass-encased shelves and refrigerators full of cakes, pastries, sandwiches, and more. The smell of fresh-baked buns made her mouth water. The bakery had four circular tables, two on either side of the entrance. A young Japanese-looking couple sat at one of them, eating matcha cookies and speaking in Portuguese.

Kiyoko and Gabriel ordered thick slices of torta de frango and glasses of juice. He paid—Kiyoko was broke. "I should sell some things," she said. "You shouldn't have to pay for me, especially now that you're on vacation and not getting reimbursed."

He held up a hand. "I am happy to buy anything you need."

They sat at the furthest of the two empty tables to the right of the door. Gabriel slid his chair so his back wasn't to the entrance. "I like to see my surroundings," he said.

"Do you think we'll have more trouble?"

"I'm never getting caught unprepared again." He ate a forkful of torta—chicken, peas, and corn in a pastry crust.

"I'm getting a cupcake afterward," she said.

Gabriel blinked. "I don't know how you eat so much and stay so thin."

"Super energy. Waylee's the same way." She had a bite of torta. The chicken and vegetables were flavored with garlic and tomato. She lowered her voice. "How can we find out more about this John Hill guy?"

Gabriel put his fork down and leaned forward, speaking quietly. "I thought you were going to run an image search on the Comnet."

"That was if we got a photo. Without it, we'd get millions of matches. We don't even know for sure he's American."

He nodded. "I am not trained as a detective."

"Well, neither am I. Are there any police we can trust?"

"I don't know."

The bell on the bakery door jingled. A man in jeans and a leather coat entered. He wore a rigid plastic mask of some man she didn't recognize. Kiyoko almost peed herself. "Gabriel!"

Another masked man followed the first, then two masked women.

If I cower, we'll die. An invisibility spell would be ideal. Kiyoko reached into her carry bag and pulled out her smoke grenade.

The masked people whipped out pistols and submachine guns. Gabriel reached inside his outer shirt for his guns. He didn't have his data glasses on.

Kiyoko pulled the pin of the smoke grenade and pointed it at the attackers. White smoke billowed out. She waved it, forming a dense cloud that stank of sulfur, burning metal, and chlorine.

The attackers fired, an onslaught of loud bangs. Something hard hit her in the collarbone, followed by another. A bullet whizzed past her head. People screamed. Gabriel grunted and shot back, loud rapid bangs.

The smoke grenade, still belching white, got too hot to hold. She chucked it at the attackers and dove beneath the table.

The attackers' masks had eye and nostril holes. Kiyoko pulled out her pepper spray gun and fired at the four shapes in the smoke, spraying from right to left at face height. The attackers screamed.

Gabriel kicked his chair at them, ran, dodged, fired on the move. Non-stop bangs from the attackers' guns, thuds against the table, crashing glass all around.

Kiyoko kept spraying. She couldn't see the attackers now through the foul smoke and tears in her eyes. Something hit her right arm just above the elbow. It burned like a blowtorch.

One of the attackers dropped, then another, although it was hard to be sure. Kiyoko ran out of pepper spray and pulled out her stun gun. It was impossible to see through the white smoke, though. She didn't want to hit Gabriel.

The shooting stopped. Kiyoko glanced at her arm. Blood streamed from a hole in the blouse sleeve. Just below the armor, bad luck.

She started crying, then forced herself to stop. *I'm a princess.*

More gunshots, then silence.

Kiyoko's hands and arms shook as she gripped the stun gun. Everything hurt. Her stomach contracted and her two bites of torta spewed onto the floor. She threw up again, mostly bile-tasting liquid.

Someone pulled her up. "Kiyoko?" Gabriel's voice.

Right next to her, he was close enough to see. His blazer and shirt were torn and the adaptive fiber undershirt full of circular indentations. His face was pale. Blood streamed from his right ear. Half the ear was missing. It seemed like his left ear stuck out even more now.

"You're hurt," she said.

"I'd be dead if not for the armor. And you. Most people freeze when attacked but you took their sight away."

"I'm a princess," she managed.

He nodded. "Your arm." He threw off his shredded blazer, then pulled off the remnants of his shirt and wrapped it around her bleeding arm.

"The attackers?" she asked, feeling faint.

"Two down, dead or close to it. I hit the other two but they got away. Piranhas I presume from the masks. They had armor and not all my rounds went through."

Kiyoko turned her head just in time to avoid retching on him.

⋆ ⋆ ⋆

Dalton

Sitting with his laptop on the saggy mattress of his guesthouse room, Dalton was typing a status report on the Ares network when he received a message on his comlink from De Barros. The fat drunkard had ironically picked the codename "Jaguar."

```
Jaguar: Can't meet.
```

Dalton responded from his randomly chosen username for this mission.

```
Hurricane40: Why not?
Jaguar: Can't get away. I'm sending you the interview
video.
```

Their secure chat program didn't allow attachments, so De Barros sent a link to a Comnet address. Dalton had Martinez check it out first. The Ares IT specialist gave the okay and Dalton clicked the link.

As expected, it was video of an interview with Lee and Demopoulos. More important, it included a walk around the air force base. A lot of guards and security cameras. Getting to the targets would be difficult.

De Barros sent another message while Dalton was studying the video in detail.

```
Jaguar: Another shootout in Liberdade.
```

De Barros had told Dalton that the Piranhas had embraced their suggestion to kill Da Silva. They had been staking out Liberdade, something they were supposedly good at, but avoiding their quarry's apartment building, which was being watched by police.

```
Hurricane40: What happened?
Jaguar: Two Piranhas dead. Da Silva in hospital but
alive.
Hurricane40: Piranhas worthless.
```

Jaguar: I wasn't finished. We can charge Da Silva with murder and get him out of the way. The delegado is my good supporter, and I know a prosecutor who will take the case.

Hurricane40: Excellent. What is a delegado?

Jaguar: Brazil's system differs from USA's. The delegado de polícia draws up the arrest warrants and decides which cases will be prosecuted. He outranks me but I know his big secret and have him by the balls.

No wonder De Barros hasn't been fired yet, even though he drinks on the job.

Hurricane40: What secret?

Jaguar: It is too unpleasant to talk about.

In other words, he doesn't want me to co-opt his leverage.

Hurricane40: What happens once Da Silva's charged?

Jaguar: Depends on the preliminary hearing. I have enough evidence for trial and will hope for detention. But even if he is released until trial, he will have to wear a tracking bracelet. Pingyang also. I will contact the prosecutor and judge and make sure.

Hurricane40: And you can monitor their whereabouts?

Jaguar: Yes I will know where they are at all times.

Hurricane40: Good. It could be useful to have Pingyang. We can use her to get Lee and Demopoulos.

Jaguar: Yes. Now the delegado will cooperate for free but this prosecutor requires a fee for his risks.

Of course.

Jaguar: Most of his colleagues are strict so he must be careful.

Hurricane40: How much?

Jaguar: R$200,000. You can transfer to my account.

Probably the son of a bitch will keep half of it for himself.

Hurricane40: That is too much.

Jaguar: That is the price. And for a judge, more would be needed. I would not bother though, the case will be difficult to win if Da Silva has a decent advocate.

No shit. It was self-defense.

Hurricane40: We only need the tracking bracelets. How do I know this prosecutor will get the money?

Jaguar: By the results, porra. I must go now. Make
sure you wire me the money before the end of today.

Another expense. Less money for me and my kids.

Hurricane40: What about getting custody of Lee and Demopoulos?

Jaguar: I am working on that. I must go.

De Barros logged off.

Dalton typed a report to Petrov and sent it to his network box. Petrov
responded a few minutes later via network chat.

Spica77: What is the timeline?

Hurricane40: Jaguar was not specific. Military is less
pliable than his usual network.

Spica77: Need timeline ASAP. Need this wrapped up to
focus on Haiti follow-up.

*Security for MediaCorp's research facility on Gonâve? Or a more aggres-
sive task? Best not to ask.*

Hurricane40: Wilco

Hurricane40: Why isn't there a reward for Pingyang?

There was a pause, then:

Spica77: No Interpol notice filed. She is a person of
interest by U.S. FBI but no warrant filed. Guyanese accomplices have warrants and blue notices as persons of
interest but no reward or red notice for arrest and
extradition.

*The FBI apparently didn't have anything solid on Pingyang. Why not take
something to a grand jury anyway? Grand juries almost never turned down
U.S. attorneys. It was a rubber stamp process.*

Hurricane40: Oversight. Aiding and abetting and acces-
sory after the fact are easy to apply. Doesn't matter if they can't convict. If we get a red notice for
Pingyang, we can remove her from the field and use her
as leverage.

Spica77: Agree. Your police background is helpful.
Will channel suggestion to relevant officials.

After the chat ended, Dalton messaged Kozachenko:

Be patient but stay ready. We will act soon.

20

Waylee

When Waylee arrived at the Lewis F. Powell, Jr., United States Courthouse in downtown Richmond, Virginia, the marshals gave her a new jumpsuit, green instead of orange. Then they locked her in a small cell in the basement, which was cold and reeked of paint fumes.

She had to stop the despair that weighed down her shoulders and jellied her spine. The medicine seemed to help. She could at least reason now, although her thoughts flowed like sludge.

Her talisman, the printout of Pel's blog posting, had been stolen from her. But she'd already committed it to memory. "Waylee Freid is quite possibly the most courageous, selfless person of our time. . . ."

And she had five years of memories to draw on. Like their first kiss, which quickly turned into their first fuck. He'd had a crush on her since seeing her fronting Bombshells for Breakfast, then they ended up in a band together. It was just a matter of time.

It was after Dwarf Eats Hippo's second show, a backup gig at Club Antiseen. Everything had gone perfectly and the crowd had loved them. They'd packed their equipment and were grooving to the headliner when their fingers twined and their eyes locked.

It was unexpectedly exciting, like someone had flipped on banks of strobe lights and smoke cannons. He had a girlfriend, she had a boyfriend, but she and Pel were like opposite magnet poles, pulled together by universal laws of physics in an act of completion. Lips and tongues lashed together, hands gripped flesh, and all reason sloughed aside as they plummeted together off a cliff, ditching everyone else and fucking like rabid weasels in the back of the van.

Pel was still her lodestone, her hearth stone, her ballast stone.

Even an imaginary Pel was better than no Pel at all.

A few hours later, two new marshals, thirtyish white men wearing dark suits, brought Waylee to a small meeting room. They removed her shackles and stood by the door. A young African-American woman wearing a gray pant suit rose from a plastic chair. "Ms. Freid?"

"That's me."

"I'm Veronica Jones, Ms. Martin's assistant on this case." She didn't offer a handshake. "Now, jury selection begins tomorrow and your trial will begin immediately afterward."

That quick? "Weren't you supposed to prep me or something?"

"Well, you're just an observer in jury selection. And the trial too, unless you testify, but that's typically not a good idea."

"Don't I have a say in my fate?"

"You can bring that up with Ms. Martin. I'm just here to get your measurements." She pulled a small camera out of her purse, with a laser aperture next to the lens.

"What for?"

"You don't want to go to court wearing that prison garb, now do you?"

Waylee nodded. "What are my chances?"

"We'll do the best we can." Ms. Jones looked at the marshals. "Do you mind waiting outside? And no peeking."

The two men shrugged and left, locking the door behind them.

"Clothes off," Ms. Jones ordered. "You can keep the undies on."

Feeling a little embarrassed about how skinny and frail she'd become, Waylee pulled off her green shirt and pants.

Ms. Jones pointed the camera at her. "This will record your measurements and skin tone and when I get back to the office, order a loaner suit from Court Supplies. We'll have it before tomorrow. Turn please."

Waylee turned in a slow circle. "What's the judge like?"

Ms. Jones slipped the camera back in her purse. "You can put your clothes back on. Uh, Judge Mahle—he's your judge—he's a former prosecutor. Conservative, but not as ideological as the latest batch. That's pretty much all I know about him. It's not something we've got control over, so don't fuss yourself about it."

*　*　*

Kiyoko

Through the sixth-floor window of Kiyoko's pastel-colored hospital room, the sun neared the horizon. Reclined on her industrial-looking bed, Kiyoko replayed her near death over and over. Poor Gabriel had suffered another set of wounds on her behalf. Despite the fuzziness from the pain medication, her fingers twisted knots into the detergent-infused sheets.

A police guard sat in a chair in the hallway. The police had confiscated her and Gabriel's weapons and body armor before escorting them to the hospital. *Why?* They were the victims, not the attackers. And they'd been put in separate rooms, even though they had empty second beds.

Kiyoko's right arm was bandaged and in a sling. The bullet had passed through her triceps without hitting the bone, the doctor had said. And she had a "clavicle fracture"—a broken collarbone—from bullet impacts to her body armor.

She hadn't been a hospital patient since she was six, a few months before she and Waylee ran away. Her mother had discovered her secret crayon drawings of her parents as fanged monsters being slain by a knight on horseback. Feng—she hated admitting he was her father—tore them up and shouted obscenities. She cringed and cried, he told her to shut up, she wailed in terror, and he twisted her arm so hard it broke. Waylee called the cops and they brought an ambulance.

The doctor and nurses had been nice to her at the hospital and gave her ice cream but her mother took her home the same day. The cops had thrown Feng in lockup where he belonged, but a judge let him out the next day.

Her comlink buzzed.

`Gabriel: Doctor gone. I planned to see you but guard will not let me leave the room.`

Why text instead of video chat? He must not want the guard to overhear. Kiyoko's writing arm was disabled, so she tapped the voice to text icon and put the microphone to her lips, speaking quietly in English.

"Why not? We're on the same floor."

`Gabriel: Orders. That's all he would say.`
`Kiyoko: Well then I'll come visit you. I'd feel better if we were together.`

Gabriel: Me too. They moved patients to give us our
own rooms. I heard a nurse complain about it. I do not
even need a room, I am fine.
Kiyoko: Me too. Sort of. I thought the armor was supposed to protect us.
Gabriel: It did. Not perfect though, momentum gets
through, just not the bullet itself. But I was hit
seven times and only have bruises. And lost half an
ear.
Kiyoko: Can they fix it?
Gabriel: Doctor said I can schedule plastic surgery.
Brazil is #2 after USA in plastic surgery procedures.

Kiyoko sent a happy cat emoji, followed by a string of hearts.

"Why did the Piranhas attack us like that?" she whispered in her comlink microphone. "What was the point?"

Gabriel: I have been thinking about that. Revenge
probably, but possibly someone paid to kill us.
Kiyoko: Why?
Gabriel: To get us out of the way. Especially me.

And they were trapped in these rooms with no way to defend themselves. "We have to get out of here," she whispered.

Gabriel: Agree. I will call SSG.
Gabriel: Did you contact Charles and Pel?
Kiyoko: Yes, we chatted. I told them what happened today, but said we were fine, just minor injuries. Pel
said De Barros interviewed them yesterday. I told them
to be careful and he said the same thing.

Kiyoko heard the door open. Panicked, she whipped her head around.

Her friend Reiko entered, wearing a short flowery dress. "Yahho!"

Kiyoko exhaled and voiced a quick text to Gabriel. "Reiko's here. We'll
come over." She turned to her friend and spoke in Japanese. "Reiko, wonderful to see you." Reiko only understood a little English, and Kiyoko still
struggled with Portuguese. "Your dress is very cute."

Reiko nodded. "Thank you."

Kiyoko threw the starched bedsheet aside and slipped out of bed. Forced
to wear a hospital gown, she wasn't properly dressed for visitors, and with
an arm in a sling, changing would be a challenge.

Reiko waved a hand. "You don't need to get up. Are you fine?"

Kiyoko felt dizzy from the synthetic painkillers and sat back on the bed. She had already filled in her friend—it was in the news anyway that Pel and Charles had international arrest warrants and kidnappers had tried to cash in. "I won't be able to do much for a while. I have to wear this sling for four to six weeks. But I'm alive. It was pretty scary."

She plucked her carry bag from the bedside table and gave Reiko the apartment keys. Pel wouldn't approve, maybe not even Gabriel, but they would probably have to move anyway. "Please don't let anyone know you have my keys, and don't make copies."

"I won't."

"I sent all the instructions for Nyasuke to your Comnet account. Hopefully they'll release me tomorrow but the doctor said they had to observe me, and then the police said they needed me to stay put until they finished their investigation."

"I got the instructions. Nyasuke is such a cute cat. I love the vlog you keep for him."

"He is a sweetie. Best cat ever." They talked about cats for a while, then Kiyoko returned to crisis mode. "We might need to move."

"You think you might be attacked again?"

"This is twice now. Can you help me find a storage place? I can make costumes for anyone who helps move our stuff."

Reiko waved away the offer. "I'm happy to help however I can, and I'm sure the rest of the community is too. I can even help you find a secret new home."

"Thank you so much!"

"No problem! It's terrible someone would try to kill you."

"Can you help me change? I want to see how my boyfriend is doing."

Reiko asked a lot of gossipy questions, then talked about her own boyfriend, who was a game designer but had never fired a real gun.

Kiyoko examined her clothes as they talked. The blouse was tattered and bloody. Even the skirt was ruined beyond repair. She sighed and tossed them in the trash can.

"Come on," she told Reiko. "Let's go see Gabriel." She'd just wear the hospital gown until the doctor said she could go home.

The guard stood when she opened the door. "Onde vai?"

The translation program on her comlink displayed, *Where are you going?* Not that she needed simple phrases like that translated.

"I'm going down the hall to visit my boyfriend," she said in Portuguese.

The guard pointed into the room. "You must stay here for your protection."

"It's just down the hall."

He scowled. "You must stay. Don't make me lock you in."

"Why?"

"Orders. You must stay in your room until this situation is resolved."

He had a gun and even if he didn't, it would be foolish to challenge him. Kiyoko said goodbye to her friend and returned to her apparent prison.

* * *

Gabriel

Shirtless upper body covered with bruises and bandages, Gabriel sat on his hospital bed, data glasses projecting a keyboard onto his meal tray and recording his finger movements. First thing, contact SSG dispatch and ask for a lawyer.

Black-outlined white letters projected over his vision.

SSG-CC: After hours. Can you wait until tomorrow morning?

Gabriel summarized his situation and asked for an attorney to call him as soon as possible. Then he messaged Alzira and Nicolas.

Neither one was online. Alzira was probably with her fiancé and Nicolas with his latest conquest, whoever that happened to be.

Okay, time to research this De Barros bastard. SSG's search engine could access all the public records in Brazil and a lot that weren't public.

Olivier de Barros, São Paulo Polícia Civil. Age 48. Reached inspector quickly but hadn't advanced since. As a child, lived in Miami, Florida, USA while his father worked for an import-export firm. Married and divorced twice, children with both spouses, paying alimony and child support. Owned an apartment in Jardins, an upper-class region west of the city center, plus a house on the beach.

No way he could afford all that on a police salary. *Typical.*

The door opened. Gabriel shut off the keyboard projector.

A bulky mustached sergeant in the state military police entered, followed by two young soldiers. The sergeant pulled handcuffs off his white belt. "The doctor says you can be moved. They need the space."

Gabriel closed the Comnet portal and planted his feet on the floor. "What do you mean moved?"

"You're under arrest. Murder."

"What the hell? I need to make a call."

"Esquece isso! Forget it. Let's go."

Gabriel ignored the police sergeant and spoke into his data glasses. "DG, chame a SSG."

"Serviços de Segurança Globais," a woman's voice answered.

"Da Silva. I'm being arrested. I need that lawyer now. Emergency."

"That's enough." The sergeant approached with the handcuffs while the two recruits stood by, eyes darting as if they expected the worst.

Gabriel could probably take all three of them in a fight. But that would bring the whole weight of the law down on him. "DG lock." He put on his torn shirt and blood-stained blazer, folded his data glasses, and slipped them in the front pocket of his shirt.

The sergeant, his breath smelling of indeterminate street food, put on the cuffs. He patted Gabriel down and took his data glasses.

"I need those."

"You'll get them back if you're released. Let's go."

* * *

Kiyoko

After an awful dinner of lukewarm rice and beans, the door of Kiyoko's hospital room opened and Inspector de Barros entered. He wore data glasses, and was accompanied by a big man in his twenties with close-cropped hair, wearing jeans, a black T-shirt with "POLICIA" in vertical white letters, and a gear belt with handcuffs and a stun gun. Both men wore badges pinned to their shirts.

Kiyoko's fingers gripped her bedsheets. De Barros must have ordered their guards and separate rooms. Had he come to kill her? Hopefully that would be too hard to cover up.

"DG, grava," Inspector de Barros said. The record light on his data glasses turned red. "Good evening, Miss Pingyang."

She didn't respond. If he was working with the CIA, or whoever was behind Pel and Charles's kidnapping, was he planning to extradite her too?

"That's two gunfights now," he said. "Please tell me what happened today."

"I already made a statement to the officers at the scene."

"Yes, I watched it. But I would like to hear it myself."

She remembered Francis's advice when the FBI arrested her in Baltimore. Don't speak to anyone besides an attorney. "I would like to confer with a lawyer first."

Behind the data glasses, his eyes narrowed. "It is your duty to cooperate with an official investigation."

She remained silent.

"Very well. It is my duty to inform you that you are under arrest as an accomplice to murder."

Did he say murder? "What? What are you talking about?"

The T-shirt and jeans cop pulled the handcuffs from his belt and stared at Kiyoko's sling.

"We were attacked," Kiyoko told the detective. "We had to defend ourselves, we're lucky to be alive."

"Witnesses say that Sr. Gabriel fired first during Sunday's incident."

"They pulled guns on him, you heard that."

"There was no corroboration of that." He looked at the other cop and snapped his fingers.

The man said something in rapid Portuguese, including the phrase "is it necessary."

The inspector called him an idiot, and the flunkie cuffed Kiyoko's free wrist to the constrained one. It hurt despite the painkillers.

"Where is Gabriel?" she asked. "Can I see him?"

"He has already been arrested."

Hopefully his company would help him. "What are my rights?" She had no idea.

He grunted. "You have the right to counsel and so forth. But first you must come to the station for booking. And I will need your comlink."

The T-shirted cop frisked her and took her belongings, putting them in a clear plastic sack. At least he didn't grope her. But what would happen now? Her knees shook as her enemies escorted her out of the room.

21

Gabriel

Gabriel stood in a crowded preventive detention cell with thirteen other male prisoners, most of them young. It was hot and stank of body odor and shit from the clogged toilet in one corner. Three walls were concrete and the fourth steel bars with white paint flaking off. There were no cots or chairs.

Hopefully he wouldn't be here long. He'd gone through booking and SSG had sent a lawyer for his custodial interrogation, where he repeated his story for the fifth time. The lawyer, Eduardo Bicudo, whom he'd met at headquarters earlier, had promised to get him out on bail and get an expedited decision by the judge. "SSG can't allow the precedence of a body-guard punished for doing his job," Sr. Eduardo had confided.

A wiry light-skinned man in his twenties swaggered up to Gabriel and looked him up and down. "What's with the ear?"

It would be bandaged until he got a prosthetic, assuming he could navigate the health care and insurance systems. "What's it to you?"

The man sneered. "You look like an asshole, one big ear and one missing ear."

Gabriel had never been in a holding cell but knew all about the monkey dance, the status game that young men felt obliged to play. There was a lot of that growing up, although he was too scrawny and shy then.

If the man was serious, he would have thrown a punch instead of an insult. Gabriel thrust his shoulders back and stuck his face inches from the presumptive alpha, staring him in the eyes. "You're fucking with the wrong man."

The man blinked, glanced down, and backed up a step.

Gabriel stared at the others. They weren't armed, so worst case, he'd get more bruises. "I'm not in the mood for any shit. If you want a fucking fight, let's get it over with."

No one took him up on it. But he wondered if anyone in here was in As Piranhas, or if someone would pay a guard to kill him.

And what about Kiyoko? He had no way to contact her. Was she still in the hospital? Or had she been arrested too?

* * *

Kiyoko

Kiyoko's second arrest was worse than the first. For starters, she had no clothes, only an embarrassing polka-dotted hospital gown and pants. And at least in Baltimore, they spoke English. Inspector De Barros, the possible CIA liaison, disappeared and her booking was done entirely in Portuguese. They had her comlink so she couldn't translate.

"Por favor fale mais devagar," she repeated, along with "Não entendo." Her basic knowledge of Portuguese didn't include judicial procedures. "Quero um advogado," she asked several times.

They didn't bring her a lawyer. Instead, a pair of policemen threw her in a stinky cell with no beds and a single shared toilet. The police didn't return her purse or comlink but let her keep her plastic bag with her antibiotics, bottle of painkillers, and fresh bandages.

The eight other prisoners eyed her like she was fresh meat.

"Ola," she said. "Chamo-me Kiyoko."

Their looks were far from friendly. One of the women, twice Kiyoko's age, snatched her plastic bag.

"Give that back! I need that!" With one arm in a sling, Kiyoko couldn't fight back.

Half the prisoners converged on the plastic bag and argued in rapid Portuguese. They split up her pills and even kept the bandages.

"Doente sem as pills." She didn't know the word for pills, or how to conjugate the future tense of "sick."

The women laughed.

She pointed at her bandaged arm and pleaded for some of the antibiotics at least. "Preciso dos antibióticos. Por favor? Alguns?"

The woman who took her bag glared at her, then looked at the others and snapped her fingers. "Dê-lhe alguns comprimidos."

They gave half her antibiotics back. Hopefully that was enough to stave off infection, which used to be the most common cause of death from battle injuries.

Kiyoko settled in a corner and prayed in whispers. *Bast, Tara, Wong Tai Sin, by your power, protect me and Gabriel from harm, and heal our injuries.*

* * *

Gabriel

"Da Silva!" A voice from outside the cell woke Gabriel. During his eight years in the special forces, he'd learned to sleep anywhere, but his back ached from leaning against the concrete, and his chest bruises and shredded ear felt worse. No painkillers, not even aspirin.

A guard unlocked the door, two others behind him holding batons. "Lawyer's here," the guard said.

They cuffed him and led him down the hall, past other crowded cells, through a pair of gates with electronic locks, and into a concrete-walled meeting room. Dressed in a dark pinstripe suit, the SSG lawyer, Sr. Eduardo, rose from a small table and shook Gabriel's hand. After the guards left, Sr. Eduardo motioned to the chair on the opposite side of the table.

Gabriel sat, still in handcuffs. "This is a pile of shit."

Sr. Eduardo nodded. "Of course it is. But I'm confident we'll beat all the charges. The evidence is incontrovertible that you acted merely to defend yourself and your clients. This is just an inconvenience, and like I said before, SSG is committed to squashing any charges against its employees in the reasonable conduct of their duties."

"Where's Kiyoko?" Gabriel asked.

"You mean your client, Kiyoko Pingyang? Former client, I should say?"

"Yes, that's her."

"I don't know. But if you want I'll look into it after your custody hearing."

The hearing room was in the same building as the holding cells, but was decorated like a regular courtroom, minus the jury box and spectator seats. A stern-looking judge stared at a bank of computer screens atop a raised desk. A youngish man from the Ministry of Public Prosecution sat at a small table to the right, typing on a data pad. They looked up as Gabriel and Sr. Eduardo entered.

Six charges of murder were about as serious as it got. But Sr. Eduardo said his client was a national hero, citing his service in the Special Forces and all the lives he'd saved over the years. In contrast, the people he shot were scum with long records and initiated the shooting. Gabriel was just trying to stay alive and protect his clients.

The judge agreed, saying Gabriel didn't need to be detained. But he had to post bail, stay in São Paulo until the trial, and wear a tracking bracelet.

"I shouldn't have to wear such a thing," Gabriel told Sr. Eduardo.

Sr. Eduardo relayed the complaint to the judge.

The judge frowned. "It's that or a holding cell."

While Sr. Eduardo stayed behind to pay the bail, a pair of guards escorted Gabriel back to the cell block. A middle-aged technician fastened a black GPS monitor to his ankle and activated it. "If you leave the city limits," he said, "it will let us know, and will also make a very loud siren noise. If you take it off, it will do the same thing."

The guards led Gabriel through a black steel door into a lobby. It was a big open space full of plastic chairs, most of them occupied by bored or anxious visitors, and a reception desk behind bulletproof Plexiglas.

The guards uncuffed him and left without speaking. Sr. Eduardo strode toward him. With him were five SSG soldiers in fatigues. Comrades, brothers in arms. They greeted him with handshakes, hugs, and shoulder pats.

"You look like shit," a bulky soldier named Matheus said.

Gabriel's shirt was ripped and his jeans torn and spattered with blood. And instead of a right ear, a bandage was taped to his head. "You always look like shit," he managed.

Matheus laughed and drew back a fist, pointing it toward his arm, then put it down, perhaps realizing even a play tap might hurt.

"Let's get your things," Sr. Eduardo said, and led him to the reception desk to fill out a litany of electronic forms on a data pad.

They didn't return his weapons or armor, only his wallet, keys and data glasses. His guns and ruined armor had been entered as evidence. He put on the data glasses, unlocked them, and checked his messages. He had a top priority text from Kiyoko, sent yesterday: De Barros arresting me. Need lawyer.

"We have to find Kiyoko," he told Sr. Eduardo, feeling anxious. "She's been arrested too."

"I understand she and her friends are not SSG clients anymore."

"Not at the moment, but we should still help. Moreover, without her, the Piranha scum would have killed me in the cafe. She is very brave."

One of the soldiers, a wiry man named Oscar, smirked. "Are you banging her?"

He was, but he wouldn't turn his girlfriend into gossip material. He kept at the lawyer, wishing he had Kiyoko's gift for words. "She is probably being held here too, if there's a women's wing. Are you going to help?"

Sr. Eduardo sighed. "I'll look into it. Let's get you home, though."

Gabriel didn't know him well enough to trust that he'd follow through. "I'll go with you."

The lawyer asked the balding duty officer about Kiyoko. He looked on a computer screen, then said, "Yes, she's here."

"Can we see her?" Gabriel asked.

The reception officer raised an eyebrow. "That is impossible."

"I'm representing her," Sr. Eduardo said. "When can I see my client?"

The receptionist passed him a data pad and had him fill out a visitation request.

"You promise you will get Kiyoko out?" Gabriel asked Sr. Eduardo on the way out, sunshine just a few steps away.

"She didn't break any laws. I expect a quick dismissal." He stopped just short of the glass door. "Unless for some reason they decide to deport her."

22

Waylee

Waylee's guards removed her shackles before escorting her into the courtroom for the first day of the trial. She wore a white high-necked blouse and a dark blue skirt suit that Ms. Jones's computer had picked out. She'd showered and brushed her hair, even put on lipstick, and felt almost like a normal person.

The courtroom was brightly lit, with royal blue carpeting and right-angled walnut furnishings. Every seat except the audience benches had an adjustable computer screen. The air was as chilly as her cell and smelled like wood polish and carpet cleaner.

The guards escorted her to a wooden table with an olive-hued plastic mat on top, behind which sat her public defender, Ms. Martin, and her assistant, Ms. Jones. They glanced up from their laptops, which had curved screens and thin plastic carapaces that wrapped around the sides. The prosecution team's laptops were identically cloaked.

Waylee spotted some familiar faces in the audience, like Ms. Van Hofwegen and some of her FBI interviewers. The jury seats were empty.

Ms. Martin pulled out an empty swivel chair to her left. "Please, sit."

Waylee sat in the faux-leather chair. One of the guards stood just past the table and the other remained by the door, along with a third guard. Raised against the opposite wall, an unsmiling man with more wrinkles than hair stared at a computer monitor. Judge Mahler, dressed in a black robe as if he were Death.

"We're doing opening statements this morning," Ms. Martin said. "There will be a break, then the prosecution will bring forth their first witness."

"Who's that?" Waylee asked. Ms. Martin wasn't very good at keeping her informed.

"Caleb Mercer. A guard at the MediaCorp broadcast center."

Mercer was the bald guy manning the gate when they entered. Dingo and M-pat, who'd been disguised as MediaCorp guards, had thrown him quite a beating on the way out. Unfortunate, but otherwise they'd all be in prison, not just her.

Judge Mahler looked up from his computer monitor. "Welcome to everyone that's here. We are here to commence the trial of the United States of America versus Waylee Freid. Is the prosecution ready to proceed?"

The prosecutor, Assistant U.S. Attorney Todd Lachlan, got up from his crowded table on the other side of the room. "Yes." Lachlan was somewhere between Ms. Martin and Judge Mahler in age, but athletic looking, with luxuriant black hair and broad shoulders.

"Is the defense ready to proceed?" the judge asked.

Ms. Martin stood. "Yes."

A court officer brought in the jurors and administered an oath, then the judge read a long statement from his computer screen about how the trial would work. Waylee barely heard his words as she fought creeping waves of fear. The wrath of the entire federal government was focused on her.

"We'll hear first from Mr. Lachlan on behalf of the United States," the judge finished.

The dark-haired, blue-suited prosecutor rose and nodded at the judge. "Good morning, your honor." His tone was relaxed and confident.

He strode to the jury box. "Good morning, ladies and gentlemen of the jury. Thank you for your service. On Sunday, February 4, Waylee Freid, born Emily Smith, led a vicious and deliberate attack on the facilities broadcasting the Super Bowl. In the process, she and her accomplices injured twelve people, some of them severely, damaged the facility's computer infrastructure to a point that took it days to repair it, and disrupted a broadcast that tens of millions of people were watching. Her purpose? To broadcast illegally obtained information that she twisted into a series of falsehoods to smear the President of the United States in hopes of embarrassing him and driving him from office. All so she could advance a radical leftist agenda—nothing less than the destruction of our way of life."

Waylee nearly jumped from her seat to challenge the man's lies, but her lawyer gripped her arm. "Don't do anything, don't say anything," she whispered through gritted teeth. "This isn't the time."

The prosecutor spent over an hour summarizing her leadership role in harboring a fugitive hacker, infiltrating the presidential fundraiser, committing unprecedented computer crimes, and breaking into the Media-Corp broadcast center. He omitted the fact that snipers on Homeland helicopters shot out her tires and almost killed her when her car crashed. He spent another half hour painting her as a radical leftist whose boyfriend belonged to the "notorious cyberterrorist group called the Collective," and said she harbored a deep hatred of Media Corporation and the president.

He concluded with a long list of charges. "The people will prove these charges beyond a reasonable doubt. The evidence is overwhelming. The only verdict you can return is guilty." In a quieter voice, he added, "Thank you for your time."

"Thank you, Mr. Lachlan," the judge said as the prosecutor returned to his seat. "Ms. Martin?"

Waylee's lawyer rose and approached the jury with fidgeting hands. "Members of the jury. Mr. Lachlan makes a lot of bold claims. But the question is, can he prove them? He told you a story about a group of people that snuck into a fundraiser, entered Media Corporation's complex in Virginia, and broadcast a video during the Super Bowl. But can he prove that Ms. Freid, who by the way has no criminal record whatsoever, participated in these actions, much less organized and led them? No, he can't."

Waylee had considered inventing a story, but decided against it. She hated lying, and wouldn't be painted as a liar.

"Remember," Ms. Martin continued, "those accused of crimes are innocent until *proven* guilty. We are only considering Ms. Freid's guilt, no one else's, and as you will see, the prosecution lacks the needed evidence."

They couldn't deny all the evidence. Charles had stayed in Waylee's house and fled from police with her. Waylee had been caught with the Tania Peart mask, with which she entered the broadcast building and its server control room. And the prosecution had DNA evidence that she had worn it.

On the other hand, the prosecution overreached by portraying her as the group leader. They made their decisions collectively. Waylee came up with a lot of ideas—that's the way she was, especially when hypomanic – but she never coerced anyone.

"Yes, Charles Lee stayed in the house that Ms. Freid lived in," her lawyer continued. "But is there any proof Ms. Freid knew he was a fugitive? And yes, she entered MediaCorp's broadcast center in Virginia. But she didn't open any locks, didn't hurt anyone, didn't damage anything, and didn't tamper with any of the computer systems. There is no proof she was involved in any of the computer crimes alleged by the prosecution. She doesn't even have the necessary skills."

Ms. Martin didn't mention the presidential fundraiser. If necessary, they could admit she attended but as a journalist. All she did was record conversations that she participated in, which was perfectly legal.

"The only just and lawful verdict you can return," Ms. Martin concluded, "is not guilty."

* * *

Kiyoko

'PINGYANG, KIYOKO' appeared on the screen over the door terminating the long white hallway.

"It's your turn," the lawyer told Kiyoko.

Well duh. She was next in line and her name was on the screen in big letters. She chose not to antagonize her lawyer, though. A graying man in a dark pinstripe suit named Eduardo Bicudo, he worked for SSG. Sent by Gabriel, her archangel.

The uniformed young guard removed her handcuffs, relieving some of the pressure from her aching, sling-confined right arm. He prodded her forward with a hand on the back of her now-filthy hospital gown. Sr. Eduardo trailed.

They entered a small courtroom with faux-mahogany paneling. At least she was out of that foul-smelling jail cell and its rotating crowd of unfriendly prisoners. And if this detention hearing went well, she'd be out for good, either on bail or her own recognizance. If not—best not to think about it.

To her right as she entered, a balding man with glasses in a dark gray suit sat behind a raised curved desk with computer screens and a touchpad. Ahead, a dark-haired man stared at a data pad on a small table. Her guard didn't follow them in, but another one stood by the entryway door. He was wearing a holstered pistol.

Kiyoko followed Sr. Eduardo past the balding man and dark-haired man to a table with three padded chairs. Her chair creaked as she sat.

What were Brazilian courts like? This was her first time in any courtroom at all. Her heart thumped like it was trying to escape. Could anyone else hear it?

Sr. Eduardo pulled his data pad out of an inner jacket pocket and stretched it to maximum size. He leaned toward Kiyoko and spoke quietly. "I will argue for your immediate release. This is not the old days where you could be detained indefinitely and tortured."

Torture? It could be worse? "This whole thing is ridiculous," Kiyoko said. "I'm the victim, not the perpetrator."

The judge said good day and something about beginning and Kiyoko Pingyang. He didn't bang a gavel or anything. Behind his glasses, his eyes were half-lidded with boredom.

The man at the small desk pulled a curved microphone toward his mouth and spoke Portuguese into it. Kiyoko was too tired to translate. *Too bad I don't have my comlink.*

"That is the public prosecutor," Sr. Eduardo whispered in English. "He is summarizing the case against you. He is prosecuting Sr. Gabriel's case too."

"Is this the same judge who heard Gabriel's case?" Kiyoko whispered back.

"No, different. It is like a lottery."

When the prosecutor finished, the judge pushed a small box to the edge of his raised desk and turned it, revealing it to be a speaker.

The judge said something in Portuguese and the speaker translated in American-accented English. "Miss Pingyang, I understand you are an American and do not speak much Portuguese?" The voice sounded as human as BetterWorld simulations, but in an even cadence and unemotional tones.

"It's your turn," Sr. Eduardo told her, and pushed a microphone to her. "You can answer in English and the judge's and prosecutor's computers will translate."

"I speak some Portuguese," Kiyoko spoke into the microphone. "But not technical stuff, and I'm very tired." Her eyes burned from the lack of sleep. "And I am an American citizen, yes, but I am a legal resident of Brazil."

"Yes," the judge's translated voice responded. "You were granted residency status under conditions of political asylum?"

"Exactly."

"Now first I am required to inquire about your condition and how you were treated during your detainment."

"Very poorly."

The judge's eyebrows raised.

She had the initiative. "First, I shouldn't have been arrested at all, since I didn't do anything illegal. Second, I was pulled out of a hospital while being treated for gunshot wounds and then my medicine was taken from me. If not for my lawyer, I would have run out of antibiotics, and I had no painkillers. I couldn't sleep, the pain got so bad."

Bad was an understatement—it had been more excruciating than anything she'd felt in her life, and the guards and other prisoners had ignored her pleas for help. Thank the gods for Sr. Eduardo bringing ibuprofen, which had reduced the pain to a more tolerable level.

"Not that there was any place to sleep anyway," Kiyoko continued. "And I haven't been able to change my bandages." They oozed red and were probably full of hungry bacteria.

Sr. Eduardo leaned into the microphone and spoke in English, presumably for her benefit. "Miss Pingyang was held in detention longer than the legal maximum of 24 hours before disposition."

"I apologize for that," the judge said. "But the hearing was arranged as rapidly as possible."

"Her treatment was outrageous," Sr. Eduardo said. "The state owes her an apology and should return her to medical care."

The judge sighed. "Do you have all the medicine you require now?"

"Yes," Kiyoko responded.

"You are charged as an accomplice to six counts of murder. These are very serious charges."

"And unfounded," she said.

"Please do not interrupt. Now this hearing is not about the likelihood of your guilt regarding the charges. We are only here in regards to your detention, and whether or not you should be released until trial. First, the crimes are serious. And because you are a foreign national, there is a high flight risk." He paused.

"São Paulo is my home," Kiyoko said. "And I don't have a passport. Brazil granted me asylum, so why would I leave?"

He nodded. "Do you have anything else to say?"

"Look at me. Do I look like a danger to society?" She looked pathetic in her dirty hospital gown, unkempt hair, and sling. "Please do what's right and let me recover from the unprovoked attack that almost killed me."

Her lawyer spoke quietly in her ear. "Please let me take it from here."

That sounded reasonable. Brazilian law was his specialty, not hers. She nodded.

"I will argue for your release on medical grounds," he told her. "Further, there is no evidence you can disturb, you are not a flight risk, and you are not a threat to the public order."

He slid the microphone over and spoke at length in Portuguese. Then he answered questions from the judge.

At the end the judge nodded. Translated through the speaker, he said, "This court finds that Miss Pingyang will be released on her own recognizance until the time of her trial. Given her financial situation, no bail is required. However, she must sleep at her address in São Paulo each night and wear a tracking bracelet, which will be installed immediately following the conclusion of this hearing."

Not good, but far better than jail.

* * *

Gabriel

Showered and wearing fresh clothes, Gabriel returned to the detention center and waited for Kiyoko. If they let him out until the trial, they'd let her out.

Sr. Eduardo joined him. "She's on her way out. Didn't even have to post bail."

Gabriel hugged the lawyer, aggravating his sore chest in the process. Half an hour later, the metal door to the jail wing opened and Kiyoko entered the lobby, feet dragging, eyes red and puffy, clad in a dirty hospital gown and pants. Her right arm was in a sling and she clutched a plastic bag with her left hand.

Their eyes locked. She brightened and ran to him. With her sling they couldn't really embrace. But they kissed for a long time.

Sr. Eduardo coughed. "I bill by the hour you know."

Gabriel looked at him. "Let's get out of here then."

"Thank you so much for getting me out of jail," Kiyoko said as they retrieved her things.

"You shouldn't have been locked up in the first place," Gabriel said.

She lifted her right pants leg, revealing a tracking bracelet around her ankle. "They put this thing on. And told me not to leave the city."

He lifted his pants leg. "I have one too. They seem to be waterproof. And if you take them off it notifies the police."

"Yeah, they told me that. So what happens now?"

"It's all bullshit. Sr. Eduardo will take care of it. Let's go home."

* * *

In case the Piranhas or anyone else fucked with them again, SSG left Gabriel and Kiyoko more weapons and armor, and fixed the doors and surveillance system. The judge didn't say anything against re-arming, and it was Gabriel's profession, after all.

"We should find the attackers who got away," he asked Nicolas Pistario, who had come along with the techs. "Can't rely on the police to catch them."

According to the crime blogs, São Paulo police only had a 10% clearance rate.

Nicolas nodded. "We can do better than that. We'll shut the whole gang down. An attack on one of us is an attack on all. We'll make sure they never bother anyone again."

Gabriel checked his new guns, same type he usually used, a Glock semi-auto and an Auratus needlegun. He synced them to his data glasses and ran the diagnostics program. "When do we start?"

Nicolas looked him up and down with raised eyebrows. "You need to rest, you look terrible. More important, you have that tracking bracelet. Come on, we can't have you along."

23

Kiyoko

Pain woke Kiyoko early the next morning. At least she was in her own bed, with her champion beside her.

Sidestepping the clothes and cat toys on the floor of her wardrobe-lined bedroom, she trudged naked to the bathroom and popped a codeine pill in her mouth. Ibuprofen hadn't been strong enough, and the stuff they gave her at the hospital was too strong.

Gabriel, also naked, was sitting up when she returned. "How are you feeling?" he asked.

She snuggled against him on the bed. "Like I've been in battle and lost most of my hit points."

He kissed her. "You were in battle. And you did quite well."

She remembered something. "Today's my birthday. I'm twenty now. Can you believe it? I was gonna plan this big party but after the kidnapping I forgot all about it."

Gabriel kissed her again. "Happy birthday. You should have told me. If I'd known, I would have bought a present."

She ran a hand down his shoulder and bicep. "I have a naked hunk in my bed who can fight off gangs of armed criminals. What more could I want?"

Nyasuke jumped onto the bed and meowed. Kiyoko shooed him out of the room. "We have human business to attend to."

Gabriel grinned when she returned to the bed. "Your cat is jealous, I think."

"He likes you, actually. He can sense you're good for me." She paused. "I do have a birthday wish, but it's not something we can fulfill by ourselves. We'll need the help of the gods."

"What is it? I will grant you anything you desire. Within reason, of course."

Adoration gave way to guilt for all the trouble she'd caused him, and might continue to cause. "I desire safety for Charles and Pel, and freedom for Waylee." *And an end to MediaCorp's tyranny, but one thing at a time.*

"Charles and Pel are safe on the base," Gabriel said.

"I hope so."

"As for your sister, you are doing everything you can."

"Which so far is practically nothing."

Gabriel rubbed her shoulder. "Let me know if there's anything I can do. But I will also get you a present."

Kiyoko lay back against the fluffy pillows. The codeine was starting to kick in and her head felt warm and fuzzy. "If you want to give me a nice present now, you can make me feel super good."

After another amazing round in bed, Gabriel made breakfast. Toasted French bread, cheese, and coffee—nothing elaborate—but it was still the best breakfast ever.

Kiyoko wanted him again afterward, but it would have to wait. Still a little high, she went into her VR room and donned her immersion helmet and gloves. It would be a while before she could wear the rest of the suit.

First thing was to search for news about her sister. No messages from Francis Jones, which meant he was still being held incommunicado. She ran her news trawler for 'Waylee Freid.'

The leading hit was a video link titled "Waylee Freid trial begins." From MediaCorp, of course. A news broadcast from yesterday.

"I'm standing outside the Lewis F. Powell courthouse in Richmond, Virginia," a handsome man of indeterminate age said. He recapped the charges, painting Waylee as a public menace. "No cameras are permitted in the courtroom," he said then, "and the prosecutor isn't saying much."

The video ended without providing any useful information. Nothing from Waylee's defense. Kiyoko ran more searches, but couldn't even find her new lawyer's name. Probably a public defender. *May Waylee be cleared of all charges,* she prayed.

She then logged onto the Crypt-O-Chat room and sent Charles and Pel a chat invite. She set the helmet to transcribe voice, which was a lot quicker than typing.

Princess_Kiyoko: Are you there, shonen-tachi?

The response took a couple of minutes.

Godwin: ?

Pel and Charles didn't have a voice transcriber, most likely.

Princess_Kiyoko: How are you doing?
Godwin: C moping. We both say happy birthday tho.
Princess_Kiyoko: You remembered! :) ♥♥♥
Godwin: Of course. And without a comlink reminder.
We'll celebrate when we're together again.

Kiyoko sent an animated dancing cat.
Godwin: You're in a good mood. How is W?
Princess_Kiyoko: I don't know but she's strong and
she's in the right.

Hopefully her antidepressants are helping.
Godwin: Both true.
Princess_Kiyoko: Tell Charles I'm sorry about Adri-
anna.

She opened her image library and swiped over a hugs emoji, a kitten
with outstretched paws surrounded by hearts. It wasn't much but it was the
best she could do at the moment.
Godwin: C says someone has to pay.

Kiyoko agreed but didn't respond.
Godwin: At first I thought she wasn't worth the grief
but she was his first and death is hard.
Princess_Kiyoko: You guys have had it tough. I should
have been nicer to you and promise I will be from now
on.
Godwin: Not sure what you're talking about but not important.
Godwin: C wants to know who killed A.
Princess_Kiyoko: Are you sure the chat's secure?
Godwin: Double Ratchet-based encryption protocol that
combines a forward-secure ratchet with a zero round-
trip authenticated 4096-bit key exchange. Unbreakable
even by quantum computers.

Kiyoko replied with a confused cat emoji, then told Pel everything she
knew about As Piranhas, Inspector De Barros, and his apparent ties to a
CIA agent that went by the name John Hill. She closed with the attack at
the cafe, how she and Gabriel were arrested and jailed, and were awaiting
trial with tracking bracelets on.
Godwin: De Barros interviewed us. He said he'd try to
get us back home but we're still stuck at AFB. AF offi-

cer told us we have to stay put until they get orders
to contrary.
Princess_Kiyoko: Gabriel says Brazil's the most bureaucratic country on Earth. But we think you're safer
at Campo de Marte. Don't trust De Barros. Don't go
anywhere with him.
Godwin: Yes you told us before.
Princess_Kiyoko: You're a tech genius. Do you know how
we can get these tracking bracelets off without the
police knowing?
Godwin: Never tried. No idea. But I can look into it.
You should look too. The darknet is your friend.

Pel was being snippy but she couldn't blame him. People were after him.
And he wasn't getting laid while high on codeine.

Princess_Kiyoko: Gabriel and I are working to expose
De Barros and Hill to get them off our backs.
Godwin: Good, let us know how we can help.
Princess_Kiyoko: Stay put & stay safe, that's how.
We'll find friendly police and gather evidence against
De Barros. We'll see how he likes being arrested.
Godwin: Friendly police? LOL. But go ahead and try.

✳ ✳ ✳

Pelopidas

Pel was researching border crossings into Argentina, in case they had to
flee Brazil, when someone knocked at the door. He logged out of Crypt-O-
Chat, which deleted his conversation with Kiyoko, powered off the TV, and
hid his makeshift antenna behind it.

More knocking at the door.

"Yeah?"

The door opened. Two men in camouflage Air Force fatigues with holstered pistols stood there. No name tags or rank insignia.

"You must come," the shorter of the two said, his heavily accented voice
firm.

"To where?"

Short Guard said something in Portuguese, then "Come, please."

Charles was already in the hall with two other guards. "What's going on?" he asked Pel.

"English anyone?" Pel asked. "Inglês? Where are we going? Onde vamos?"

Short Guard frowned and put a hand on his holster.

Not good.

One of the guards led them down the hall, Short Guard between Pel and Charles, and two more took the rear. They exited the officer's quarters, walked through a parking lot and down a tree-lined road, and approached a white concrete wall with a guard station.

Were they being released? Or transferred? "What about our stuff?" Pel asked Short Guard. Not that they had anything other than the clothes and toiletries the Air Force gave them.

No answer.

At least three state police cars sat on the other side of the guard station, white SUVs with zig-zagging red, grey, and black bands on the side. Gray-uniformed men stood in front. And Inspector De Barros.

Fuck. "Run, Charles!" Pel bolted.

Behind him, men shouted in Portuguese. "Pare! Pare!"

They wouldn't shoot him, would they? Pel ran into a grassy area with scattered trees. He wasn't sure where to go, just to put as much distance as possible between himself and Inspector De Barros.

Someone crashed against him from behind and knocked him to the ground, forcing the air out of his lungs. More men piled on, grabbing his arms and pinning them behind his back.

With angry shouts, they kept him there, face pressed into the grass, then someone snapped handcuffs onto his wrists.

* * *

Dalton

Seeker111—Martinez—messaged Dalton.

SharkFeed999: Info you need to know.

Dalton logged onto their current chat channel and sent an encrypted message:

Here. Waiting.

Martinez responded a few seconds later.

Seeker111: We've been monitoring De Barros per your request.

Dalton didn't trust the fat detective, and he remembered Petrov didn't, either.

```
SharkFeed999: And?
Seeker111: He initiated contact with MediaCorp Secu-
rity and has been exchanging messages. Some of the
messages have a size typical of video. The messages
are encrypted, with too many bits to crack. He has
also exchanged messages with avatars of U.S. Homeland
Security agents. Also encrypted, no reasonable chance
of breaking.
```

Son of a bitch.

```
SharkFeed999: How many messages? When did he send
them?
Seeker111: I will send you a log file.
SharkFeed999: Where does De Barros live?
Seeker111: Hold on.
```

After a while, Dalton received an address and coordinates in the Jardim Paulista neighborhood.

It was only a few blocks from the Hotel Tiberio. No wonder he knew the neighborhood so well. Yet he never said anything about it, as if he didn't want Dalton to know where he lived.

Prudent. I wouldn't want me to know where I lived either.

Dalton normally communicated with De Barros via encrypted Comnet messages or chat, usually voice. He called De Barros as soon as he ended the chat with Martinez.

No answer. He left a message to call back ASAP.

Next he called the Air Force base at Campo de Marte, speaking through a real-time translator and voice modulator. "This is Kevin Brock. I'm with Interpol. I'm calling about two prisoners you're holding, Pelopidas Demopoulos and Charles Lee."

After several transfers, a man told him, "They're not here. State police picked them up."

Dalton was too angry to thank the man before hanging up. He left another message with De Barros, then contacted Martinez again. It was news to the rest of Ares too.

De Barros would pay for his treachery.

24

Waylee

The prosecution brought forth witness after witness. A middle-aged Homeland Security technician displayed pictures on the computer screens on the wall and in front of every seat. First Waylee and Pel, then Waylee as Estelle Cosimo and Pel as Greg Wilson, then pictures of the real Estelle and Greg. "You can see that despite the makeup, hair dye, and contact lenses, that this is Waylee Freid, not Estelle Cosimo. Analytics confirm this."

The technician then displayed a voice analysis, and spent a good hour going over arcane statistical procedures and data. "We can conclude from the data that there is a 99.9% probability that Waylee Freid entered this fundraiser disguised as Estelle Cosimo."

Waylee's lawyer tried to cast doubt on the analysis, but the technician didn't budge. Well coached, Waylee thought, like all the witnesses.

* * *

Kiyoko

Abandoning the codeine for less effective but less impairing ibuprofen, Kiyoko returned to Miranda Rossi's office at the Ministry of Foreign Affairs. Gabriel joined her. Ms. Rossi, or more properly, Sra. Miranda, had given her an emergency appointment when Kiyoko told her the CIA was trying to kidnap or kill them.

"I'm sorry about your difficulties," the puffy middle-aged bureau chief said in English.

"Obrigado." Kiyoko told Sra. Miranda about the kidnapping and assassination attempts, about Inspector De Barros, his dubious wealth, and his connection to an American agent. Gabriel added a few details.

"They're still after us," Kiyoko said. She wasn't sure this was true, but it was likely. "Can Inspector De Barros be removed from office?"

"I will inform the federal police and request an investigation," the woman said. "Will you be available to speak with them directly?"

"Yes, of course. And can you guarantee we won't be extradited?"

Sra. Miranda leaned back. "The National Committee for Refugees approved your admission. You have papers of asylum and residency. You should be safe from a legal perspective. Only the president, through the Ministry of Foreign Affairs, can approve an extradition request, and is unlikely to reverse her original decision."

"Is there a way we can get citizenship sooner? Like right away?" That would make extradition nearly impossible. And in Brazil, they wouldn't have to renounce their U.S. citizenship.

"You applied just two months ago. You must live in Brazil at least four years, be fluent in Portuguese, and have a stable job."

As they exited the building, Kiyoko asked Gabriel, "Do you think we're safe now?"

He blinked. "The government is a many-headed snail. I don't think Sra. Miranda will trick you, but it is always good to have backup plans."

She stopped and grabbed one of his hands with her free left hand. "What if we get married?"

He blinked, then smiled. "I thought the man was supposed to propose marriage."

"No, I'm serious. And maybe we can find wives for Pel and Charles. It worked for our friend Dingo, he married his girlfriend Shakti who's Guyanese, and they gave him some sort of provisional citizenship right away."

Hard to believe she referred to Dingo as a friend, the way they used to fight. But Waylee's operation against MediaCorp brought everyone together.

"So you just want to use me to stay in the country?"

She squeezed his hand and kissed him. "Of course not. If I could marry anyone in the whole world it would be you. This is just fate speeding things up."

He sighed. "Let me be honest, Kiyoko. I do love you."

Oh no. "But?"

"But it is a serious decision. If we marry, we will have to have children and devote ourselves to them. My mother will be very happy about that, but are you prepared for such a thing?"

That hadn't occurred to her. "It wouldn't have to be right away, would it?"

"That tells me you are not serious."

WRATH OF LEVIATHAN ◆ 227

With all their other problems, this was too much. "Just forget it," she said. "Forget I mentioned it."

* * *

Gabriel

Gabriel and Kiyoko returned to her apartment. She kissed him as soon as they entered. "We shouldn't fight. I need you. And I love you more than I've ever loved anyone."

He gripped her waist and his mouth pressed against hers. Kiyoko unfastened her sling and then they were all over each other, removing each other's clothes, only bandages remaining. She leaned naked against the entryway wall, perfect legs spread for him, her injured arm held aside. A beautiful angel with a broken wing. "Te quero, meu amado!" she beckoned.

After they finished, they moved to the couch and laid together, limbs entwined. "We could marry," he suggested, "and not have children right away. Many couples do that. And of course there must be no danger from killers."

She squeezed him, then yelped.

His muscles tightened. "What's wrong?"

"My arm. I keep aggravating it."

He relaxed a little. "You should put the sling back on."

"And nothing else? Would that be sexy?"

He met her lovely eyes. "On you, yes."

She kissed him, her lips warm and moist. "So you do want to marry me?" she asked. "Yes, I would love to have kids with you, but you'd have to give me some time. I can't even think about it now."

A negotiation. Frankly, he wasn't ready for children either. Maybe when he was promoted and not working in the field. On the other hand, he was pushing thirty already. If they waited another decade, he might be too frail to play football with them.

"Five years maximum," he said.

Her smile vanished. "That's not the kind of thing you can dictate to me."

"Forget I said a number. We both agreed to marry, we can work everything out later. As long as you promise to take this seriously."

"Of course I do." She ran a hand over his chest. "I can't believe I'm getting married. It never, ever crossed my mind before. But I want to be with you forever."

They kissed again and soon she was on top of him.

Eventually they dressed and contacted the SSG lawyer, Sr. Eduardo. His serious-looking face appeared on a window in the big living room wall screen. He was at his office desk in the SSG headquarters at Congonhas Airport, shelves of law books behind him.

"Any word on our cases?" Gabriel asked.

"No, it's too soon. I'll let you know when I need anything." He leaned forward as if to end the chat.

"I have a question," Gabriel said.

Sr. Eduardo leaned back. "Yes?"

"Kiyoko is concerned she and her friends will be deported." He summarized what they knew about Inspector De Barros and his possible ties to the CIA, but also Sra. Miranda's assurances that their asylum papers should protect them.

Kiyoko leaned against his side, looking into the camera. "I wanted to know if you could help me get citizenship. Gabriel and I have proposed marriage. What's the procedure from there?"

Sr. Eduardo blinked. "First, congratulations."

"Thank you," she said.

Gabriel's eyes locked with hers and his heart fluttered out of control. "I would never meet someone as perfect as Kiyoko if I searched the world for a thousand years."

Kiyoko squeezed his hand. "You are so sweet."

Sr. Eduardo typed on a keyboard and looked at something on his screen. "This is not my specialty. But the government will want proof you're in a real relationship, not just using a loophole. Are you cohabiting, for example."

"We're sharing a bed," Gabriel said. "How's that?"

Beside him, Kiyoko blushed.

Sr. Eduardo came close to smiling. "That's certainly a good start. You should file as soon as possible. I'll send you a link." He looked at his screen again. "Be advised it takes a year or two after that to be naturalized. And it doesn't make you immune to crimes committed before citizenship."

"They don't have anything on me," Kiyoko said. "Just that the FBI told me to stay in Baltimore and I left."

"And what about Sr. Charles and Sr. Pelopidas?"

"Uh . . . well they're on the most wanted list, but it's political. They didn't hurt anyone, just the price of MediaCorp stock and the president's re-election campaign."

Sr. Eduardo sighed. "Mitigating circumstances won't erase legal charges." He typed on his keyboard again. "But you're in luck, Brazil does not normally extradite to the U.S. since their punishments tend to be overly harsh. Including the death penalty. And we canceled our extradition treaty with the U.S. two years ago. Part of our declining relations since your President Rand was elected and fancied himself leader of the whole world."

Gabriel nodded. "He's an arrogant son of a whore."

"He's not the leader," Kiyoko said. "Luxmore pulls the strings."

"Regardless," Sr. Eduardo said, "the Brazilian president and Supreme Federal Tribunal have to approve an extradition. On paper, anyway. There are loopholes, and if an Interpol warrant is served for pre-asylum crimes, a willing judge might be able to overturn the asylum and transfer custody. Especially if they've been designated terrorists, as your friends were."

"That's ridiculous! Pel and Charles never hurt anyone!"

Sr. Eduardo ignored her. "It is a gray area and there isn't much precedent to go on. Again, this isn't my specialty."

"How can we find out if an Interpol warrant is served?" Gabriel asked. "Can you find out before it's too late?"

"I'll look into it."

Kiyoko bit her lip when the video chat ended. "Maybe we should find a lawyer who knows extradition law better."

"We can't afford a lawyer of our own," Gabriel said. "But Sr. Eduardo has lots of friends. He'll find the right person to call. We're lucky he's spending the time on us."

Kiyoko headed for her VR room. "I'm going to do some research." She stopped in the doorway and turned. "You found out where Inspector De Barros lives, right?"

"Yes. He lives in the Jardim Paulista neighborhood. It's just a few blocks from the Hotel Tiberio, where the American named John Hill was staying."

"We should put a camera outside his apartment. We've got plenty of them."

"That is true."

"I'll look at street imagery and any public cameras I can access and try to find a good spot."

Gabriel put on his data glasses and forwarded his research on De Barros to Kiyoko's private dropbox.

Kiyoko donned her VR helmet and gloves and disappeared into the Comnet.

Nicolas called a few minutes later, using his secure SSG number. "We found the Piranhas hideout," he said. "Went in with state military police. They took fire so they sent in robots with explosives and took down the building. We're doing mop-up now."

"Thank you. I only wish I was there."

"I know. But the tracking bracelet."

* * *

Kiyoko

Kiyoko woke the next morning feeling generally anxious, but relieved that As Piranhas were no more. According to Gabriel's colleague Nicolas Pistario, there were no survivors. Even though the gangsters were her enemies, she chanted a quick prayer for their souls.

Her anxiety returned. What would their enemies' next move be? *I really am turning into Pel.*

Gabriel was already up. Her fiancé! They were getting married! She kissed him. "Bom dia, my wonderful champion!"

He kissed her back and they poured bowls of Pokémon Cereal for breakfast.

Kiyoko had started divining the day's events by the mix of grain and marshmallow shapes that appeared in her bowl, but was still working on a consistent interpretation system. She poked through her cereal, inventorying the characters. No Happinys, Chanseys or Meowths.

Then she saw it. Absol, who appears before disasters. "Shit."

"What is it?" Gabriel asked from the other side of the small table.

She held up the tufted quasi-feline marshmallow. "It's Absol. Something bad is going to happen today."

Gabriel put down his spoon. "Kiyoko. If there's one thing I learned in the army, it's that something bad might happen every day. You just have to be prepared for it and find a way to take the initiative. What's the best way to survive an ambush? Attack the attackers."

He was right of course. Princesses and champions made their own luck.

Kiyoko hopped on the Comnet after breakfast. First thing was to check on her sister.

No news since the MediaCorp report a few days ago. She called the public defender's office in Richmond, using a location scrambler. An office assistant answered.

"Is someone there representing Waylee Freid?" Kiyoko asked.

"I'm sorry, that sort of information is confidential."

"I'm her sister."

"We can only answer queries in person, and you'll have to bring proper ID."

Kiyoko willed herself not to curse at the woman. "Can I leave a message?"

"Do I have your permission to record it?"

"Yes. Please ask Waylee Freid's legal representative to contact Kiyoko Pingyang, her sister, at Princess_Kiyoko@mico.net.br. I need to know how she's doing. It's very important."

The office assistant promised to pass the message along if Ms. Freid was represented by someone in their office.

What about Pel and Charles? She hadn't heard from them since yesterday. They spent nearly all their waking hours on the Comnet. Either they lost their connection or they'd been moved. Was that Absol's warning?

She tried again.

`Princess_Kiyoko: Please msg. Worried.`

Charles and Pel still hadn't responded an hour later. "Can you call the base?" she asked Gabriel.

"Of course." He put on his data glasses and spoke in Portuguese for a while.

"They wouldn't even admit your friends were staying there," he told Kiyoko.

"Then how do we find out? They wouldn't let us on the base."

"I'll call Nicolas. SSG has many contacts in the government. Someone should be able to help."

Gabriel received a return call about an hour later.

"Pel and Charles have been transferred to state custody," he said when the call ended.

Taiko drums pounded Kiyoko's blood into pulses of shrieking ice. "No! No, we can't let this happen. Call Sr. Eduardo. We have to do something!"

The Absol warning had been right.

25

Kiyoko

What was De Barros's plan now that he had custody of Pel and Charles? Sr. Eduardo hadn't called back yet.

Kiyoko checked her name crawler. She'd set up a program that searched the Comnet for her name and her friends', giving priority to U.S. and Brazilian government sites and Interpol.

Pel and Charles were still on the Interpol wanted list. But now she was too. And Shakti and Dingo. Not M-pat, who didn't live in the band house and had survived the initial investigation.

'WANTED BY THE JUDICIAL AUTHORITIES OF UNITED STATES FOR PROSECUTION / TO SERVE A SENTENCE'

Pel and Charles, like Waylee, had been charged with just about everything short of murder. Kiyoko, Shakti, and Dingo were charged with aiding and abetting terrorists and being accessories after the fact. The FBI was offering $100,000 rewards. A lot less than for Pel and Charles, but $100,000 would go a long way in Guyana.

Shakti and Dingo also had covert accounts in their Crypt-O-Chat room, although Pel had discouraged their use, insisting it only be used for emergencies. Kiyoko pinged their aliases and sent links to the wanted lists.

Shakti's alias contacted her an hour later.

Pachamama999: How r u?

How to be sure it was really Shakti and not a trap? Could Homeland or MediaCorp have infiltrated their chat room? Unlikely, but if she were Pel, she'd be super-careful at all times.

Princess_Kiyoko: Do you remember my wedding gift?
Pachamama999: You didn't have any money but you sewed my wedding dress. It was so beautiful, yellow and orange with flowering vines but it only took you a couple of days.

Princess_Kiyoko: I've made so many dresses I can almost do it without thinking.

To verify her own identity, Kiyoko described a Mori Girl outfit that she made for Shakti when she first moved into the Band House.

Pachamama999: I loved it. So earthy, like me, but so faerie, like you.

Princess_Kiyoko: I wouldn't call myself faerie, but thanks.

Pachamama999: You kissed me on the lips before you all left Guyana. When no one was looking. It made me wonder if you liked me. I know you've had girlfriends but you know that isn't my thing.

It was definitely Shakti.

Princess_Kiyoko: I love you. As a true friend, not in a romantic way. I didn't know if we'd ever see each other again. I'm sorry, I shouldn't have kissed you. I don't know why I did it. But since no one could see us it makes a good verifier.

Pachamama999: At least you didn't tongue. So can we talk about our pursuers?

Princess_Kiyoko: The terrorists are calling us terrorists.

She summarized everything she, Pel, and Charles had gone through since arriving in Brazil. She said Charles and Pel were in state custody now and might be picked up by the CIA, which was probably also behind the kidnapping and assassination attempts.

Pachamama999: Pel was right all along :(

Princess_Kiyoko: To make things worse, even though we were the victims, my fiancé and I are being charged for shooting some of these gangsters. Well, he did the shooting but I supposedly helped. But we were just trying to stay alive and save Pel and Charles. The police put tracking bracelets on our ankles.

Pachamama999: Fiancé?

Princess_Kiyoko: Yes!! Can you believe it? So ecstatic!! He is a demigod!

Not a full god since he wasn't bulletproof. But not a mere mortal either. Kiyoko summarized her relationship with Gabriel and said they hoped to get married soon.

234 ♦ T.C. WEBER

```
Pachamama999: Congrats!!! So happy for you! Dingo and
I have had our difficulties. Although weirdly, being on
the run brings out the best in him. We're actually in
hiding now. I was fighting the international logging
and mining companies raping Guyana, and I got a tip
their bully boys were planning to kill me. We had to
leave Georgetown and hide in the country.
Princess_Kiyoko: I was hoping you two were safe at
least. :(
Pachamama999: Let us know how to help.
```
Kiyoko sent a string of heart and cat hug emojis.

* * *

Sr. Eduardo finally called back. Kiyoko sat on the sofa with Gabriel and put the lawyer on the wall screen. "Srs. Charles and Pelopidas are being held at the state police headquarters under protective custody," he said.

"We heard," Kiyoko said.

"They are being held pending review of an Interpol red notice, which is like an international arrest warrant."

She'd been over and over this with the ministry. "But they have residency. They're here legally. Sra. Miranda from the Ministry of Foreign Affairs promised they wouldn't be extradited. And Brazil withdrew from its extradition treaty with the U.S."

"That doesn't cover Interpol warrants. Brazil is an Interpol member." He looked down. "Article 28 of Law No. 6,815 determines that a foreign national admitted to Brazilian territory as a political asylee must comply with all duties imposed on him/her by international law, along with the current domestic laws and all additional duties established by the Brazilian government."

"But the ministry said their actions were political, so the indictments were irrelevant."

He looked up again. "I don't think their situation has been tested in the courts, not where a red notice was issued or allegations of terrorism. Our government branches do not all agree on everything." He glanced down briefly. "Srs. Charles and Pelopidas are also being questioned about illegal activities performed in Brazil. Cybercrimes. This could really hurt their case."

It was unlikely Pel and Charles would have left footprints of anything they'd done. "What cybercrimes?" Kiyoko asked.

"All I was told," Sr. Eduardo responded, "is that it's an ongoing investigation. To be honest, the state police has been citing cybercrime lately to get federal grant money. This investigation could be one of those ploys. Or it could be a reason to hold your friends, assuming a judge complies. Hold them until someone serves the Interpol warrant."

Her knees were shaking. She gripped them, forced them under control. "Well how do we get them out? Can you represent them?"

"They are no longer clients of SSG. I am assisting you, Senhorita Kiyoko, because Sr. Gabriel is a valued part of our company and your cases are linked."

Gabriel leaned forward. "We owe them. They were clients at the time they were kidnapped, and all this shit comes from that."

Sr. Eduardo didn't respond.

"I'll pay the costs," Kiyoko said. Whatever it took. She could sell their VR gear. After that—follow up on Gabriel's bikini modeling suggestion? Could they use a graphics program to remove the bandages and bruises? Could she pretend not to be embarrassed?

"I cannot represent them," the lawyer said. "But I know someone who can, someone we work with, and I will ask him to give you a special deal. His name is David Calvo. He speaks very good English. I will have him contact you."

"Does he know extradition law?" Kiyoko asked.

"He will research whatever is needed."

They thanked him and he signed off.

Kiyoko called Sra. Miranda but had to leave a message. She said Inspector de Barros had tricked the federal government and was planning to have Pel and Charles extradited under their nose, all for his own personal profit. "Please call back, and please move them back to the air force base before it's too late!"

Kiyoko pressed her hands together and shut her eyes. She prayed to the gods for guidance.

She felt the sofa cushions shift and heard Gabriel's faint breathing. Anxiety faded to peace, replaced by warmth. She wasn't alone in the universe and things weren't hopeless.

She opened her eyes and regarded the wonderful man next to her. "Gabriel, if it looks like Pel and Charles will be extradited, will you help me free them?"

He blinked. "Free them? Us?"

"If the legal route fails. We'll track them and intercept before they're taken out of the country. Just like you did when As Piranhas kidnapped them."

"That was different. It was an obvious kidnapping. Extradition is a legal procedure."

She put her hands on his. "If they're extradited, it's because of that corrupt cop. You heard Sra. Miranda. The federal government granted them sanctuary."

"As I said, our branches of government do not always agree. But if we do what you suggest, we will be breaking the law. And what are our chances of success? I told you what happened on the *Tropical Breeze*. Three hostages were killed. What if that happens to Pel or Charles? Can you live with that?"

Good point. "And you promised our safety would be your top priority." She squeezed his hands. "We'd have to be careful. But remember these assholes want our friends alive, so they're not going to shoot them."

"Two bystanders were hit when I tried to stop the Piranhas kidnapping. We were lucky it wasn't more. When bullets fly, people get hurt."

She nodded. "You're right."

"And if we succeed . . ." His eyes roved. "Then what?"

"They could hide out until things are settled. Or go back to Guyana."

His thumbs fidgeted. "We would have to hide too. We would have to remove the tracking bracelets, which means jail if caught. And I do not want to move to Guyana."

"São Paulo is huge and we have friends here. We could hide until the extradition danger is over."

He hesitated, then said, "There are many places to stay anonymously if we pay cash."

"And my friend Reiko promised to help."

He met her eyes and exhaled. "I hope this plan will not be necessary. But we can at least prepare. It's always good to be ready and to ensure success."

My champion. She hugged, then kissed him. "Like I said, hopefully it won't come to that. For now, we can gather evidence against Inspector De Barros. We'll get Pel and Charles back under federal protection, and send De Barros to jail where he belongs."

26

Kiyoko

Kiyoko and Gabriel took a bus to the Rua Santa Ifigênia neighborhood, a downtown shopping area that specialized in electronics. Just two kilometers from Liberdade, it was one of the few places in the city Pel had visited. Wearing his stupid beard and dark glasses disguise of course, and with Gabriel along for protection.

This was Kiyoko's first time there. Beneath drizzly skies, electronics and computer stores stretched forever in every direction, the streets and sidewalks crowded with cars and pedestrians. So many people, a pink noise din of crunching tires and footsteps and conversations, almost like Feirinha da Liberdade. In store windows and above the awnings, flashing lights, LED ticker displays, and hologram videos competed for attention.

It didn't take long to find a store carrying GPS microchips the size of rice grains. Better, they had slightly bigger ones with amplifiers and batteries, and short antennae thinner than hair. According to one of the technicians on staff, the batteries were good for about a month if she set the GPS to transmit every ten minutes while stationary and every minute while moving. They could also receive commands to change their transmission rate, if she wanted more frequent signals.

She bought two sets with a cryptocurrency card and they took a bus home. She almost suggested shopping for engagement rings, but they had neither the time nor the money. Soon, hopefully.

In her living room, Kiyoko melted wax from an unscented candle and embedded each GPS and its antenna inside a nostril-sized clump. She set up a tracking app and confirmed that the systems still worked. Then she programmed the app to alert her if the signal strength increased along with the position changing, like if they were moved out of the police station. *I could be a hacker like Charles, just give me time.*

She showed her creations to Gabriel. "All we have to do now is get these to Pel and Charles and we'll be able to follow them wherever they're taken."

"They're at the police station," he said. "We can't go there, especially with these bracelets on."

True. "Can we get Sr. Eduardo to pass them along, maybe through that lawyer he recommended?"

Gabriel shook his head. "Lawyers don't do things like that. At least not SSG lawyers."

"What about your buddy Nicolas? He's like you, not afraid of anything."

"It's not that we don't feel fear. It's that when we have a job to do, we do it. Missão dada, missão cumprida! Mission given, mission accomplished." He squeezed her hand and faced the wall screen, which was playing a Harajuku fashion show without sound. "Wall screen, call Nicolas. English translation below."

Nicolas answered with video disabled and said he couldn't talk long. He agreed to help deliver the GPS trackers, though. "Easy task. I just need enough warning to adjust my schedule."

After they ended the connection, Kiyoko told Gabriel, "We need to monitor Inspector De Barros and see if he meets with this John Hill guy or someone else suspicious. Figure out what car he drives if we can, then trace it on the public cameras." Gabriel had only found his address. "Even better," she added, "maybe we can tap his comlink or hide a microphone in his clothes."

Gabriel stared at her. "How are we supposed to do that?"

Everything seems so easy on Nakano High School Detective. Or with Pel and Charles around. Kiyoko had searched the public cameras in the Jardim Paulista neighborhood, hoping for real-time coverage of De Barros's apartment building. They were password protected but Charles had set up a Collective router for her, and the passwords, which no one ever bothered changing, were posted on one of the boards. Unfortunately, none of the real-time cameras had a view of his building entrance or the garage.

"We have all those micro-cameras Pel bought," Kiyoko said. "And you found out where De Barros lives. Trouble is, we have these damn tracking bracelets on our ankles. Surely De Barros or one of his stooges on the state police are monitoring them."

"I could ask Nicolas or one of my other colleagues to do it," Gabriel said, "but it would be trouble for SSG if they were caught."

"I'll do it then. Can they track us on the metro?"

"Yes, there is full wi-fi and cell coverage and the bracelets communicate on both. Also GPS signals. But some of the pedestrian tunnels are unwired, especially the new ones."

"I'd gnaw my leg off," Kiyoko said, attempting to lighten the mood, "but then I'd have a hard time running if it came to that."

Gabriel smiled. "You have very nice legs. It would be a crime to destroy one."

"What if we wrap the bracelet in aluminum foil or something, block the signal?" Pel had promised to send her instructions on how to disable or fool their trackers, but had never followed through. He must have been moved before he had a chance, and didn't have Comnet access anymore.

Gabriel shrugged. "I'm not an expert on these things."

Kiyoko put on her VR helmet and gloves and scanned the darknet. Charles and Pel were brilliant. But more often than not, they just looked up what they needed to know and adapted it.

According to a technical article, they could indeed block the signal with aluminum foil. But if the police didn't receive anything, an alarm would sound.

Kiyoko had watched Pel build the Faraday bags that he, Waylee, M-pat and Dingo placed their comlinks in before they set off their EMP bomb to free Charles from detention so many months ago. At least, she watched him for a few minutes and listened to his explanation.

They could build a Faraday cage by lining the inside of a closet with aluminum foil. They could even remove the data card and spoof its signals through the Comnet, but that was a much bigger challenge. The trouble was taking the bracelet off without breaking the alarm cable, and then putting it back together again. She couldn't find a solution to that. Too bad Pel wasn't here.

Their only option, then, was to snip off the bracelets inside the closet. It would just look like the battery died. It might give them extra time to escape since the police wouldn't receive a tampering alarm.

Kiyoko finished researching. Gabriel had his guns apart in pieces and was putting them back together again. "What are you doing?" she asked.

He looked up. "Just checking everything. I haven't used these weapons before. I need to take them to the firing range too."

"Okay, well let's put out a camera first. And buy some boxes of aluminum foil. Cash if we have enough."

* * *

Kiyoko

That evening, Kiyoko and Gabriel took the metro blue line to Luz station and entered the unfinished underground walkway they'd taken to the Ministry of Foreign Affairs office. Like Gabriel, Kiyoko wore long pants to hide her tracking bracelet. Gabriel carried disguises in a backpack.

Once their comlink signals disappeared, they ducked into an unfinished bathroom. They changed clothes. Kiyoko opened her makeup kit and darkened her skin. She put on a black wig and mirrored data glasses that matched Gabriel's. They wrapped aluminum foil around their ankle bracelets. Finally, she took off her sling.

They'd be invisible, but had to hurry before the cops sent someone out to check.

They hopped back on the metro, headed south again, transferred to the green line at Paraiso, and got out at Trianon Masp. They walked south on Rua Pamplona, into Jardim Paulista, an upscale neighborhood southwest of Liberdade and the city center.

Gabriel scanned the monotonous high rises and shops as they walked, most of them freshly painted. "Must be nice to afford to live here."

"Why?" Kiyoko asked. "Liberdade has a lot more character."

"It's very safe, I am told. All the banks and consulates mean more police attention and private security."

She squeezed his hand. "You're the ultimate warrior. I don't see why you need to worry about that."

He looked in her eyes. "It's good for children to grow up somewhere safe."

More talk about children. Could she do that? Could she be someone's mother? It seemed like an alien notion, something that vanilla people did after they settled into boring nine to five jobs. But Gabriel wasn't vanilla, and he seemed to really want kids. She decided not to respond, and focus on their mission.

They weaved their way to De Barros's block, a series of tall, new-looking apartment buildings. De Barros's building was painted tan. All the apartments had glass doors that opened onto balconies. The perimeter was protected by a tall fence of thick black metal bars, with strategically placed floodlights, cameras, and motion detectors. A guard bunker sat to the side of the otherwise swanky entrance. An underground parking garage entrance was to the left of the building, protected by a thick gate. It looked like a place for bankers and stockbrokers, not cops.

A hedge lined the sidewalk on the opposite side of his street. Kiyoko activated the microcamera she had taken from Pel's door and inserted into a bracket with a battery pack.

She glanced around. No one was watching. No one obvious, anyway. What if the guard was monitoring them? What if De Barros was looking out his window? "Block the view, would you?" she asked Gabriel.

He stood between her and De Barros's building, pretending to call someone on his data glasses.

Kiyoko clipped the camera to one of the branches where it would be shadowed by leaves, and adjusted the angle until she could see the pedestrian and parking garage entrances on her data glasses.

Still no one looking, as far as she could tell. "Muito bom," she said quietly.

They continued down the street and made their way back to the metro, then back the way they came. The batteries would only last a few days. But maybe they'd learn something useful by then.

* * *

Dalton

Dalton waited in a stolen white delivery van with Kozachenko just up the one-way street from De Barros's apartment building. It didn't look much different from the other buildings in the neighborhood, eighteen stories of well-maintained concrete and glass with heavy security. No doubt someone was watching the perimeter cameras. It would be too difficult to break into.

"This guy's got the balls to screw Ares?" Kozachenko asked from the driver's seat.

If there was one thing Dalton was good at, it was making people regret crossing him. "He won't have balls when I get through with him, that's for sure."

Dalton wasn't sure when De Barros would come home, just that he wasn't there at the moment. They'd parked while he was supposedly on shift, and hadn't seen any lights on in his apartment. Nor had their directional mike picked up sounds.

At 8:05, their quarry's black sports car approached. Three hours of tedium over at last. "Here he comes!"

Kozachenko swung the van into the street and stopped it perpendicular to the flow of traffic, blocking the road. Dalton jumped out with a stun gun. Metal typically disrupted its electromagnetic pulses, but not glass.

The first rule of combat—one of the rules, anyway—was to hit hard, fast, and by surprise. Dalton sprinted to the car and fired at the mustached detective through the windshield before his surprise could give way to action. De Barros spasmed, then slumped in his seatbelt, pistol still in its holster.

Up the street, horns honked at the inconvenience of being stuck, but the closest drivers hunkered down, trying to be invisible.

With his other hand, Dalton tried the car door. Locked of course. He pulled out a small thermal charge mounted on suction cups. De Barros's car was bulletproof, but this would burn a hole through just about anything. He pressed the trigger button, which had a five second delay, and stuck it on the passenger door against the lock.

The thermal charge flashed brilliant white, leaving a blackened hole where the door latch had been. Dalton grabbed the handle, which was well away from the scorched section, and yanked the door open, swinging it upward. He shot De Barros with the stunner again, then climbed into the car and injected sedative into his carotid artery.

Kozachenko ran to the driver's side, a few seconds late.

Dalton released De Barros's seatbelt and reached across his girth to open the driver's door. "Grab him, would you?"

Kozachenko pulled the unconscious fat detective out of the car. "Son of a bitch is heavy."

Dalton slid out of the car and grabbed the detective's legs, and together they threw him in the back of the van.

They sped off. No sirens yet. But there would definitely be a search. Cops stuck together no matter what country you were in.

* * *

Kiyoko

As Kiyoko left another message for Sra. Miranda, her comlink emitted a camera alert tone. She finished her message and opened the camera feed. Nothing visible, but lots of honking from off screen.

She loaded the stored video file and displayed it. Scattered cars drove past De Barros's apartment building, then nothing, then a white van sped past.

She routed the feed to the living room wall screen. "Gabriel, come see this!"

Gabriel sat next to her on the sofa and she replayed the video. Then she opened another window and brought up the nearest public camera.

A black sports car sat in the middle of the street. Other cars began to inch around it. Police sirens sounded in the distance. "What do you think it means?"

Gabriel shrugged. "Wish I knew."

Maybe it had something to do with De Barros and his CIA buddy. Or maybe not. She set a news crawler to track any mention of either, or any mention of crime events on that street.

* * *

Dalton

Dalton drove to the forested hills north of the city and parked at the end of a long dirt road, far from prying ears. He climbed into the back of the van, where Kozachenko had tied De Barros spread eagle to the floor, running thick wires from his wrists, ankles, and neck through holes and gaps in the metal ribs holding the panels together. Dalton slapped the fat detective until he woke.

De Barros shouted in Portuguese. Dalton's data glasses translated them as pleas and curse phrases.

Dalton slapped him again. "Shut the hell up."

To emphasize the point, he pulled off the inspector's left shoe, then the smelly blue sock. "Hammer."

Kozachenko passed him a heavy claw hammer. De Barros's eyes widened. "No, no, there's no need for that."

Dalton ignored him. De Barros twisted his foot back and forth but couldn't move his leg much. Still, it made aiming difficult.

With his left hand, Dalton pinned the fat man's foot to the hard plastic floor mat. With his right, he swung the hammer against the toes. He hit the middle two and heard a crack.

De Barros screamed.

Dalton brandished the hammer at his face. "I said shut the hell up."

The screams diminished to whimpers. The inspector's toes reddened and oozed blood.

"Do you know why you're here?"

De Barros shook his head.

Dalton swung the hammer against his foot again, smashing the big toe.

More screaming. Dalton punched him hard in the Adam's apple, not hard enough to break it, but hard enough to shut him up. "If you want to live, you'll cooperate."

Tears dripped from the corners of the man's eyes. "Puta que pariu . . . What do you want?"

"What do you think, you motherfucker? You're trying to fuck me out of four million dollars. Worse, you're fucking Ares. Your employer. That's an automatic death sentence. Did you really think you'd get away with it?"

"I . . . I just moved them to a better holding place. They were unreachable on the air base."

That was true. "You brokered a separate deal with MediaCorp and Homeland Security. Hoping to get the reward for yourself. When are they picking up Demopoulos and Lee, and how are you planning to transfer them?"

De Barros shook his head. "No, that's not true, please, please."

Stubborn greedy bastard. Dalton swung the hammer against the man's foot over and over until he was pretty sure all the bones up to the ankle were broken.

De Barros had passed out so Dalton had to slap him awake again. Then he pulled off the other shoe and sock. "Who's coming to pick up Demopoulos and Lee, and when?"

De Barros whimpered.

"I'm this close to smashing your fat head in. Just answer the questions and you can limp your way out of here."

"How do I know you'll let me go?"

"Because you can still be useful to us. I won't even dock your percentage that much. Just the cost of this hammer." He waved it.

De Barros nodded. He breathed in and out. "It's all legal. I know this judge, he arranged the transfer and he's bypassing their asylum status. He knows all the loopholes. As soon as that's all complete, a team will fly in from the USA and pick them up."

"Are they paying you?"

"$4.5 million." He sniffled. "Wire transfer. The judge gets half."

"Who's the judge?"

"Judge Rocha. He's giving them Pingyang too." De Barros raised his head and peered at his ruined foot, then bit his lip.

"You can get that fixed when we're done," Dalton said.

"Pingyang's a troublemaker," the detective said, "and we can't have her around complicating our lives. And she's worth $100,000 now."

"When's this pickup supposed to happen?"

"Any day now. The judge said it wouldn't take long."

"Fuck. Okay, here's what you're gonna do. Good job getting Demopoulos and Lee out of the air base. Where are they being held?"

"State police headquarters."

"Call your colleagues and arrange an Interpol pickup. The agent's name is Kevin Brock. He looks like me. He'll be with a Ukrainian named Aleksi Andrusenko. Looks like my colleague here."

Kozachenko leaned in front of De Barros and waved.

"Once we're safely out of the country," Dalton continued, "I'll have you released. So it's in your interest to speed things up."

De Barros made the calls as instructed. His comlink was voice-activated, speaking the phrase "meu mina." Dalton recorded him saying it so he could unlock his comlink if needed.

"I'll need all your passwords," he said after De Barros hung up.

The treacherous bastard was reluctant but two smashed right toes later he gave them up.

"What do we do with him now?" Kozachenko asked.

Couldn't take the chance he'd wreak some kind of vengeance. *The hell with him.*

Dalton lifted the hammer and swung it at De Barros's forehead. It hit with a loud crack. The detective went into convulsions, eyes rolled up, limbs thrashing against the wires.

Kozachenko turned green and looked away, even though he'd killed plenty of people before. Maybe not so close up, though.

Dalton hit the skull again, harder, heard a wet smack, and the thrashing stopped. He kept pounding away until the head was a misshapen mess and the face unrecognizable. He made sure to knock out all the teeth.

He untied the corpse, dragged it into the scrubby trees, soaked it in gasoline, then lit it with a match. The fire spread into the trees so they took off.

Then they drove to within walking distance of a bus stop, changed into clean clothes, and set the van on fire.

27

Waylee

Waylee's trial had been a disaster so far. The prosecutor's team had terabytes of DNA and video evidence, and a long string of witnesses, including Amy Hill and six other turncoats from Friendship Farm, who testified that Waylee was the group's leader, was crazy, and had planned the fundraiser infiltration and the Super Bowl preemption. The prosecutor also had charisma, an easygoing style that made you cling to every word.

Ms. Martin had no alibi witnesses and only a handful of experts, and her cross-examinations had seemed inadequate. The best she'd done was portraying the Friendship Farm traitors as brain-addled stoners.

Throughout the trial, the jury members squinted at Waylee with tight jaws and downturned mouths, but refused to meet her eyes. They'd convicted her already.

"Can we try plea bargaining again?" Waylee asked her lawyer in their meeting room.

Ms. Martin sighed. "We're in the middle of trial. The prosecutor's offer is still on the table, though – reduced charges and sentences if you recant your video and testify against your co-conspirators."

"Forget it." Despite the anti-depressant medications, a dark cloud settled over Waylee. "Can I just plead guilty to the lesser charges if they drop the ridiculous ones, like cyberterrorism?"

Ms. Martin typed on her data pad. "I'll talk to Mr. Lachlan, but he hasn't budged since I started, and it's unlikely he'll bargain now."

In her head, Waylee played "DNA," one of her more upbeat Dwarf Eats Hippo songs.

We're ninety nine percent the same,
Our basic needs a common frame.

Todd Lachlan, Judge Mahler, President Rand, and Bob Luxmore had powerful positions but were mistake-prone mortals just like she was.

They're not gods or beings enlightened,
They're just people with thoughts misguided.

The song summoned enough energy for her to press on. When the game was fixed, kick the table over.

Jury nullification – that was the key. There was this organization called the Fully Informed Jury Association that advised jurors to acquit defendants if they disagreed with the law, even if they believed the defendant committed the crime. Prosecutors and judges had no power to retaliate against the jurors. The problem was, almost no one knew about jury nullification.

"As it stands," Waylee told her lawyer, "I'm doomed. The jury thinks I'm a terrorist out to kill them in their sleep. If I can speak directly to the jury, show them I'm a decent human being, tell them why I did what I did, show that I'm on their side and the government isn't, maybe they'll acquit me."

Ms. Martin frowned. "We've been over this. While establishing character or intent might win some sympathy, assuming you can pull it off, it's dangerous. Mr. Lachlan gets to cross-examine you, and you have to answer."

Lachlan would probably hurt her, but her case looked hopeless. She had to do something. Just like she'd always done, fight seemingly impossible odds. "Can I speak without interruption?"

"The prosecution can object to individual parts, but they can't stop your overall testimony."

"Then I want to do it. Can you bring me cases to study, anything you can find about successful trial outcomes for direct action protesters, and anything involving necessity defenses or appeals for jurors to vote their conscience?"

Ms. Martin's eyes roved, like she wanted to leave. She snorted. "I advise against it. Judge Mahler runs a tight ship and Mr. Lachlan could tear you apart."

Am I just supposed to give up? "It's my only hope. I'm the defendant and I choose to do it."

* * *

Kiyoko

Kiyoko's news crawler told her there had been a kidnapping in the Jardim Paulista neighborhood. No one had the event on video, but statements to local media and on social networks said a white van pulled in front of a black sports car, blocking the road. Two men with guns got out, set off an explosive charge against the passenger door, and dragged an unconscious man out of the car and into the van.

No word on the victim, but the state police had begun a massive manhunt. Kiyoko's camera showed police congregating in front of De Barros's apartment building and going in and out. A suited man with the uniformed police spotted the camera in the hedge and reached fingers toward it.

Kiyoko cut the signal and turned off the camera program in case it could be traced back to her. "Gabriel, I think Inspector de Barros might have been kidnapped."

"What?" He put on his data glasses and contacted SSG.

"You're right," he said when he finished the call. "Our favorite police inspector has been kidnapped. His car was bulletproof but they were prepared for that. They used a military-grade thermal charge to melt the door lock."

"As Piranhas?"

Gabriel shook his head. "No, they're finished. My guess is De Barros cheated the people he's working with, the CIA or whoever. Unless it's for something else he's done."

"That makes it even more important to get Pel and Charles out of custody and get away from here. I'll call Sra. Miranda again, but we need to get those GPS transmitters deployed right away."

＊ ＊ ＊

Pelopidas

Pel sat alone in a tiny, new-looking holding cell with only a metal toilet and an air mattress. The police hadn't taken any statements or told him his rights or anything.

How long would he be here? Was he being charged? Turned over to the FBI or CIA? Was Charles in another cell like this?

A guard opened the door. "Advogado."

He led Pel to a small meeting room with a folding table and three plastic chairs. One was occupied by a stocky dark-haired man with wire-rimmed glasses, wearing a dark gray suit and a red tie. In the other sat a brawny man with a buzzcut, wearing a blue blazer that was at least a size too small for him.

Both men stood. The stocky man with glasses shook Pel's hand. "David Calvo. I am a defense attorney with Reus, Borges and Jones." His English was excellent.

The buzzcut man introduced himself with a firm grip. "Nicolas Pistario. Serviços de Segurança Globais." His voice sounded congested, like he had a cold.

Gabriel's company to the rescue. Again. "Why am I here?"

"From what I understand," Mr. Calvo said, "the state police may hand you over to Interpol."

Pel's bladder threatened to give way. "Interpol?"

"Yes, they conveyed an international arrest warrant on behalf of the United States. Brazil currently has no extradition treaty with the USA, but honors Interpol requests."

Fuck. Fuck! "That's quite a loophole. What about Charles?"

"He is in the same position. I will meet him also."

Pel tried to suppress the panic rattling his bones. *Focus.* "But the government granted us asylum. I have a residency card, it's back at my apartment, assuming no one took it."

Mr. Calvo nodded. "Yes. And your friend Senhora Kiyoko received assurances from the Ministry of Foreign Affairs that you will not be extradited. However, the Interpol warrant is problematic. I have been researching the matter and will argue that you cannot be extradited without approval from the president, which I believe is unlikely to happen. In the meantime, you will receive a custody hearing and I will argue for your release."

"Argue for? What are my chances?"

Mr. Calvo remained impassive. "I think the law is on your side, but of course I am your lawyer."

"Why are they doing it? Inspector de Barros. He's working for the CIA, I think. But why?"

"I was briefed about this inspector. Certainly he has many assets compared to his inspector salary, and must be doing something on the side. Police salaries are not very high, so side work is common—some legal, some not legal. Corruption is less than it used to be, but it is still there. There is a very large reward for you and Mr. Charles and it is not surprising people want to collect it."

The buzzcut man, Mr. Pistario, stood to the side, not paying attention to them, just watching the door.

"And now I must take my leave," Mr. Calvo said. "I will accompany you at your hearing and handle your case."

"Thank you." Pel shook his hand and he left. Pel's palm oozed cold sweat.

Mr. Pistario remained in the room. He waited until the door shut, then reached a thumb and finger into his nose.

Pel couldn't help but cringe. Most people just used a finger to pick their nose, and didn't do it in front of clients. Another layer of insanity.

Mr. Pistario pulled a solid looking piece of snot out of his nose. He wiped it on his shirt beneath the blazer, then approached Pel with it.

"No thanks, I'm not hungry." Despite the joke, Pel backed up a step. Was the man crazy? Or brain damaged?

The buzzcut man whispered. "Forgive me, my English is poor. This is gift from Kiyoko."

It didn't look like a standard booger. It was pretty big. It looked like a ball of wax.

"GPS inside. You put in nose like me."

Oh. It was so Kiyoko or SSG could follow if he was taken somewhere. He felt like fist-bumping the man and praising Kiyoko for her ingenuity. And it meant Kiyoko had a backup plan in case legal measures failed. Hard to believe this was the same girl who painted rainbows and unicorns on her door in Baltimore.

Mr. Pistario pointed to his other nostril. "I have one for Carlos too."

"Charles?"

"Yes. I see him next."

Pel accepted the wax booger, breathed deeply, and shoved it up his right nostril until it lodged. He suppressed the urge to sneeze.

* * *

The next day, a guard led Pel and his stocky lawyer, Mr. Calvo, into a fluorescent-lit room with two faux-wood tables. At the far table, a well-groomed middle-aged man in a gray suit sat behind a computer screen. Two dark-haired men sat at the near table. Everyone looked up as they entered.

Mr. Calvo motioned to a pair of empty chairs at the near table. "Please sit."

Pel sat, cuffed hands on his lap. Mr. Calvo took the adjacent chair and started up a data pad. "I will speak on your behalf," he said.

The men spoke in Portuguese for a while. Finally, the man at the far table said something in an officious tone.

Mr. Calvo frowned and leaned toward Pel. "The judge said you are a high flight risk and must remain in detention. You must stay in your current cell for safety reasons, he said."

Pel's chest tightened. *I'm stuck here?* "What do you mean safety reasons? Never mind—what happens now?"

"There will be an extradition hearing tomorrow, and then either you stay here or an Interpol agent picks you up and flies you to the USA."

* * *

Kiyoko

"There's been a development in your case," Sr. Eduardo told Kiyoko via video chat.

"Good or bad?"

"You must appear before a new judge."

"Why? Let me guess, they're planning to extradite me?"

"They didn't say so, but your friends appeared before the same judge this morning. Judge Rocha."

"What happened?"

"I talked to their attorney. The judge ruled that they must stay in state custody. There is an extradition hearing tomorrow. Also before Judge Rocha."

So much for their asylum. Was Judge Rocha on the CIA or MediaCorp payroll? Like Inspector de Barros? "Please call Sra. Miranda in the Ministry of Foreign Affairs," Kiyoko said. "Tell her she has to stop this. Hold on, I'll give you her contact info."

Kiyoko opened her contact list and swiped Sra. Miranda's email address and voice number over to Sr. Eduardo's box. "When do I have to turn myself in?"

"The police are picking you up. They may be on their way now."

Shit! She closed the connection.

"Police are on the way," she told Gabriel. "We have to run." They couldn't go far if they wanted to help Pel and Charles, but they couldn't stay here either.

Gabriel stared at her. "Run?"

Kiyoko fought the waves of panic. "We're all being extradited. I can't let that happen." She set the wall screen to display all the camera feeds. Nothing unusual yet.

Gabriel nodded. "We will get in more trouble. But I won't let you be extradited."

She changed into her escape outfit—adaptive fiber undershirt, white blouse to hide the armor, short black skirt, light denim jacket that she left unbuttoned, running shoes, big purse, and black wig. And a belt with two stun guns in makeshift holsters. She had two smoke grenades and pepper spray in her purse. She left the sling off—she was fine without it as long as she didn't carry anything heavy with her right arm or do gymnastics.

Gabriel changed too—body armor, loose shirt, cargo pants, and data glasses.

"You could stay here," she told him as she pulled her new bug-out bag out of the closet and put on her mirrored data glasses.

Gabriel checked his weapons. "You don't know the city like I do." He threw on his backpack. "We are a couple. We go together."

Kiyoko sent a voice message in Japanese to her friend Reiko. "I need to go away. Take care of Nyasuke-kun please and the apartments as we discussed. If you can sell our VR gear and other electronic equipment, please send most of the money to my lawyer so he will continue to represent us." She added Sr. Eduardo's contact information. "You can take any favorite clothes and costumes. Thank you very much! All the best! See you!"

The wall screen showed two white police cars with zig-zagging bands pulling up to the building. Shit, they were already here! They had planned for a reasonable amount of lead time.

"Let's get these trackers off!" she said in English.

They squeezed into the aluminum foil-lined closet, struggling for room among the dresses. Kiyoko picked up the clippers from the floor and snipped Gabriel's ankle bracelet, then hers. They didn't make any noise but would be sending out an electronic alarm. Blocked, hopefully, by the surrounding foil.

They pulled off the snipped bracelets and hurried out of the closet, not opening the door any more than necessary.

The police would have a hard time getting to them. She had changed the elevator code to their floor and the new stairwell door was impervious to anything short of explosives. "How do we get out of here without the cops seeing?"

"We can't. They'll be in the lobby by the time we get downstairs. They might even be in the stairwell. There's no fire escape, they took Pel's rope during the investigation, and the next buildings are too far to jump to. We have a choice—surrender or fight."

"Fight? Kill cops?"

"No, just incapacitate them."

"We can't surrender. If we do, there will be no one to help Pel and Charles and Waylee."

Gabriel grinned. "Be ready with your stun gun. We will both need to fire."

Kiyoko picked up her cat and kissed him goodbye. "I'll see you again, my little nyan-nyan. I just can't take you with me now. Reiko is very nice and loves cats. You be nice to her."

Backpacks on, they ran to the elevator. It didn't have a floor indicator but she could hear it moving. They unlocked the stairwell door on the opposite side of the hall. She looked down.

Two men in black clothes, body armor, and baseball caps—civil police by the look—were coming up the stairs. Not running though. She leaned against the stairwell wall so they couldn't see her.

Gabriel did the same and took the lead. Kiyoko hugged the wall, stun gun in hand. They descended, a step at a time, while their adversaries ascended at a faster pace. The lead cop wore data glasses. Probably they could tell the ankle trackers had been disabled.

When they were only one floor apart, Gabriel nodded. They leaned over the railing and fired their stun guns at the two cops.

It didn't seem to do anything. Something in their body armor? They fired again. Again, no effect.

The cops drew their pistols.

Kiyoko and Gabriel threw themselves backwards just as loud bangs echoed through the stairwell.

Acting on instinct, Kiyoko pulled the pin out of a smoke grenade and tossed it at the two cops. Thick white smoke billowed out.

Gabriel traded his stun gun for a real one, his needler.

"Don't," Kiyoko whispered.

Gabriel pressed his lips together and reholstered his gun. "You're right." He vaulted over the railing and into the smoke below.

* * *

Gabriel

Kiyoko was right. Gabriel couldn't shoot cops, even if they were dirty. And these might just be following orders.

It was a short drop to the adjacent flight of stairs. He landed on the lead cop's shoulders and heard a grunt. They tumbled backward onto the landing, against the second cop, into the thickest part of the metallic-smelling fumes. Gabriel fell hard on his back but his backpack absorbed the blow. Good thing he didn't take it off.

The man he'd landed on was on his back next to him, groaning and breathing hard. He'd dropped his gun and his data glasses had come off. The second cop had fallen on his ass but still had his pistol in his right hand.

Gabriel had practiced Brazilian jiu-jitsu for so many years the moves came without thinking. Still on his back, he pivoted toward the second cop, grabbed the man's gun, and twisted it out of his hand. He shoved one foot against the man's hip, wrapped the other leg around his back and pulled him face down.

Through the smoke, Gabriel saw the first cop getting up. He was in leg range too. A kick to the back of the knee and an ankle sweep sent him tumbling again.

The second cop grabbed Gabriel's arm, trying to get his gun back. Gabriel yanked the man's arm forward, pulling him off balance and toward him. He twisted and head butted the cop in the nose. The man howled.

Gabriel leapt to his feet, kicked the cop against the wall of the landing, then pointed his new gun at the two smoke-shrouded sprawled men. "Don't make me shoot you."

They held up their hands. Blood streamed from the second cop's nostrils.

Kiyoko raced down the stairs. She picked up the first cop's data glasses and gun and pointed the gun in their general direction.

Gabriel snatched the cops' handcuffs off their belts and cuffed them to the railing. No time for anything fancy. He took the second cop's comlink and dropped it down the stairwell, where it smashed against the floor at the bottom.

"Let's go," he told Kiyoko.

Kiyoko took off her data glasses and put on the cop's. They hurried down the stairs to the ground floor and opened the door to the hallway. A young couple, residents, stood there staring, but no police.

"DG, traduz Português para Inglês," Kiyoko spoke to the cop's data glasses. "Translate all voice and text," she added.

Gabriel ran out the building's back door, Kiyoko close behind. They sprinted across the wide alley and into the small grocery store next door.

Gabriel slowed and called a taxi on his data glasses. He arranged a pick-up two streets over.

Kiyoko faced him, big police glasses over her eyes. "Cops on the elevator are assisting the ones in the stairwell," she said in English. "I'm running the audio through a translator—my Portuguese still isn't good enough." She paused. "The police have called for reinforcements."

Unfortunately there was a police station a few blocks away, on the other side of the Avenida Radial Leste highway. Wouldn't take long for them to get here. And civil police headquarters was only a few kilometers north.

"They called for a helicopter too," Kiyoko said.

That would take longer, at least fifteen minutes. But still, they had to get out of Liberdade.

They sprinted to the pickup point, Kiyoko huffing with the big backpack on. A white electric sedan with a "Taxi" sign on top pulled up.

Still breathing heavy, Kiyoko pulled off the police data glasses and tossed them down a storm drain, followed by the pistol. Gabriel ditched his police gun too.

Sirens sounded from two directions. The police were typically sluggish except when one of their own was assaulted. Then they turned into a swarm of angry assassin bees.

They jumped in the back of the taxi. "Carrão," Gabriel told the driver. A random district to the east, away from the police. "Rápido, por favor."

The driver, a thick-jowled man with a bald spot, turned and stared at them. "The police, are they after you?" he asked in Portuguese.

Kiyoko responded first. "Não." *No.* She waved her stock of cash and shouted in Portuguese. "My sister is giving birth and we need to be there!"

The driver stared at the wad of bills and nodded. He accelerated away, toward Carrão.

Their ultimate destination was to the west. Gabriel had picked out a family-run pousada in the Pinheiros district, one that was cheap and accepted cash off the books. They'd switch taxis and walk, taking a circuitous route.

And then what? They'd be hunted until the federal government took action against Inspector de Barros. No telling how long that would take, or if it would even happen at all. And if this Judge Rocha decided to extradite Pel and Charles, which was likely, he and Kiyoko would have to figure out where they'd be taken and if there was any way to intervene with even a remote chance of success.

28

Waylee

"Do you solemnly swear to tell the truth, the whole truth and nothing but the truth, so help you God?" the dowdy-looking female clerk asked Waylee.

Right hand raised, Waylee responded, "I do." If there was a God, he/she/it should be impeached for dereliction of duty, but this wasn't the time to argue theology.

The judge directed her to the witness chair. Waylee sat in a faux-leather swivel chair in a polished walnut box just below the judge's platform. It had a blank computer monitor and thin directional microphone with a sound baffle. She felt weird sitting in front of a microphone instead of gripping it and pacing a stage.

Her attorney, Ms. Martin, approached the witness stand. Waylee had spent twenty hours a day researching and preparing her testimony, and they had practiced and probed for holes.

"Good morning, Ms. Freid," Ms. Martin began. "How are you?"

"I've been better." She was supposed to say she was doing fine, but couldn't force the lie out.

Ms. Martin licked her lips. "Could you please introduce yourself to the jury?"

Waylee looked at the jury sitting in two rows of six, not more than ten feet away. They were all from the Richmond area. Seven white men, four white women, and one black woman. All older than she, most much older. No visible tattoos or unorthodox hair. At least her lawyer had culled out anyone with ties to MediaCorp.

"Hi, I'm Waylee Freid. F-R-E-I-D." She wasn't supposed to say anything else.

"And how old are you?" Ms. Martin asked.

"I'm 29." Hard to believe she was almost thirty. On the other hand, that meant a life sentence would stretch forty or fifty years unless she killed herself, which she'd almost certainly do.

"And what line of work are you in?"

"I'm a journalist. And a musician."

Ms. Martin asked her to describe her journalism career, how she raised her much younger sister, how she'd lived in the same house with the same boyfriend for five years, and how she helped keep her neighborhood together in the face of collapsing city services and emboldened drug gangs. It all showed that Waylee was responsible and cared about others.

"Have you ever been convicted of a crime as an adult?" Ms. Martin asked next.

"No." She was no Black Blocker like Dingo, and prior to breaking Charles out of juvenile detention, hadn't participated in direct actions or demonstrations, to safeguard her supposed journalistic objectivity.

"Have you ever been charged with a crime as an adult?"

"No."

"Now to fast forward, so to speak, can you describe the events leading to your interviews at the Smithsonian Castle?"

At the prosecution table, Mr. Lachlan stood and faced the judge. "Objection, your honor. The defense is calling for a narrative response."

Ms. Martin turned. "Your honor, we are merely breaking the timeline into manageable chunks. Let the defendant tell us what happened in her own words."

Judge Mahler nodded. "I'll allow it, as long as the witness sticks to the facts. Objection overruled. You may proceed."

"Thank you, your honor." Ms. Martin looked at Waylee and folded her hands.

Waylee had been a performer for ten years, fronting various bands. And although she rarely took advantage, she knew how to charm. She'd charmed President Rand himself into admissions of collusion with Media-Corp. Could she charm these twelve jurors into agreeing that her actions were justified?

Waylee locked eyes with each juror and tried to build a subconscious bond of empathy. "First, I admit to some of the charges."

Mouths fell open. She had their attention. And the prosecutor might let her speak for a while.

"Some, not most," she continued. "I'm a journalist and I've been investigating MediaCorp for a long time." She described how as a reporter for the *Baltimore Herald*, she uncovered evidence of Media Corporation's secret deals with the government. "MediaCorp, their board members, and their foundations and PACs gave over a billion dollars to Al Rand, the president before him, and key Congressmen."

Mr. Lachlan stood. "Objection, your honor. Relevance?"

"Can I finish what I was saying?"

"Your honor," Ms. Martin said from her position near the witness stand, "the witness is describing the events leading up to the alleged crimes."

"I'll allow it," the judge said, "but the witness should stick to the relevant facts. Ms. Martin, am I to gather from your client's admission that you plan to change your plea?"

"Not at this time, your honor."

The judge blinked, then looked down at Waylee. "The witness will proceed. Please be brief."

Waylee's fingers were shaking. *Stop that.* "As I was saying, my investigation showed how Media Corporation gave over a billion dollars to key politicians. And during the big Internet upgrade, these same politicians leaned on the FCC, exempted MediaCorp from antitrust laws, and rubber-stamped every one of their requests. In fact, MediaCorp lobbyists drafted the regulations and enabling legislation almost verbatim. They were allowed sole ownership of the backbone and switches, a power which they immediately abused to seize control of everything we see and hear online."

"Objection, your honor," Mr. Lachlan said. "Witness is ignoring your instructions."

The judge glared at Waylee. "This is your last warning."

"I'll move on to what MediaCorp did in response to my investigation." She described how MediaCorp bought her newspaper, along with every other for-profit media outlet in the region. They killed her story, then fired her. They bought the Independent News Center's building and forcibly evicted them with military crowd-control weapons. Before she was fired, Waylee covered the eviction for the *Herald*. She was badly injured even though she identified herself as a journalist. "Dozens of people were hospitalized, not just me. Some were just kids."

The jurors hung on to her words but Judge Mahler began to scowl.

Waylee was having trouble staying focused. Was her hypomania coming back? She'd been pretty stable since the antidepressants took hold. But the medicine only addressed part of her condition.

"Now can you describe the events at the presidential fundraiser?" Ms. Martin asked.

Waylee described her plan to interview President Rand and Bob Luxmore. "Yes, I impersonated someone to get in," she admitted. "But the American people have a right to know what their elected officials are up to. Their decisions shouldn't be shrouded in secrecy. Or made at an exclusive fundraiser organized by MediaCorp." As an example, she summarized a discussion between a mining company CEO and the House Natural Resources Committee chair about relaxing regulations and eliminating the EPA.

"So you recorded some of these conversations?" Ms. Martin asked.

"Yes. That's why I went. To let people know what was going on behind their back."

"Now what about the events of February 4? Can you describe what happened that day?"

Waylee said she tagged along behind some other people and entered the MediaCorp broadcast center. "The doors were open already, and I didn't touch any computers. My one regret was using a stun gun on an employee, who then fell and hit his head. But he'd just hit me in the face with a stapler—sounds funny, I know . . ."

Some of the jurors smiled.

"But it hurt like hell. Anyway, I'm sorry he hit his head when he fell."

Ms. Martin elicited more details, then addressed the judge. "I'd like to play the video now."

He nodded. "Go ahead." He'd already allowed it.

Still on the witness stand, Waylee watched as her lawyer addressed the jury. "I'd like to show you the video that was broadcast during the Super Bowl," Ms. Martin said. "The prosecution only showed stills from it, but I think it's important we see it in its entirety."

A technician tapped a button. The presidential seal appeared on screens all over the courtroom, followed by President Rand speaking on the Smithsonian stage. The guests, all senior officials or ultra-wealthy donors, were tagged with their name and affiliation.

Waylee, disguised as Estelle, asked the president why ordinary Americans should vote for him.

"People are surprisingly easy to influence once you know how their minds work," his media advisor said.

Bob Luxmore stepped forward. "People are generally stupid. That's why they need people like us to tell them what to do. Plato's philosopher-kings, bred and educated to make the right decisions."

"Exactly," the president said. "Most people don't know what's in their best interest."

"What about all men and women being created equal?" Waylee/Estelle said. "That governments should consent to the will of the governed?"

The president laughed.

"So MediaCorp persuades the public to support you."

"Staying on message, we call it. We're headed toward a world where MediaCorp knows everything about everyone. But we're on the same side. We help each other out."

The feed split into three windows, the left-most displaying an email from the president's media advisor, the middle showing a memo from MediaCorp's news director to their staff, and the right playing the news as broadcast. All three contained the same content. Then it switched to their emails about Justice Consiglio's sex site visits, with the right window showing him shaking hands with the president.

The video returned to President Rand at the fundraiser. "He can turn anything into a public issue," he said. "Name a person alive who doesn't have skeletons in their closet."

The video continued, detailing how MediaCorp and the president's party worked to suppress democracy, and what they planned for the future. At the bottom of the video, a caption invited viewers to virtual links administered by the Collective: "Discover more at /MenOfGold, and discuss at #FooledNoMore."

Somehow the court had managed to find jurors who hadn't seen the video before. Their reactions varied from wide eyes to anger-flared nostrils to bored slouches.

"Why did you create and broadcast this video?" Ms. Martin asked Waylee.

"All you have to do is tear your eyes away from MediaCorp's propaganda and look around." Waylee described Baltimore's descent into squalor, largely the result of fiscal crises and ideology-driven 'belt-tightenings.' Libraries and rec centers closed, schools consolidated, crime rose, businesses fled, and the cycle worsened each year.

Mr. Lachlan stood. "Objection, your honor."

Part of Waylee wanted to stop but it wasn't the part in charge now. "There's plenty of money and resources to solve the world's problems. But the handful of people who control most of the world's wealth and power live in their own stratosphere and want to keep it that way. And Media-

Corp is their biggest mouthpiece, manufacturing fake realities and keeping people distracted and divided."

The judge was telling her to stop. She did. "Your honor, I'm answering my attorney's question. I'm trying to explain why I did what I did."

"Your honor," Ms. Martin added, "we're establishing motive. Perfectly reasonable."

"The court doesn't need to hear the witness's political opinions," Judge Mahler said. He turned to Waylee. "And when you hear the word 'objection,' you are to stop speaking. Have I made myself clear?"

"Absolutely, your honor," she said, trying to look contrite. "But this is all part of my investigation of MediaCorp and therefore relevant to the case."

"Proceed," he said. "But mind the court rules."

Waylee looked each juror in the eye. "As the video and supporting documents show, MediaCorp and their allies have rigged the political system. They've destroyed journalism and critical inquiry. They decide what people see and hear. That's why I broadcast that video, to show what's going on behind our backs.

"Let's face it, the wrong person is on trial here. Why isn't Bob Luxmore on trial for violating anti-trust laws and buying off politicians? Why aren't those same politicians on trial for accepting bribes and favors?"

Lachlan all but shouted. "Objection, your honor."

The judge scrunched his wrinkled face. "Objection sustained. Ms. Freid is the one on trial here, not Bob Luxmore."

Waylee leaned toward the jury. "As jury members, the Constitution gives you the right to vote your conscience."

"Objection."

"If a law isn't just, or is being used unjustly, you can reject it. Juries rejected the return of slaves in the 1800's and acquitted peace activists in the 1900's. You have the right to acquit me, to make a statement against—"

"Objection!" Lachlan had a pained expression on his face.

"Sustained." Judge Mahler glared at Waylee, who had barely begun her argument. She had to tell the court what Luxmore might do with his planned brain interfaces.

The judge turned to the jury. "The jury will disregard all suggestions by the witness about how to render a verdict." He stared at Ms. Martin, still standing near the witness booth. "I consider nullification arguments to be jury tampering, and will not have it in my court. Is that clear?"

Ms. Martin's shoulders drooped. "Yes, your honor."

He leaned toward Waylee. "You have stretched my patience, Ms. Freid. One more word like that, and I will find you in contempt."

Lachlan barely suppressed a grin as he sat back down at the prosecutor's table.

"No further questions," Ms. Martin said, ending Waylee's defense prematurely.

Lachlan took Ms. Martin's place by the witness stand. He smiled at the jury and shook his head. "I should thank you, Ms. Freid, for admitting your guilt and making my job that much easier."

"I'm not guilty of any real crimes compared to Bob Luxmore and President Rand—"

The judge rapped his gavel, cutting her off again. "Just answer Mr. Lachlan's questions."

Lachlan paused. "Let's start with your name. You were born Emily Smith, correct?"

"What does that have to do with anything?"

"Yes or no?"

Waylee tamped down her temper. "Yes."

"And you changed your birth name after blinding your stepfather, gouging his eyes out with your bare hands?"

Ms. Martin leapt to her feet. "Objection, your honor."

"Prosecution," the judge said, "is this line relevant?"

"It is. The defense painted Ms. Freid as a saint when her history suggests otherwise."

"You are reaching, Mr. Lachlan," the judge said. "I'm going to rule for the defense and ask the jury to disregard the question."

Waylee leaned toward her microphone. "I'd like to answer the accusation, though." Feng had tried to rape her and she was just defending herself.

"The question has been stricken, Ms. Freid," Judge Mahler said.

The prosecutor returned to the attack. "When you were six, your father jumped off a bridge and killed himself, is this correct?"

"So I've been told."

"And he was diagnosed as a paranoid schizophrenic?"

"Objection," Ms. Martin said. "The witness is not a psychiatrist."

"Sustained," the judge said.

The prosecutor didn't look phased. "Here's a question you are qualified to answer. Your mother drank a lot, correct?"

Waylee seized the opportunity. "That's why I had to raise my sister. She'd probably be dead if not for me."

"Please limit your responses to yes or no."

Fuck you. "Yes, she was an alcoholic, which is why I am not. She taught me how not to live."

The judge glared at her. "Just answer the questions, Ms. Freid."

The prosecutor went on to grind through Waylee's cyclothymia diagnosis while she was at the University of Maryland. Ms. Martin objected twice but was overruled.

"Now, Ms. Freid," the prosecutor said, "let's talk about the crimes you've been accused of. You permitted Charles Marvin Lee to stay in your home last December, didn't you?"

"Objection," Ms. Martin said. "Beyond the scope."

"Overruled," the judge responded. "You opened up a two year timeline."

The prosecutor repeated the question.

"Yes," Waylee answered. "Lots of people stayed at our house."

"And you knew Mr. Lee was a fugitive from justice, correct?"

She couldn't lie—the breakout was on the local news every day and she was a news junkie. "Yes."

The jurors leaned closer. One gasped.

"He was harshly punished for a harmless prank," Waylee continued. "If it hadn't been MediaCorp he pranked, he'd only have received probation."

"You helped break Mr. Lee out of the Baltimore City Juvenile Correctional Facility, didn't you?"

"I did not." She had to lie about that, or she'd be fucked. And they had no evidence linking her to the breakout.

His voice rose and he stabbed a finger at her. "You broke him out to help with your operations against Media Corporation, didn't you?"

"No." She would not be bullied.

"But you helped him escape when the police came to your house to recover him, correct?"

"Yes. He didn't want to go back. He was bullied in detention and afraid for his safety, but the authorities did nothing to stop it."

"And then you worked together to take over BetterWorld avatars and hack their users' computers, isn't that so?"

"I don't even have an account on BetterWorld."

"Yes or no?"

"No." And she was telling the truth—it was Kiyoko who'd helped him.

The prosecutor went on and on. Waylee had prepared and practiced for weeks, but it was like trying to fight a grand master martial artist with superpowers. She was just a normal human who'd been ground down by months of hospitalization and imprisonment.

Her lawyer cringed as if putting her on the stand had been a huge mistake. Which it probably was. By agreeing to testify, she was compelled to answer all of the prosecutor's questions.

"Now let's talk about your presence at the broadcast center. You were observed conversing with the other intruders, as if they were friends. Or comrades. One even shared a ride with you." He described Charles's disguise. "You knew him, didn't you?"

She had to lie here too, or the prosecutor would force her to testify against Pel, Charles, and everyone else. "Everyone wore disguises and I didn't know who they were."

"But you coordinated with them. How could you not know who they were?"

"It's like online avatars. You don't necessarily know who the person behind the disguise is, but that doesn't stop you from interacting with them."

"The other intruders were Charles Lee, your boyfriend Pelopidas Demopoulos, and two others you knew, weren't they?"

"I don't know who they were."

He stabbed a finger at her. "You're lying, Ms. Freid. We've already heard witnesses testify that you were the mastermind behind this whole string of crimes. Why don't you just admit it?"

She fought the urge to slap him in the face. He was just trying to rile her. "I'm a journalist, and shouldn't even be here."

The prosecutor questioned her for two more hours, jabbing away at her story, before saying "that will be all."

Simultaneously exhausted and exhilarated, thoughts racing and skidding in her head, Waylee tried to meet the jurors' eyes.

Most of them looked away.

* * *

Kiyoko

Their pousada was just a house with guest rooms. Kiyoko and Gabriel had a room in the basement. The bed was a double-sized cot with a sagging mattress, the air was stuffy, and the only lighting was from bare LEDs in old incandescent sockets. But it was cheap and the owner, a diminutive woman named Sra. Agatha, didn't ask any questions.

Using her new comlink, voice only, Kiyoko reached Sra. Miranda. "I've been trying to get hold of you."

"Yes, I received your messages and spoke with your lawyer." Her voice sounded tense. "I understand you are a wanted fugitive?"

"I'm not going back to the U.S. You promised that wouldn't happen."

"Ms. Pingyang, I contacted the federal police. But then you violated a judge's orders by removing your tracking bracelet, then assaulted two police officers."

"I didn't hurt anyone. But this Judge Rocha could be working for the CIA, just like Inspector de Barros. Please, can you check into it?"

"Ms. Pingyang, you should turn yourself in. There is no way I can help you while you are violating Brazilian law." She clicked off.

I might have ruined everything. Sra. Miranda might even report the contact. To be safe, Kiyoko shut off the comlink and removed the battery. Gabriel had already done the same with his data glasses and backup link.

The federal police regional superintendent might act to stop Charles and Pel's extradition. And their attorney, David Calvo, might triumph at the hearing. But it wasn't in Kiyoko anymore to rely on others.

"Gabriel," she asked, "if this judge hands my friends over to the CIA or Interpol, how do you think they'll try to get them out of the country?"

His forehead wrinkled and he didn't respond right away. "They won't try Campo de Marte again. Commercial flight out of Congonhas? SSG has their headquarters there, so that would be a convenient destination for us."

"And less likely that they'll go there."

He nodded. "Although they may not care about SSG anymore since we lost our contract. Guarulhos is the main airport, but it's outside the city. It has an Air Force base too, BASP." He frowned. "Of course they could use helicopters or VTOLs and leave from anywhere."

"So we have no idea where they'll go."

He shrugged. "We should be flexible."

"We can intercept them before they get out of the city. We need a hotel with a parking spot"—their pousada didn't—"and a car ready to go. In case the worst happens. We can jump in the car if I get a GPS alert."

He frowned but didn't object. "I'll call Nicolas. See if I can borrow a car."

Kiyoko said a quick prayer to the gods. Then she remembered her conversation with Gabriel after the Pokémon divination. Heroes didn't rely on others. Heroes made their own luck.

* * *

Charles

A guard led Charles and his lawyer, Mr. Calvo, into the police house meeting room again. The GPS in his nostril irritated his nose and made him feel constantly watched. It was Kiyoko's, though. Her tracking him wasn't like the police tracking him.

The same judge, middle-aged white man in a suit, sat at the far table behind a computer screen. Same black-haired prosecutor or whatever at the near table. No Inspector de Barros. Maybe the bastard was out eating donuts, or whatever cops in Brazil ate.

Mr. Calvo steered him to the near table, sat next to him, and opened his data pad. The three Brazilians spoke in Portuguese, too fast and complicated to follow.

Was Kiyoko tracking him now? Charles hadn't seen her since he and Pel were kidnapped. And Adrianna murdered. The thought still raised a lump in his throat. Why would someone kill a hot girl like her, who probably never hurt anyone in her life?

And what was up with Kiyoko and Gabriel? She liked him, beyond doubt. They were probably banging by now. His stomach burned.

The barbs didn't last long. He had no right to be jealous, she had every right to be happy, and Gabriel was pretty kick ass, he had to admit. More important by far, he and Pel were fucked if they got sent back to the States. Considering what Waylee was facing, he'd probably get life in prison. It would be worse than death.

Mr. Calvo's voice rose and his round face reddened.

"What's going on?" Charles asked him.

His lawyer held up a hand and spoke in stiff English. "The judge has already made his decision, it seems. This meeting is just a formality."

"What the hell does that mean?"

Mr. Calvo didn't answer. There were more exchanges in Portuguese.

Then the judge leaned back in his chair and said a few things that sounded official.

The guard grabbed Charles's arm from behind. Another guard had joined him and grabbed Charles's other arm. They lifted him out of his chair.

"What's going on?" It was bad. Game over, he could tell.

His lawyer sighed. "The judge has ruled for extradition. You will be held here until an Interpol agent arrives to transport you to the U.S. for trial there."

Charles tried to squirm out of the guards' grasps but they were strong and he had handcuffs on. "No! No fucking way! Can't you appeal?"

The guards shoved Charles out of the room and dragged him back down the hallway, cursing in Portuguese. He couldn't see their faces, but they were probably smirking.

Instead of taking him back to his cell, they hauled him into a brightly lit room. In the center of the room, a potbellied guard with glasses slipped on rubber gloves.

* * *

Kiyoko

"Here we are," Nicolas Pistario announced over his broad shoulder as the rolling steel door slid upward. Tryst São Paulo, a 'love hotel' that provided anonymity and wasn't far from where Pel and Charles were being held. Nicolas parked their rented four-door electric sedan inside a small garage.

As soon as the door lowered behind them, Kiyoko, sitting in the back seat with Gabriel, grabbed her backpack and hopped out. The electric pink door to their room had the number 127. The numeral one represented a leader. Two was the number for partnership. Seven, the number for perfection. Auspicious.

Nicolas, who had traded his combat fatigues and armor for a silk shirt and tight jeans, slid a cryptocurrency card into a reader next to the door. "It's a little expensive," he said in Portuguese, "but it's worth it, having a garage. And no hidden cameras inside."

"How do you know?" Kiyoko asked.

"I know which ones have cameras and which don't. But also I have checked."

"He knows these things," Gabriel said in English. "He has an appetite for married women. "Something about the thrill of the conquest."

"Yuck." *Marriage should be sacred.*

The room was cheesy beyond belief, with red wallpaper, colored lights, a circular bed, and ceiling mirrors. A white data pad sat on a shelf next to a stainless steel hatch.

"Anything you want," Nicolas said in English, "food, drinks, sex toys . . ." He winked at them. "You order on the data pad and insert a currency card, and it is delivered by dumbwaiter. No one sees you or knows who you are."

Gabriel patted him on the back. "Thank you for your help."

"Try not to damage the car, please. I will take a taxi back."

Kiyoko caught Gabriel's eyes as soon as Nicolas left. As cheesy as this place was, every bit of it pointed to sex.

* * *

Kiyoko lay naked on their circular bed, her skin hot as fire, snuggled against her champion's warm, sweaty body. His bruises were fading, although he still had bandages on his arm and ear. What was left of the ear, poor guy.

Gabriel kissed her ear. "What are you thinking about?"

"This would be like a honeymoon if we weren't in such big trouble."

"At least we aren't being shot at."

"How much more money do we have?" Her e-card was empty.

"My bank account is certainly frozen but I have almost five thousand reais on two e-cards, plus a little in paper. That should give us a month or so."

"You're supposed to be making money protecting us," Kiyoko said, "but you're spending it instead."

"We are almost married now. What is mine is yours."

"You are the sweetest man in all the universes." She kissed him, then hugged him tight.

"Do you miss your cat?" he asked.

"Of course. But Reiko cached a video. My little nyan-nyan misses me but everything's okay." She switched topics to something more strategic. "Why didn't the stun guns work?"

"They must have conductors in their clothes or body armor that block the electromagnetic waves."

"Can we do that?"

"Maybe we can make suits of aluminum foil, except they wouldn't be very practical."

Gabriel's data glasses chimed. He put them on. "Fala." A pause, then his face fell.

Bad news.

"I understand," Gabriel said in Portuguese. "What now?"

When the conversation ended, Gabriel turned to Kiyoko. "That was Sr. Eduardo. Judge Rocha ruled for extradition. Interpol will come soon to pick up Pel and Charles."

Her stomach seized and she leapt to her feet. "What do we do? What do you mean by soon? Can't their lawyer appeal or something?"

Gabriel held her arms and Kiyoko realized she was shaking.

"Sr. Eduardo doesn't know exactly when," he said, "and the judge said his ruling was not subject to appeal."

Bad, bad news. "Why not?"

"It's an administrative matter, apparently. And the judge said they should never have been granted residency in the first place."

What now? Plan C—their last option? Kiyoko had yet to receive a GPS signal from Pel or Charles. The cells were in the basement, so maybe there was too much concrete and steel in the way. Or maybe the GPS's had been discovered and confiscated.

She locked eyes with Gabriel. "If we get a signal, we need to move right away."

"Our bags are packed," he said. "But we must practice putting our armor on quicker, and prepare for combat. We will be up against professionals."

29

Waylee

The day after Waylee's ordeal on the witness stand, they returned for closing arguments. Waylee struggled to control jittery hands and dissonant sprinting thoughts as the marshal removed her handcuffs. Her hypomania had fully arrived, like fast-pounding guitar riffs screeching with feedback.

She plopped down next to her lawyer and her assistant at the defense table. The courtroom had not a single flow or curve. It was all right angles, sharp and cruel, daring her to approach so they could slice into her flesh and scrape gouges down her bones.

Breathe. In. Out. In. Out.

Ms. Martin leaned toward her and spoke in low tones. "Judge Mahler called me into his chambers after we adjourned yesterday. He was very clear about not employing nullification arguments in his courtroom."

"I'm not a lawyer," Waylee said, "but I call bullshit on that." *Bull motherfucking shit!*

Ms. Martin frowned. "It's his court, his rules. I could lose my license. Not to mention the possibility of imprisonment and a hefty fine. Jury nullification isn't very popular."

Maybe the jury would consider it anyway—that she was on their side and MediaCorp and the government had to be stopped. *They had to be! Open your eyes and step up!* Her toes fought to carve exits from her shoes.

The judge called the court to order and the jury filed in. The prosecutor, Todd Lachlan, strode across the blue carpet and stood in front of the jury box, shoulders back and arms welcoming. Smugly self-confident as always. Did he dye his hair?

Lachlan thanked the jury for their service, then summarized his case. He claimed the evidence was overwhelming. "Multiple witnesses testified that Ms. Freid was the leader of this conspiracy."

Why did Amy have to fucking sell out like that? And the other Friendship

Farm turncoats? I'd rather die than sell anyone out. What ever the fuck happened to loyalty and principles?

"And Ms. Freid herself confessed that she harbored Charles Lee, assumed a false identity to infiltrate the event at the Smithsonian, and collaborated with others to enter the Media Corporation broadcast center . . ."

How could she have been so stupid? Her fingers jittered beyond her control.

Of course the prosecution had copious evidence anyway. Between MediaCorp's control of the Comnet and Homeland's armada of drones and satellites, the government watched everything and knew everything and had nearly unlimited power. *Gods wish they were so powerful. All hail Al Rand, fuck tool of Satan!*

"What is cyberterrorism?" Lachlan asked the jury, as if he expected an answer. "U.S. code defines it as 'the premeditated use of disruptive activities against computers and/or networks, with the intention to cause harm or further social, ideological, religious, political or similar objectives.'"

It was one of last year's laws passed by President Rand's Congressional lickspittles to suppress dissent. Up to twenty years in prison. Direct actions to address social issues had always been illegal for the most part, but under Rand, they were harshly punished. *Fuck tool of Satan!*

"Ms. Freid, under the law, is a cyberterrorist. Think about that. A terrorist. Not only that, she was the leader of a terrorist cell, or at least one of the leaders, and this cell injured numerous people and caused significant harm to our nation's political system and self-confidence."

Not enough harm, not yet anyway. If you call transforming oligarchy to democracy 'harm.'

"To not convict Ms. Freid, when the evidence is overwhelming, is to invite further terrorist attacks. The Comnet taken down. The power grid taken down. Innocent people killed and maimed by bombs."

Absurd exaggerations. Waylee fought the impulse to jump onto the table and scream. *Fuck you, Lachlan, you goat whore of evil incarnate!*

"America could descend into anarchy."

'Anarchy in the U.K.' played in Waylee's head, with 'U.K.' changed to 'U.S.A.'

"The nation asks the jury to return a verdict of guilty on all counts. Thank you."

Waylee's defense attorney walked up to the jury box. She paused before speaking. "Good morning ladies and gentlemen. I think we'll all agree this has been a long and complicated trial. But in all this time, the prosecution has not been able to prove their case beyond a reasonable doubt."

She limited her arguments to the lack of evidence linking Waylee to any of the computer or conspiracy crimes, which comprised the bulk of the charges. The prosecution was relying on hearsay from witnesses who were threatened or paid.

Should we have changed some of the pleas to guilty? Too late now.

Ms. Martin didn't say anything about the importance of Waylee's cause, or that her actions were justified.

Can you fight the system if you're a part of it? Of course you can, you just have to use different methods.

Waylee's fingertips were drumming against each other. She halted them. She felt an inappropriate yearning, another hypomania symptom. When was the last time she'd had sex? It had been months. Would she get conjugal visits if convicted? Pel couldn't visit, obviously. She'd have to learn to love women. Fuck the patriarchy anyway.

"The prosecution has failed to prove guilt beyond a reasonable doubt," Ms. Martin concluded. "The only reasonable verdict is not guilty on all charges."

Ms. Martin was a decent lawyer, Waylee thought. Now it was up to the jury. *Please think big picture and please be decent humans.*

* * *

Dalton

The São Paulo police headquarters was a massive new building downtown, made of reinforced concrete, with an underground garage entrance for official vehicles and a visitors' garage across the street. Following instructions, Dalton parked his small rented passenger van, which was painted baby blue, in the visitors' garage.

The headquarters entrance had a red, white and green São Paulo coat of arms and "Palacio da Policia" over the double doors. Palace of Police.

Dalton stifled a chuckle as he walked up the steps. Just behind him, Kozachenko said nothing.

They walked through a body scanner. They hadn't been dumb enough to carry any weapons with them. A uniformed flunkie escorted them to an office in the basement, where they met a higher-ranking uniformed flunkie at a desk behind a curving computer screen.

Dalton showed his fake Interpol ID and introduced himself. "Kevin Brock. This is my colleague, Aleksi Andrusenko."

Kozachenko nodded but didn't say anything. Talking wasn't his specialty.

The thirtyish man held out a hand. "Caio Medina, prisoner administration." His English was heavily accented. "You are from the United States?"

Dalton didn't want to engage in small talk. "Born there, but I live in the E.U. now, as does my associate. We're here to take custody of Pelopidas Demopoulos and Charles Marvin Lee so they can stand trial for their crimes."

Officer Medina moved fingers across his computer screen. "Yes, you are expected." He passed over a data pad. "Please fill out these forms and sign."

"Do you have Kiyoko Pingyang in custody yet?" he asked. "She's also on the list."

The officer looked at his screen. "How do you spell that?"

Dalton spelled it for him.

He typed on an old-style keyboard, then stared at his monitor. "Pingyang, Kiyoko. Our records tell me she was arrested and processed, but released until the time of her trial. Then an order was issued to bring her in for an extradition hearing but she disabled her tracking bracelet and fled, along with one Gabriel da Silva, who faces multiple charges."

Incompetent fools. "When do you expect to find her?"

He shrugged. "I am not on that assignment."

She was only worth $100,000 anyway. Dalton looked at the data pad the officer gave him. The forms were all in Portuguese so Dalton put on his data glasses and set it to translate. Ares had sent him a list of the questions in advance and suggested answers.

The man looked over Dalton's responses and tapped fingers against his computer screen. "*Bom*. Now you have transportation?"

"Yes. In the visitor garage."

"Please bring it to the back of the building and we will have your prisoners ready in fifteen minutes."

Dalton held out a hand. Except for Pingyang's disappearance, everything had gone perfectly. "Thank you."

Kozachenko hesitated, then shook the officer's hand too.

* * *

Kiyoko

Kiyoko's data glasses beeped with the grating pitch of the tracking alarm. Pel and Charles were out of the building and moving. At least the GPS was working and they had a chance. "Gabriel, we've gotta go! They're being moved!"

They threw on their armor and outer shirts, grabbed their bags, and jumped in the car. Gabriel took the driver's seat. Kiyoko pressed the garage door button and plopped in the passenger seat. Her data glasses overlaid two sets of graphics over her vision. On the left, a map with a flashing red circle at the police station and a car icon at the love motel. On the right, navigation directions.

Gabriel backed out of the garage. Beneath an overcast sky, they headed for the police station.

* * *

Dalton

Two police officers led Demopoulos and Lee, who had wrist and ankle cuffs on, out a rear door of the headquarters building, and to Dalton's small passenger van. Two other officers stood by, 'supervising.' The prisoners yelled and struggled, as if they had the slightest chance of escape.

The police had more data pad forms for him to read and sign. He had been expecting these ones too.

"We need the cuffs back," one of the officers said in English. "Do you have your own?"

"Yes, of course." Dalton put the new cuffs on before letting the police remove the old.

He strapped the prisoners in the backmost of the two bench seats behind the driver and shotgun seats. Then he handcuffed Lee's left ankle to Demopoulos's right. It wasn't as secure an arrangement as he'd like, but they would have a hard time reaching the sliding passenger door, which had an override lock anyway, and an even harder time reaching the driver.

As soon as the police went back inside, Dalton duct taped his prisoners' mouths shut. Then he covered their heads with dark blue pillow cases. The first time Dalton tried to take the two hackers, Lee had frozen in terror like most people do in crises. Demopoulos, though, had fought back and cost them crucial time. Dalton wouldn't underestimate him again.

Kozachenko belted each hooded prisoner hard in the jaw. Their heads snapped back, then the two shook and squirmed.

"Don't disfigure them," Dalton warned.

"Da, da, I am careful."

"That's a warning," Dalton told the prisoners. "My colleague will be watching you and he enjoys hurting people. On the other hand, if you co-operate, he will not have to hit you again."

Dalton pushed the ignition button of the electric van. He looked at Kozachenko. "Keep them under control."

"No problem."

"DG, navigation." A transparent map appeared on the right side of his vision, and an arrow pointed out of the back alley.

"Proceed to Rua Washington Luis and turn right," his bone conduction transducer said in a pleasant female voice. "You will reach your destination in approximately 1 hour, 5 minutes."

They were to meet an Ares VTOL at an abandoned field south of the city. It was a long drive but Campo de Marte had been a disaster that Ares didn't want to repeat. Prudent choice, especially with Da Silva still at large.

The *Polemos* was well beyond helicopter range, but within VTOL range if they added external fuel tanks. Would have been easier if they'd rented a helicopter and transported the prisoners from the police station roof, avoiding the wretched São Paulo traffic, but the police bureaucrats had refused, citing security reasons.

"Music?" Kozachenko asked.

"Just watch the prisoners," Dalton said. "You can listen to all the music you want when we're done."

This was it! He'd make the case to get De Barros's cut, and settle for half. Two million dollars, tax free. His kids could afford any college that accepted them. And he'd have enough left to retire from this shit.

* * *

Gabriel

Gabriel drove south on Corredor Norte-Sul, a divided six-lane road that cut through the city. Full of cars, of course, but at least they were moving. In the passenger seat of their borrowed sedan, Kiyoko tracked Pel and Charles on her data glasses, complaining that she kept losing the signal.

They still hadn't seen their quarry, the people who'd taken Charles and Pel on behalf of Interpol. Gabriel had had to cut west from Avenida Do Estado and was trying to make up the difference, dodging in front of cars without being too obvious.

They entered a long tunnel, poorly lit by widely spaced fluorescent bulbs. "Are they still on the expressway?" he asked Kiyoko.

"Yes. They're about a kilometer ahead, past the tunnel. It's confusing because the road keeps changing names, but they're still going straight."

Where were they headed? Congonhas airport? Out of the city? To the coast? "DG, call Nicolas," he ordered his data glasses.

After a pause, a small icon of Nicolas's face appeared in the lower left part of Gabriel's vision. "Fala."

"Someone took Lee and Demopoulos from state custody. They're headed south on Corredor Norte-Sul. You could intercept."

"You know SSG cannot interfere with an Interpol operation. Especially since they are not our clients anymore."

"Yes of course. But you could personally. Come on."

"I don't think that's a good idea," Nicolas said. "I gave you as much help as I could. Besides, I am working now. Do you think I sit in the office and play video games?"

"Can anyone else assist?"

"I will ask, but you are probably on your own. You are top notch, though. I think you can handle this."

"Please try to get me assistance. DG, end call." The Nicolas icon disappeared.

They exited the tunnel and re-entered street level. Still staring forward through her data glasses, Kiyoko said, "We're a little closer now."

"Nicolas said we're on our own," Gabriel said.

"Can we pull it off? I assume they'll have guns."

"We beat those bastards twice, you and me. We can do it again, as long as there's not too many of them. It's what I'm trained for. We'll try to stun them first, but do anything necessary to free Charles and Pel unharmed."

Kiyoko blew him a kiss. "You are a super amazing champion. You can count on me."

"Please be careful. I could not face life if you died."

"Likewise."

Gabriel took a chance and entered the bus lane, speeding down it and ignoring the honks of irritated drivers in the regular lanes.

Bus ahead. He had to swerve back into the car lanes. "We're a lot closer," Kiyoko said.

"Can you see them?"

"Not yet."

Gabriel spotted the big orange and white striped platform that marked the northwest boundary of Congonhas airport. "Are they turning off?"

"No," Kiyoko said, "still going straight."

They passed businesses and hotels, the airport itself hidden except for descending and ascending planes. The monorail appeared on their right, paralleling the road.

"I think it's that light blue van up ahead," Kiyoko said, her voice excited. "Three cars ahead. Yes, it's the van."

The other cars near it were two-seaters or motorcycles—poor candidates. "Great." He didn't move closer—didn't want to alarm them.

There was far too much traffic on the road to intercept. He'd just follow for now. The monorail loomed above and stretched into the distance along the expressway. "Kiyoko," he said.

"What is it?"

"Please look up the engine position of the van ahead of us."

"What do you mean, engine position?"

"Is the engine in the front or the back of the van? Most of the time it is in the front, which is inconvenient for us."

"DG, zoom in." She huffed. "Moving around too much." A pause. "DG, identify vehicle brand and display picture, cutaway."

Another pause. "Engine and electronics are in the front," she said. "Just forward of the front wheels and just above."

As he guessed. "Obrigado."

"De nada." After a pause, "It looks like they're leaving the city."

"Maybe to meet a helicopter or boat. Or both."

"There will be more of them wherever they're going," she said. "It'll be harder to fight them."

"I agree. We should intercept before then. As soon as traffic lightens and there's someplace to pull over."

The monorail crossed over the road and curved off to the left, and they entered a skyline of cranes and half-finished apartment buildings. Some sort of redevelopment effort, but he didn't know southern São Paulo well and wasn't even sure what the neighborhoods were named.

The roadsides opened up at last, biofuel and charging stations and auto shops along the road, a forest of apartment buildings beyond. Traffic lightened a little and slowed.

The road would never be empty. Gabriel wasn't sure if he'd ever seen a road in São Paulo that wasn't crowded except in the middle of night. He accelerated until they were one car behind the blue van, one lane to the right. There were two hooded figures in the back seats of the van and two people in the front. The middle seats were empty.

"You'll have to steer," he told Kiyoko.

"Take the wheel from where I am?"

"Yes, I will keep my foot on the accelerator but I can't shoot and watch the road at the same time."

"Shoot?"

"Just to disable their vehicle, to slow them down."

Gabriel pulled out his needlegun. He rolled down the driver's window and accelerated around the car in front. Kiyoko grabbed the steering wheel.

The fortyish Slavic-looking man in the passenger seat stared at him as they pulled even with the van. He had a pistol in his hand. They had been too obvious.

Gabriel almost went for the man with the gun, but couldn't bring himself to shoot at law enforcement. He fired half a clip of fletchettes at the van's engine section instead.

The Slavic man shot back. Bullets smacked through the windshield.

Gabriel hit the brakes. There was a crash and shudder from a car hitting them from behind. He hoped Nicolas had insurance.

Belching blue-gray clouds, the van slowed to a halt next to a fuel and recharging station. There was a big convenience store past the pumps. Gabriel pulled behind the van, hitting it just hard enough to spoil the aim of any weapons.

"Make a smoke screen!" he told Kiyoko while unbuckling his seat belt. "But keep your head down!" He slapped a new clip into his needlegun.

"On it." Kiyoko ducked below the dashboard, readied a smoke grenade and opened the passenger window.

Gabriel swung open his door. Instead of using its thin aluminum and plastic as cover, he hurdled over it and slid down the front hood, needlegun in right hand, stun gun in left, then hugged the back of the van.

Visible through the van's back window, the two prisoners crouched down, bags or pillow cases on their heads. The driver and passenger pointed pistols in his direction.

Gabriel didn't have a clear shot and ducked as they fired. Small bits of safety glass rained down on his head. White smoke billowed around him from Kiyoko's smoke grenade.

More gunshots. People refueling their vehicles ran for cover, some of them screaming. On the road, cars screeched to a halt and smashed into each other.

The van's passenger door swung open and the Slavic man ran out. Going for Kiyoko! Gabriel lost him in the smoke.

Kiyoko leaned out her window and fired her stun gun in the man's direction. "Got him," she said. Stun guns had a much wider spread than pistols.

Gabriel heard sprinting footsteps to his left. Something punctured his neck and spurted out the other side.

He swung around. The driver—the man who went by John Hill—had exited the van, outflanked him, and was shooting at him from the road.

I fucked up. Gabriel felt like he was drowning. He coughed a spray of blood and fired both weapons, the needlegun and stun gun, at the driver.

He was taking more hits. His head hurt. The sound of gunfire disappeared, replaced by a loud high-pitched ringing.

Gabriel kept firing. The world constricted to a tunnel, only his enemy visible, gun recoiling upward, desperate anger on his face. Crosshairs fixed on his enemy's chest, on his head.

The enemy fell backward in a blur. The tunnel collapsed into blackness. He couldn't see. The guns dropped out of his fingers. *Where did they go?*

Hospital. Hospital. He couldn't see or speak and started to panic.

Kiyoko. Her beautiful face shone through the darkness, her powerful soul melded with his. Bliss, warmth, vertigo.

His head smacked hard against something.

* * *

Kiyoko

Through the cloud of white smoke, Kiyoko saw the Slavic man drop his pistol and crumple to the ground. His head hit the pavement. He looked unconscious but she shot him again with the stun gun just to make sure. Shots rang in rapid succession to her left, almost like machine guns.

Keeping the car and van between her and the gunfire, Kiyoko ran forward. She kicked the Slavic man's pistol beneath the van. Southbound traffic had stopped and northbound had slowed, drivers rubbernecking at the smoke and damaged cars.

The driver's seat was empty. Wearing dirty green T-shirts and camouflage pants, blue pillowcases on their heads, two figures huddled in the back seats. Pel and Charles, presumably.

The sliding side door was locked. She opened the front passenger door, reached past the bucket seat and pressed the side door lock. "Pel? Charles? It's Kiyoko."

Muffled grunts. They must be gagged beneath the hoods. They raised their heads a little.

Kiyoko thrust back the side door and jumped in. She pulled off her friends' hoods and tore the strips of duct tape from their mouths. Charles screeched in pain.

"The keys," Pel said, breathing heavily. "The driver has the keys to the cuffs."

The gunfire had stopped. Kiyoko leaned toward the left windows.

The driver, the American who went by John Hill, lay on his back in the street, white button-up shirt tattered and bloody, a pool of crimson expanding beneath him.

Where was Gabriel? She could only see white smoke behind the van. To her right, the Slavic man was still unmoving, but she stunned him again anyway, then scrambled over the driver's seat and out the open door.

Behind his data glasses, the American's pupils were fixed wide. He was either dead or in shock. *Focus.* She took the data glasses and rifled through his pockets. A wallet, passport, second gun, two knives, keycard for the van, and finally, a ring of simple metal keys. She took the ring and dashed back into the van.

She unlocked the wrist and ankle cuffs on Pel and Charles. "We should hurry."

Charles rubbed his lips and wrists, and stared at the smoke. "Yeah, let's jet."

Pel's eyes darted wildly. "Who are these assholes anyway? One of them has a Russian accent."

"I'll take their pictures so we can figure out who's after us," she said.

"DG, record video." She ran back to the driver, still motionless, and zoomed in on his face. She grabbed his wallet and passport and an Interpol ID.

Pel and Charles scrambled out the side door. Kiyoko ran around the front of the van and joined them. She recorded the unconscious Slavic man's face and pointed at him. "He's just stunned. We should cuff him."
Then find a place to hide out, maybe head to Guyana.

Pel dashed back for the handcuffs and Kiyoko took the Slavic man's passport, wallet, and ID. Passports had radio chips and probably the ID cards did too, so she wouldn't keep them, just record the info. And of course data glasses emitted all sorts of signals. Pel must have been thinking the same thing—he pulled off the man's data glasses and tossed them into the road.

Where was Gabriel? As Pel cuffed the Slavic man, she ran back into the smoke. "Gabriel!"

She found him on the other side of the car, on his back, bleeding from the head and throat. He wasn't moving. Blood was everywhere, gurgling out of his neck and holes in his head.

Her heart stopped beating. "Gabriel!" She knelt next to him. Behind the data glasses, his eyes were shut. "We have to get him to a hospital!" she screamed.

The worst bleeding was from the throat. Kiyoko pulled off her denim jacket and wrapped it around Gabriel's neck, tying the sleeves together. She ripped off her blouse next, exposing the armor beneath, and wrapped it around his head.

Behind her, Pel said, "Let's . . . Let's get him in the car."

"Keep pressure on his wounds." They pulled him into the back of the car. Pel hopped in with him, keeping hands against Gabriel's neck and head.

Maybe SSG could help. Kiyoko grabbed Gabriel's data glasses and hopped into the driver's seat. She gave her own glasses to Charles, who had taken the passenger seat. "Find the nearest hospital," she told him.

"DG, call Nicolas," she ordered Gabriel's glasses.

An icon of Nicolas's face appeared. "Fala," he said.

"This is Kiyoko. Gabriel's been shot. Neck and head, it's really bad. Please help!"

"Merda! Onde estão?"

She sent him her GPS coordinates. Then she heard sirens.

"We gotta get out of here," Charles said. "Turn right out of this ethanol station and I'll give you the back way to the hospital. There's one ten minutes away."

Traffic and police permitting. She backed away from the van. The smoke grenade was still on the hood, pumping out white clouds. "Get that thing off," she told Charles. She couldn't find the windshield wiper button. "Shit!"

Charles fumbled for the smoke grenade, and batted it off the hood.

Kiyoko backed away from the assholes' van. Something scraped and clumped. The bumper had come off.

Car still worked though. She accelerated out of the fuel station and turned right on the side road. "You still there, Nicolas?" she spoke in her data glasses mike.

"Yes. I am scrambling a helicopter and a doctor. There is a hospital ten minutes from you—"

"Yes, that's where I'm going."

"We will meet you there," he said, "and make sure there is no waiting."

"Turn right onto Avenida Santa Catarina," Charles said from the passenger seat, "and that'll take you the rest of the way."

Avenida Santa Catarina was narrow and crowded, only one lane in each direction, with shops on either side. She drove as fast as she could, weaving into oncoming traffic and then back again to pass cars in her way.

"He's not breathing," Pel said from the back seat.

No! "Pump his heart! Give him mouth to mouth. Do something!"

Kiyoko forced the panic down, tried to still her mind, focused on the road and getting Gabriel to the hospital. She prayed to every god and goddess she'd ever heard of, hoping at least one would listen. *Please grant us a miracle! Please save Gabriel!*

"There," Charles said. "It's that white building up on the left."

"That's a hospital?" It didn't look very big.

"That's it."

It got bigger as she approached, wings of multi-storied white paint and aquamarine glass. The biggest building, a towering structure off in the back, had a helicopter landing pad on top that stretched out beyond the building walls.

A military-looking helicopter was flying in fast from the north. SSG?

"Where do I go?" Kiyoko asked Charles.

"I don't know."

"Well figure it out!"

He pointed at a wavy-tiled driveway with in and out arrows. "That looks like an entrance."

She pulled in. There was a thick barred gate across, separating her from the courtyard. "Fuck!" She could see the main entrance just beyond, 'Hospital Municipal Vila Santa Catarina' on the sign above the glass doors. She slammed a fist against the horn and kept it there.

A scowling guard ran out a pedestrian gate and said something in Portuguese. Something about official use only.

"Emergência," she told him. "Meu noivo está morrendo!" *My fiancé is dying.*

The guard ran back to where he came from. The gate slid open to the right on a narrow track.

Kiyoko drove in and stopped in front of the entrance. Pel and Charles helped her carry Gabriel inside. He wasn't breathing and his pupils were huge and unmoving. He felt extra heavy, arms and legs flopping. A white uniformed nurse and a white coated doctor, both women, rushed toward them.

30

Kiyoko

Standing in the antiseptic-smelling waiting room, Kiyoko could tell from the grim look on the doctor's face that the news would be the worst possible.

"I am sorry," he said, and the rest didn't register. She wasn't even sure if he was speaking in English or Portuguese.

"Wait—what?"

"Mr. Da Silva—your fiancé—was dead on arrival and could not be resuscitated."

It hit her—*yes of course—he was shot in the head—those holes—who knows what inside—all that blood everywhere—you don't come back from that especially once you stop breathing . . .* Her eyes filled with water. She gasped for air that wouldn't come. Gabriel was gone forever. *He's dead he's dead he's dead.* The room spun and blurred and faded.

Someone held her, kept her from falling. Pel. "I'm sorry, Kiyoko."

"We're supposed to get married," she managed, tears pouring down her cheeks.

"I didn't know. I knew you liked each other. Almost from the beginning."

"He sacrificed himself for you and Charles. And me . . . It's all my fault."

"No, it's not your fault, Kiyoko. It's the people who kidnapped us and shot him. It's their fault. And the people who gave the orders."

"No no NO NO NO!!!"

Charles stood close, looking at the white tiled floor, feet shifting. "Sorry Kiyoko. At least he got the other guy too."

More tears gushed out. Charles couldn't help but be clumsy, but what an awful thing to say. The horror overwhelmed her and she wailed and shook.

Nicolas Pistario replaced Pel, wrapping big arms around Kiyoko, somehow calming her a little.

"Please don't blame yourself," he said. "Gabriel was a soldier. That's what we do, risk our lives for others." He wiped moisture from his eyes. "I served with him in the Special Forces. We are like brothers." His voice choked. "I should have helped him, and perhaps he would not have died. Instead I was a coward, worried about my job."

"We had a whole amazing life to look forward to and now it's never going to happen. He's gone forever." Her thoughts clouded and she sobbed from the pain that was getting worse and worse, with no end in sight.

"Whatever you need," Nicolas said, "ask me. I will help you. Anything."

Nicolas let go. Charles led Kiyoko to a seat. He sat next to her and held her hand, tears in his eyes. "I . . . I always had this thing for you, you this amazing princess and all. But I know . . . I know how you feel. My mom when I was a kid, and Adrianna. I'm really sorry. I wish so hard this hadn't happened."

"Thank you Charles." She wiped her eyes with the back of her hand and looked at the others, trying to focus. There was quite a crowd around her. "Thank you everyone."

She couldn't say anything else. There was nothing to say. The gods had forsaken her in the worst way possible. She started to scream.

* * *

Waylee

Waylee had a hard time tracking the monotonous days in her cell, but the jury took its time. That had to be good, right? That there was enough doubt to argue over?

Her hypomania disappeared but not before she scrawled out hundreds of pages of politics, philosophy, and poetry. All of which needed editing to make coherent. She addressed each page to her lawyer so it couldn't—hopefully—be seized.

Finally she was escorted back into the courtroom. Her lawyer glanced up from her concealed laptop screen but didn't say anything.

For once, Waylee didn't have anything to say either. She sat in her swivel chair and tried not to scream. Papers rustled throughout the courtroom, fingers tapped against keypads, and low voices murmured. Chilly, desiccated air hissed from vents high overhead.

The jury filed in. One of them, a heavyset woman, coughed. Waylee gripped the arms of her chair.

The judge spoke. "Mr. Foreman, would you read the verdict, please?"

Waylee's palms skidded down the chair arms on a veneer of sweat.

The middle aged foreman stood and stared at a small data pad. He adjusted his glasses and cleared his throat. "We the jury find the defendant, as to count one, harboring a fugitive—"

Make a statement, set me free.

"—Guilty."

Waylee's fingernails dug into her palms. *No, no. Please stop there.*

"Count two, conspiracy to commit computer and wire fraud—"

One of the weaker charges. *You have to rule not guilty.*

"—Guilty."

Her faint hope disappeared.

"Count three, illegal interception and disclosure of electronic communications, guilty."

That was it, they'd find her guilty on all counts. She and her lawyer had fought so hard. It wasn't fair.

"Count four, cyberterrorism, guilty."

Cyberterrorism—up to twenty years in prison. And a precedent that could end online activism.

The foreman went on and on but there was a roaring of waves in Waylee's ears, like a dark ocean crashing over her and drowning her forever.

* * *

Pelopidas

Gabriel's SSG colleague, Nicolas Pistario, settled Pel, Kiyoko, and Charles in a house on the periphery of São Paulo, near the zoo. It was a two-story, three-bedroom townhouse, flush against its neighbors, no yard, and a racket of people, cars, and helicopters all day and most of the night. It belonged to a friend of an SSG employee who was trying to sell it, and contained furniture and a stocked kitchen, but not much in the way of decoration. Kind of like Pel's apartment in Liberdade.

Pel, Charles, and Kiyoko were officially wanted by the state police, but the federal police had intervened. They just weren't allowed to leave the country and had to check in every day. The feds had also launched a corruption investigation, but didn't provide any details.

Their grumpy backup minder in Liberdade, the dark-skinned woman named Alzira, took the living room sofa. "I am very sorry about Gabriel," she told them in thickly accented English. "And not being by his side again when he needed help. He was a good man. I will try to fill in. SSG will help as much as you need." Tears welled in her eyes but she brushed them away.

The apartment had a Comnet connection, wall screen, and two data pads. Charles got to work right away, setting up encoded browsers and fake accounts with login locations in other cities and countries. Pistario and one of his colleagues brought over the gear from their old apartment. Pel had wiped the computers and VR controllers and would have to reinstall the operating systems and applications.

Kiyoko was a wreck and wouldn't stop crying. After Pistario and the other SSG man left, she fell to her knees on the living room carpet and steepled her hands together. "Guanyin, White Tara, bodhisattvas of compassion, please turn back time and change what happened. Don't let Gabriel die."

Pel found a nearly full bottle of cachaça in a kitchen cupboard and offered to make her a drink, but she shook her head. "I'm not going to drown my feelings. I want the bodhisattvas and gods to see my suffering so they'll intervene. And I want Gabriel to know how much I miss him."

Pel didn't argue. He'd let her grieve how she thought best. *I'll drink for both of us.* "Anyone else want a drink?"

Alzira declined, and kneeled across from Kiyoko. "Let us pray together."

Charles raised his hand. "I'll take one."

Pel waved him over. "Look up how to make capirinhas. Gabriel said they use limes and sugar."

Charles found the recipe on the Comnet and Pel found the ingredients. It was pretty simple, almost as simple as Dingo's wobbly recipe.

Pel made himself and Charles a drink and they sat at the dining room table. "To Gabriel." He lifted his glass. "He died for us. He fucking died for us."

Charles clicked glasses with him. "To Gabriel. And Adrianna."

"And Adrianna." *Even if she was a possible spy.*

The capirinha was both sour and sweet. A metaphor for life. It kept Pel from crying.

"Poor Kiyoko," Charles said.

"I know. You should give her some space, you know."

He frowned. "Don't be a dick. It ain't like that now. I just wanna help."

"Sorry. You're right, I was being a dick. I've been doing that a lot."

They clicked glasses again.

"I don't know about you," Charles said, "but I'm tired of getting owned by these chumps."

"Yeah, me too." Pel took a long sip of his drink. "I took all these precautions, and they didn't help. I might as well have gone to the hacker spaces like Kiyoko suggested. I should have been out doing shit instead of hiding."

"We defended Waylee on the Comnet, you with your blog pieces, me griefing trolls."

"Yeah. But we need to do more. First thing, figure out who those two assholes were. And who they were working for."

Charles fist-bumped him. "No doubt. Fuck their shit up, whoever was behind it. Then get the Collective back in the game and throw down on MediaCorp."

* * *

Kiyoko's Japanese-Brazilian friend Reiko came by with her cat and some of her things. That seemed to help. Kiyoko held her cat almost constantly, stroking his cream-colored fur.

Pel took stills from the video Kiyoko captured with her data glasses, then he and Charles scoured the Comnet to identify their attackers.

Pel had given the men's passports and IDs to Nicolas Pistario at the hospital but had photographed them first. The shorter, stocky man had two passports—John Hill, which he used at the Tiberio hotel, and Kevin Brock, which matched his Interpol ID. Neither person was real, but that was as far as they could get. The man was a ghost.

The other man with the Slavic features, who the police had picked up after the petrol station gunfight, had the name Aleksi Andrusenko on his passport and Interpol ID. But after an exhaustive search, his picture showed up in a Ukrainian police database. His real name was Yegor Kozachenko, age 40, Ukrainian national. Four years in the Ukrainian Army, followed by six in various militias. He was convicted for armed robbery and murder and given a ten year sentence, but was released after two years. Current employment unknown.

When Pistario visited the next morning, Pel told him what they'd learned about Kozachenko, and how the police had been scammed. Pistario copied the database info to his comlink.

"Any news on Inspector De Barros?" Pel asked. There was nothing on the news or discussion boards.

Pistario shook his head. "Still missing."

"I bet he's dead," Pel said. "Police get anything out of Kozachenko?"

"He insists he is Aleksi Andrusenko from Interpol and they should release him. But the police sent his image and name and document number to Interpol and they replied there is an Aleksi Andrusenko but he looks different. The state police arrested him for impersonating a police officer and are holding him until they find out who he is."

Charles turned and shook his head. "All they had to do was go through databases and run a photo search."

"The police," Pistario responded, "have a state of 250,000 square kilometers and more than 50 million people to patrol, but a tiny budget. They need much more money to do the job right."

"We don't know who those men work for," Pel said. "We assumed CIA, and this John Hill guy being a ghost would back that up. But they seem a little reckless for government spooks."

"Spook?" Pistario asked.

"Spy."

"Maybe private sector like me," Pistario said. "Gabriel thought the CIA would not take such chances to kidnap you. I will see what I can find out. And maybe the police can press Mr. Kozachenko to a confession."

"You mean torture?"

"Torture is illegal. But there are ways. And police do not like to look foolish."

* * *

Kiyoko

Nicolas Pistario, Alzira, and four senior SSG officers, all wearing dark suits, carried Gabriel's coffin across Cemitério do Morumbi's expanse of neatly mowed, bright green grass embedded with bronze and stainless steel plaques. A curtain of trees blocked the lower parts of the surrounding apartment towers. Unfairly, it was a warm, sunny day. Wasn't it supposed to rain on funerals?

Following Western custom, Kiyoko was dressed in black—for the first time in her life. She had volunteered to help carry the coffin but had to settle for walking behind it. Not even directly behind—his parents, two brothers, three sisters and other relatives all got priority.

Why couldn't she have met her fiancé's family while he was alive? Hiding and being on the run was no way to live. At the funeral service, held at a public mourning building the day after the coroner's office released Gabriel's body, everyone had been angry at her.

"My son died because of you and your gringo friends," his mother had shouted at her in Portuguese.

Kiyoko had tried to stay calm. "I miss him too," she managed. "We loved each other and were going to get married."

"He told us that. He should have married long ago and then he would be alive with children."

Gabriel's colleagues had come to Kiyoko's rescue. "He was a soldier," Nicolas told the grieving relatives. "He died a hero. You should be proud of him."

"We are all proud of him at SSG," the company president had added.

When they reached the grave site, a priest and attendant waiting there, the SSG soldiers lowered the coffin into the deep hole using thick straps. Kiyoko found a place by the hole. Pel and Charles stood just behind her. Gabriel's family and friends, SSG colleagues, and men in army uniforms crowded around. Hundreds of people.

"Oh gods and goddesses," Kiyoko whispered, "please admit Gabriel to paradise. He deserves it more than anyone. And please let him know I'll join him as soon as I can."

Sra. Miranda and other government officials stood on the periphery. The bureau chief had offered condolences at the mourning building, apologizing for the government being too slow and for corruption in the local police and judiciary. Kiyoko had collapsed in tears. "You promised me we'd be safe. Why couldn't you have helped us?"

Kiyoko tried to be brave as the coffin disappeared into the ground but Gabriel's sisters and aunts wouldn't stop crying. His mother howled and tore at her hair. Kiyoko's strength disappeared. Her knees shook and the horizon spun.

Pel held her in his long arms and kept her from falling. He didn't say anything. He and Charles had been quiet the whole terrible day, from the service in Portuguese to the ride to the cemetery.

Screaming about unfairness, Gabriel's mother tried to throw herself into the pit with the coffin. Half blinded from tears, Kiyoko reached for the woman but Gabriel's brothers intervened first, pulling their mother back and trying to comfort her.

A priest spoke in Portuguese. Kiyoko understood some of it but her mind wandered too much to focus. Her champion, the man she was destined to be with, maybe have children with, had been stolen away. Killed by someone with no name.

* * *

Pelopidas

Pel was sitting on the living room sofa, reinstalling software on their computers and VR gear, when he heard the front door lock turn and the heavy deadbolt slide. His muscles seized and he whipped his eyes toward the camera feeds on the wall screen.

He relaxed. It was Pistario. Data glasses obscuring her eyes, Alzira rose from her chair and faced the door, but didn't pull out her gun.

Pistario entered, sporting a black eye. "I have good news."

"We could use some good news." Pel went upstairs to retrieve Charles and Kiyoko. Kiyoko was cradling her cat and still wearing the black dress they'd rented for her. Her eyes were red-rimmed from crying. She sat next to Pel on the sofa, making room for Charles.

Pistario remained standing. "All charges have been dropped against you."

The air lightened. They were a little bit safer now. Even Kiyoko brightened, and hugged her cat.

"Kozachenko decided to cooperate," Pistario continued.

Everyone leaned forward. "What did he say?" Pel asked.

"He works for a private security firm like SSG, only much bigger. They are called Ares International."

Pel had heard of them. Everywhere you saw conflict in developing countries or failed states, Ares was there with bodyguards or mercenaries. They'd been involved in the recent coup in Haiti.

"After his initial hearing," Pistario said, "the police put him in a cell by himself and then threw me in there for disorderly conduct."

Pistario pointed to his black eye. "Kozachenko is a good fighter but I am younger and faster and he was very tired and hungry. I hurt him a lot and let him know that he would be found guilty and as soon as he arrived in prison someone would slice off his cock."

Charles grimaced. "Damn."

Pistario continued, "The prosecutor made it clear he would go to prison for thirty years unless he cooperated. And his public defender advised the same. Kozachenko hoped his employer would send someone but they never did. So he confessed everything in return for fewer charges and a jail where he would be safe. I watched on video."

"What else did he say?" Pel asked.

"He confessed to working for Ares but said the other man was the boss."

"John Hill? Did you get his real name?"

Pistario nodded. "Dalton Crowley. An American, former military, former police detective. He was a field manager for Ares, like me except he was always in combat somewhere and had a high body count."

"So they were both mercenaries?"

"Yes. The U.S. government and Media Corporation promised millions of dollars."

Pel wanted to hear everything. "What else did he say?"

"Kozachenko kept saying Crowley was the boss and he just did what he said. Inspector De Barros also worked for Ares, under Crowley. But after they tried to kidnap you and failed—"

"Thanks to Gabriel," Kiyoko interrupted.

"Yes," Pistario said, "thanks to Gabriel. And Pel. You delayed them."

"I was hoping for better than just a delay," Pel said.

"When the kidnapping failed," Pistario continued, "Inspector de Barros decided on a new approach, using Judge Rocha, and contacted U.S. Department of Homeland Security to get the money for himself. Crowley became very angry and kidnapped de Barros, tortured the information out of him, then beat him to death with a hammer. He burned the body."

Pel cringed. These people made Baltimore gangs seem like girl scouts.

"Kozachenko confessed to helping kidnap the inspector," Pistario said, "but said he had nothing to do with the murder."

"Who killed Adrianna?" Charles asked.

"He wasn't there. But he said Crowley liked to talk about her and said it was a shame she had to be killed."

Charles's voice rose. "Who killed her?"

"One of the Piranhas, he didn't know who. They are all dead or in prison now so whoever it was, there was justice. Crowley gave the order and he is also dead."

"Did Adrianna work for Crowley?" Pel asked.

"She recorded video of your apartment layout and security systems and was supposed to let his team in. Crowley told her he worked for Interpol."

"I knew it. That's why she was standing by the door when the kidnappers came."

Charles seemed to shrink into the sofa. His face sagged like a popped balloon.

I should have mentioned my suspicions earlier. "I'm pretty sure she liked you regardless," Pel told him.

Kiyoko's eyebrows knotted in anger. Her cat sensed something and stiffened. "So this Crowley asshole and all the others were being paid by the U.S. government and MediaCorp?"

"Only if they delivered. But there was an agreement. Some people in the U.S. government and in MediaCorp told Ares that they wanted Charles and Pel, but it was too risky to do it themselves. Kozachenko said that they helped Ares with information, and there was space for more contracts if the capture went well."

"So De Barros is dead," Pel said. "What about the judge?"

"He was arrested and is being charged for corruption."

"Good." *No wonder the police dropped the charges against us.* They all stemmed from police and judicial malfeasance.

Kiyoko released her cat and clenched her fists. "Rand and Luxmore were behind this whole thing. Gabriel's death is their fault." Her face contorted into a snarl. "They should pay."

31

Kiyoko

Huddled in her creaky bed with Nyasuke and one of the data pads, Kiyoko searched for news about her sister. Beyond the bed, rain drummed against the blinded window.

Forget the gods. They don't care about me. They took everything and won't answer my prayers.

"Waylee Freid has been found guilty on eighteen counts," an impeccably groomed man announced over MediaCorp's "Top News" Comnet feed. "And there's more to come. But the court agreed that she was a terrorist leader and belongs in prison."

The program gave a highly biased recap of Waylee's harboring of Charles, the infiltration of the New Year's presidential fundraiser, the BetterWorld and comlink hackings, and how she and others broke into MediaCorp headquarters during the Super Bowl and broadcast a subversive—and fake—video.

"Fake?" Kiyoko challenged the data pad screen. "You're the fake ones." She snatched one of her pillows and hurled it against the wall. Her cat leapt from the bed and scurried for cover.

"Nyasuke, I'm sorry. I didn't mean it. Come back."

He didn't return. On the data pad, the news switched to an interview with the lead prosecutor, Assistant U.S. Attorney Todd Lachlan. "Justice was done here today," the prosecutor said. "There are still a number of charges that will be tried later in Virginia and Maryland courts, but the jury agreed that Ms. Freid was guilty of the federal charges. The other perps are still at large but we'll bring them to justice soon enough."

"What happens now?" asked the interviewer, a blonde woman with a smile as fake as the news.

"There'll be a sentencing hearing in a couple of months. Ms. Freid will be sent to a federal prison and await the state trials. When all is done, I expect she'll spend the rest of her life in prison."

Kiyoko's eyes filled with tears. *My poor sister.* Then her fingers quivered with anger. They curled into fists and flew toward the data pad. She diverted the blows at the last moment, pounding the mattress over and over.

It wasn't the gods—they didn't take Gabriel and Waylee. MediaCorp and President Rand and their henchmen did. And we're nothing to them. Just hairs to brush out of the way while they choke the world to death. They have to be stopped. They have to pay.

Not bothering to change out of her pajamas, Kiyoko marched downstairs into the living room, inserted herself between Pel and Charles on the sofa, and replayed the broadcast for them.

Pel's lips trembled. "She can appeal, right?"

Kiyoko didn't answer. Waylee's court-appointed, probably overworked lawyer could appeal the verdict. But what were the chances it would do any good? The system was rigged.

Maybe there was another option. Waylee always said if the game was rigged, kick over the table.

Like her sister, Kiyoko had changed her name after they fled the Philadelphia darkness. Kiyoko for purity and goodness, Pingyang for the Chinese princess who recruited an army and overthrew an evil regime. The world needed a Princess Pingyang more than ever now.

"You heard the prosecutor." Her fists clenched, nails digging into the palms. "There's still a huge bounty on us. The government and MediaCorp will never stop persecuting us. Well, I'm going to fight back. That's what Waylee would do."

Charles fist-bumped her, lightening her mood a little. "I'm with you," he said. "I fucking hate those motherfuckers. Let's break Waylee out and put Rand and Luxmore in jail. She broke me out. I owe her."

Fear and doubt started to displace Kiyoko's anger, but drowned beneath rising excitement. *Gabriel's death won't go unanswered.* "We can do it. We can free Waylee and bring down President Rand and MediaCorp. If it's conceivable, it's possible."

"Yeah, we got that Super Bowl video out," Charles said.

Pel blinked. Then he nodded. "I'm with you too. I'll do whatever it takes to free Waylee. You know that." He leaned toward her. "I told Charles earlier, I'm sick of being a victim. If we're going down, we might as well go down fighting. And like Dingo and I used to say, the best defense is a surprise attack."

Kiyoko hugged him. "You're your old self again. Maybe stronger. I don't know who I am yet—I know I'll never be the same. But I know who I want to be."

Princess Pingyang.

* * *

Kiyoko sat in one of the dilapidated stuffed chairs in the living room, VR helmet and gloves on. The helmet masked out the incessant traffic and helicopter noise and helped her concentrate.

They were in a race and hadn't even started the car. According to online articles and documents, federal sentencing processes averaged 75-90 days, but might be as quick as a month or two. They had to strike before Waylee was transferred to a prison, where they'd never be able to reach her.

Where was she now? That was easy to find. Waylee was being tried in the Lewis F. Powell, Jr., United States Courthouse in downtown Richmond, Virginia, and held in a basement cell there.

Kiyoko looked up the courthouse specs. It was a new building, built like a fortress, and a U.S. Marshall's Service office was based there. Not an easy place to break into—they would be heavily outnumbered by armed professionals.

The only option was to intercept the prisoner van between Richmond and wherever they were taking Waylee. According to speculation on the Comnet, that was the federal Supermax in Florence, Colorado, where she'd spend the rest of her life in solitary confinement. Burial in hell.

Regardless of her destination, U.S. marshals would drive her in a prisoner van or car to the Richmond airport and put her on a small plane. Possibly with other prisoners, but most likely not. There weren't any other "terrorists" being tried at the Powell courthouse now.

Kiyoko reported her findings to Pel and Charles, who were also doing Net research. Then she logged onto BetterWorld.

Getting to the U.S. and buying what they needed would be expensive. Kiyoko could sell her clothes and VR gear, but that wouldn't come close. Charles and Pel had led a group of hackers that pillaged money for the Super Bowl op, but Homeland and Interpol had crushed the Collective, at least temporarily, and Charles and Pel already had time-consuming missions.

Yumekuni was the only option. MediaCorp had restored her Better-World avatar and realm, stating in writing that they found no evidence of wrongdoing. They'd done so to infect her with spyware and pinpoint her location, but no matter their intentions, she was clearly Yumekuni's owner again, and could sell it if she wanted.

Kiyoko set up a private chat room and invited her friend Abrasax, who had helped her defeat Prince Vostok in BetterWorld, and later, helped destroy a Homeland spy drone. Remembering how big her friend's avatar was, Kiyoko maximized the room dimensions and set the texture to a field of purple flowers.

Abrasax teleported in a few minutes later, a massive gold dragon with folded wings and a swishing tail. "How fare thee, Princess Kiyoko?"

Wearing a white mourning gown and her tiara of office, Kiyoko bowed. "Not well. My real-world fiancé was murdered." The sorrow and anger returned. Would they ever go away?

Abrasax shed a tear, which splashed onto the flowers like the contents of a goldfish bowl.

Kiyoko recapped her troubles, omitting a lot of the details. "I am broke, and must, unfortunately, sell Yumekuni. Can you help?"

"There must be another way. Yours is the loveliest realm on the continent."

True. The elaborate palace, the Vale of Waterfalls, the Magical Woods, the lifelike NPCs . . . Kiyoko had put years of work into Yumekuni, hours each day, and re-invested all the lease income and production profits, increasing its size, *qi* storage, and infrastructure without scrimping on details.

Abrasax bared long white fangs. "What if Prince Vostok bought it?"

"That's where I need your help. You have a friend who's a realtor?"

"Yes. Miss Francesca."

Kiyoko forced herself to continue. "I'd like to break up the realm into affordable chunks and auction them off, but keep out jackdogs like Vostok. Only good alignments need apply."

Her heart clenched. Gabriel was murdered before he could set up an avatar. She never got to share the creation of her life with the love of her life.

Abrasax craned her gold-scaled head forward. "Are you sure you want to do this?"

No, not at all. But I have to. Kiyoko felt hollow inside and the beginnings of another long cry. "Please don't make me change my mind."

* * *

Shakti and Dingo contacted Kiyoko via Crypt-O-Chat, offered condolences about Gabriel and Waylee, and volunteered to help. "Waylee's my best friend," Shakti messaged, "and Luxmore and Rand are the world's biggest threats. Besides, we're being hunted too."

Kiyoko thanked them and messaged M-pat. He'd stolen all the vehicles they used to free Charles and break into the broadcast center. Old commercial vans and trucks mostly, but he knew how to disable the GPS and wireless on newer models too. And he was almost as good as Gabriel in a fight, and stayed cool under stress.

About an hour later, Kiyoko's data pad played an old Wu-Tang Clan tune, signifying that M-pat had logged on to Crypt-O-Chat.

Ujamaa1: Miss you, girl.

They chatted about the neighborhood for a while, then Kiyoko told him about their attackers and Gabriel's death, and who was behind it.

Ujamaa1: Motherfuckers. You don't deserve that shit.

Gabriel's expressive eyes and sculpted torso flashed into Kiyoko's mind. The anime figurines on her bedroom shelves shook as he thrust and thrust and brought her to orgasm. *Not now.*

Princess_Kiyoko: They should pay.

Ujamaa1: No doubt.

Princess_Kiyoko: Listen, I really need your help.

Ujamaa1: This gonna get me in more trouble?

Princess_Kiyoko: Not if we plan well. You know Waylee might get life in prison?

Ujamaa1: Fucking feds. I hate em.

Princess_Kiyoko: We're freeing her during transport. We need a couple of cargo vans, same as last time. And your tactical skills if you're willing.

After a few seconds, he replied,

Ujamaa1: Latisha got another kid on the way.

Princess_Kiyoko: Congrats!

Her mood quickly plummeted. Gabriel wanted kids. *Now it'll never happen.*

Ujamaa1: Tell you what, I'll get you whatever you need but gotta skip the main event.

Understandable, and still very helpful. Kiyoko thanked him and they brainstormed a while. She committed the details to memory since the text would disappear as soon as she logged off, and notes could be incriminating.

Finally, to see if Nicolas and Alzira would help. Kiyoko waited for Nicolas's daily visit, then directed everyone to sit in the living room. She remained standing, like Waylee used to do.

Kiyoko didn't have her sister's charisma and way with words, but this was a friendly audience. "Nicolas," she began. She continued in Portuguese. "You promised me anything I need."

Nicolas straightened in his chair. "Yes, of course."

"I need your help to free my sister."

He blinked. "From prison in the U.S.?"

"No, while she's being transported. We're putting a plan together but need your help." She looked at Alzira, sitting across from her comrade. "Yours too."

Nicolas rubbed his temple. "I did promise to help you, but I didn't mean something like that."

Disappointing but not surprising. "Can you at least help us sneak into the U.S.?"

Alzira stared at her. "You want to go to the USA where you can be arrested? You are safe here."

"We're not safe here," Kiyoko said. "And it's the only way to save my sister from life in prison," she added in English.

"We survived that Ares team," Pel said, "but barely. And it cost Gabriel's life, plus a lot of others. There's still a huge reward for us, so it's only a matter of time before someone else tries. We'll never be safe as long as President Rand and MediaCorp run things."

"No one is safe as long as they run things," Kiyoko added. "But when we free my sister, she'll become an instant celebrity, and Rand and Luxmore better look out. No one can plan and inspire like Waylee."

"Okay," Nicolas said. "What kind of plan do you have?"

"You must promise not to tell anyone."

"Of course. You have my word."

Alzira agreed also.

Kiyoko described how they used an EMP bomb and stun guns to free

Charles from the Baltimore Juvenile Correctional Facility last year. "And we've learned a lot since then."

"We just have to get on the JPATS scheduling system," Pel added. "To find out when she'll be moved."

"JPATS?" Nicolas asked.

"Justice Prisoner and Alien Transportation System," Pel said. "Head-quartered in Kansas City. They arrange all the prisoner transportation, but keep the schedules secret. They likely use a standard airline database, though, and I downloaded a general schema."

"We'll find a way to own them," Charles added.

Kiyoko looked Nicolas in the eyes. "So will you help?"

"I will see what might be possible," he said. "Whatever we do, SSG must not be implicated."

"Of course," Kiyoko said.

Alzira still looked baffled. "I can not believe you consider such a thing. But obviously you made your decision. I will also help as circumstances permit. We are Gabriel's comrades and we are your comrades."

Kiyoko practically jumped out of her shoes. It wasn't exactly enthusiastic support, but far better than 'no.'

One last thing. Nyasuke was reclined on the back of the sofa behind Pel and Charles, watching her like the others. It would be far too dangerous to bring her cat on such a mission. She'd have to leave him with Reiko again.

Would she ever see him again? Or would she end up dead or in prison? And worse, what about her friends? How could she put them at such risk? What the hell was she thinking?

Pel was staring at her. She realized she was trembling.

"Don't worry, Kiyoko," he said. "We're in this together."

32

Kiyoko

Kiyoko gripped the arms of her form-fitting seat as the small private jet raced down the Campo de Marte runaway. São Paulo's endless skyscraper lights sparkled farewells through the darkness.

Goodbye.

The plane leapt into the air. In the seat facing her, Nicolas gave her a thumbs up. The jet was owned by a "friend" of his, some businesswoman. It wasn't free but at least it was a special price, with no security checks. They'd land in the Bahamas and then try to sneak into Florida by boat.

Across the narrow aisle, Charles shut his eyes like he was about to die. It was only his second time on a plane too. Across from him, Pel stared out the window, his face tense.

Kiyoko returned her gaze outside. São Paulo's receding forest of lights stretched to the horizon. Gabriel was buried somewhere down there. She wished she'd looked at a map beforehand so she could wave in the right direction.

Her vision clouded with tears. Which was okay. She'd cry the whole flight if she had to. When they landed, there would be no more time for that. They had a partial plan, but there were still so many unknowns, and difficulties ahead beyond fathoming.

They'd have to figure it out. She owed Gabriel. She owed her sister.

"Ironic," Pel said.

Kiyoko realized her teeth were grinding. She unclenched her jaw and turned to face him. "What?"

"We did everything we could to stay in Brazil, and now we're going back to the U.S. anyway."

Kiyoko leaned across the aisle and touched his fingers. "Yes, but there's a difference. We're not going as prisoners. We're going as liberators."

An advance look at *Zero-Day Rising*
Book 3 of the BetterWorld trilogy

1

Bob

Unfettered by small-minded decrees, humans are limited only by their own imagination and intellect, heroes able to transform the world. Unfettered by the physical world, humans have no limitations at all. This is the promise of BetterWorld, the transformation of humanity itself; an opportunity for every man, every woman, and every child, to become a god.

Bob Luxmore finished his monthly letter to the shareholders, who were mostly small-minded themselves. They needed reminders that MediaCorp had responsibilities beyond quarterly profits.

He ran the sensitivity filter, which changed the phrase "become a god" to "become a creator." Ridiculous, like all its suggestions. He sent the letter to his office staff to finesse, then swiveled his data screen aside and glanced out the window next to his form-fitting seat. They were flying over scrubby hills dotted with shacks. Ahead, more sea.

"Almost there," his new communications aide, an attractive but prim brunette, said from the seat opposite him.

Good. The VTOL was cramped compared to his other jets, but it was the only one able to land at MediaCorp's research facility on Gonâve Island. Gonâve was situated between the two Haitian peninsulas like a piece of meat being devoured. They must be passing over the upper jaw.

Bob returned to his data screen and skimmed the financial and asset statements regarding the Fantasmas na Maquina acquisition. The upstarts actually thought they could steal his ideas, not to mention his customers. And they hired criminals like Kiyoko... he couldn't remember her last name. They'd probably hired those cyberterrorists Lee and Demopoulos, too. He'd been tempted to purge the entire company, but that would have been a waste. As with past acquisitions, they'd keep the best assets.

Bob logged out as the jet slowed and redirected its engine thrust. They landed on cleared ground surrounded by a high concrete wall and patrolled by Ares International guards.

"We're here!" the communications aide said.

If you're not going to say something worthwhile, keep your trap shut. Bob was tempted to fire her, but maybe he'd just transfer her. That's what he'd done with the last one.

Amidst his aides and bodyguards, ten in all, Bob exited the plane and entered a hellhole of humid heat. Sweat began to drip inside his Savile Row suit.

The facility director, Keith Sherman; the chief scientist, Darla Wittinger; and a host of underlings greeted them. Sherman was taller than him—most men were—and looked down as they shook hands.

"Let's get out of this heat," Bob told the crowd. "The day's half over already."

It was a short walk to the reception building, where after retinal and DNA scans, they took a long escalator down and boarded an underground tram. The tram passed the first two stops, marked only by letters, then stopped at 'C.'

Director Sherman unlocked a steel door with his badge and led them into a hallway with labs off both sides, visible through polycarbonate windows. They stopped outside one of them.

"Mr. Luxmore, Dr. Wittinger, if you please," the director said. He turned to the others. "There isn't enough room inside for everyone, I'm afraid. My assistant will direct you to Conference Room C-3 for your first meeting."

They'd be talking protocols and getting in the technical weeds—the type of stuff Bob usually understood, but didn't have time for. That's what underlings were for. His aides could message him if something important came up.

Sherman opened the lab door. Inside, Dexter Ramsey, the Assistant Director of Science and Technology with the U.S. Department of Homeland Security, was talking to a pair of MediaCorp technicians, as was a second guest, a heavyset woman who probably worked for DHS as well. The facility's communications director and a security officer stood next to the outsiders. All visitors, no matter who, were chaperoned inside MediaCorp facilities. Especially since the Super Bowl fiasco.

Ramsey, whose hair was starting to turn as gray as Bob's, held out a hand. "Mr. Luxmore. Good to see you again."

Bob shook it. "Likewise."

Ramsey introduced the heavyset woman as Dr. Dowling, a DHS psychiatrist who wanted to see MediaCorp's new technology in action. "This could revolutionize prisoner interrogation," the woman said.

"I hear you've made a lot of progress," Ramsey added.

"That's a question for Mr. Sherman and Dr. Wittinger," Bob said.

Dr. Wittinger smiled. "We've made remarkable progress since this facility opened."

She had been developing brain-computer applications for nearly thirty years, and was probably the most talented researcher in the field. Which was why Bob paid her so much and gave her whatever resources she needed. And on Gonâve, especially with a pliable new government in Haiti, there were no regulators or third-party meddlers to shackle her or her staff's imaginations.

Dr. Wittinger ushered them to a tinted glass window along the far wall. On the other side, a young Haitian woman sat on the bed of a comfortably appointed suite. She stared at them.

"She can't see us," Director Sherman said. "It's a see-through wall screen."

The one-way screen was too expensive for the consumer market—at least for now—but might have government applications. When invoking national security, nothing was too expensive for governments.

"Fascinating product," Bob told the DHS guests. "I'll have someone put a demo together for you."

One of the MediaCorp technicians, wearing augmented reality glasses and haptic gloves, moved his fingers in the air. A box popped up on the one-way window, showing wildebeest trying to cross a river. One of the creatures was grabbed by a crocodile and pulled, struggling, beneath the water.

"We're looking at subject 273," the technician said. "She's watching a nature show on the wall screen."

"Can you put one of those wildebeest in the room?" Dr. Wittinger asked the technician.

"Yes, just a sec." The technician muttered commands into his jaw microphone. Two more boxes popped up on the big window. In the upper one, a three-dimensional wildebeest appeared in the room with subject 273, not moving except for the twitch of its tail. The lower box showed the same image, only more crudely rendered. The Haitian woman recoiled in shock, then smiled and reached a familiar hand toward the ugly creature. Obviously she'd seen this sort of trick before.

Dr. Wittinger turned to address Bob and the others. "The subject has a polyflex neural interface in her skull, between the cortex and the dura mater. It's printed with AI processors and memory circuits that exchange signals directly with the brain. By placing it beneath the skull, we improve signal fidelity far above EEG-based interfaces." She smiled. "We've had some big breakthroughs. First, we were able to grow special brain cells from stem cells. They're more adaptive than prior types and connect to different parts of the cerebrum. They serve as interpreters, if you will. Second, the AI processors are just remarkable." She looked at Bob. "As you know, every brain is organized differently..."

Bob twirled a finger for her to stay on track.

She spoke faster. "But the AI system trains itself to the user. It's orders of magnitude faster than anything developed before, although it still isn't instantaneous, obviously." She touched a finger to her ear. "The subjects have a fiber-optic jack behind their right ear, which provides the best signal, naturally. But there's also a wi-fi antenna that runs along the neck. That's what we're using now with subject 273. We're sending the wildebeest image, autocorrected to fit in the room configuration, and the bottom image is what she's seeing broadcast back to us. Transmission never seems to be as good as reception—it has to do with the statistical interpretation of neuron signals—but that's something we're working to boost."

"But the user *can* send basic information," Bob asked her, "like speech and movement intentions, that could be interpreted by the BetterWorld servers?"

"Yes. There's a training process, but yes."

"We've made a game out of it," Director Sherman added. "And I'm sure the BetterWorld designers can improve it, come up with fun high-res adventures or combat that teach the user and AI how to work together."

That was the designers' job—keep the users happy and wanting more. "How much resolution can you simulate?" Bob asked Dr. Wittinger.

"Plugged in, we're getting closer to BetterWorld quality. Better in the case of smells and tastes—and who wants to stick electrodes on their tongue or pay for a chem synthesizer that has to be refilled every week? The user has to train on the system a while, but—"

"How long is a while?"

She hesitated. "It depends on the scene complexity. We've observed that children acclimatize quicker than adults, so I think the key is to start people as early as possible, maybe in infancy."

Bob shook his head. "Eventually, hopefully, but for now we need to focus on teens and adults. I need specifics—how long it takes to train and how you can improve it. The average American has the patience of a gnat."

She nodded and spoke quietly into her wristband comlink.

This technology will change everything! Bob would get the PR staff to put a campaign together. No more clunky gear, especially for taste and smell. Direct exchange of thoughts all the way across the world. Immersion indistinguishable from reality. They'd have to appeal to early adopter types to be beta testers, maybe get some celebrities in on it. Maybe even some porn stars—you could be right there with them in the middle of the act.

There was a hitch, though. "Won't skull surgery turn people off?" Bob asked.

Dr. Wittinger frowned. "We're not at the marketing stage." Her eyes lit up. "Maybe we could go through the sinus. It would be tricky, though. I think you'd need a trained doctor no matter what."

Not what he wanted to hear. "Work on that. We need a procedure people can do themselves."

Dr. Wittinger blinked, then spoke into her comlink again.

The Homeland psychiatrist, Dr. Dowling, pointed at the window. She didn't seem interested in BetterWorld. "This is subject 273?"

"Yes," Dr. Wittinger said.

"How many do you have in total?"

"Eighteen still active at the moment. Most of the subjects were for preliminary tests and we've let them go." She glanced away. "And the others—there were some complications. But we've learned from our mistakes."

The psychiatrist peered at Dr. Wittinger. "What sort of complications?"

Bob interrupted. "Just some failed tests from what I understand." He addressed Ramsey, who was the more senior of the two officials. "But you can't be afraid to make mistakes if you want to get anywhere." Risk had built MediaCorp into the most innovative and influential company in human history.

"These subjects you've allowed to return to their homes," Ramsey asked Dr. Wittinger, "do they still have the implants?"

"No," Dr. Wittinger said. "We take them out."

Ramsey frowned at Bob and Sherman. "Even so, aren't you afraid they'll talk?"

Bob let Sherman answer, since he had first-hand knowledge. "They've all signed non-disclosure agreements," the lab director said, "and they receive annual stipends. And we're monitoring them, just in case. Not that they know much of anything."

"The damaged cases," Dr. Wittinger added, "are still in the compound while we monitor them and work on patches."

Dr. Dowling opened and closed her mouth like a goldfish. "What kind of damage are we talking about?"

From what Bob had been told, complications had ranged from disorientation to seizures to persistent aphasia or loss of self-awareness. He had to deflect her again.

"That's extraneous to our DHS contract, and privacy concerns prevent us from going into details."

Ramsey gave a half smirk, like he knew Bob was bullshitting, but otherwise didn't seem interested. He pointed at the Haitian woman behind the glass.

"What about accessing memories? That's what the grants were for. And the monitoring software."

Dr. Wittinger nodded. "I was getting to that. We're still working out some kinks, but yes, you'll be able to download memories. Monitoring, that's the easy part. As long as the subject doesn't know they've been operated on, we can transmit optical and audio signals with the wi-fi, then decode them at the lab. It doesn't have to be real time; we can store up to a week on the polyflex depending on the amount of memory and the degree of sample density and compression."

"How would they not know they'd been operated on?" Dr. Dowling asked.

"Our laser's precise enough that we don't need to shave the head," Dr. Wittinger said, "and we put everything back the way we found it. We use a bioglue—much better than sutures or staples."

"What about transmitting thoughts?" Ramsey asked.

"Like I said earlier, everyone's brain is different, so there's a training process required, until the user and the AI can communicate with minimal error. The subject would certainly be aware of it."

Ramsey frowned again, but Sherman said, "I don't believe that was in the scope of the grant."

"But we'd be happy to explore additional lines of research," Bob said, not wanting to lose the possibility of more funding. "Why don't you come up with another wish list and we can discuss it."

Dr. Wittinger had the technicians carry out a series of demonstrations.

They'd obviously practiced because the Haitian woman looked almost bored as they had her ride a bike and fly a plane in brain-only virtual reality. They had her read a book next. Her internal antenna broadcast a legible, though imperfect, facsimile of the text. Not that Bob could decipher it anyway—it was in Creole.

Ramsey smiled. "Can we access her memories now?"

The technician with the augmented glasses spoke into his jaw mike loud enough for everyone in the room to hear. "I'd like you to think back to your first day here. Is there anything specific you can remember? Concentrate on it."

A translator program repeated his words in Creole.

The window with the subject's wi-fi broadcast showed a woman's hand filling out forms. The page was fuzzy except for certain questions and answers, like 'Edikasyon: *Lekòl segondè*' and 'marye oswa yon sèl? *Sèl.*'

"What's interesting," the technician said, "is that the forms were originally in French, but she's remembering them in Creole. She's writing down that she completed secondary school, which is something to be proud of in Haiti. And she's unmarried—which we require, since our subjects can't leave the compound. She volunteered for the study, if I remember right, because we promised a university scholarship."

"I'm impressed," Bob told his employees when the demonstration ended. "And I'm not easily impressed."

Ramsey nodded. "I'm impressed too. Are we ready for the next phase, then?"

"Did you bring your mystery subject with you?" Bob asked. Homeland's priorities weren't exactly MediaCorp's priorities, but the government had sunk a lot of money into this. They were entitled to their return.

"I did not. But I can get the subject on the next flight, along with our interrogation team, assuming your people are ready and have the space."

Bob didn't wait for his employees to reply. "They'll be ready and they'll make space. Do you mind if I ask who this prisoner is?"

Ramsey half-smiled. "I can't answer that now, but I'll fill you in when they arrive."

More Sci-fi from See Sharp Press

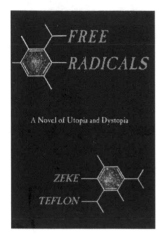
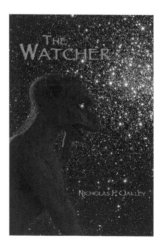